## She did not w...
## hungered for it.

Jeb's mouth was on hers, delicious as salted caramel. Haley knew that this was an experience she would never forget: the sound of the billowy sails flapping in the Atlantic breeze; the July sun beaming down bright and hot, shining a million tiny fractured lanterns over the choppy caps of blue water; the smell of briny ocean spray; this handsome man, hard with muscles and a gorgeous smile, kissing a practical woman who'd forgotten what it was like to have fun.

She should break off the kiss. She knew it. *Do something!* Anything! Just stop kissing him!

But she did none of those things.

Instead, she twined her arms around his neck and pulled him down on top of her.

Haley couldn't think straight. Acting like this was so unlike her. She felt as if she were channeling some spritely mermaid turning the tables on a handsome fisherman by catching him in her net. Oddly thrilling, that image.

*You are in such trouble,* whispered her brain…

Dear Reader,

One of the fun things about being a writer is the research. On the surface, research might sound boring. Dry and dusty. Hours spent poring over books. Except, that's not the kind of research I'm talking about. For *Smooth Sailing,* my research entailed going to a marina and asking to be taken out on a sailboat. It meant taking a class in sailing and spending hours talking to avid sailors. Now that's just downright fun.

I learned boating safety, the difference between the sails, the names of all the ropes, the way to properly launch a sailboat, how to trim the sail, how to throw a line, tie up the boat, how to recover from a capsize and how not to panic if you fall overboard. What I took away from this experience is that sailing is really complicated and I have a whole new respect for the sport and the people who sail.

What I hope is that my dedication to research paid off and you'll be able to experience sailing right along with the hero and heroine of *Smooth Sailing*, Jeb Whitcomb and Haley French, who fall in love on the high seas. It's a grand adventure and I thank you for taking the ride with me.

*Smooth Sailing* is the second book in the STOP THE WEDDING! series. I hope you'll be on the lookout for the final installment in the trilogy, *Crash Landing*. Until next time…

Happy reading,

*Lori Wilde*

# SMOOTH SAILING

BY
LORI WILDE

First published in Great Britain 2013
by Mills & Boon, an imprint of Harlequin (UK) Limited,
Eton House, 18-24 Paradise Road, Richmond, Surrey TW9 1SR

© Laurie Vanzura 2013

ISBN: 978 0 263 90307 2
ebook ISBN: 978 1 408 99674 4

14-0513

Harlequin (UK) policy is to use papers that are natural, renewable and recyclable products and made from wood grown in sustainable forests. The logging and manufacturing processes conform to the legal environmental regulations of the country of origin.

Printed and bound in Spain
by Blackprint CPI, Barcelona

**Lori Wilde** is a *New York Times* bestselling author and has written more than forty books. She's been nominated for a RITA® Award and four *RT Book Reviews* Reviewers' Choice Awards. Her books have been excerpted in *Cosmopolitan, Redbook* and *Quick & Simple*. Lori teaches writing online through Ed2go. She's also an RN trained in forensics and she volunteers at a women's shelter. Visit her website at www.loriwilde.com.

To my students, past, present and future.
Helping you has made me a better writer.
Thank you.

# 1

**Forward**—*Toward the bow*

A PEACOCK COULDN'T have strutted more gloriously than Jeb Whitcomb taking the outdoor makeshift stage. A self-satisfied grin graced his tanned handsome face, his blue eyes crinkled seductively at the corners as he joined the governor at the podium. The sleeves of his white work shirt were rolled up to his elbows, revealing powerful forearms dotted with hair a shade darker than the milk-chocolate locks swept rakishly off his forehead.

"In appreciation of your hard work, dedication and monetary contribution to rebuilding the island of St. Michael's, we are bestowing you with the first Jeb Whitcomb humanitarian award," Governor Freemont announced and passed the gilded trophy to Whitcomb.

From the audience, Haley French, R.N., rolled her eyes. Whitcomb might have everyone else on the island snowed, but Haley saw through the charming smile and sexy swagger. He hadn't really come here to help the residents of St. Michael's; his visit had all been about plumping up his ego. Whenever there was a camera about, Whitcomb was in front of it.

Cameras flashed. Reporters tossed questions. The crowd applauded.

Haley's best friend, Ahmaya Reddy, poked her in the ribs with her elbow. "Don't be rude. Clap."

Halfheartedly, Haley joined in the applause, but she frowned. "He's grandstanding."

Whitcomb launched into what was clearly an off-the-cuff speech.

"He's a bona fide hero," Ahmaya argued. "St. Michael's couldn't have recovered as quickly without him."

"He's self-centered."

"Oh, yes, self-centered people give up a year of their life to rebuild islands they have no connection to."

"That's precisely my point. He has no connection to St. Michael's. Who anointed him our savior? I question his motives. Ever notice how he always has hangers-on following him?"

Ahmaya shrugged. "He's handsome, rich and fun to be around. Who wouldn't want to hang on?"

"Rebuilding an entire island wiped out by a hurricane shouldn't be fun."

"You'd think not, but somehow he managed to get everyone to pull together. That's why he's getting the attention, not to mention the award. His ability to get people to work in harmony."

"He's just doing it for the attention. It strokes his ego."

"So what if he is?" Ahmaya asked. Okay, Haley was being a bit harsh, which was not like her, but

Whitcomb seemed to bring out the worst in her. "The results are the same. People have homes again and essential services have been restored because of Jeb's generosity."

"He's impulsive."

"Oh." A sly smile crossed Ahmaya's face. "I get it."

"Get what?"

"The reason why he rubs you the wrong way."

Haley crossed her arms over her chest, canted her head. "Care to enlighten me?"

"He doesn't live up to your expectations."

"I have no expectations of him."

"No?"

"He's nothing to me."

"I thought you two—"

"We certainly did not." Haley bristled.

"But almost."

Haley's cheeks heated. Yes, she'd almost had sex with Jeb Whitcomb several months back when they'd both served on the hospital rebuilding committee. Thankfully, she had not gone through with it.

"Wait a minute." Ahmaya snapped her fingers. "It's not Jeb who didn't live up to your expectations. It was you. You're mad at him because you violated your own code of ethics when you—"

"Let's stop talking about him, okay?" To get Ahmaya to shut up, she purposefully fixed her attention on the stage.

Jeb had a microphone in his hand. He paced the length of the stage, whipping up the audience with his passionate vision of what St. Michael's could become. Haley knew how dangerous his passion was. He'd had her under his spell, however briefly. He paused in midstride, peered out at the audience and his gaze landed on her.

For one heart-stopping second, their eyes locked and Haley's throat tightened. Darn it, she could not glance away.

Jeb held her pinned to the spot, his eyelids lowered slightly, and his voice took on a seductive quality. Or maybe she had merely imagined it. "Since this is my last day on St. Michael's, I'm having a party on my yacht and everyone is invited," he announced.

A cheer went up from the assembly.

He tossed the microphone to the governor and stalked offstage with a jaunty spring to his step, his entourage of sycophants trailing after him. The crowd gathered around, patting him on the back, trying to shake his hand, but he seemed a man on a mission.

It took Haley a few seconds to realize he was headed toward her. Oh, hell, no.

She spun on her heel. Should be easy enough to disappear in this throng. She rushed forward. Her toe caught on a power cord snaking across the ground and she tripped. *Way to watch where you're going, French.* She put out her palms to catch herself and ended up sprawled on the ground. Oh, she hated being vulnerable.

From behind her came a familiar chuckle. He was already upon her. Before she could scramble up, Jeb's hand went around her waist, his citrusy scent enveloping her as he helped her gently to her feet.

"Easy there, baby," he crooned, bending down to dust the dirt from the knees of her scrubs.

She wrenched away from him, stepped back, breathless and despising herself for it. *Hands off the goods, buster.* Worst of all, she couldn't help meeting his eyes.

There he was standing so close to her in his white shirt, pressed khaki shorts, yachting cap and boat shoes, looking every inch the wealthy windblown yachtsman. Everyone else faded away and it was just the two of them.

His light blue eyes regarded her with a lively sense of humor. It was that sense of humor that had been her undoing. She wasn't going to fall for it. Not twice. No way. No how. He was finally leaving the island. Yay! She'd never have to see him again.

"You're coming to my party, right?" His fingers lightly stroked her upper arm.

No way.

"It wouldn't be a party without you," he went on.

"I've got to wash my hair," she lied. On second thought, why lie? Maybe she would wash her hair. Wash that man right out of it.

"All you need is to lose a few of these pins." His fingers went from her shoulder to her hair, which was pulled up into a tight bun. It was far too intimate of a gesture. He plucked bobby pins from her hair, one by one, and the locks fell loosely to her shoulders. "There, much better."

Haley jerked back, pulse thumping hard. *Oh, no. Do not like this. You are not allowed to like this.*

The expression in his eyes was one of total amusement. He knew he'd made her uncomfortable and he was enjoying himself.

"I'm a stickler for clean hair. I make it a policy to wash it every day." She stuck her chin in the air.

"I know," he murmured, his voice warm and cozy. "You do love your rules."

Who was he to act as if he knew her? Just because they'd almost— Well, never mind what they'd almost done—she was determined to forget it. What really chafed was that *he'd* been the one to pull the plug on their encounter.

"Gotta go." She pointed her feet away from him, but for some unfathomable reason, she did not move.

"I should have known you wouldn't come to my party," he said. "Little Miss Straitlaced."

"Just because I don't want to attend your bacchanal doesn't mean I'm straitlaced."

"Bacchanal?" He sounded amused.

"It's a word. Look it up."

"You're chicken."

She straightened. "I'm not afraid of a thing." *Watch out. Noses grow when lies are told.*

"I disagree. You're terrified of having a good time."

She sniffed. "My idea of a good time and your idea of a good time are two very different things."

"I know. Beating myself up is not my favorite pastime."

She curled her upper lip, determined not to smile back at him. "Well, have a nice party and a safe trip." He'd nailed her, but good. Well, not nailed her in the sexual regard. *Pegged her*—that was better terminology. He'd pegged her. Must hate him for that if nothing else.

"Are you going to miss me when I'm gone?" He leaned down, his grin widening.

*All night long.* "Not in the least."

"I suppose I asked for that."

"You did."

He batted his eyes at her. "I'm going to miss you."

"Whatever for?"

"You're the only one on this island who keeps me on my toes."

No, sir. She would not let this man turn her into mush. She was better than that. "You want to be on your toes? Wear high heels."

He threw back his head and laughed heartily. "I also love your sense of humor."

"I wasn't trying to be funny." She folded her arms over her chest.

"You're also the only one who doesn't like me, and I can't figure out why."

Haley scoffed. "Not everyone has to like you. Why do you care whether I like you or not?"

"Because I like *you*."

"You like everyone."

"True," he said, taking a step closer. "But not as much as I like you."

She put up her hand like a stop sign. "You don't like me. You like a challenge."

His crystal-blue eyes glittered. "I have to admit, I do enjoy a challenge. The more you resist, the more I want you…" There was a long pause that set her heart to rocking, before he added, "At my party."

"You can want in one hand and spit in the other and see which fills up first."

Jeb laughed long and loud, showing off a row of straight white teeth. That was the problem with the man. He was too perfect and every woman wanted him. Just like the blonde who was sidling up to his elbow and fluttering her false eyelashes at him.

"Your adoring public awaits."

"What?"

She nodded at the woman.

Jeb barely cast the platinum blonde a glance and quickly swung his gaze back to Haley. "Come to my party."

"I don't think so. It takes my hair a really long time to dry," she quipped.

She could not let him know how much he got under her skin. If he knew that he was a major star in her sexual fantasies, she would never hear the end of it. She refused to be like all the other women simpering at his feet.

Yes, he was good-looking. Yes, he was rich. Yes, he had personality and charisma oozing from his pores. Those were exactly the reasons she was not interested. Jeb Whitcomb was a very superficial man.

"It's the last time you'll ever see me." A hangdog expression crawled over his face. "Don't you want to say goodbye?"

"Goodbye." She wriggled her fingers at him.

"The party won't be the same without you."

"You won't miss me."

He canted his head, his eyes drilling into her like lasers. "Ah, see, but that's where you're wrong."

"It's not going to happen, Whitcomb."

He shrugged. "A guy can always dream, can't he?"

"As long as it stays a dream."

He reached out, touched the back of her hand. A shiver ran straight through the middle of her. "I am going to miss you, Haley."

"That makes one of us."

"Ouch." The grin was back as he clutched a hand to his chest. "You play for keeps."

"Don't ever forget it."

The blonde at his elbow edged closer, cleared her throat. "Mr. Whitcomb, I'm from *Metropolitan Magazine* and I want to do a story on you."

Jeb turned to the woman. "Yes?"

With her hand still tingling from his touch, Haley took advantage of his distraction and slipped off into the crowd. Great. She felt like a James Bond martini, shaken and not— Oh, who was she kidding?

She was both shaken *and* stirred.

HALEY STALKED OFF with a purposeful bounce, her honey-colored hair flowing around her shoulders, those blue scrubs stretching across her sexy rump as she marched away.

Jeb grinned, put a palm to the nape of his neck and licked his lips. *Wow, you can park that swing in my backyard anytime.* He tilted his head, honed in on her narrow waist and curvy hips.

His pulse pounded and his body stiffened. In spite of the cool ocean breeze swaying the palm trees, a simmering heat moved through him. He chuffed out a breath, struggling to regain his equilibrium. Truth was, he really would miss her. He enjoyed their sparring matches. She was sassy and saucy and didn't take anything off anyone.

The last person who'd challenged him that same way was his ex-girlfriend, Jackie Birchard. Out of the dozens of girlfriends he'd had, Jackie was the only one to dump him. It made her stand out in the crowd. The one woman he couldn't charm.

That was, until he met Haley. Too bad they'd never hooked up, although they'd come pretty damn close.

Jeb smiled, remembering. He could have gotten her into bed if he'd wanted. When they'd made out on the beach at sunset a few months back, sparks had ignited unlike anything he'd ever felt before, and that was saying something. Haley had wanted him as much as he'd wanted her, maybe even more so, although chances were good that she would never admit it.

But, surprise, surprise, he'd been the one to put a stop to things before they'd completely lost control.

He'd stopped for two reasons. One, he knew Haley would have regretted it the morning after. She was such a stickler for protocol, held herself and others to high standards. Two, he'd been trying to prove to Jackie that she was wrong about him. He wasn't a self-absorbed playboy with no depth of character. He could restrain himself.

No matter how difficult it had been to break that kiss and send Haley home with their desires unfulfilled.

Ah, well, you couldn't win them all, right? It was time to move on. His work on St. Michael's was done. He'd achieved what he'd set out to achieve. He'd helped rebuild the island. He could return home with his head held high.

"About that interview, Mr. Whitcomb," said the blond reporter with a smile that sparkled like prisms.

Matching her smile, Jeb turned and led her away, but he couldn't resist one last glance over his shoulder at Haley.

She paused and looked back.

Their eyes met.

*Gotcha! Protest all you want, sweetheart—you do want me.* Boldly, he winked.

Her cheeks reddened and her eyes narrowed in a scowl. She ducked her head and flounced from his view, leaving Jeb sorely regretting the night that they'd never had.

HALEY LAY STRETCHED OUT on her twin bed in the one-bedroom bungalow she shared with Ahmaya. She was eating Oreos, twisting the cookies apart and scraping the white filling off with her front teeth before gobbling up the dark cookies. Oreos were her go-to comfort treats when she was stressed or frustrated, and yes, she knew the drawbacks of de-stressing with a sugar fix, but when she was feeling like this, she didn't care.

The quarters were basic and cramped, but a long sight better than the tent they'd lived in after Hurricane Sylvia. She was trying not to think about Jeb, but he kept popping into her head at the most unwanted times.

Why?

Yes, he was wealthy, handsome and self-confident, but he was also full of himself and far too free with his affections. Imagine! He'd called her *baby* and took the pins out of her hair, and she'd just stood there and let him. Unexpected goose bumps lifted on her arms and she hugged herself.

Ahmaya stood in front of the mirrored closet door, examining her reflection as she got ready for the party. "What do you think about this skirt?"

"The hem is too short."

"Perfect," Ahmaya purred.

"You're going to wear it anyway?"

"I am. If you think it's too short that means it's exactly the right length."

Haley sat up. "You're saying I'm a prude?"

"Uh-huh, kinda." Ahmaya ran her fingers through her straight, glossy black hair.

"I'm not a prude," she argued against the heavy feeling in the pit of her stomach. Was she? She didn't mean to be; it was just that she had certain principles and she wasn't going to compromise.

"Prove it."

"What?"

"Prove you're not a prude."

"I don't have to prove anything."

"You don't curse."

"So what?"

"Prudes don't curse."

"I believe in having a wide vocabulary. Is that so wrong?"

"Prudish."

"What?" She raised her arms. "I should go around swearing like a sailor to prove I'm not prudish? Okay, then." Haley let loose with a few descriptive curse words.

Ahmaya looked surprised. "I had no idea you knew those words."

"I'm a nurse. I've heard a lot worse than that. It's just that cursing seems so crude and uncivilized."

"Sometimes—" Ahmaya grinned "—it's fun to be uncivilized."

"If you say so."

"Prude."

"Are we back to that?"

"It's the truth of your being."

"I don't think *prude* is the right word. *Prudent,* if you wish, but not *prudish.*"

"Hmm." Ahmaya stepped into a pair of mile-high stilettos. "Prove it."

"I just did."

"Not by cursing, by coming with me to Jeb's party. I need a wing woman."

"You don't need a wing woman."

"Everyone needs a wing woman."

"Call Jessie. I'm sure she'd go."

"She's stuck working second shift."

"Ahmaya, I don't want to go."

"But you're the one with a car."

"It's only a half mile. You can ride your bike."

"In this?" Ahmaya swept a dramatic hand at her sexy outfit. She had a point. Jimmy Choo didn't pedal well. Her friend dropped on her knees in front of Haley, pressed her palms together. "Please, please, please. I'll do the crash-cart checks for you all month."

Haley sighed. "You know parties aren't my thing."

"Seriously, it's great that you're all into altruistic causes and saving people and everything, but you can't work or think about work 24/7. You need to lighten up. Let your hair down."

That remark had Haley remembering how Jeb had pulled the bobby pins from her hair. She suppressed a shiver. He'd kept her bobby pins. It would serve him right if she went to his party and demanded the return of her bobby pins.

"You are the dullest twenty-seven-year-old I know." Ahmaya pouted.

Ouch! That hurt.

Haley considered self-discipline her strong suit, not a flaw. It was what had gotten her through nursing school with a 4.0 grade-point average. An accomplishment she was very proud of.

"One little bitty party isn't going to kill you. Everyone is going to be there. Look at it as a networking opportunity." Ahmaya batted her long, dark lashes. "Pretty please?"

"Oh, all right, but I'm only staying for one drink and then I'm out of there."

"You'll drink really slowly, right?"

"An hour. I'll stay an hour. If you're ready to go in an hour, you can leave with me. If you're not, then you'll have to find your own way home."

Ahmaya's face dissolved into a happy smile and she extended her hand. "Deal."

Huffing out a sigh, Haley shook her hand.

"Now," Ahmaya said, "we have to find you something sexy to wear."

"No, we don't. Jeans and a T-shirt will do just fine."

Ahmaya looked aghast. "Shut your mouth. This is a par-*tay*. You're not going looking like a schlub."

"I came here with the Red Cross and I stayed to work. I have scrubs and jeans and that's it."

"Ah." Ahmaya's eyes glistened. "But *I* have party clothes. My sister sent me a big box of them last month."

"You wear a size four."

"You're not that much bigger than me. I bet we can squeeze you into my blue Ann Taylor Loft spaghetti strap. Ann Taylor sizes run big, and blue is your color." Ahmaya dug in her closet, found the dress, tossed it to Haley. "The dress is a little bland for my taste anyway. Should be right up your alley."

"I'm not much for florals. Too girly."

"No excuses. Try it on." Ahmaya sank her hands on her hips.

Reluctantly, Haley stripped off her scrubs and put on the dress. It hugged her curves and the hem fell halfway up her thigh. *Hello, where's the burlesque stage? Gypsy Rose Lee is in the house.* She tugged at the bottom of the dress, trying to lengthen it. "It's too short."

"You've got dynamite legs. Why are you so scared to show them?"

"I'm not scared. Just not interested in looking like a hoochie mama."

"You're saying I'm a hoochie mama?"

"The dress isn't snug on you and you're two inches shorter than I am."

"Celebrate your curves, Haley. I'm jealous."

"It's too tight in the boobs."

"It's perfect. That's the way a sexy dress is supposed to fit."

"I'll need a strapless bra."

Ahmaya's eyes danced mischievously. "Go braless."

"My nipples will show."

"I have Nippies you can wear. No more excuses."

"What are Nippies?"

"Gawd, do you live under a rock? They're nipple covers."

"I live on a hurricane-devastated island. My concerns run more toward basic human necessities than fashion."

"You can say that again. Can you for once not be a Debbie Downer?"

That startled her. "Am I really a killjoy?"

"Yeah, kinda. Not everyone lives by your work-work-work credo, and you know, sometimes people need something fun to take their minds off the bad things that have happened. Jeb totally gets that."

Her friend's comment stopped Haley in her tracks. It wasn't the first time she'd heard that she was too focused on hard work and doing things by the book. Did everyone think she was a hard-ass? Yes, she was very careful by nature and thorough in forming her opinions, and she had high principles. Why was that a bad thing? Why did she so often feel out of step with others her age?

"Haley, if you're not perfect every minute of the day, the world won't come to an end," Ahmaya said, her voice softening. "Please just try to have fun tonight. Will you promise me that?"

She really did want to fit in. Wanted people to like her. "I'll try, but the main reason I don't want to go is that Jeb Whitcomb will be there."

"Of course he'll be there. It's his party."

"He's just so cocky. He thinks that all women want to fall at his feet."

"Most of them do."

"Not me."

"Do you really want to make him suffer?"

That intrigued her. "How would I do that?"

"Show up looking gorgeous. Let him see what he'll never have. Rub it in."

Hmm. She liked that. Little Miss Sadist. "Okay, I'll do it."

"Yay." Ahmaya clapped. "Now, will you let me do your makeup?"

Haley started to resist—Ahmaya had a tendency to overdo makeup application—but she quickly thought better of it. She was determined to prove she could be a party animal just like everyone else, even if it killed her.

But most of all, she wanted to give Jeb Whitcomb a good-riddance send-off he wouldn't forget.

# 2

**Luff**—*The flapping motion of the sailcloth when a sail is undertrimmed*

JEB WAS IN HIS ELEMENT. He loved throwing parties, loved crowds. Having people around amped him up, fed his energy.

It wasn't even sunset and the party was already rocking. Wang Chung was urging "Everybody Have Fun Tonight" from the sound system. People were bobbing and weaving to the beat. The bartender he'd hired was imitating Tom Cruise moves from *Cocktail*. The yacht overflowed, people spilling out onto the gangplank and dock. The caterers dished up delectable canapés—prawn spring rolls, Thai chicken skewers, langoustine pastry puffs, smoked-salmon crisps, mini Yorkshire pudding with roast beef and horseradish, and mushrooms stuffed with lump crab meat. Japanese paper lanterns and flickering citronella candles provided intimate lighting. The air smelled salty and calm.

He stood smiling, dressed in a blue button-down

silk shirt, chino slacks and deck shoes without socks, a tumbler of finely aged Scotch and water in his hand. Great turnout. Then again, the turnout for his parties was always great.

But one person was missing. The person he most wanted to see.

*You really didn't think she'd show, did you?*

No, he hadn't. Why did she snub him so vigorously? Why did he care so much to begin with? He was supposed to resist the allure of other women so he could win Jackie back. His ex-girlfriend would have to be impressed with all he'd accomplished on St. Michael's. He'd proven he wasn't a dilettante and that he was serious about helping others.

The hospital administrator came over to thank him again for his contributions. Jeb leaned in, pretended to listen intently, but his gaze kept straying to the dock, watching the arriving guests.

No Haley.

What was the big deal? He should be happy to have that contentious female out of his life for good. He would be on his way home to Florida tomorrow. He should be thinking about Jackie. She would be so surprised to see him.

Yes! Going home. He missed Miami and he was turning flips at the thought of seeing Jackie again and showing her how he'd changed, but he couldn't help wishing he could have said goodbye to Haley. He would miss the way she challenged him at every turn. Not too many people did that to him.

Jackie did.

It had just been so long since he'd seen Jackie that he was imbuing Haley with his ex-girlfriend's traits.

That was all this was. That was all it could be, because he'd given up being a ladies' man and he was damned proud of his restraint.

A year.

It had been a year since he'd been with a woman. His longest record since he'd lost his virginity at sixteen. *See, Jackie, I have changed!*

The governor and his wife joined Jeb's conversation with the hospital administrator. Jeb winked at the wife, a dumpy woman in her mid-fifties wearing a colorful muumuu. "You're looking beautiful tonight, Mrs. Freemont."

She blushed like a girl and ducked her head. "You're such an outrageous flirt."

From eight to eighty, most women were so easy to charm. Look them straight in the eye, pay them a compliment and mean it. That was the essential part. You truly had to love women. Add a conspiratorial wink and they were putty.

All except for Jackie.

And Haley.

"You don't have drinks," Jeb said to the Freemonts. "Let me rectify that right now." He motioned for one of the waiters roving through the crowd with trays of hors d'oeuvres to come over. He gave their order to the waiter, turned back to pick up the thread of the conversation when his attention was immediately snagged by a leggy honey-blonde sauntering up the gangplank.

She wore a skimpy little blue dress with tiny white flowers scattered over the material, and her breasts moved with such a pert bounce he had to assume she was not wearing a bra.

Instantly, his body lit up.

His gaze trailed from the blue four-inch stiletto sandals on her delicate little feet, up the length of those amazing calves and back to the nip of her narrow waist to the boldly unharnessed breasts, and finally, he glanced at her face.

His heart did a double take.

No way! This could not be Haley French looking like a supermodel with her perfectly arched eyebrows and glossy pink lips.

His eyes bugged out and his tongue stuck to the roof of his mouth. He knew she was pretty, yes indeed, but he had absolutely no idea she could look like this. Stunning.

"Excuse me," he said smoothly to the Freemonts and the hospital administrator, then set down his drink and made a beeline straight for Haley.

Her eyes widened and she reached for the elbow of the dark-haired girl beside her. She said something short and succinct to her friend, shook her head, spun on her heel and hurried back down the gangplank.

"Wait!" Jeb called, pushing through the crowd.

But Haley didn't even glance around. Her friend stood on the gangplank looking bewildered.

"Jeb, hey, I've been wanting to speak to you," someone said.

"Great party." A beautiful woman clutched at his arm.

A man clapped him on the shoulder. "We're going to miss you on St. Michael's."

"Excuse me, excuse me." Jeb shook off the people. Why was he so desperate to prevent her from leaving?

He blew past Haley's friend, reached the end of the gangplank. Haley was a good twenty feet ahead of him. She was already off the dock and climbing the stairs to the marina parking lot.

"Haley!"

She didn't turn around.

He was running now. *Definitely uncool. Ruining your image, dude. Stop it.*

Jeb reached the bottom of the stairs just as Haley crested them. "Baby, don't go."

She stopped in midstep and spun around to glower at him. One sexy gam perched on the landing, the other on the step below. "Excuse me?"

"Baby, please don't go."

"Baby? Did you just call me *baby?*"

He shrugged, chagrined. "Sorry. Figure of speech."

"Do I look like an infant to you?"

"No, ma'am. Not in any way, shape or form."

Slowly, she came back down the steps toward him, her eyes blazing fire. His pulse hammered hotly through his veins. "The word *baby* is also often used as a term of endearment between lovers," she said.

"Uh-huh." He nodded.

"Are we lovers?"

"Unfortunately, no." What was he doing? Jackie was the one for him. He was trying not to seduce other women, and for a whole year, he'd been a very good boy. He should just tell Haley goodbye and go back to the party.

"I am not an infant and we are not lovers, correct?"

"Correct."

"Then under no circumstances are you to call me *baby.* Got it?"

He gave a jaunty salute. "Got it. No *baby.* Not now, not ever. The word is stricken from my vocabulary."

"Good. Even among lovers I find the word off-putting. Infantilizing each other isn't the way to build a mature, loving bond."

"You have strong opinions about it."

"I do."

"You really don't like me all that much, do you?"

"Not especially."

"Why did you come tonight?"

"My friend Ahmaya needed a wing woman and a ride. She doesn't have a car."

"You were just going to go off and leave her?"

For one second, she looked shamefaced, but quickly recovered. "Ahmaya's a big girl. She can take care of herself."

"And yet, you came with her." Jeb raked his gaze over Haley. "Looking like that, I might add."

A pink blush crept up her neck. "It's Ahmaya's dress."

"You're stunning."

"Oh, I feel so special," she said snidely. "I bet you said that to only a couple dozen women today."

"More like a baker's dozen," he teased.

Her shoulders relaxed a little at that and a tiny smile briefly lit her lips. Small victory. With Haley, he'd take his triumphs where he could get them.

"Are you still planning on running away?"

"I'm not running away."

"Seems to me you are."

"I can't run in these shoes. I was walking away or, more accurately, hobbling away."

"Why?"

"I don't like parties."

"Why not?"

"They're too crowded. I don't like crowds."

"Uh, you forget I saw you in action in those relief camps right after Hurricane Sylvia. The tents were packed tighter than sardine cans and you were right in the middle of it."

"That was different. I was helping people."

"C'mon back to the party," he coaxed. "I'll let you give the Heimlich maneuver if anyone chokes on a canapé."

There was that brief smile again.

His heart gave a strange bunny hop. He held out a hand. "C'mon."

They stood there a moment; Haley posed on the top steps, Jeb at the bottom, groveling, palm outstretched.

"Don't leave me hanging, ba—" He almost said *baby* but stopped in the nick of time.

"Why should I come back to your party?"

"For one thing, you're a good friend. Ahmaya needs you."

"Low blow."

"I'll use any tool in the arsenal."

"Why?"

"Why what?"

"Why do you care so much if I'm at your party or not?"

It was a very good question. He didn't have a glib answer handy and ended up just blurting out the truth. "I've got enough yes-men and yes-women around me. I need someone who knows how to luff a sail."

"A what?"

"There are no brakes on a sailboat. The only way to slow down is to luff the sail. That means to undertrim the sail so it doesn't catch any wind."

"In other words, I'm a brake, huh?"

"Well, you know you are a stickler for rules, etiquette, proper behavior and all that." He waved a hand.

"A wet blanket."

"I didn't say that."

"A Debbie Downer."

"I didn't say that, either."

"Why would you want a brake at your party? Parties are supposed to be go, go, go. No-holds-barred. Looks like you'd want an accelerator, not a brake."

"Don't be offended by the brake comment. A brake is a good thing," he said. "A brake is very necessary. A brake keeps you safe."

"Like a mother?"

He shoved fingers through his hair. "This isn't going well, is it?"

"Not in the least." She folded her arms over her chest, but the smile was back and stayed a fraction of a second longer this time.

"Come luff my sails, Haley."

She hesitated. Ha! He had her.

"You're already dressed to impress. Why waste it?" he cajoled.

"I don't know why I'm even considering this."

"'Cause part of you doesn't really want to spend tonight all alone washing your hair."

"I don't mind being by myself."

Man, she was a hard nut to crack. "Okay," he said. "But you don't know what you're missing." Taking a calculated risk, he turned to go.

"Wait."

He grinned, stopped, but did not turn back around. "Yes?"

"I *am* pretty hungry. I'll stay for a bite to eat." The sound of her mincing down the metal stairs in her stilettos rang out into the twilight.

He bent his arm at the elbow, signaling for her to take it. To his surprise, she did.

"Only because I'm wearing high heels," she said, reading his mind as she slipped her arm through his.

Her touch ignited a firestorm inside him. Jeb gulped. Good thing he was sailing out tomorrow—one more day around Haley and there was no telling what might happen.

HALEY HAD NO IDEA WHY she'd allowed smooth-talking Jeb Whitcomb to coax her into coming back to his party.

Partially, it was true that she was hungry and hated to cook for just herself, plus, there was her promise to Ahmaya, but there was another part of her that she didn't really want to poke. The part that *liked* being around Jeb.

The minute they reached the deck of his sailing yacht, Haley let go of his arm. She was disturbed to find herself breathless.

"What would you like to drink?" Jeb asked.

"You don't have to get my drink."

"It's no problem." He lifted a finger at a white-gloved waiter waiting at the ready.

Haley supposed a lot of women fell for the master-and-commander routine. Your every wish was his command. Seductive, for sure, but she mistrusted anything that wasn't hard-won.

The waiter appeared at his side.

"Could you please bring Miss French a…" Jeb looked at her expectantly.

"Diet cola."

"Seriously?"

"I don't drink."

"Not ever?"

"Rarely. New Year's Eve. Wedding toasts. That kind of thing."

"This is my going-away party."

"So?"

"You're not going to toast my journey?"

"I can toast with diet cola."

He got a knowing look on his face. "Aha."

"What?"

He shrugged. "Nothing."

"The 'aha' meant something."

"It's not important."

"Then why did you say it?"

The corner of his mouth tipped up. "I've figured out something about you."

She pulled her lips downward. "And what is that?"

"You're afraid of losing control."

"What's wrong with that?"

"I never said anything was wrong with it. Just had a lightbulb moment."

"I like to keep my wits about me."

"Make an exception," he said.

"You want me witless?"

"Maybe."

"Why?"

"To prove you can let your hair down."

"I don't have to prove a thing to you."

He leaned closer. "No, but wouldn't it be fun to stop thinking so much for once and simply let go?"

"Five minutes ago you were telling me you needed someone who knew how to luff a sail."

"If the sailcloth stayed luffed, you'd never set sail."

"Nothing wrong with dry land."

"You're not a sailor?"

"Landlubber all the way. That's me." She groaned.

The waiter cleared his throat.

"You're holding up the poor man," Jeb said. "What'll you have? And no diet coke unless it has rum in it."

She thought about sticking to her guns, but it was easier just to give in, and at some point, you couldn't fight everything, right? *Pick your battles, Haley. Everything is not worthy of a crusade.* She recited her mother's frequent advice. "White wine, something with a low alcohol content and sweet."

"Uh," he said sounding mildly amused. "I had you pegged for something tart, like a salty dog."

"What's a salty dog?"

"Grapefruit juice and vodka with a salted rim."

"When it comes to alcohol, the sweeter the better." She crinkled her nose. "I don't like the taste."

"Bring her a glass of Luccio Moscato d'Asti," he told the waiter.

The waiter actually bowed, clicked his patent leather heels and departed for the open bar.

"What's Moscato whatever?"

"Light, white dessert wine, five percent alcohol. Couldn't get a kitten drunk on it. You'll love the stuff."

"Sounds perfect." She spied Ahmaya in the center of a clot of men—so much for hope of rescue on that score.

"Come." Jeb took her by the elbow and escorted her toward the buffet.

She wanted to resist out of general principle—he was far too proprietary—but the deck was crowded, and in these ridiculous stilettos, it was nice to have him threading the needle to the food. But what disconcerted her most was the feel of his skin against hers. Just like she'd enjoyed that kiss he'd given her on the beach several months back. Which, if she were being honest, was at the heart of why she wanted to avoid him.

He handed her a plate and the waiter brought her drink. Solicitously, Jeb held the wineglass for her while she filled her plate. The gentlemanly shtick was all part of his seduction ritual, no doubt. *Don't fall for his courteous manners. It's a trap.*

"You're not going to have anything to eat?" she asked him.

"When I eat, I'm not giving my guests my full attention."

"Well, feel free to mingle." She waved him off. "Don't let me hold you back."

"Ah, but you're one of my guests. I want to make sure all your needs are met."

Her stomach grumbled, so she loaded up on food while he waited, and then he guided her down three steps to bench seating on the lower deck. Two people were sitting there, but he went over and whispered something to them and they got up. He turned to smile and waved triumphantly at the vacated seats.

"You ran them off?"

"I politely asked if they'd mind giving up their seats for a lady whose feet were hurting."

"Hey, I can eat just fine standing up."

Jeb sat and patted the spot next to him. "Please, have a seat, Haley."

The way he said her name, as if it were the most elegant sound on earth, sent tingles zipping through her. Reluctantly, she sat and perched her plate on her knees, which she kept firmly pressed together in the too-short dress. Instead of meeting his gaze, she concentrated on pulling a morsel of chicken off a wooden skewer.

"I'm glad you came tonight."

"That makes one of us."

"You love busting my chops."

She grinned. She did.

"How's the wine?"

"Haven't tasted it yet." She took a sip. Ooh, it went down sweet and smooth. "I like it. Reminds me of Kool-Aid."

"Wow, something you approve of. Duly noted."

"No need to note it. This is the last time we'll ever see each other."

"You sound happy about that."

Not happy. Relieved. And grateful that she'd managed to avoid his charms and stay out of his bed, although she'd had a near miss.

He reached out to touch her hand. "I'm going to miss you, Haley. I've never met anyone quite like you."

She slipped her arm away. "Great puff pastries. Kudos to the caterers."

"I'll pass along your compliments to the chef."

An awkward silence passed between them.

"You're one of the hardest workers I've ever had the pleasure to know," he said.

"Thank you." What was he getting at?

"And I admire how straightforward you are. No beating around the bush."

"Speaking of that." She dusted off her fingers with a napkin. "Let me just set you straight. There's no way I'm spending the night with you. Not if it were my last night on earth."

"Whew." Laughing, he leaned back in his seat and wiped a palm over his forehead in mock relief.

Whew? Haley scowled.

"Because the last thing in the world I ever want to do is have sex with you," he said.

She stared at him, stunned, her jaw unhinged. He did not want to have sex with her? "Excuse me?"

"Don't get me wrong. It's not because you're not desirable, because you most certainly are in a tough-girl, nothing-touches-me-emotionally kind of way."

"Then what the hell is this full-court press about? Begging me to come to your party, getting me food and wine, *touching* me like you mean business."

He held up a palm. "Wait a minute. Let me get this straight—you want me to want you, but you're not about to sleep with me?"

Haley pursed her lips guiltily. Yeah, well, sorta. "I want to be the one woman who won't fall at your feet."

His grin turned wolfish. "You almost did."

"But I didn't."

"Only because *I* called it off."

"I would have called it off. You just beat me to it."

"We'll never know, will we?"

She put her plate aside. She really wanted more of

those crab-stuffed mushrooms, but she did not want to sit here with Jeb Whitcomb any longer. "You are driving me bonkers."

"Right back atcha, baby."

"Don't call me *baby!*" How was it that this man could ruffle her so easily? She hated that.

"Why not? You're acting like one. I was trying to pay you a compliment and you got all twisted off for no reason. You have a tendency to do that."

"Yeah? Well, you have a tendency to believe you're God's gift to women. News flash, you're nothing but a rich frat boy swooping in with your money to make yourself feel good."

"What's wrong with that? I feel good, people get the help they need."

"Because you sail away to your fancy life, leaving people longing for you."

His smile turned knowing and he lowered his voice. "Are you longing for me, Haley?"

"Yes, longing for you to be gone." Wine in hand, she flounced away.

# 3

**Safety harness**—*Personal gear that attaches to a tether to keep the person on board*

JEB TOOK A LONG PULL off his Scotch and water; the synapses in his brain were alight with lusty and inappropriate impulses. He'd pissed her off.

Oh, she was gorgeous when she was mad and she had the world's cutest scowl, hands down. He followed her up the steps, back to the bridge. She circled the boat.

He licked his lips.

She ended up talking to one of her coworkers starboard, but every now and then, she'd dart a glance in his direction. When their eyes met, she'd quickly glance away. *Can't handle the heat, huh, angel?*

*Corner her. Kiss her,* hissed one of those lusty, inappropriate impulses.

Nope. No way. He'd lasted this long without giving in. He could certainly last one more night. Haley deserved much better than a quick one-night stand, but even a pious man had his share of sexual fantasies, right? And when it came to the pious spectrum, Jeb slid to the not-so-much side of the scale.

She was unlike the sophisticated society women that he usually dated, women who could shrug in and out of an affair like their designer clothes. Haley was honest and down-to-earth and direct, and he was a jerk for even entertaining the fantasies dancing around in his head.

He made the rounds, talking to his party guests, but no matter where he was on the boat, his gaze was drawn back to her again and again. A full moon climbed the sky, setting the mood and tugging at the tides. Haley stood in shadows with her head tilted up, bathing that side of her face in moonlight, and she let out a light laugh that stirred his desire.

*Do something. Move. Drink. Eat. Talk to your other guests. Just stop staring at her!*

He went toward her. She stood with her back against the mainsail mast, her spine as straight as the post. She had great posture, shoulders squared and alert.

People stood around her, drinks in hand, but he saw none of them. Moonlight glinted off her eyes; her lips were painted deep pink. He realized it was the first time he ever remembered seeing her wear lipstick. The wind ruffled her hair, which for once was not pulled into a stern ponytail or tight bun. The breeze molded the dress to her slender figure, hugging her hips and stopping several inches above her knees.

His mammalian brain whispered, *Claim her.*

*Resist. You are not going to succumb. One more night and you'll be out to sea. Within a week, you'll be holding Jackie in your arms and the wait will be worth it.*

*Love the one you're with,* prodded the most primal part of him.

He snuffed that out.

Or at least tried to.

Haley was watching him warily.

He moved closer.

She slunk away.

Seeing her in this environment—*his* environment—was novel and exciting, and he simply reacted, moving forward as she slipped away from him behind other guests.

The chase was on.

The part of his DNA that was thousands of years old stirred, eager for the hunt. His body quivered and his heart hammered against his rib cage. All his senses were aroused.

His civilized veneer vanished. Raw, aching need took over. Need so strong it scared him.

*Back off! Wake up. Snap out of it.*

Treacherous body.

He shook his head but could not seem to stave off the sense of urgency shoving his blood through his veins. He was a lion and she was the most beautiful lioness on the plains. She mesmerized him and he was aware of everything about her. It was disorienting, this acute sense of awareness.

His muscles were tensed, the hairs on his arms raised, a thrill shivered through his nerve endings. He felt well and truly alive, but the jolt was nerve-frazzling and worrisome.

Around and around the boat they went, Jeb pursuing, Haley fleeing. It was fun and he was quite enjoying himself, even though he knew nothing would come of this strange cat-and-mouse game. Didn't want anything to come of it.

Until a group of people cornered him for a toast and Haley gave him the slip.

HEART IN HER THROAT, a helpless smile on her face, Haley hid behind a large man to catch her breath and then rushed down the steps as best she could to the lower deck. What was this weird game they were playing and why was she playing it? Why didn't she just leave?

Why? Because Jeb had lit a fire inside her that scared her silly. Being with him was like driving a Ferrari on the Autobahn with a learner's permit. Roadkill. She'd been there before. Refused to be there again.

She had to get off this boat. Coming to the lower deck had been a mistake. He could corner her down here.

Alarmed by that thought, she moved to climb the steps but she wasn't accustomed to stilettos. It took more skill than one might suppose. She tripped and nose-dived forward, wine splashing out of her glass. She would have hit the deck if a masculine hand hadn't reached out to catch her.

"Are you okay?"

She glanced up to see Rick Armand, a respiratory therapist who worked at St. Michael's General Hospital. He'd asked her out several times, but she'd put him off. She considered him a bit smarmy with his oversize porn-star moustache and the way he clicked his tongue and used his fingers like pistols, pretending he was shooting her. Still, she let him rescue her from Jeb. "I'm fine."

"You lost your drink," Rick said. "Let's get you another."

She was about to say no, when she glanced back to see Jeb giving her the eye. "Yes, that sounds good. Make it a salty dog, please," she said extra loudly so Jeb would hear.

Rick took her empty wineglass and gave it to a passing waiter. "Would you like to come with me?"

Yes…yes, she would.

She accepted Rick's hand and allowed him to lead her to the bar. It took everything she had in her not to look back to see the reaction on Jeb's face. She wouldn't give him the satisfaction of knowing she cared what he was thinking about her going off with Rick.

As they stepped up to the bar, Rick placed a hand to the small of her back. Haley moved sideways and Rick dropped his hand. "Salty dog for the lady," he told the bartender. "And I'll have a beer."

"Thank you," she told him.

"I've never seen you looking like this," Rick said, raking a lascivious gaze over her. "I like it."

"Moment of temporary insanity," Haley mumbled and tugged at the hem. A bandanna had more material in it. How did Ahmaya wear these skimpy dresses without feeling overexposed?

"I like it."

The bartender placed their drinks on the bar. Rick reached over, plucked a pink flamingo stir stick from the holder, dropped it into Haley's drink and stirred the salty dog before handing it over to her.

"The alcohol tends to settle to the bottom. You have to stir it to make sure it's completely mixed. Don't want that last swallow to be pure alcohol. Might go straight to your head." Rick leered as if that was exactly what he was hoping would happen.

See, this sort of thing was precisely why she didn't like wearing short skirts and stilettos. It had guys dripping all over her.

"Thanks for watching out for me," she said sarcastically and stirred her drink vigorously.

"My pleasure." Rick showed a row of small, crowded teeth. Shark.

What was she doing here with this dweeb? Oh, yeah, avoiding Jeb. She looked around for him, didn't see him. Thank heavens.

They stepped away from the bar, walking to the back of the boat. Aft, she thought it was called. She touched the straw to her lips, took a swallow of the salty dog. Not bad. Tangy. Salty. Tart. She took another sip. Hmm, on second thought, it had a weird aftertaste she didn't really like. Maybe she could dump the drink overboard.

"Your eyes sparkle in this lighting," Rick said. "And with the full moon behind you, the night is picture-perfect."

"Um."

Rick started telling her about the souped-up Camaro he'd ordered and was having shipped in from the States, expounding at length on exactly how much he'd paid for it. Like, really, who cared if he'd blown a year's salary on a car?

He pitched forward. "You're not drinking your drink."

"It tastes a little weird."

"Do you want me to get you something else?"

"No, I'm fine."

Rick held up his beer mug. "A toast?"

"To what?"

"To seeing people in a different light."

Why not? "To seeing people in a different light," she repeated.

They clinked glasses. Feeling obligated, Haley took another swallow. What was that weird aftertaste? It was just supposed to be grapefruit juice, vodka and salt.

"And to a beautiful night." Rick raised his mug again.

"To a beautiful night." This time, she barely sipped the drink. Okay, she was definitely going to have to pour it overboard when Rick wasn't looking.

She meandered toward the edge, but before she could get there, a woozy sensation hit her and she wobbled on her heels. Whoa, those salty dogs sneaked up on you.

"Are you all right?" Rick loomed over her.

*Back off, dude.* "I'm fine." She didn't want him to know she was feeling tipsy. "I just need to, um…go powder my nose." *And get away from you.*

It occurred to her that she was spending the night running away from men. She knew that most women would love to have two guys vying over them, but Haley found it annoying more than anything else.

"Could you excuse me?" she asked, pushing her drink at him.

He curled his hand around the glass. "Sure, I'll be waiting right here."

Making sure to take careful steps, she maneuvered through the crowd. She longed to go home, but she couldn't drive like this. Not with her head swirling. She'd go to the restroom, splash some cool water on her face and then go find Ahmaya and see if she was in any shape to drive them home.

Seriously, she was such a lightweight. A few sips of wine and a quarter of a salty dog and her knees were buckling.

Carefully, she made her way from the bridge to the main deck. The party was in full swing. People were dancing all over the place to The Red Hot Chili Peppers singing "Under the Bridge." How appropriate. She realized that Jeb must have handpicked songs for the evening. Slick. What else would she expect from him?

"Bathroom?" she asked a woman she knew from the hospital.

"The one on this level is occupied, but I heard there's an en suite in Jeb's cabin on the lower deck."

"Thanks," Haley said. Wow, was she actually slurring her words? This was why she didn't drink. She could not hold her liquor.

As she clung to the stair railing that led to the lowest deck, her head spun so wildly that she had to stop several times and take a deep breath. Finally, after what felt like a hundred years, she stumbled into the bedroom.

Jeb's bedroom.

A strange feeling passed through her as she stared at the bed and vividly imagined herself in it with Jeb. *Oh, knock it off.* She had to get into that bathroom and put some cold water on her face.

She sank against the door, clicked it locked in case anyone else wandered this way. She needed privacy until the dizziness passed. After a minute, she lurched toward the bathroom door. Heat swamped her body. Her mouth was like a desert. And those damn stilettos were anchors on her feet.

This didn't feel right. Sure, she was a lightweight drinker, but this...this was more than being tipsy. This felt *wrong*.

Her vision blurred. She couldn't think. *Help!*

She heard a knock on the door.

"Haley?" It was Rick.

He was the last person she wanted to see.

The door handle rattled. "Haley, are you in there?"

She might not want to see him, but she was feeling very weird and maybe he could help her. She opened her mouth to answer, but belatedly, it occurred to her that Rick might have put something in her drink. The salty dog had a funky aftertaste and he'd stirred it before he'd passed it to her.

Had she been drugged? How naive was she to have trusted him?

Her heart thundered in her chest as the truth of it hit her. Rick was a predator prowling outside, waiting to pounce. Thankfully, she'd had the presence of mind to lock the bedroom door.

The bathroom was so close and yet seemed a hundred miles away. Screw it. She was going to lie right down here on Jeb's bed for a couple of minutes, just until the dizziness passed and Rick went away, and then she'd go find Jeb and tell him what she suspected had happened to her.

Jeb would know how to handle that lowlife Rick. A charming playboy Jeb might be, but oddly enough she trusted him. Beneath that party-hearty attitude, he *was* a good guy. She had to admit that.

Satisfied with her plan, Haley flopped headfirst onto the mattress and that was the last thing she remembered.

THE LAST GUEST LEFT at 3:00 a.m., as the cleaning crew Jeb had hired swept down the deck. By the time he paid the cleaners, the caterers and the parking-lot attendants, he was so exhausted he could barely keep his eyes open. The party had been a resounding success, but even in the midst of that knowledge, he was disappointed, because at some point during the night, Haley had slipped away without saying goodbye.

He'd been on the lookout for her, but hadn't managed to see her again after she'd gone off with Mustache Rick. He'd found Rick, who was frantically searching for Haley, so he figured she'd given the smarmy respiratory therapist the slip, not him. Still, he would have liked one last conversation with her.

Never mind. He had other things to think about. Like getting home to Miami to see Jackie. He couldn't believe it had been a year since they'd spoken, and he was eager to see her again and show her how much he'd changed.

He thought about his last conversation with Jackie, when she'd broken up with him. It had come as a shocker—because no woman had ever broken up with him. Jackie had been on her father's research ship, the *Sea Anemone,* and he'd sailed up and tried to get her to blow off work and go sailing with him.

"Some of us work for a living, Jeb," Jackie had said, clearly irritated with him.

"I work for a living," he'd protested, giving her his biggest smile and an endearing wink.

"When was the last time you built something?"

Hmm, well, it had been over a year since he'd completed the Miami Beach condos, but everyone knew the Florida real-estate market was in the toilet. His strategy was simply to wait it out and have a good time while doing it. "I'll be ready when the market turns around."

"You have the luxury of waiting. Most people don't, Jeb. You squander your time."

"I don't see things that way."

"I do and I just don't think this relationship is working. We're too different."

That comment had smacked him upside the head. "I can change."

"Seriously? You come from money. It's all you've ever known. You don't really have to work. You're a playboy at heart. I mean, c'mon, just look at the name of your yacht. *Feelin' Nauti.* You summed yourself up quite neatly."

"But don't we have a lot of fun together?" he'd wheedled.

"Yes, that's precisely the problem. All we do is have fun together."

"What's wrong with that?" he'd asked, puzzled.

"Nothing as long as it's in small doses. But my life is ninety percent work, ten percent play. You, on the other hand, are completely the reverse. Ten percent work, ninety percent play. It's not a lifestyle I desire."

That had thrown him for a loop. All his life he'd been complimented on his ability to light up any room he walked into and now here was Jackie telling him that wasn't necessarily a good thing. "So let me get this straight. You're breaking up with me because I'm too much fun to be around?"

"Precisely."

"I'll work."

"Prove it."

"How?"

"Go do something useful."

"Like what?"

"I don't know. Find someone to help. Find something bigger than yourself to be a part of. Figure it out."

"If I do that, will you give me a second chance?"

"Jeb—"

"Please," he said, "don't cut off all hope."

She sighed. "All right. I'll give you a year. If you can get involved with something meaningful and prove to me you've changed, we'll see."

"You won't regret it," he said, but she'd already turned back to her research materials.

The first thing he'd done was change the name of his boat to *Second Chance,* even though it was supposedly bad luck to change the name of a boat. The very next day, Hurricane Sylvia had churned up the Atlantic and a few days later slammed into St. Michael's. Bad luck for St. Michael's, but Jeb had taken it as a sign and he'd headed out to help rebuild the devastated island.

Jeb smiled smugly. Jackie had given him a much-needed wakeup call, and she was going to be so impressed at how he'd changed.

He shut off the lights, blew out the candles and stood on the deck in the moonlight. He was damned proud of what he'd done. He'd gone from thinking only of himself to putting others first, and he was so grateful to Jackie for setting him on this path. He couldn't wait to tell her about it.

Bed. It was time to go to bed, but he didn't have the energy to head down to his bunk on the lower deck.

He stretched, yawned, completely exhausted. His eyelids were heavy. He walked to the blue-and-white-striped bridge hammock, stretched out, cupped his head in his palms and stared up at the stars.

"I'm coming home a changed man, Jackie," he murmured and instantly fell into a deep sleep.

## 4

**Crab**—*To compensate for current or leeway by correcting the heading to one side of the actual course*

THE SOUND OF HIS CELL PHONE announcing a text message woke Jeb at dawn. Bleary-eyed, he pulled a palm down his face, blinked at the pink rays of sun pushing up over the crystal-blue water.

*Ding.*

The cell phone in his back pocket reminded him about the text.

He blew out his breath, dropped his feet over one side of the hammock and fished in his back pocket for his phone. The text was from Jackie. His pulse leaped and he grinned widely.

Until he read the message.

To our closest friends and family. You are invited to the Fourth of July wedding of Coast Guard Lieutenant Commander Scott Marcus Everly and Jacqueline

Michele Birchard at 4:00 p.m. aboard the *Sea Anemone* docked at Wharf 16, Key West, Florida.

We know our union is quick and unexpected, but when you've found your soul mate, there's nothing to do but take the plunge. We would love to have the pleasure of your company. RSVP to Jackie @ JackieBirchard@seaanemone.com.

Jeb's smile vanished. A muscle at his right eye jerked repeatedly. He had to read the text four times before the words finally sank in. Jackie was getting married on the Fourth of July. Six days from now. The precise number of days it would take *Second Chance* to sail from St. Michael's to Key West in calm waters.

And she'd invited him to the wedding via text message!

"A bit cowardly, Jackie," he murmured. "You could have had the decency to pick up the phone and call me."

He got to his feet, shoved his hands through his hair, paced and cussed a blue streak. How could she do this to him? She'd promised she would give him a year to prove he could change, and now she'd gone and gotten herself engaged to some guy in the Coast Guard? What the hell?

Jeb had to admit his feelings were hurt.

To top it off, she'd used the words *soul mate*. Jackie did not talk like that. She didn't believe in stuff like that. What had happened to her? She could not be thinking clearly. She must be caught up in some kind of lust-fueled haze, like the one he'd gotten ensnared in when he almost had sex with Haley on the beach. It happened. He understood. He could forgive her. What he couldn't do was let her make the biggest mistake of her life.

Distressed, he punched Jackie's number into the keypad.

She answered on the second ring with a cheery, "Hey, Jeb, long time no hear."

How could she sound so casual?

"I just got your text message," he said tersely.

"Will you be coming to the wedding? I know it's short notice, but it would mean a lot to me to have you there."

"Jackie, you can't marry this guy."

"Why does everyone keep saying that to me?"

"Who else said it to you?"

"Boone, for one." Boone was Jackie's half brother. "He was a bit of a jerk about it, too," Jackie continued. "At least I know you're not going to be a jerk. You're never a jerk about anything."

"Well, I'm with Boone on this one. You can't marry this guy."

"I can and I will. I'm in love, Jeb. For the first time in my life. Truly, madly, deeply, forever and ever in love."

"Okay, who are you and what have you done with Jackie Birchard?"

"I've changed, Jeb."

"I've changed, too, Jackie. I've changed so much and I miss you. You can't marry this Scott guy because I'm the man for you and I can show you if you just give me a chance."

"Jeb." She laughed. "You don't love me."

Laughed! She was laughing at him.

"But I do, Jackie, I really do."

"You think you love me because I'm the only woman who has ever turned you down. The only woman who's ever challenged you and called you on your crazy lifestyle."

Not the only woman. Immediately, Jeb thought of Haley.

"How long have you known this guy?" he demanded.

"Only a month, but the time doesn't matter. Not when it's the real deal."

"Listen to yourself. Do you really hear what you're saying? You're marrying a guy you've only know for four short weeks."

"It's all the time I need."

"Jackie, you've got to believe me—"

"Are you coming to the wedding?"

"I'm coming to Key West. Right now. I'm on my way. It'll take me six days to get there, winds willing. I'm on St. Michael's."

"You on the *Feelin' Nauti?*"

"I changed her name."

"Bad luck." Jackie hissed in a breath. She was a smart, educated woman working on her Ph.D. in oceanography, and yet, she had a sailor's innate superstition. It came naturally to those who spent their lives on the sea and understood that there were certain things beyond your control. Not breaking certain rules could make a sailor feel safer. It was psychological. They both knew it, but ingrained patterns of behavior were hard to break.

"It's not bad luck. I changed her name because of you."

"What are you calling her these days?"

*"Second Chance."*

"Oh, Jeb."

"Promise me you won't get married until I get there."

"I can't promise that. The wedding is at four."

"Then I will find a way to be there before four."

"Good, should I put you down for fish or filet mignon?"

"What?" he asked, thrown off by the question.

"Fish or beef. For the reception head count."

"Once I get there, there won't be a reception."

"Oh, Jeb, you are so funny. I can't wait to see you again."

"Jackie, I'm being serious—"

"Gotta go, honey, another call is coming in. I've been nuts with the RSVPs. See you on Saturday, if not before."

The dial tone sounded in his ear.

Honey? Jackie had called him *honey*? As if he was some maiden aunt or the flower girl or something.

He thought about calling her back, but he realized no matter how hard he tried to tell her that he'd changed, she'd simply have to see it to believe it. Okay, he deserved that. He'd been fickle and shallow in the past, but his year on St. Michael's truly had transformed him. The only way that Jackie was going to know he was serious was if he showed up at the wedding, got down on bended knee and asked her to marry him instead of Scott.

After all, she'd only known Scott a month. How serious could it really be if she'd only known him a month? She and Jeb had known each other through nautical circles since they were kids. His family had helped finance many of Jack Birchard's research trips before he'd gotten as famous as Jacques Cousteau. That was how Jackie knew him so well. Even before they dated, she'd heard of all his exploits. That was the main strike against him. She'd witnessed his dating history firsthand.

There was only one thing to do. Sail to Key West immediately and confront Jackie face-to-face.

THE ROCKING MOTION was so nice, a gentle lullaby soothing Haley's splitting headache. Her eyes were closed and her thinking was fuzzy. She should open her eyes and see where she was, because she'd forgotten, but a provocative fragrance distracted her.

What was that enticing scent? It smelled like sea and cotton linen and masculine man.

Jeb.

It smelled like Jeb.

Mmm, Jeb.

Dreamily, in spite of the headache, her mind conjured up her favorite image of Jeb Whitcomb.

November.

It was last November on Divers' Beach at sunset.

After a taxing twelve-hour shift at what was then a makeshift tent hospital, Haley had decided to take a long walk to clear her head. She'd been working nonstop since she'd arrived with the Red Cross on St. Michael's the previous June and she was close to the breaking point. She just needed some alone time and Divers' Beach was the most secluded stretch of sand on St. Michael's. Especially since Hurricane Sylvia had driven many people to leave the island for good.

The beach had been cleaned up, but there were still

big piles of brush stacked up in the tree line awaiting disposal. Her heart ached for the damage her adopted home had suffered.

As a child, she'd spent her summers on the island. Her parents were teachers and each year they volunteered as instructors for a program to help disadvantaged children get the education they needed. It was a win-win situation. Free vacation for her and her sister and brother, while underprivileged children got the assistance they needed. The experience taught Haley the power of giving to others.

That was when she happened upon Jeb, who was up to his waist in the surf, the golden rays of the evening sun glinting off his bare chest. At first, she thought he was dangerously swimming alone—which was sort of what she might expect from a guy who liked to test limits, except he never went anywhere alone—and then she realized there was a flailing seagull in the water beside him.

Jeb approached and soothed the frantic bird, and then he plucked a plastic six-pack ring holder from around the gull's legs. Freed, the bird launched itself into the air. Jeb stood there watching it soar, a happy smile on his face, unaware he was being observed.

When he turned back around and spotted her, he looked chagrined for a fraction of a second, as if embarrassed to be caught saving a seagull's life, but then quickly he started preening, flexing his biceps and strutting like a badass, almost killing the tender scene she'd just witnessed.

He sauntered ashore, water rolling off his body, black swim trunks clinging to his hips. Haley gulped, noting they were completely alone on the beach.

"Hey," he greeted her, stuffing the plastic six-pack holder into the pocket of his swim trucks. "Fancy meeting you here."

The previous day, they'd had an argument at the meeting of the hospital planning committee. He wanted to put an open-air solarium in the middle of the new hospital. She thought the money would be better spent on more monitoring equipment. He'd won, of course. He was paying for the hospital, after all, but she did have to give him props for at least hearing her out, and then today, the administrator had told her that Jeb had cut an extra check to cover the equipment, too.

She was still in her hospital scrubs. She hadn't taken the time to change. Home at this point was still a communal tent in the town center.

"Thanks," she said, always able to admit when she was wrong about someone. "For buying the equipment."

"Thank *you*."

"What for?"

"Making sure that my priorities were straight. Notice that no one else on the committee protested my plans?"

"No one ever goes against you."

"Except for you." He'd grinned at her as if that was a good thing.

She found herself softening toward him, but that scared her because she was just as attracted to him as everyone else. She was *not* going to give in. She'd done the hero-worship thing before and that had turned out badly.

"Where's your entourage?" she asked.

"I gave 'em the slip." He winked conspiratorially.

She warmed from the inside out. "What for?"

"Sometimes a guy just wants to be alone."

"I'm shocked," she teased. "I never considered that you got tired of being adored."

"It's not all it's cracked up to be," he answered in a moment of honesty that took Haley by surprise.

"Well…" she said. Could it be more awkward between them? "I'll leave you to your privacy."

He put out a hand to touch her arm.

Her skin ignited. Like gasoline on a fire.

"Don't go," he said.

"I don't want to intrude."

"You're not." His smile was soft and inviting and she just swooned. "May I walk with you?"

She nodded and he fell into step beside her.

They walked along in silence for a while and then stopped to watch the sun slide down the horizon. It winked out, leaving a salting of stars in its wake.

"It's very peaceful," he said.

She took a deep breath, acutely aware of how close he was to her, how good he smelled and how kind he'd been to rescue that seagull. It was the only excuse she had for what happened next.

"Haley," he murmured and lowered his head. "You've bewitched me."

"What?" she squeaked.

"I can't seem to stop thinking about you."

"Me?"

"You."

"But why? I'm nothing special."

"You underestimate your beauty."

Yeah, right. Here she was with no makeup on, hair pulled back in a ponytail, wearing shapeless green hospital scrubs, and he was telling her she was beautiful. In a pig's eye. "I'm fully aware of my physical attributes. I have nice legs, I'll grant you that, and decent hair, but I'm no supermodel. I have a gap between my teeth and my eyes are just a little too wide set and my chin is too pointy—"

"All those things come together to create an interesting face. Do you know how deadly dull most supermodels are? After a while they all look alike. Be proud of your distinctive looks. You're an original."

"Oh," she said because she was embarrassed by his compliments. She wasn't accustomed to being buttered up and Jeb was slicker than olive oil. She could not forget that.

"But as pretty as you are, it's not your looks that intrigue me." He stepped closer.

"No?" She was barely breathing now.

"Nope."

She gulped.

"What I like most about you is your ethics."

"Yeah, that's so sexy. Guys tell me all the time I have gorgeous ethics."

"They do?"

"I'm being snarky."

"And your dry sense of humor. I like that, too, although I'm not sure I'm sharp enough to always get your jokes."

"You're being humble?" Haley put a hand to her forehead and pretended to faint.

"I like how grounded you are and how you set a good example for those around you."

"What's this all about, Whitcomb?" she asked suspiciously. "Why are you flattering me?"

"It's not flattery. I'm being sincere."

She eyed him speculatively.

"I know we butt heads and I want to smooth things out."

"Ah, you mean you want to convert me to your way of thinking."

"No," he said, "not at all. Didn't I mention that I like the way you challenge me? I just want to be clear that a little healthy disagreement is a welcome thing."

"I'll remind you of that the next time I disagree with you."

"Do that." He nodded vigorously.

She wasn't sure what to do. She'd never really seen this side of him. Of course, she'd never really been alone with him, either.

The water lapped at the shore, a whispering, seductive rhythm. The breeze ruffled the leaves of the palms and the air smelled of coconut. The moon started its ascent up the sky.

Jeb peered deeply into her eyes. His lips were so close, just inches away, and his chest was so bare, his skin so tanned and her knees so weak. Such enticing lips they were, angular and full, but not too full. What would his lips taste like? How would they feel against her mouth? What would they make her feel?

She got trapped in his eyes. Trying to snap out of it, she lowered her lashes and her gaze became tangled up in the stunning view of his muscled torso. Jeb was like a pirate ready to plunder a cargo ship weighted with gold. Within her personal space, his unique masculine scent claimed her.

"This is nice," he murmured. "Being here with you."

"Nice," she echoed.

"You know," he said, "if I didn't—"

But he never got to finish, because damn her, she'd just acted, which was something she never did—no one had ever accused her of being spontaneous—but in the moment, she went completely off the rails, flung her arms around his neck and kissed *him*.

Haley didn't know who was more surprised, her or Jeb.

For a second, he simply stood there not kissing her back and she'd thought, *What have I done?*

Then he groaned low in his throat, gathered her in his arms and pressed her to his chest. The chest she'd just been aching to touch. His abs were as taut and hard as she had imagined they would be.

He made a deep, pent-up sound as his lips assailed her, his tongue striking like heated lightning on a still, cloudless day. Her body was stunned, thrilled. He tugged gently on her ponytail, tilted her head back and thrust his tongue farther inside of her.

She clung to him.

Moaned. Pulled him down to the sand. The soft-packed damp earth was cool against her spine and he was astride her, his knees sunk into the sand. He stared down into her eyes with wonder and shock. He was hard and she was—oh, this was the shameful part—she was whimpering for more.

Her fingers plucked at the waistband of his shorts.

His eyes darkened.

Her heart thumped.

His hands were all over her, burning her up, building sweet pressure within her body. Construction. He was a builder and she was the structure he was erecting. His lips laved hers, a pleasing foundation, a solid beginning, the underpinnings.

He used small, quick kisses. And long, big, bold kisses that lasted for minutes. And at last, when she was certain that he couldn't possibly do more, he covered her mouth with a kiss of considerable duration. A kiss that sizzled with energy and, like a tower of blocks, stacked one atop the other, rising higher and taller, reaching for the stars, sweeping the top of the moon, climbed to dizzying heights that promised she'd never, ever feel anything like this again.

Just when she was about to rip off her clothes, bare herself to him and beg him to take her right there on the sand, Jeb had stood up and stepped away from her.

"I can't do this," he said hoarsely.

"Please," she begged. Yes, she'd begged. "You can't leave me like this."

"Haley—" he shook his head "—you deserve so much better."

He was turning her down?

Shame shot through her. She couldn't even interest a playboy? She jumped up, dusting off the seat of her scrubs.

"I don't mean to hurt you. Another time, another place and I'd be all over this, but there's someone else and—"

"Stuff it, Whitcomb," she'd growled to hide her deep humiliation.

"Haley." The pain in his voice sounded genuine, but she wasn't sticking around to find out. She'd run from him then, as fast as she could.

She shoved the memory out of her mind and her

eyes flew open. She stared up at the ceiling, and for a second, she was disturbed to see she wasn't in her bed.

Where was she?

It hit her. Bricks. Tons of them. Falling in on her. The party. Rick. The suspect salty dog. Staggering to the bathroom.

She'd spent the night in Jeb Whitcomb's bed! Fully dressed in Ahmaya's sexy Ann Taylor Loft spaghetti-strap dress and ridiculous stilettos. She had to get out of here.

Now.

She leaped off the mattress, landed wrong, staggered against the door. Strange, it felt as if the boat were moving—probably just the wake from a passing speedboat rocking the yacht in the marina slip. Except this motion felt a lot stronger than simple wake ripples.

It felt as if they were under way.

But they could not be under way. Jeb wouldn't leave the dock with her on board. Surely he knew that *someone* was on board. His bedroom door had been locked. He had to know she was in here. Bedroom doors did not lock themselves from the inside. Besides, hadn't Ahmaya come looking for her? Wasn't her friend concerned?

Alarmed, she unlocked the door and lumbered out into the hallway. No one was around, but the lower deck was as neat as a pin. Someone had cleaned up and she hadn't even heard it? How long had she been out? Luckily, today was her day off from work, but still, this was unsettling. Where was Jeb?

Slowly, she climbed the stairs to the next deck. "Hello?" she called out. "Jeb? Anybody?"

No answer.

With a sick feeling settling in the pit of her stomach and her head throbbing as if there were a miniature construction crew up there whacking down walls with a sledgehammer, she eased up the final set of stairs to the bridge and looked around.

She spied Jeb at the helm with his back to her, his whiskey-colored hair blowing in the breeze, a serious set to his shoulders.

Reality hit like the slap of a palm against her cheek. Not only were they under way, but it was also late afternoon, and there was nothing around as far as the eye could see except for miles and miles of turquoise ocean.

# 5

**Sheet**—*The line used to let out or trim in a sail*

"WHAT ARE YOU DOING?"

Startled, Jeb whipped around to see a woman standing behind him. The hairs on the nape of his neck lifted. What the heck?

It was Haley, her hair in a mad tangle, her dress rumpled, her eyes blazing sparks.

His stomach lurched. He was so stunned to see her there that all he could say was "I…I…um…uh…I…"

"Where are we? Where are we going? Why are we not in the marina? Why are you kidnapping me?" She spit out rapid-fire questions, her tone accusatory.

Flabbergasted, his jaw dropped. "Kidnapping you? Why are *you* stowing away on my boat?"

"I didn't stow away. It was not my intention to stow away. I am not a stowaway."

"And yet here you are." He engaged the autohelm so he could give her his full attention and turned to face her.

"You took off without my permission."

"Clearly, you spent the night aboard without *my* permission." He raked his gaze over her. How could he not have known she was on board? "Or without my knowledge."

"Turn this boat around and take me back to shore," she demanded.

"Excuse me?"

She raised her chin, indignant. "You heard me."

Jeb laughed.

"Stop laughing at me." She scowled. "This isn't the least bit funny."

"It's a little bit funny."

"Not from my perspective."

"Seriously, French, do you ever see the humor in a situation?"

She looked hurt then, but quickly blinked it away. "I was a bit rude earlier. Excuse me. It was just an eye-opener to wake up and discover I'm out to sea."

"Apology accepted."

"Now, please return me to shore."

Jeb shook his head. "Sorry, no can do."

She stepped closer. "Why not?"

"For one thing, we've been under way since dawn."

"What time is it now?"

"Three-fifteen p.m."

"Three fifteen! That means we've been gone—"

"Eight and a half hours."

The column of Haley's throat moved in a visible gulp. "You have to take me back."

"I don't like this situation any better than you do, but I can't." He was already wondering how this was going to look to Jackie, showing up at her wedding with another woman. He couldn't show up at the wedding with Haley. Once he'd cleared customs and immigrations in Key West, he'd stick her on a plane back to St. Michael's. Jackie would never know.

"What do you mean, you can't?"

"I have to get to Key West by Saturday. It's doable, but only if the winds and currents cooperate. If I take you back, I don't stand a chance. We have to crab the tempestuous Gulf Stream and that's always a crapshoot, although luckily, the weather report indicates smooth sailing."

"Crab?"

"In order to compensate for the Gulf Stream current, you have to sail a bit to the side of the actual course in order to reach it."

"I get it. Moving sideways like a crab."

"That's it."

She surprised him by plucking the sunglasses from the pocket of his shirt, her fingers lightly—accidentally—grazing over his nipple, and his body responded immediately.

Dammit!

She slid his sunglasses onto her face, and a surge of something dark and sexy moved through him.

"Go right ahead. Make yourself at home. What's mine is yours," he said.

"Do you mind? I have a headache, and since you did kidnap me—"

"Didn't kidnap you. Had no idea you were on board."

"Nonetheless, I'm out to sea against my will without my sunglasses."

"Too much wine last night?"

"Too much salty dog with some kind of drug in it."

"What?" Alarm rippled through him.

"Why else do you think I was passed out in your bedroom for sixteen hours? Alcohol alone wouldn't knock someone out that long."

"Cabin."

"What?"

"A bedroom on a boat is called a cabin."

She waved a hand. "Whatever. Anyway, I have a strong suspicion that creepy respiratory therapist Rick Armand spiked my salty dog with something."

Part of him wanted to say that if she hadn't tried to escape him by running off with Armand that it wouldn't have happened, but another, stronger part of him had a vivid image of grabbing Armand by the throat and shaking him until his eyes popped out of his head or his mustache fell off, whichever came first. "The creep drugged you?"

Massaging her temple, Haley told him what had happened to her the previous night.

"I'm truly sorry," he apologized, "that this happened to you at my party."

"It wasn't your fault. Rick is a sleazebag. I already suspected it, but now it's confirmed. I was going to make a report to the St. Michael's police, but by the time I get there the drug will long be out of my system and there's no way I can prove he did it. All I can do is warn the women at the hospital to be wary of him."

"I'd help you do it, too, if I were going back."

She grimaced. "So I *am* being kidnapped."

"Not kidnapped. Whisked away for a few days. Think of it as a vacation. When we get to Florida, I'll put you on a plane back to St. Michael's."

"In the meantime, I'm stuck with you."

"Is that so horrible?"

Her grin was tiny. "Could be worse, I suppose. I could be stuck out here with Rick the dick."

"Over my dead body," he said vehemently.

"So why are you crossing the Gulf Stream?"

"I have to stop a wedding."

For the first time since she'd come onto the bridge, she looked something besides distressed, upset or angry. Curiosity sparked in her eyes. "Whose wedding?"

"My ex-girlfriend is getting married to a guy that she's only known for a month."

"And you don't think she should marry him?"

"She should marry me," he declared.

"You?" Haley hooted as if it was the funniest thing she'd ever heard.

Annoyed, Jeb frowned. "Why do you find that so humorous?"

"Hey, five minutes ago you were accusing me of not having a sense of humor. I just never pictured you as the marrying kind."

Actually, neither had Jeb, but since Jackie had started him off on his personal journey, he really had started to change. Going to St. Michael's was the most monumental thing he'd ever done.

"So what's the story?" Haley sat down on the hammock and reached down to unbuckle the stilettos from around her gorgeous feet.

It did weird things to him to think about her sweet fanny sitting where he'd just been sleeping. It felt strangely intimate. Just as intimate as when he thought about her having spent the night in his bed, and dammit, he'd missed it.

Seriously, what was wrong with him? He was talking about marrying Jackie, and here Haley's delicious bare pink toes wriggling against the deck were turning him on. Maybe he hadn't changed as much as he'd thought.

Haley rocked gently in the hammock, swinging back and forth with mesmerizing motion.

*Jackie, Jackie, Jackie,* he chanted to remind himself of his goal. He was going to Key West to stop Jackie from marrying this Coast Guard Scott character.

Jeb tried to call up his former girlfriend's face, but to his complete shock, for one blind instant, he could not remember what Jackie looked like. When he tried, he couldn't picture anyone except for Haley. Alarmed, his mind raced through his mental cache of old girlfriends—Kellie, Ashley, Heather, Robin, Brenna, Jane, Erin, Sophia, Lucy, Emily, Rachel, Jackie.

Nada.

He couldn't call up any of them because the woman in front of him was absorbing every bit of his attention.

*A leopard can't change its spots,* Jackie had told him.

Jeb was determined to prove that wasn't true. He could settle down. More than that, he *wanted* to settle down. This was all a startling new development.

Haley put out a toe to the bench seat. "Have a seat and tell me about her."

"Who?"

"This woman you're crabbing the Gulf Stream for."

"You don't want to hear about her."

"Why not?"

"Why?"

"Because," Haley said, "this is the most real I've ever seen you. For once, instead of being a guy regularly idolized by adoring females, you're the one behind the eight ball."

"You're enjoying my misery, aren't you?"

She slanted her head, grinned and winked. "Not at all. I just enjoy getting a glimpse at the human being lurking behind the slick facade."

MAYBE IT WAS BECAUSE she was overwhelmed at finding herself all alone with Jeb Whitcomb in the middle of the ocean on his yacht with St. Michael's eight and half hours behind them. Maybe it was the lingering effect of being drugged and the dull headache that had settled behind her eyes. Or maybe it was the fact that what Jeb was doing was so romantic it disarmed her.

"Jackie's the reason that we…that you…that we didn't do it that night on the beach?" she asked.

"Yep."

"Well," she said, "that makes me feel a little better. I thought it was me."

"Oh, no, ma'am. Not you. Not by a long shot. In fact, your very sexiness is what had me turning tail and running. I was not going to fall back into old habits."

That should have cheered her up, but it didn't and she couldn't say why.

*Aw, c'mon. You know the reason why. You're jealous of this Jackie woman.*

He kept talking about her, which was annoying, particularly since Haley was the one who had encouraged the conversation in the first place. Then he told her that Jackie was the daughter of the world-renowned oceanographer Jack Birchard. But of course, Jeb was in love with someone of his own ilk…a rich celebrity type. It was stupid of her to think he might fall for a lowly nurse.

*Holy Oreos.*

Was that what she was secretly hoping? That Jeb would fall in love with her? Ashamed of herself, Haley pushed his sunglasses farther up on her nose, thankful that her eyes were hidden from him. She didn't want him seeing her thoughts written on her face.

She should get over herself and be happy for him. Well, except that the woman he was in love with apparently loved someone else. Wasn't that just the way of love? Fickle. Stupid. Love oughta be banned.

"So," he said, "I do appreciate your patience and understanding."

"I gotta call Ahmaya." She jumped up. "She's going to be freaking out."

"You might not be able to get cell-phone reception out here. We are pretty far from shore."

"I have to try." Where was her purse? Down in Jeb's cabin, no doubt. "I'll be right back," she said and hurried to the lower deck.

She found her purse on the floor of his bedroom, fished out her cell phone and put a call in to Ahmaya.

"Haley!" Ahmaya answered on the first ring. "You naughty girl."

"Naughty?"

"Spending the night with Jeb Whitcomb after you pretended not to like him. I knew you really had a crush on him."

"I did not spend the night with him."

"Your car was still in the marina parking lot when I left the yacht at two o'clock."

"Why didn't you come looking for me?"

"I did. You were nowhere to be found and now I know why."

Static crackled over the airwaves. "Ahmaya, I don't know how long the connection is going to last, so just listen to me."

Quickly, she explained the situation.

"That's awful!" Ahmaya said. "I knew that Rick couldn't be trusted."

"Anyway, will you tell the director of nurses I had an emergency situation?" That was true enough. "And I need to take a week of vacation."

"Okay. I'm sorry, Haley."

"What for?"

"You finally get to be all alone with Jeb and you find out he's got a thing for another woman. That's gotta hurt."

"I'm fine, really," she said, but her heart gave a strange little tug.

"Be—"

The phone cut out.

"Ahmaya? Are you there?"

Nothing.

"Ahmaya?"

Dead.

Well, at least she'd gotten through long enough to let Ahmaya know where she was. Sighing, Haley hung up. She'd just lost her last contact with the outside world. It felt monumentally scary to realize she was out on the open sea. Stuck in this skimpy party dress. For six days. With Jeb Whitcomb.

Six days.

And five *nights*.

Right. Too bad she couldn't stay down here in the cabin for the duration of the trip. Her stomach rumbled, reminding her of one major reason she couldn't stay down here. She hadn't eaten anything since the hors d'oeuvres the previous evening and she was starving.

As if by magic, she caught a whiff of something delicious. Bacon. Yum.

Drawn by the scent, she went to the galley.

Jeb stood at the stove frying up bacon through a brown haze. Oops. Not a brown haze. Brown lenses. She was still wearing his sunglasses. She slipped them off her face and she could see him clearly now. Far too clearly if the truth be told.

His feet were bare, showing off very sexy toes. Who knew toes could be sexy? His hair was windblown, his cheeks bronzed. He looked every inch the wealthy yachtsman.

"Did your call go through?"

"Just in the nick of time. I lost the signal, but Ahmaya's going to make my excuses to the director of nurses."

"I appreciate your being such a good sport about this, Haley, but I shouldn't be surprised," he said. "You're at your best when you're helping people."

"Hey, I'm simply along for the ride, reluctantly, I admit, but there's nothing to be done about it. I really can't expect you to spend over eight hours returning me to the island when you're on a mission to win back the woman of your dreams."

"Thanks for understanding." He pushed a tall glass

of iced tea toward her. "Drink. It's easy to get dehydrated on the water, and after what Armand pulled, you need to flush out your system."

"Thanks." She took the glass of tea. It was so refreshing and cool, she sucked down the whole thing in nothing flat.

"I thought you might be hungry, too." He flipped bacon.

"I could gnaw the arm off that chair."

"No need. I'm making BLTs. You do eat meat, don't you?"

"I try not to eat red meat too often, but I love it." Unable to resist the enticing aroma any longer, she reached over to filch a piece of bacon from the cooling rack. Crisp, crunchy, salty. Perfect. "May I help?"

"You can slice up a tomato." He pointed at the garden-ripe beefsteak tomatoes in the wicker basket on the table.

"I can't believe you know how to cook," she said, plucking a tomato knife from the Calphalon knife block resting on the granite countertop.

"Why's that?"

"I figure you grew up with cooks and servants at the ready to do your bidding."

"I did," he admitted. "But my mother believed her sons should know how to prepare a meal, so she got the cook to teach us."

"The cook?"

"We had live-in help."

"Smart mother. I like her style."

Jeb shot her a sideways glance. "She would like you, too. You're not an Airy."

"An Airy?"

"That's what she called my girlfriends. Airy, short for *airhead.* Except for Jackie. Jackie is the opposite of an airhead."

"Like me?"

"Like you," he echoed, his gaze warming her skin.

"So you date airheads for fun, but when you decide to get serious, you go in the other direction."

"I was never serious about Jackie until she dumped me. We've known each other since we were young and she was more a friend than anything else, but when she told me she had no interest in life with a playboy, well, I gotta admit that it hurt my feelings."

"I'm liking Jackie more and more."

"Because she hurt my feelings?"

"Because she pushed you in the right direction." This was such a bizarre conversation to be having with the man she was half hung up on. Okay. She was admitting it. She liked Jeb. Stupid time to find out. Or maybe she only liked him because she knew there was little danger of him liking her back now that he was hot to stop Jackie from marrying someone else.

"Honestly," he said, "I never thought Jackie would get married. She's so wrapped up in her work."

"Maybe that's why you were dating her in the first place." Haley washed two plump tomatoes in the sink, scrubbed the tender red skin. "Because she wasn't a threat to your bachelorhood."

"Then why do I want her back?"

"Because you can't have her. We always want most what we can't have."

He shifted his stance to look at her. "Do you really believe that?"

She shrugged. "It's a theory."

"I just know I have to see her."

"So," Haley said, desperate to talk about something else besides the love of his life, "how many brothers and sisters do you have?"

"Two half brothers and a half sister. Three stepsisters and a stepbrother."

"That's a lot."

"My parents—" he waved a hand "—have trouble staying married."

"No full siblings?"

"Nope."

"Where are you in the birth order?"

"My dad had a daughter when he married my mother. They had me and then got divorced. Dad remarried a woman with two daughters. My mother remarried a man with a son. Then my mother and her second husband had a son and daughter and my dad and his fourth wife—"

"Fourth?"

"It seems to have stuck this time. He and Pam had a son. My half-brother Benjamin is five."

"And your mother?"

"She and Chet have been married twenty years now, so that's working out, too."

"I'm dizzy just hearing about it. How do you keep up with everyone?"

"It's old hat to me." He shrugged.

"I bet Christmas at your house is wild."

"I got tons of presents. When parents feel guilty for not giving you enough attention, they tend to buy your love."

Poor guy. It sounded as if he'd been shuffled from

pillar to post and been bought off. No wonder he was a bit materialistic. "What does your dad do for a living?"

"Runs the family business."

"Which is?"

"Shipbuilding."

"You weren't interested in that?"

"I like building houses. It's nice creating homes for people."

"That sounds odd coming from a playboy bachelor."

"Construction is in my background, but I want to blaze my own trail. Besides," he said a bit sheepishly, "I mostly build vacation condos."

"Did you take a big hit when the housing bubble burst?" Haley concentrated on neatly slicing the tomatoes and tried to ignore how close they were standing to each other and how good it felt to be near him.

He nodded. "But I have a trust fund from my grandparents and it gives me flexibility to do other things."

"Like rebuilding St. Michael's."

"Yes."

"Which you wouldn't have done if Jackie hadn't dumped you."

He shrugged, looked chagrined. "Probably not."

"So Jackie did a lot for your personal growth."

"She did." He turned the gas burner off and blotted grease from the bacon with a paper towel. "What about you? Do you have any brothers or sisters?"

"One of each. Both younger."

A head of iceberg lettuce rested beside the sink. He picked it up, smacked the bottom against the counter and pulled the core from it. He tore the sturdy leaves with long, tanned fingers.

Giddy buoyancy bubbled up inside of her. She had no explanation for it. It was probably a residual effect of being drugged the night before.

"Tim is in the Peace Corps after getting his degree in sociology, and Phoebe is still in college studying green technologies."

"Sounds like you come from a family of helpers."

"I do," she said proudly. "My parents are teachers and every summer they take part in a teachers-without-borders program. When I was growing up, St. Michael's was where they volunteered. They've been married thirty years and are as much in love today as on their wedding day."

"That's great," he said, sounding slightly wistful. "I can't imagine what that's like."

He spread out the lettuce, which glistened with the water he'd rinsed the leaves in, on another paper towel. Then those long fingers were at the loaf of artisan sourdough bread, slicing through the brown crust to the soft white center. A delicious shiver skipped down her spine. Why did she find watching him make sandwiches so erotic?

"Could you get the mayo from the fridge?" he asked.

Happy to have an excuse to step away from him, she hurried to the compact refrigerator and retrieved the mayo. This was craziness. She couldn't allow their proximity to throw her.

She cracked open the fridge. A package of double-stuffed Oreos sat on the top shelf.

"Oreos," she exclaimed. "They're my favorite, and you keep them in the fridge, too!" She might be in

love. Any guy who kept her favorite cookie in the refrigerator was a man after her own heart.

"Where else would you keep them?"

"Exactly." She grinned at him over the refrigerator door. "Ahmaya says I'm nuts for taking up fridge
space with them, but cold Oreos are so good."

"The best."

"Do you break them apart, eat the filling out, then
eat the cookie?"

"Is there any other way to eat Oreos?"

"I love the creamy center."

"Why do you think I get double-stuffed? Twice the
creamy goodness."

"You know, Whitcomb, you might not be such a
bad guy after all," she said.

His eyes twinkled. "If I had known we'd bond over
cold Oreos, I would have gifted you with a refrigerator full of them months ago."

She ignored that statement and passed him the
mayo. "Here you go."

Their knuckles brushed in the handoff and her
stomach did a stupid flip-flop thing. Motion of the
ocean. Boats rolled. Exactly. That was part of the problem. Being at sea set up a certain rhythm, sweet lull-
ing, a dulling of one's internal warning system. Or
at least that was what seemed to be happening in her
case.

Jeb slathered mayo on the sourdough bread, topped
it with the bacon, lettuce and slices of beefsteak tomatoes she'd cut up. "Simple, but elegant and delicious,"
he proclaimed and handed her a sandwich on a plate,
took the second one for himself and she could have
sworn he added in a soft mumble, "not unlike you."

"What?" she asked, her heart suddenly pounding.

"Up top for the view?"

She blinked. "Huh?"

"To eat," he clarified and she felt silly for thinking he'd said that simple-but-elegant-and-delicious comment about her.

She touched her temple. "Right now I feel too much like a vampire to go into the sunshine."

"Right. I forgot."

They sat at the table across from each other. Haley dug into her sandwich. It was so good and she was so hungry that she had to remind herself to slow down.

"I like watching you eat," he said.

Feeling self-conscious, she stopped chewing.

"You're not one of those girlie girls who pick at their food. You go at it with gusto."

"You talking about the airheads?"

"I am."

"Does Jackie eat with gusto?"

"Actually, no. Jackie's head is so wrapped up in her research that she doesn't even take time to enjoy the food she eats. She is usually reading oceanography books or studying nautical charts or writing a paper and would chew shoe leather if you stuck it in front of her for breakfast. But you," he said with admiration in his voice, "you enjoy every bite."

"It probably comes from being a nurse and having to grab meals when and where I can. I appreciate any food I can get."

"You're fun to cook for."

"It's fun to eat what you cook."

He grinned at her and leaned in closer. Even through the mouthwatering aroma of bacon, bread and tomatoes, his scent wafted over her, that clean sunshine smell that spelled *J.E.B.* She had a wayward urge to bury her nose against his neck and take a lingering whiff.

"Dessert?" he asked.

"If you're talking Oreos, yes." She grinned. "My one great temptation."

"The only one?" he drawled, strolling over to the refrigerator to retrieve the Oreos.

"The only one I'm admitting to," she said in a tone far sexier than she intended.

"Why, Haley French, are you flirting with me?" He returned to the table, opened the package of cookies.

She lowered her lashes, gave him an enigmatic smile. Hey, this was fun. No wonder Ahmaya was an outrageous flirt. She reached for a cookie, twisted it apart and scraped the filling with her teeth. From her peripheral vision, she saw Jeb do the same thing, his movements mirroring hers. "Mmm."

"It's odd—" his fingers twisted apart a second cookie, one hand moving clockwise, the other counterclockwise "—that we've worked together for almost a year but we hardly know anything personal about each other."

"What's the point of getting to know each other better? You're gone from St. Michael's and there's the whole Jackie thing."

He stared at her with expressive eyes, and it might have been her imagination, but he looked slightly hurt. "Didn't mean to step on your toes. I know I do that a lot. Just thought it might be nice to know more about each other. Never can tell when you'll need a friend."

"I'm sorry," she apologized. "I can be a little

prickly sometimes. Not the best defense mechanism in the world, I agree."

"You feel like you need a defense mechanism against me?" He sounded surprised.

"You have a way of taking over every room you walk into. It can make those of us who are less secure feel threatened."

"You?" His mouth dropped. "Insecure? You are the most capable, competent person I've ever met."

"In my job, okay, I know what I'm doing, but in social situations? Where small talk and charming repartee are de rigueur? Not so much."

"You do better than you think you do."

Flustered, she glanced away and mumbled, "That's kind of you to say, but untrue."

"So," he said, "what should we talk about?"

That was the sixty-four-thousand-dollar question since they had absolutely nothing in common. "You're the suave, debonair one here. You pick."

"How about hobbies? What do you do in your spare time?"

"I pretty much work all the time or volunteer."

"Do you like movies?"

She shrugged. "As much as the next person, I guess."

"Sports?"

"Doing or watching?"

"Either."

"Not fond of watching sports on TV, but in person on a balmy summer night, baseball isn't bad. I'd much rather participate in a sport than watch someone else having all the fun."

He propped his cheek in his palm and studied her

as if she were the most fascinating person on earth. He had a way of making her feel special that she found unnerving. "What sports do you participate in?"

"Nothing much these days, but I used to be a marathon runner."

"That's impressive. Built for the long haul, huh? How'd you pick up the sport?"

"I started running to get over—" She stopped. She wasn't going to get into that. It was too personal of a topic to discuss with him. She shook her head. "Never mind why I started. Running cleared my head."

"Why did you stop?"

"Hurricane Sylvia."

"The bitch," he teased. "I run."

"I know. I've seen you on the beach."

"And you've never been tempted to join me?"

Tempted? Oh, yeah. That was precisely why she had not joined him. "I always had too much to do."

"C'mere." He motioned to her with two fingers.

"Huh?" she asked. What was he up to?

"Lean forward."

She reared back.

He laughed. "You always do the opposite of what I want you to do."

"What is it?"

"You're very suspicious."

"Some guy drugged me last night. Don't you think I'm justified?"

"I'm sorry about that, Haley." His eyes darkened. "I'm so glad you were able to lock yourself in my cabin. If Armand had touched one hair on your head…"

He let the sentence stay unfinished, but the expression on his face said it all. He would have made sure Armand would have paid for his actions. Too bad Jeb hadn't been there to watch out for her when—

Nope. She was *not* going to think about that.

"Seriously, lean forward."

Nervously, she leaned in toward him and all her muscles tensed.

He extended his hand toward her face.

She jumped.

"Easy, there." The pad of his thumb whisked against her bottom lip. "You've got a tiny dollop of Oreo cream. All gone now."

She felt her face heat.

"Maybe someday you'll tell me," he said, wiping his hands on a napkin, then balling up the napkin and tossing it onto his empty plate.

"Tell you what?"

"Why you're so jumpy around me."

"Probably not," she said. "I won't ever see you again after Saturday."

"You know—" his gaze locked on hers "—I can't help but feel that's a terrible shame."

*You and me both.*

What was going on with her? She had to get this under control or she was not going to be able to survive six days—*and five nights*—alone with him on this sailboat.

How had she gotten herself into this fix? More importantly, how was she going to get out of it unscathed?

# 6

**Preventer**—*A line or other device used to prevent the boom from accidentally moving from one side to the other*

JEB SPENT A RESTLESS NIGHT in the hammock. He'd insisted that Haley take his cabin and she'd only marginally argued with him about it, but no matter how he tried to block it out, he kept thinking about her down there. How she might be curled up in the middle of his bed, wearing one of his T-shirts that he'd loaned her since she didn't have anything to sleep in.

Finally, he fell asleep around two o'clock in the morning, but even as he slumbered, Haley invaded his dreams. He kept seeing those pert high breasts of hers, dreamed of those long legs wrapped around his waist, inhaled the scent of her hair, which smelled faintly of strawberries. He'd sat up bathed in sweat. Tossed. Turned. Marinated.

He knew what this was. Haley was his last temptation, the final test to see if he could truly remain faithful to Jackie. Haley was the universe's way of making him prove he was worthy of Jackie. Why else had fate put her right here on his boat in the middle of the deep blue ocean?

Actually, it was quite poetic when he thought about it. This last challenge to prove that the play had gone out of the boy.

This was his second chance. Time to take a stand. He was a full-grown man and his future lay ahead of him. He was excited about it. The thought of commitment didn't scare him as it once had.

Comforted, he went back to sleep only to repeat the Haley dreams all over again.

This time, the changing wind woke him.

Jeb didn't need a weather vane to tell him which way the wind was blowing. He'd been riding the ocean for so long that he could feel the shift before it happened, that brief, silent pause before the change occurred.

Dawn heated the water's cool shimmer. The wind blew toward Florida at a sweet clip. Jeb grinned. Today, they would sail.

He got out his maps and charts and hurried down to the galley to make breakfast before they pulled up anchor. On his arrival, though, he found Haley standing at the stove in his T-shirt, drinking coffee while she scrambled eggs. Toast popped from the toaster.

"You're up," he said.

"Surprise. I thought I'd do the cooking today since you did it yesterday."

The hem of his T-shirt hit her midthigh. He didn't want to notice, but c'mon, how could he not? He was only human and her legs were fantastic.

"Excellent," he said. "We can get a jump start on

the morning. The wind is up and at our backs. We're sailing today and we'll make better time."

"That's thrilling." She buttered the toast.

He poured himself a cup of coffee and spread out the charts, checking his coordinates and seeing whether he needed to alter the headings so the boat "made good." Haley put a plate of eggs and toast in front of him and sat down across from him.

"That looks very complicated," she said.

"Sailing is a complex endeavor."

"But fascinating."

"You can never learn all there is to know about the sea. I discover something new every time I'm on the water."

"I'm fascinated by your fascination."

"Do you know anything about sailing?"

"Not in the least."

Jeb grinned, shook his head. "I have so much to teach you, Grasshopper."

Haley salted her eggs. "Um…I found a pink bikini in the bottom drawer of your dresser. I wasn't snooping, I promise. I was looking for a pair of socks. My feet get cold at night."

Somehow, he found that completely endearing.

"The bikini is my size, and since we're on the water, I was wondering if it might be okay to wear it."

Okay? For Haley to wear a bikini? That was like asking if it were okay to frame the *Mona Lisa*.

"Sure."

"I mean, I don't want to offend the woman it belongs to. Does it belong to Jackie?"

"Jackie? In pink? Not hardly." Jeb had no idea whose bikini it was, but he didn't want to tell Haley that it could belong to any number of women, so he told a little white lie. "It belongs to one of my sisters."

The happy smile on Haley's face told him the white lie was the right move. "You're sure she won't mind if I wear it? I washed out the dress I wore on board."

"No problem," he said hoarsely as a shiver went straight to his cock. This talk of women's clothing was stirring him, especially in relation to Haley. "Go ahead and change and I'll meet you up on deck." He finished his coffee. "It's time to get sailing."

*Because I have to get to Jackie as fast as I can before I do something with Haley that I'll live to regret.*

HALEY WAS EXCITED.

She stood in the cockpit, listening to Jeb explain the parts of the sailboat and what they were called. There was a lot to absorb. There was the mast—the vertical pole that supported the sails. It rose up in the center of the sailing yacht. There was a horizontal pole called the boom. It supported the bottom of the mainsail.

"What do you like most about sailing?" she asked.

"The playing field is constantly changing. No two days are alike."

"The playing field?"

"In other sports, the playing field is always the same—the baseball diamond, the basketball court, the football field—but in sailing the playing field is the wind and the water, Mother Nature at her finest. You can never control or predict her." His eyes tracked over Haley's face. "A bit like you."

Haley's cheeks heated at his appraisal.

"The boom swings from side to side as the boat turns," Jeb said, going back to the lesson. "So be careful not to get in the boom's way as it swings or you could end up in the ocean."

"So now I know what the saying 'lower the boom' means."

"This is the mainsail. You'll also hear it referred to as the main. A sail is nothing more than a big sheet that catches the wind to help move your boat faster through the water."

She wrung her hands. "Should I be taking notes?"

"You'll pick it up as you use it. *Second Chance* has a headsail. Smaller boats often don't."

"What's the headsail?"

"It's the sail here in front of the mast. There are different types of headsails. One type is a jib."

"Jib. Jeb. Easy to remember."

"This headsail is a spinnaker. You use it when sailing downwind. We'll be using it today since we're going with the wind."

"Got it."

"Now, each part of a sail has a name, too."

"Yipes. My brain is getting overloaded."

"You know medical terminology—nautical terms are a piece of cake compared to that."

"Easy for you to say. You cut your teeth on this lingo. But I'm ready. What are the parts of the sail?"

"The head is the top corner of the sail." He indicated the top.

"I bet that term gets teenage boys laughing."

"And some immature adult males, as well. The tack is the front bottom corner of the sail."

"Head, the top, just like it sounds. Tack, the front bottom. Got it."

"The clew is the back bottom corner of a sail. The foot—"

"Let me guess,' she interrupted. "It's the bottom of the sail."

He grinned at her. "I knew you were bright. The leech is the back edge of the sail and the luff is the front edge."

"I thought you said the luff was like a brake."

"*Luff* has multiple meanings. When used as a noun, *luff* refers to the forward edge of a sail. When *luff* is used as a verb, it refers to the flapping motion a sail-cloth makes when it's undertrimmed. *Luff* can also be used as an adjective. As in luffing sails can't generate any power.

"And these are the battens." He showed her the solid slats that were inserted into pockets along a sail's leech in order to help the sail maintain its shape.

"I think I've got it."

"Don't forget the lines."

"Lines?"

"Ropes with a specific purpose."

"This is starting to sound like a bondage film," she teased.

His grin turned wicked. "And what would you know about that?"

"Just because I work all the time doesn't mean I don't know what goes on in the world."

"Hmm." He sent a look over her that had Haley flushing.

"The ropes," she prompted and then cringed because it sounded as if she was too eager to know more about ropes.

"The ropes." The way he said it sounded so seductive. "The Cunningham is the control-line system near the tack of the sail used to adjust the luff tension."

The word *tension* hung in the air, a taut line between them.

"I'm guessing that's so you can tighten or loosen the sail. Speed it up or slow it down?"

"Something like that." He lowered his eyelids to half-mast. "This is the halyard." He tugged on the thick rope that ran up the mast. "It's used to pull up the sail. You'll be doing that in just a minute."

"Me?"

"You."

"All by myself?"

"All by yourself."

"What if I mess it up?"

"We start over.

"This rope that's mounted on the boom—" he touched it "—is called the outhaul and it's used to control tension on the foot of the mainsail."

"You need ten hands to be a sailor."

"Doesn't hurt." He went on to tell her the names of the remaining ropes and what they did, and then he introduced the equipment that adjusted the ropes, including the block, the clear and the winch. By the time he was done, she was thoroughly confused.

"Whew," she said. "I'm so not ready for a pop quiz."

"But you now know enough to hoist the mainsail."

"I do?"

"Yep."

"I'm glad one of us is confident in my abilities."

"The first thing you do when preparing the mainsail is to insert the battens, which I've already done.

Then you attach the tack. C'mere and I'll show you how." He motioned to her and she stepped over.

"It's starting to sound like learning the human skeleton. The hip bone is connected to the thigh bone..."

"An apt analogy," he said. "Now we attach the clew with a shackle and then we feed the luff."

"Ropes, shackles, feeding the luff, this is a very kinky sport." Oh, wow, why had she said that? She was officially babbling. He was going to think she was flirting with him. She wasn't flirting with him.

Was she?

*Stop it. Just stop saying anything remotely suggestive.*

He simply chuckled and continued with his instructions. Once everything was harnessed and in place, they double-checked the sails. "Okay," he said, "I'm going to steer us into the wind and then we'll hoist the mainsail."

"I'm nervous. What if I ruin something? This is a very expensive boat."

"I'm right here to help you. You're brave as hell, Haley French. I've seen you in action. Compared to heading up a hurricane refugee camp, sailing is a piece of cake."

Once he had the boat in position, he guided her over to the winch and slipped his arms on either side of her waist to show her how to wrap the halyard line in a clockwise direction around the winch drum.

"Just enough times so you can hold the line without it slipping, but as the sail goes up, you'll need to add another wraparound or two," he explained.

His breath was warm on her ear. It tickled and she

almost giggled but managed to bite back the giddy sound.

"Now what?" she asked, resisting the urge to lean back against him just so she could feel his muscled chest against her spine.

"You get to jump."

"Off the board?"

"Nope, on the halyard line. Remember what the halyard line does?"

"Raises the sail."

He chucked her under the chin gently. "Good job."

"Tell me what to do."

"Stand at the mast where the halyard is just above your head."

"Let me guess, I jump up to yank the halyard downward."

"Exactly. I'll be in the cockpit taking up the slack in the line by pulling on the rope that's wrapped around the winch."

"I think I'm beginning to see how this works."

"When the sail reaches the top, the load will increase so that jumping will no longer be effective. At that point I'll grind the winch until the sail is at the top."

"Ooh," she said, "there you go with the dirty words again."

*Holy Oreos, French. Will you stop with the flirting? The man is hung up on another woman. Just shut your gob already.*

What was really disconcerting was the fact that she never acted like this. Ever. What was it about Jeb that turned her into a silly schoolgirl? She was acting like an eleven-year-old backstage at a Justin Bieber concert.

"Ready?" Jeb asked.

"Ready," Haley confirmed.

"Pull the halyard."

She jumped for the halyard line, grabbed it and started tugging. Jeb had moved to the cockpit, taking up the slack. As they worked together, the mainsail began to rise.

The sail flapped gaily. She was so relieved. This was fun. She suppressed the urge to do a little jig. But halfway to the top of the mast, the halyard hung up and no matter how hard she pulled, she could not get it to budge.

"Er, Jeb," she called over to him. "I think I goofed up."

"The luff is jammed. Common occurrence. Best way for you to learn. Just stop pulling on the halyard and I'll show you how to clear the jam." He crooked an index finger for her to come over to where he was standing.

The second she was within touching distance of him, every nerve ending in her body tingled and sang. *Really, Haley? This is getting pathetic.*

They got the sail back on track and Haley got her body under control, sort of. They pulled and tugged, winched and ground until the mainsail reached the top of the mast and it filled with wind. Once it was fully hoisted, Jeb showed her how to secure the halyard with the jammer and they moved on to the spinnaker.

Once the sails were hoisted, she and Jeb cleaned up the spaghetti of rope lying about the deck. When it was over, she was perspiring and a little breathless from all the unusual exertion.

Jeb took up his place at the helm and Haley was free to take a seat and enjoy the fruits of their labor, and oh, my goodness, it was exhilarating. She never expected sailing to feel so freeing.

Her hair blew across her face with the wind at their backs, her bare feet rested on the slick, polished fiberglass, the sound of the sails flapping and the rigging clanging against the mast, the beer that Jeb had passed to her cool in her hand.

It was so peaceful. The water was so utterly blue, the sun so shimmery bright it bleached everything it touched. She took a sip of the beer and it slid back sweetly bitter on her tongue. Her gaze gathered the horizon. A few cheerful white clouds played tag across the sky, and in the distance, she saw something and her heart leaped with joy.

"Dolphins!" she cried. "Jeb, it's a school of dolphins and they're swimming right along with us."

"They're curious creatures and they'll often follow boats."

"But we're going so fast and they're catching up to us! It's like they're playing chase." Her heart was thumping as she hung over the side of the boat, the dolphins overtaking them. "They've got spots on them."

"Atlantic Spotted Dolphins."

She glanced over her shoulder at him. "Not a very unique name."

"Jackie would call them *Stenella frontalis.*"

There it was. The reminder of the reason Jeb was making this journey. A bit of joy leaked out of the moment. *Good grief, Haley. Knock it off.*

She turned her gaze back to the dolphins. The lead dolphin was almost beside her. He was close to eight feet long and was speckled with swirls of white spots all over his body. A polka-dot dolphin. She laughed.

"They're not born with spots, but get them as they age. Sort of like the reverse of fawns. By the time they're old, they're covered in spots."

She rested her chin on her arm, stared out at the blue sea and the gray speckled dolphins, and a sense of utter happiness closed over her. She shut her eyes for a moment, savoring the feeling so she could pull out the memory later when she needed cheering up.

When she opened her eyes again, the exuberant dolphins were in a free-for-all around the ship. Like synchronized swimmers, they leaped and spun, somersaulted and cartwheeled. What graceful athletes. What gregarious creatures.

Their zestful sense of play reminded her of someone else she knew.

Haley peeked another glance over at Jeb.

The wind tousled his hair. His hands were on the wheel. His grin was wide and toothy, his blue eyes crinkling at the corners. Wow, he was so gorgeous.

Her heart did an aerial pirouette, rivaling the dolphins' acrobatics.

Back again she went to the dolphins, torn between the beauty of the sea and the handsome man at the wheel.

The lead dolphin made eye contact with her, barked an adorable noise that she could hear above the rush of the wind, his mouth stretched in a grin as compelling as Jeb's. As if he were saying, "Come play."

The creature seemed so self-aware, as if something

special was going on inside its head. She was awe-struck, humbled and grateful. So grateful that fate had put her on this boat to have this beautiful experience. It was worth the anxiety of being an accidental stowaway, fully made up for being drugged by Rick Armand.

She'd never felt so connected to the sea, to the earth, to the tides, to the sky. She was part of nature, not just moving through it or reacting against it. The rhythm of the ocean was within her. She felt a part of it in a way she'd never experienced before and it was a deeply moving moment.

Jeb chuckled. "It's fun to see you get so excited over something as simple as dolphins."

"It might be simple to you," she said, "but to me, it's miraculous."

"I know you've seen dolphins before around St. Michael's."

"Yes, but I've never been so close. I've never looked a dolphin in the eye and felt—"

"Connected," he finished for her.

Ah, he understood.

She was such a latecomer to the party. How had she not realized how incredibly special these wild creatures were? How strongly they could affect you. Immediately, she felt sorry for all the people on the land. For everyone who never got to experience this liberating high.

A dolphin from the middle of the pack pulled closer to the sailboat. So close that if Haley leaned over she could reach out and touch the dolphin's smooth, wet spotted back. The dolphin went down under the water, and when it appeared again, there was a sleek little surprise swimming under the scoop of its body. She was a mother!

"Oh, look, there's a baby!" Rapturously, Haley leaped to her feet.

"Haley! Be careful," Jeb called out.

She spun around to see what he was cautioning her about.

It all seemed to happen in slow motion.

The boom swung around and came right toward her, but her landlubber brain could not process the danger fast enough. By the time her muscles coiled to jump, it was too late. The boom clipped her in the midsection, knocking her to the floor of the boat.

*Ooph!*

All the air rushed from her body and Haley lay gasping like a guppy, staring up at the clear blue sky. Her ears rang and her stomach quivered.

Then a face blotted out the sky and the only thing she could see was Jeb, his brow knitted in a concerned frown.

"Haley, are you all right?"

She tried to nod, but since she couldn't yet breathe, the effort was moot.

His arms were around her, warm and comforting, and he was dragging her to safety out of the way of the boom.

"It's okay," he murmured. "You're going to be all right."

She was a nurse. She knew that. The wind had been knocked out of her, nothing more, but it was a helpless feeling, not being able to draw in air. An edgy panic hovered, waiting to attack.

Jeb crouched beside her, rubbed her back with an open palm. "Easy, easy."

The crisp cottony scent of his shirt mingled with the smell of sun and ocean and got tangled up in her nose. His chest was directly to her right. All she had to do was turn her head and her face would be buried against his chest.

She was so unnerved by the urge that she couldn't think. Couldn't speak. Still couldn't manage to breathe more than two thready, inconsequential inhalations.

"Haley." He sank down on his knees, positioning his murmuring mouth at the level of her ear. His hand felt so good at her back.

Without fully knowing why, she did turn toward him. His mouth was beside her lips now.

Almost touching.

"Jeb," she whispered and that was all it took.

His mouth was on hers, delicious as salted caramel. She knew that just like the moment with the dolphins, this was an experience she would never forget: the sound of the billowy sails flap-flap-flapping in the Atlantic breeze; the summer sun beaming down bright and hot, shining a million tiny fractured lanterns over the choppy caps of blue water; the smell of briny ocean spray; this handsome man, hard with muscles and pecan-colored hair, kissing a practical woman who'd forgotten what it was like to have fun.

Haley stored this memory in the vault of her mental photo album and swore to pull it out from time to time when she needed a reminder of how utterly sweet life could be.

Jeb had a knowing mouth. It had been places. Tasted many sophisticated things. Kissed many things:

the small of a woman's back, the nape of a neck, ear-
lobes. She wanted him to explore all those places
on her, but although hope perched like a bird on her
shoulder, she knew the bird could never fly.

Not with this man. His heart belonged to another.

She should break off the kiss. She knew it. Her
brain was yelling at her, *Do something! Anything! Just
stop kissing him!*

But she did none of those things.

Instead, she twined her arms around his neck and
pulled him down on top of her.

Who was she? What was she doing? She felt as if
she were channeling some spritely mermaid turning
the tables on a handsome fisherman by catching him
in her net. Oddly thrilling, that image.

The taste of him nested in her head, created a home
there. Fizzy champagne and chocolate-covered strawberries and buttered lobster and caviar. Not that she'd
ever eaten caviar, but he tasted how she thought caviar might taste.

*You are in such trouble,* whimpered her brain.

*Butt out,* retorted her body.

His lips sapped her energy, drained her free will
like the receding tide pulling away from the shore,
leaving boulders jutting up from the shoals, expos-
ing things better left hidden, like seaweed and broken
seashells and man-made refuse. Leaving her raw and
vulnerable and helpless to resist his touch.

The kiss was a thrill beyond thrills. She felt ripe
and achy and ready to be plucked. Rationally, she did
not want this but she hungered for it. Hungered for
him.

She tilted back her head, clung to his neck with the

curve of one arm. He took the kiss deep, his tongue sliding in to do blissful damage to her self-control. Their tongues were completely bonded as she took up the play and gave back as good as she got.

A sound welled up from deep in his throat, vibrated through him and into her, and Haley lit up. She'd delighted him!

Before her normal rational common sense could rally, before she planted her palms against his chest and pushed him away, before her sense of shame roused from having been anesthetized by Jeb's perfect mouth and energetic tongue, Haley lapped up every bit of his attention, reveling in the exquisiteness she would never experience again.

It was brilliant.

Then, as all brilliant moments must, it collapsed.

Jeb moved away, muttered an apology, cursed softly under his breath and left a frozen slab of emptiness icing up her heart.

# 7

**Lifeline**—*A line or wire all around the boat, held up with stanchions, to prevent falling overboard*

FOR THE REMAINDER of the day, Haley avoided him.

Jeb couldn't fault her. He'd behaved abominably. He'd tried so hard to be good, to resist the temptations of her gorgeous body in that tiny little pink bikini. Maybe Jackie had been right all along. Maybe he *was* incapable of commitment.

That saddened him.

He really did want to change, but was redemption beyond his control? Would pleasures of the flesh always woo him? Would he ever master his body? How could he prove to Jackie that he'd changed when he couldn't even prove it to himself?

Disheartened, he'd stayed at the helm until dusk. Haley had disappeared belowdecks after he'd kissed her, mumbling something about the sun having given her a headache. He knew the sun wasn't the source of her pain, but rather, his inexcusable behavior.

He sailed until night dropped around them like

a curtain and the smell of onions, garlic and cumin wafted up from the lower deck. His stomach grumbled and he realized he hadn't eaten anything since the scrambled eggs and toast that Haley had prepared for him that morning.

He'd just dropped anchor and lowered the sails when she appeared on the deck, moonlight shining off her guileless face.

"Dinner's ready," she said.

"You didn't have to make dinner."

"I needed a job to do." She'd put his T-shirt on over the bikini—thankfully. Her feet were bare and she used the toes of her right foot to scratch the calf of her left leg. It was a simple gesture and shouldn't have been at all sexy, but dammit, it was. "I'm not an idle person."

"I can eat up here if you like."

A slight smile flitted across her mouth. "Putting yourself in the doghouse?"

"I deserve to be there."

"Cut yourself some slack," she said. "You're only human."

That surprised him. "You're not mad at me?"

She shrugged. "Look, it happened in a split second of weakness. I'm as much to blame as you are, but we can get past this. You're in love with Jackie and I'm just along for the ride. It was never my intention to get in your way. We've got a few more days alone out here together, so let's not make a bigger deal of this than it is."

Her attitude was a relief. She didn't hold the kiss against him. Of course, he couldn't let himself off the hook so easily, but her acceptance took some of the tension out of the air.

"I made tacos. C'mon, if you're coming." She turned and went back belowdecks.

Jeb took off after her.

A moment of awkwardness settled over them, as it always seemed to do when they sat down to eat together. Down here, the confines were close and there were no other distractions. They had only each other for company.

"Your cheeks are a little red," he said. "Sunburn and windburn can leave you feeling sore. There's some aloe-vera gel in the medicine cabinet."

"Thanks, I'll put some on before I go to bed." Her long, slender fingers picked up a taco and she tilted her head to eat it.

Another awkward pause.

*Think of something neutral to say.*

"So," he said, "how long are you planning on staying in St. Michael's?"

She swallowed her bite of taco, patted her mouth— that sweet pink mouth—with a napkin. "I'm not sure."

"Where will you go after that?"

"I'm thinking about becoming a traveling nurse. My time on St. Michael's has stirred up a wanderlust I never knew I had."

"Funny." He lifted his eyebrows.

"What?"

"Just when I'm itching to settle down, you're looking to roam."

"Ironic, I suppose. The stick-in-the-mud turns adventurer and the adventurer is looking to get stuck in the mud."

"Well, I've got to say, you're one heck of a sailor."

"You can say that with a straight face after I got hit by the boom? And after you warned me about it, too."

"You haven't gotten seasick. The majority of people get seasick."

"I've never had motion sickness in my life. Cast-iron stomach." Haley patted her belly.

Helplessly, Jeb found his gaze drawn to her flat midriff. She had such a narrow waist and such nice curvy hips. He could see the outline of the pink bikini beneath his white T-shirt.

It was official. She *was* killing him. Resolutely, he turned his attention to the tacos.

Sexy, gorgeous and a good cook, too? "Why hasn't some guy already snapped you up?"

"Pardon?"

Uh. Had he said that out loud? "There's no ring on your finger and you've never said anything about a boyfriend. Do you have a boyfriend?"

"No boyfriend."

"Why not?"

"My reason for coming to St. Michael's was to help people. How effective could I be if I was off dating when I should be working?"

"Everyone needs a break now and then."

'I'm beginning to see that," she said. "Today with the dolphins, well, it was the most fun I've had in a very long time."

Thinking about the dolphins led to thinking about what happened afterward and they both lapsed into silence.

"Plus," she said, "I didn't want to start anything I couldn't finish."

"So there's someone on St. Michael's you have your eye on?" he asked, feeling an irrational surge of jealousy.

She looked him in the eyes. "It was a passing fantasy."

"Do you always finish everything that you start?"

"I'm guessing you don't?"

"Not everything needs to be finished. Some things are meant to be temporary."

"Like a meal."

"Or a spontaneous riff."

"What's a spontaneous riff?"

"I'll do one with your name."

"Do what?"

"Riff."

"Okay, go."

"First, do you have any nicknames?"

She wrinkled her nose. "I'm not a nickname kind of girl."

"Someone in your life has called you by a nickname. Mother, grandmother, best friend, siblings."

"My friends call me Hale, sometimes. And my grandmother called me Pole Bean because I grew faster than the cousins. My dad occasionally calls me Haystack."

"Haley. *H* as in home and hearth. Only one *y*, not two. Tidy. Efficient. Hayley Mills, Halley's Comet. Haley. So dubbed by Mr. and Mrs. French. Hay. Haystack. Pole Bean. Grew tall and fast. Fresh. Clean-scrubbed. Dependable. Haley. Five letters. Two vowels tucked between three consonants. Evenly spaced. Steady, but with that surprising curly *y* at the end," he spit out in rapid-fire succession. "Haley. Beach beauty.

Golden skin. Slightly sad smile. Knowing eyes. Dimpled chin. Legs like a Thoroughbred. Dolphin lover. Crusader. Stiff upper lip. Scrupulous. Noble. Makes the best kick-ass tacos in the world."

She rolled her eyes. "Let me guess, this name riffing thing is a line, right? That you use on your dates?"

Honestly, no, he did not. He'd never used it. In fact, he had no idea where it had come from. The riff had just spun glibly off his tongue, but he was suddenly terrified to admit that to her. Then he realized he'd subconsciously been riffing her name for days, maybe even weeks.

"You can stop trying to charm me. I know it's second nature to you, but there's no point. So just relax."

She was right, there was no point, but in the back of his mind, a quiet voice kept on riffing—*Haley. Nourishing as wheat. Hospital tent. Slept on my sheets. Hard worker. Rubber-soled shoes. She's no shirker. Strawberry-scented hair that should never be pulled into a bun. Eyelashes like paintbrushes. Scared now and wants to run. Heart of gold. Puts me in my place like no one ever has. Turns Mr. Slick into Mr. Lacking Confidence. Haley. Came along for an accidental ride. Righteous lips. What do you want that I can't provide?*

"There's no charming you, huh?"

"Nope."

Another awkward silence.

"With the wind at our backs, we made really good time today," he said, rushing to fill the silence. "At this rate, we'll be in Key West on Friday."

She looked relieved. "That's good, and then we can both get back to our lives."

"Yes." But it didn't feel good.

Not good at all.

JEB RIFFING HER NAME had gotten to her.

Haley didn't want to admit it, but there it was. When Jeb had said all those nice things about her, she'd found a place for him in her heart. It was corny and she just knew he trotted it out for any woman caught in his orbit, but it was endearing. Goofy, but endearing.

Dinner was over. The dishes were washed—by them, together, and that had been wonderful and awkward as they'd bumped elbows. Now Jeb had gone up to his hammock on the bridge and Haley was standing in the bathroom brushing her teeth with one of the new toothbrushes Jeb kept stocked. But of course. He was the consummate host. Accustomed to having women spending the night on his yacht.

She stared at herself in the mirror, toothbrush poking out of one side of her mouth as she vigorously scrubbed her gums.

*You're falling for him.*

Haley shook her head, spat and rinsed. No. She wasn't falling for him. She was just, well, she liked him.

*Uh-huh, tell yourself another lie.*

Okay, so what if she was falling for him? Nothing could come of it for so many reasons, primary of which was the fact that he was sailing to Key West to break up an ex-girlfriend's impending marriage.

Her heart settled south of her stomach.

How she wished she could get off this boat and go back to St. Michael's. Back to her sane, normal life filled with patients to take care of and away from be-guiling ocean waves, captivating dolphins and Jeb Whitcomb's super-sexy grin.

An overwhelming sadness washed over her. She'd never felt so cut off. It was just her and Jeb. She couldn't even call her friends or family for advice. How was she going to survive the next few days with him? Wanting him, yearning for him, but unable to have him because he wanted someone else.

A tight band of misery constricted her heart. What was wrong with her? Why did she feel so wounded when she had no right to feel this way? None what-soever.

She fingered her lips.

He might want another woman, but he'd kissed *her.*

*Only because you were convenient. Don't think it's anything more than that.*

She was well aware of that, but there was this stu-pid red flag of hope jutting up in the back of her mind. Anything was possible. Right?

Well, not this. A match between her and Jeb was impossible for more reasons than his desire for Jackie Birchard. He was wealthy and she was middle-class. He loved to play and she was dedicated to work. He was gorgeous and had women falling at his feet, while she was of middling good looks at best. She could not compete with the models and starlets and social-ites who regularly vied for his attention, nor did she want to.

Just get through the next few days. That was all she had to do.

Yeah, as if that was going to be easy. Unless she

wanted to stay in the cabin for the remainder of the trip, there was no getting away from him.

Melancholia twined around Haley's stomach, insidious as seaweed. Was she going to stand here whining and feeling sorry for herself or was she going to do something about it?

Her pulse quickened at the idea of doing something about it. *Don't think. Just act.* Thinking was what had held her back for so long.

Barefoot, she leaped over the bed, grabbed for the cabin door, wrenched it open and sprinted the length of the lower deck to the stairs. Her hand touched the cool rail, stopping her instantly.

Her feet froze on the bottom step.

What was she doing?

What did she think was going to happen when she got up there on the bridge? That they would make wild, passionate love in the hammock? And what if they did? What then? He'd sail off into the sunset with Jackie and she'd be left feeling all hurt and sorry for herself because she'd followed an urge that led nowhere.

Why did it have to lead anywhere? Why couldn't she just have a good time? Was there anything wrong with that? What was it that Jeb had said at dinner? *Not everything needs to be finished. Some things are meant to be temporary.*

No. She would not be the razor Jeb used to cut himself. He was trying to prove he was no longer a glib playboy. He was trying to settle down. She could not be the temptation that crumbled him.

Slowly, she backed away from the stairs.

*Go to bed. Start fresh tomorrow. Think about it tomorrow.*

*Yeah, Scarlett O'Hara, tomorrow is another day.*

But for now, the night stretched out long and endless, and dawn seemed a hundred light-years away.

MIDNIGHT AND JEB was wide-awake.

Again.

Normally, he had absolutely no trouble sleeping. Especially when he was at sea; the gentle ocean rocking always calmed him. But tonight, things were even worse than they'd been last night because he'd kissed Haley.

Since he couldn't sleep, maybe he should get up and sail. Sailing through the night would put them that much closer to Key West. That much closer to getting Haley off his boat and on her way. But the accommodating winds that had swept them ahead of schedule today had also rolled in a batch of thick clouds. Tonight, the moon was obscured, peeping out only occasionally, and the air smelled of rain. Did he really want to risk getting caught sailing in a storm?

Better not push his luck. With today's progress, even if they experienced unexpected delays, he would easily make it to Key West before Jackie's 4:00 p.m. wedding on Saturday.

To get his mind off everything, he started going over the coordinates. He loved mental math. Longitude, latitude, changes in altitude. Hell, suddenly he was humming Jimmy Buffett.

Better than thinking about Haley.

Except now there she was again, lodged in his brain.

Argh!

He tossed off the lap blanket he'd been using, jumped to his feet, the hammock swinging wildly in his wake. He paced the deck, listening to the noises of his boat—the creak of the rigging, the whisper of water lapping at the hull, the hammer of his pulse in his ears.

Jeb walked toward the lower deck, climbed down the stairs. Stopped. Cursed himself. Climbed the stairs again.

Wait a minute. Was that a light he'd seen underneath the door of his cabin? Was Haley awake? He turned again, went back down.

Yep. A light.

Was she still up? Or did she sleep with a light on? Was she scared of the dark?

The urge to comfort her eclipsed him. Compelled by a force he couldn't seem to resist, Jeb crept closer.

He reached the cabin. Raised a fist to knock on the door, his breathing coming hot and fast.

Lowering his fist, he rested his ear against the door, imagined he could hear her breathing on the other side.

Haley.

His hand slid to the door handle. His entire body strummed and throbbed, each nerve cell tingling with an immediate energy that left his head reeling.

Haley.

What if she had her head against her side of the door? What if her heart was thudding as crazily as his?

And what if it wasn't?

He pressed his lips to the door, silently whispered her name.

*Haley.*

What the hell was he doing? He ground his teeth, spun around, raced on the balls of his feet—so he'd be quieter and she'd be less likely to hear him and come out—back to the haven of his hammock.

He swung the hammock madly, placed a palm to his forehead, gulped in air, remembered kissing Haley, hardened. Jerk. What the hell was the matter with him? He wasn't *that* guy. Not anymore. He was done with living in the moment at the sacrifice of the future. There were benefits to controlling yourself, to self-denial, to foregoing self-indulgence for the bigger picture, greater good, yada fricking yada.

*Keep your fantasies to yourself, Whitcomb. Hands to yourself.*

A year was such a damn long time to go without the feel of a woman's body beneath his.

*Remember why you decided to stay celibate.*

*Haley.*

*What the hell? No, not Haley. Scratch that. Messed up on the name. Jackie.*

*Jackie, Jackie, Jackie.* She was the one he wanted.

*Ahem, Jackie is the one who is on the verge of marrying another man. She ain't busy pining for you.* Yeah, well, that was why he had to get to Key West ASAP to correct his past mistakes.

Redemption. That was his goal.

Well, he wasn't going to get it by chasing after Haley.

Right. Yes. He knew that. He was on lockdown. *Don't dare get out of this hammock until dawn. No matter what. Got it?*

Overhead, yellow lightning flashed. Thunder rumbled. Even the weather was warning him.

Got it. He saluted the sky. He was all wet.

A few minutes later, soft sprinkles hit the deck, dropped lightly onto his face. He pulled the lap blanket up over his head.

The wind gusted, sent the hammock swaying. Goose bumps raised on his arms. He burrowed his butt in the hammock. If only the blanket were thick and woolen.

Lightning, now vivid blue, forked from the clouds, a jagged, electric snake tongue of illumination. Thunder clashed as loudly as a car crash.

Jeb jumped.

The rain sped up, pelting him.

This was not the safest place in a storm, but he'd checked the forecast. The storm should be short-lived and pass quickly with the blowing wind.

Except the wind seemed to have stalled, leaving the black clouds directly overhead, drenching him. Jeb flopped over onto his stomach, not a particularly easy maneuver in a hammock, and huddled beneath the soaked blanket.

This was not working.

He tossed aside the blanket and stumbled to the cockpit, found a tarp and brought it back to the hammock. He unwrapped the tarp and crawled under it.

Better. At least it would keep him dry.

Rain pummeled the tarp, made a mind-numbing tapping noise.

Jeb grunted. Ridiculous. Go belowdecks. Tempted, he turned the idea over. Nice and warm and dry. Safe from potential lightning strikes.

*No can do, Stew.*

If he went down there, with Haley so close, he knew

he would knock at her door and the way she'd been looking at him over dinner—the way she'd kissed him back when he'd kissed her—told him that if he knocked, she would open that damn door and invite him inside with eager arms.

Haley. Of the strawberry-scented hair and sweet lips. Haley wrapping her arms around his neck, pulling him against her breasts. Haley—

No!

He chuffed out a breath, coughed. His throat felt scratchy. Even through the tarp, he could see the next flash of lightning, felt thunder shake the sailboat. *Seriously, dude, you could get struck by lightning.* No kidding.

Okay, fine. He crawled out of the hammock and went to the cockpit, wadded up into a tarp-covered ball. Not really much of an improvement, but at least the overhang protected him from the main force of the onslaught.

It would pass. It had to pass. Storms always passed.

Rain dripped off the tarp onto his face, rolled down his nose like copious tears. If he went to the lower deck he could just stretch out on the floor. He didn't need a cabin. Haley need never know he was inside.

But *he* would know.

*C'mon, you're not that weak. You can be on the same deck as the woman without feeling compelled to seduce her.*

That was the thing—whenever he was around her, he couldn't think straight. He wasn't himself. All he wanted to do was touch her.

No, that was a bald-faced lie. He wanted to do a

whole helluva lot more than touch her. Which was what had him so twisted in knots.

Things would change when he saw Jackie again. It had just been too long since he'd seen her. Once he looked in Jackie's eyes, he'd forget all about Haley and he wouldn't regret having kept his hands to himself.

He just had to make it through the night.

More lightning. More thunder. More rain.

Jeb sneezed, shivered. His lungs weighed heavy in his chest. He'd be drier if he took a header into the ocean. He peeked over at the stairs leading to the lower deck. Ten steps away. Twelve, max.

No. He drew the tarp tighter around him. He wasn't going to go down there. The rain would pass.

Eventually. Had to. It hadn't rained for forty days and forty nights since Noah and his ark.

Fifteen minutes later and there was no letup. He couldn't tell if his nose was running or it was just rain, but he felt as lousy as hell. He was *not* going down there. He was determined to prove he could control himself.

In the meantime, his fingers pruned and his head throbbed, but he would gut it out. Not a wimp. Not he. A true sailor could weather the elements, right?

His teeth chattered and he shivered so hard that he couldn't stop. His eyes burned hot, his bones ached and his skin felt waterlogged and tight. He'd never before been accused of being stubborn, but tonight, he stuck to his guns.

An hour later, he couldn't take it anymore. He was too damned exhausted to try anything with Haley anyway. He'd proven his point. Grunting, he heaved himself to his feet, but as he staggered up, his head spun and his knees gave out. The deck rose up to greet him.

*Congratulations, Captain, you're officially screwed.*

# 8

**Ease**—*To let out (a sail or a rope)*

ON WEDNESDAY MORNING, Haley was determined to put the previous day behind her. Fresh start. Yesterday, she'd washed out the dress she'd worn to the party and she put it on again. Even with a T-shirt over the pink bikini, the bathing suit was simply too provocative and she wasn't taking any more chances. Too bad she didn't have a parka and ski pants.

She made two cups of coffee and took them out on the bridge. The sun was up, and in places, water pooled on the deck. Had it rained last night? She thought she'd heard thunder, but she hadn't gotten up to investigate.

Haley reached the top step and from there could see into the cockpit.

Jeb lay facedown on the deck, partially covered by a tarp beaded with water droplets.

Haley gasped, and her fingers loosened. The thick earthenware coffee mugs clattered to the deck. One thumped and rolled, breaking off the handle. The other cracked into two clean pieces. Hot coffee splashed up onto her bare legs, but she scarcely noticed. Her heart vaulted into her throat.

She ran toward him. "Jeb!"

He did not respond.

She yanked the tarp off him, sank onto her knees beside him, her chest tightening, constricting her lungs. Grabbing him by the shoulders, she shook him gently, yet firmly. "Jeb!"

He let out a soft groan.

Dear God, he was burning up!

"Jeb." She patted his cheeks. "Open your eyes."

Slowly, he pried one eye open. "Pretty," he mumbled.

"Pretty what?"

He reached out a finger to touch her lips, but his hand flopped back to his side. "You're pretty," he whispered.

"You've got a fever. Did you sleep outside in the rain?" She narrowed her eyes, put two fingers to the carotid artery at his neck to count his pulse. It was pounding way too fast. "Why did you sleep outside in the rain?"

"Shh." He squeezed his eyes tightly closed. "Headache."

"C'mon." She slipped her hand underneath his armpit. "Let's get you to bed."

A dreamy grin slipped across his face. "Mmm. You, me, bed. Thought you'd never ask."

She managed to lever him into a sitting position. "Not me. Just you. All alone with aspirin and a cool cloth."

He shook his head. "Can't. Gotta sail."

"There will be no sailing today, Captain Whitcomb."

"Gotta get to Key West."

"You said yourself we were ahead of schedule."

"Gotta stop Jackie from marrying that guy."

Her heart pinched. She set her jaw. Seriously, she had to stop being jealous of this Jackie woman. So what if he'd sail with a fever in order to get to her? It was none of Haley's business. "Let's go, Romeo."

"I can sail," he insisted.

"You can't even stand up."

"Can, too."

"Prove it. Do it."

He struggled to his feet. Held out his hands. "Tada."

"You're swaying."

"Motion of the ocean, baby."

"Didn't we have a talk about this *baby* thing?"

"Oops." He plastered a palm over his mouth. "Sorry."

She couldn't stop herself from smiling. "Don't apologize. Just don't do it again."

He gave her a little salute and almost toppled over.

"You're drunk with fever."

"You might be right," he admitted.

"Finally," she said, "you're listening to your nurse."

"My nurse." He patted her shoulder.

"I'm not a lapdog."

"Nothing about you is like a lapdog," he agreed. Dark circles smudged his eyes.

She took his elbow and guided him toward the steps, steering him around the spilled coffee and damaged cups.

"Aw, you dropped the coffee."

"Don't worry, I'll clean it up later."

It was slow going. Jeb couldn't seem to pick his legs up. Instead, he shuffled along like a prisoner in shackles.

"Lean on me," she scolded.

"Don't want to."

"Why not? You're not going to overload me. I'm sturdy. I do this kind of thing all the time."

"Because."

"Because why?" Getting him to speak in complete sentences was like pulling teeth. *Don't get irritated. The man's got a fever of at least a hundred and two.*

"I like touching you too much."

Haley sucked in her breath. "Think of me as a nurse, not a woman."

"Kinda hard to do when you're built so nicely," he murmured, but he leaned into her.

She took his weight, wrapped an arm around his muscular waist. The man didn't have an ounce of fat on him, but his shirt was soaked. And his body? Have mercy, it was incredible. "We've got to get you out of these wet clothes."

"Betcha say that to all the guys."

"Stop trying to be charming for two seconds, will you? You're sick."

"Ba—" He cut himself off from saying *baby*. "That's like telling the sun not to shine."

"Hopeless, I know. Here we are at the stairs. Hold on to the rail and we'll take them one step at a time."

"I feel like an idiot."

"You should. Spending the night on the bridge in

a thunderstorm." She clicked her tongue, shook her head. "Don't worry. I won't let you live it down."

"That's what I love about you."

Love? Haley's heart somersaulted. *Chill out, it's a figure of speech.*

"You don't ever let up on anyone."

"That sounds terrible."

"Not terrible at all. You hold people accountable to a higher standard."

Holy Oreos, was she blushing?

"Whoa." Jeb stopped, clung to the rail.

She stopped, too. "Dizzy?"

"Yep."

"Here. Sit." She guided him down to the step.

They sat together, side by side, Jeb breathing fast and shallow. So was she. What the heck was this?

"Deep breath," she instructed herself as much as Jeb.

He took a few deep breaths and so did she. Nodding, he said, "Let's try this again."

It took a full ten minutes, but step by step, they made it to his cabin. Haley directed him to a chair and squatted beside him to slip off his shoes. As a nurse she dressed and undressed patients daily, but this was different. Jeb wasn't her patient and she wasn't his nurse. And even when he was sick, the man turned her on in nine hundred ways.

*Today you are his nurse. Be professional.*

Easy to say, much harder to do. His skin was thick and healthy. His muscles sublime. Even when he was sick, he was sexy.

She put his shoes aside, stood up. "Arms up."

"What?"

"We've got to get that shirt off you."

"I can do it."

Whew, that was a relief. "Okay." She crossed her arms over her chest, waited for him.

He sat in the chair, managing to look both pale and flushed at the same time. "Give me a minute. I need to rest up."

"Just let me help."

He shook his head. "Okay."

"Can you raise your arms?"

He nodded. "No."

She took the edge of his wet shirt in her hands and slowly rolled it upward. He lifted his arms as she peeled the shirt over taut, tanned abs so delicious they just begged to be licked. She had to bite down on her bottom lip to keep from letting out an appreciative moan.

Finally, she tugged the shirt over his head. His hair stood up in a mussed mess. How endearing he looked. *What? You like your men helpless?*

No, not at all, but illness was the great equalizer. It hit the wealthy and the poor alike.

He slumped against the back of the chair.

She eyed his shorts. Hmm, how to get those off? She could just leave him in them, but they were damp, too. Being wet didn't cause illness—bacteria and viruses did that—but it sure could weaken the immune system, especially since he'd languished outside in the rain all night, while she'd been peacefully curled up in his bed. *Feeling guilty now, huh?*

"Can you take off your pants by yourself?"

"Got it," he said, stood up briefly and then toppled face-first onto the bed.

Right.

"Roll over."

He grunted.

She grabbed his belt loops and tugged him over onto his back. His eyes were closed and he had a slight smile on his face. If he weren't so out of it, she would swear he was enjoying this.

Her fingers went to the snap of his shorts. Instantly, she felt him harden beneath her touch. He didn't move or say a word. His eyes were still closed. What was she going to do now? Undress him or let him sleep in damp shorts?

"Jeb."

He didn't answer.

She poked him with a finger. "Jeb."

He mumbled something barely audible.

Okay, he was out of it. The erection was just a natural response to a woman plucking at his pants. She shouldn't be either pleased or offended by it. Determined to act professionally, she quickly slid his zipper down.

His erection grew.

Beads of sweat popped out on her forehead. She gritted her teeth and pointedly looked away. Moving to the foot of the bed, she grasped the bottom of his shorts with a hand at each leg and tugged them down his hips.

Oops! His underwear came along for the ride and now he was totally naked. Haley hadn't meant to stare. She had no intention of staring. She'd seen any number of naked men in her career as a nurse but she'd never seen anyone like him. Jeb's ego wasn't the only thing that was oversize about the man. Underwear model, hell—he could be a porn star.

Haley curled her fingernails into her palms until it stung. *Put his underwear back on him.*

She hesitated, considered that, then dismissed the idea. Leaving him naked was easier than trying to wrestle him into boxer briefs. The very image brought out goose bumps on her skin. Especially when his erection was jutting up there, proud and tall.

But he was also shivering, his teeth chattering so loudly she could have danced the flamenco to them. His temperature must be on the rise. She covered him with a blanket. He looked miserable, poor guy.

She picked up his wet clothes and hung them up to dry on the towel rack in the bathroom, located aspirin in the medicine cabinets. She roused him enough to make him down two aspirin and forced him to drink a full glass of water before she allowed him to sink back into the covers.

Afterward, she fled to the bridge to clean up the spilled coffee.

When she finished, she straightened and looked out at the wide expanse of deep blue sea. As far as the eye could, see there was nothing but water and seagulls.

It hit her then. How isolated she was. On the ocean with an incapacitated skipper. What if he were desperately ill? She had no medical equipment with her and knew nothing about boats.

Holy Oreos, she was in serious trouble here.

AN ANGEL HAD TAKEN his clothes off.

No, not an angel.

Haley.

Okay, she was something of an angel. He'd admit that. Angel of mercy. *As in have mercy, she's tearing me up!*

Her fingers were cool on his skin, and her hair! So beautiful, the way it fell over her shoulders. She wore it up in that tight bun too much. Her hair should never be restrained. He wanted to touch those beautiful honey-blond strands but his fingers were too shaky.

She leaned over him, smelling of strawberries. He loved strawberries—strawberry shortcake, strawberry jelly, chocolate-covered strawberries, strawberry cake, strawberry Life Savers.

That was Haley. His strawberry lifesaver.

Yum.

Jeb licked his lips. Or at least he tried. His mouth was dry and his lips stuck together. Lip balm. He needed lip balm.

Hey? What was this? A smooth feminine finger was applying slick balm to his lips. What a soft finger. Ah, that felt much better. All he had to do was think about something and it happened. Neat trick.

*Test it.*

He grinned. He needed an angel in his bed, curled up right next to him, her sweet little fanny pressed up against his pelvis. He needed to run his hands over her curvy hips, trace over the dip of her waist, find the sweet swell of her breasts.

She ran a hand along his spine and he shuddered. Cold. He was so very cold. And hot. Hot and cold all at the same time. Blankets were mounded up on him and he was still so cold, but at the same time he wanted to kick all those covers off and feel the air cool his heated skin.

The covers lifted. There it was. Fresh air.

And the angel!

Sliding underneath the covers with him, curling against him. The push of her firm breasts tight against his shoulder blades.

Was this real? Was she in bed with him?

Or was it, as part of him suspected, nothing more than a very vivid sex dream?

Whatever it was, bring it on. Fantasy, reality, either one, he craved both, more.

She pressed her lips to the nape of his neck.

Jeb growled low in his throat. He was within inches of pounding his chest with his fists and letting out a Tarzan yell of triumph to find himself in bed with her. He turned toward her, dragged her into his arms, kissed her, hard and hot and frantic.

She laughed.

Red-hot electricity straight to his cock.

Heedlessly, he yanked the thin spaghetti straps off her dress, ripped the garment from her body.

The angel gasped, a soft, delighted sound. "Ooh, a caveman. I like that."

"Just wait," he panted.

She wriggled in his arms, the lace of her strapless bra scratching across his chest. The strip of her matching thong panties stretching against her pale skin. He clawed at the fastener on her bra, managed to get it off.

The pulse in his throat throbbed and his cock jumped.

In a feverish daze, Jeb took a deep, steadying breath and placed his hand over her heart. He wanted her. Damn, how he wanted her.

He shouldn't be doing this.

No? Why not?

Because, because…

His head was a mess and he couldn't think of a single reason why he should not be doing this. Need consumed him. He had to have her.

Now!

The way she was kissing him, the angel wanted him right back with a fire and passion that surprised him. She'd had him fooled. He'd thought she was pretty darn regimented, but woo-hoo, he was wrong about that.

She threw her head back, exposed her smooth, creamy neck to him, her honeyed hair trailing down his forearm. She was just as he'd dreamed she'd be— her body was both firm and soft and totally womanly. Her bare breasts rested against his biceps as he gently cupped her in the crook of his arm.

Unless he was dreaming now. It did feel pretty damn surreal.

But how could he be dreaming? She felt so genuine. Smelled so good. Sounded so earthy.

He pulled back, drank her in. Man, he loved the way she looked at him, with wide, knowing eyes.

She lowered her eyelids halfway and gave him a naughty expression. One come-hither glance and he was a goner.

If only he could capture this special moment, lock it in a vault, seal it in a time capsule. He smiled, then laughed and then squeezed her tight. His flesh, from his head to his toes, quivered.

She propped herself up on her elbow and ran a hand through her hair, tousling the long, loose curls. One strand fell saucily across her eye, adding to her sexual mystique. A hazy veil of white light seemed to encompass her.

Was something wrong with his eyes? Or was her halo simply that bright?

Mesmerized, he blinked.

She tucked the wayward tendril behind one ear and batted her lush eyelashes at him. Her blue-eyed gaze snagged his, bright as the Mediterranean. "I'm here to ease your fever."

"If I'm the one with the fever, how come you're so hot?"

Her gaze misted with lust. She flicked out her tongue to lick her full pink lips and Jeb forgot about everything except his driving need to sink deeply into her amazing body.

"Are you just going to stare at me all night?"

"No, ma'am." He crawled on his hands and knees toward her.

She reached up with the flat of her bare foot and pressed it against his chest, halting his progress. The sight of her sweet pink toes shot his desire into overload.

"I'm going to wear you out, Skipper. The way no woman has ever worn you out. Are you prepared for total surrender?" Her sultry laugh skipped across his eardrums.

"Are *you* prepared for everything I'm going to give you?" He narrowed his eyes.

She curled her toes into his chest. "This is a one-shot deal. Let's make it a night to remember."

"Ha! One taste of me and you won't be able to walk away after only one night," he teased, his gaze hooking onto hers.

"Where'd I put my shoes?" she teased right back.

She dropped her foot, curled up to a sitting position and reached for his shoulders.

Jeb groaned.

"Hmm." She reached down to wrap her fingers around his burgeoning shaft. "What have we here?"

His face was level with her breasts. They were gorgeous. Perfect. Full and round and real, but not too big. Just right. The size of navel oranges. He loved navel oranges. He couldn't help reaching out to cup her breasts in his hands.

He lowered his mouth, took one of her pert, straining nipples between his teeth, licked it with his tongue.

Her breath came out in a hot rush, and suddenly, she was as wild and slippery as a dolphin, pulling him down on top of her. Her greedy mouth kissing his cheeks, his chin, the tip of his nose.

Jeb's hunger equaled hers. He melded his mouth against hers and they dissolved into a tumble of arms and legs.

*Gotta have her. Gotta have her now.*

There was no fighting it.

His dick throbbed. Blood galloped through his veins, engorging him, hard and hot. His mind whirled. He wasn't thinking clearly. Couldn't even think. Primal urge overtook everything else.

Jeb had full command of her lips, but she was ready and waiting for him. She darted her sly, sweet tongue into his mouth, rushing pell-mell past his teeth. This moment rivaled the best day sailing. In fact, the dip and swoop of his blood as it rolled slickly through his veins reminded him of ocean swells.

She ran her fingers up and down his bare back, each

stroke driving the heated urgency inside him higher and higher. How could a guy's temperature be this hot and his brains not fry, his blood not boil?

Aah, wait. He *was* bursting into flames. Rocket ship to Mars. Buckle up and hang on tight.

She raked her fingers through his hair and arched her hips upward, driving him mad with the brush of her nipples beaded tight against his chest and the sight of her sweet honey hair down there—he had to have a taste!

*Here I come, baby.* No, wait, she didn't like to be called *baby* and he didn't want to call her that. He needed a nickname for her. A term of endearment he'd never used on another woman, but one that fit her perfectly.

Angel.

Good girl, always doing the right thing.

Angel of mercy.

He had to taste her goodness, inhale her and touch every inch of her sweet body. Let her halo light him up inside.

Her lips parted, supple and impatient, mimicking his every move. She dug her fingertips into his spine, squashing his chest against her breasts.

They were nose to nose, Jeb anchoring her to the mattress. He slipped one hand down her inner thigh, searching for her deep heat, finding out how ready she was for him. Gently, he rubbed an index finger along her soft flesh. "Angel."

"Oh, you devil." She sighed.

"You better believe it," he whispered as he found his target and slipped a finger into her.

She trembled beneath his hand.

He shuddered and inched in another finger. When he found her sensitive button with the tip of his thumb, she moaned and pushed her hips up.

She was the most responsive woman he'd ever been with.

"That's right, stud. You're making the earth move for me." She nibbled his earlobe. "But I don't want to do this alone. I want you to come along with me."

"I want this to last."

"All good things must come to an end," she said sagely. "Let's do it up big."

She was too damn wise for his good.

"Come," she whispered and did this crazy thing with her hand, touched some erogenous spot he hadn't known he possessed, and boom! He was off.

He couldn't hold out any longer. He pushed into her. The minute her hot, intimate folds welcomed him, he whispered, "Angel."

Her fingers were in his hair and she was rocking against him, chanting "Jeb" like a mantra.

She stopped breathing then.

Was she about to climax?

No, no, it was too fast. Jeb slowed down, pulled back. "Not yet, angel."

"Don't be contrary." She pouted.

He kissed her forehead, her eyelids, her nose, her cheeks and her chin as she wriggled impatiently beneath him. "You want me to make you come?"

"I want it now!"

"Whatever you say, angel." He dropped his feet to the floor, pulled her to the edge of the mattress. The tip of his throbbing erection hovered just outside her sweet sex. She spread her thighs apart and he nudged against her entrance.

He looked down at her naked body through the golden haze of enchantment. Her lips were pink and shiny, her hair mussed, her breasts full and luscious. Damn, but she was the sexiest woman he'd ever known.

Haley writhed against him. "Get inside me now, Skipper, before this boat runs aground."

"I can't deny you anything." He sank into her.

Haley held his hips and drew him in deeper.

They let out twin sighs.

The heat, the rocking of the boat, the heady smell of their combined sex pushed them over the edge. A few powerful thrusts and they were both lost at sea. Jeb came inside her at the same moment that Haley cried out in pleasure.

Exhausted, he clung to her, carried her with him as he rolled over onto his back. She lay on top of him now, peered down into his eyes.

Magic.

He'd always loved sex, but it had never felt like this. Freaking abracadabra magic.

Her hair trailed across his face, the scent of strawberries. He inhaled deeply, closed his eyes. Best thing. She was the best thing that had ever happened to him.

The heat ebbed away, but the glow in his heart flared brilliant and bright.

He reached to kiss her, but she was gone, and his hand hit cool, empty sheet. *Playing hide-and-seek, you little minx. Here I come.*

The pun made him smile. He opened his eyes.

Haley stood in the door, fully clothed, a tray in

her hand and a concerned frown furrowing her pretty forehead.

*Don't frown, angel.*

"Are you all right? You were making the most dreadful moaning sounds." She set the tray on the desktop, stepped over to the bed.

"What are you doing dressed?" he asked and tried to give her a rakish grin, but feared he came off looking like a sloppy drunk. His smile slipped.

She shrugged. "As if I'd be naked with you."

"You were, just two minutes ago. How'd you get dressed so fast?"

"What are you talking about?" She stepped forward, but stopped abruptly. "Wait a minute!"

Ah, crap!

She pressed her lips together and her eyes twinkled. "Were you having a sex dream?"

"No, no," he denied.

"Yes, yes." She snapped her fingers, clearly enjoying his embarrassment. "That's what all the moaning was about. If I'd known I wouldn't have interrupted you."

His chest tightened. All of that beautiful lovemaking nothing more than a fabulous dream. He forced a devil-may-care laugh. He wasn't embarrassed. By sex? No, siree. Not he. Sex was normal. Natural. *You thought you were really having sex with her.* It had felt so damned real. How could a dream feel so real?

"You *were* having a sex dream. About me. About us."

His face flamed. Jeb lowered his head. Dummy. He thought a sex dream was real. How could he have been so fooled?

"It's okay." She chuckled softly. "While I'm deeply flattered to be part of your sexual fantasies, it was all fever-induced. Nothing to be ashamed of. It happens. Simple biology."

"Just a fever." His body felt heavy and his heart shrunk in his chest. "Nothing but a fever."

She leaned over to press a palm against his forehead. It was all he could do not to twist away from her touch. "Your fever's gone. Don't worry, I'm sure the naughty dreams are gone with it."

Yes. Jeb gulped. That was exactly what he feared.

# 9

**Telltales**—*Yarn or ribbons on the luff of a sail to help with trimming*

"I MADE CHICKEN NOODLE SOUP from scratch," she said efficiently, professionally. Nurse mode. That was the best way to deal with this. It wasn't the first time she'd witnessed a patient having a fever-fueled sex dream, but as far as she knew, it was the first time she'd had a starring role in one.

"You made me soup?" Jeb's eyes widened in disbelief and he shook his head slowly. "That takes hours."

"Don't look so amazed. It's not like I had much else to do." She leaned over and fixed the blanket. She curled her bare toes against the sleek wood floor. *Stay grounded.*

She tried not to notice his bare chest—ha, as if she could—and tucked the covers underneath Jeb's arms. The man could be a swimsuit model, no doubt about it.

He wriggled.

*Hey, buddy, I'm just as uncomfortable about this as you are.*

Straightening, she smiled. Put on a happy face. It worked for him—why not give it a shot?

"You're spoiling me."

"You should be very accustomed to that." She picked up the legged tray, carried it to the bed and positioned it over his lap. She unfolded a paper napkin and spread it over his bare chest. There. Covered that dangerous puppy up.

"Mostly from people that I pay to spoil me. Not too many people do it for me spontaneously from the goodness of their generous heart."

"What about your mother? Surely she spoiled you."

"She paid the servants to spoil me. Does that count?" he quipped.

"Get out the violins for the poor little rich boy."

A fleeting look of sadness flickered in his eyes, but he quickly snuffed it out with a wide smile. He might have had a plush childhood, but she had a sense that he'd gotten lost in the shuffle of multiple marriages and divorces and blended families. Was that why it was so easy for him to go with the flow? She admired that trait. How he didn't let bumps in the road keep him from enjoying life. If only she could be more like him in that way.

"Usually, I'm the one doing the spoiling," he said.

"You are the one with the money," she pointed out.

"Why do I get the feeling that's a bad thing in your eyes?"

She shrugged, sat down on the edge of the bed. Which was odd because nurses were trained not to sit on their patients' beds. It went against everything she'd been taught, but here she was sitting on his bed. He was not her patient, after all. Rationalization did not excuse the behavior. She didn't understand why she didn't get up. "Money's not bad. It's the frivolous waste of it that gets to me."

"Like ordering important equipment instead of splurging on a pretty solarium," he said.

He was bringing that up, huh? "Well, now that you've mentioned it, yes. Solariums are nice, but not necessary. Medical equipment is a must-have."

"The patients enjoy the solarium. Boosts their spirits and a happy patient is a healthy patient."

"They live on an island. All you have to do is raise a window. No need for specific architecture that costs extra money."

"You got your equipment."

"Only after I butted heads with you. Everyone else was so eager to kiss your backside."

"Because I was the guy with the wallet."

"Don't you get tired of it?"

"What?"

"Having people like you only because you have money."

He pretended to pout. "Is that the reason? I thought it was my charm and devastating good looks."

"Are you fishing for compliments?"

"That meeting was the first time I realized just how special you were."

She ducked her head, slanted him a sideways glance. "Because I ticked you off?"

"You were the one who was ticked off," he reminded her. "I was amused. You become passionate so easily." He tracked a knowing gaze over her. "You've got a fire inside you, Haley French."

She crossed her arms over her chest so he couldn't

see the way her body was reacting under his scrutiny. "Eat your soup before it gets cold."

"Are you ever off duty, nurse?"

"It's ingrained in me. What can I say? Are you going to make me feed you?"

He raised his eyebrows. "I like the sound of that."

She snorted. "You would."

"What do you have against men with money?"

"It's not the money, per se. It's the way money makes them feel entitled. As if they can have whatever they want."

"What was his name?" Jeb asked.

"Who?"

"The rich guy who broke your heart."

Haley's eyes widened. How had he guessed? Bile burned a toxic path up her throat at the memory of Trey Goss. For the most part, she'd managed to put the past behind her. She didn't like dwelling on something she could not change. "Who says a rich guy broke my heart?"

"Why else would you have such a chip on your shoulder for wealthy men?"

"Eat."

He saluted her, picked up the soupspoon and pushed around chunks of chicken, carrots, celery, onions and egg noodles in the steamy broth. He took a few bites. "Mmm, this is really good."

Why was she still sitting here? She had no answer. No excuse other than she wanted to make sure he ate. He needed nourishment. That was the only reason. "I'm glad you like it."

"You're not eating anything?"

"I had some soup before I brought it in to you."

He ate every last drop with gusto. Great. That was a good sign. He was on the road to recovery. It was probably just one of those twenty-four-hour things. If he kept improving, she'd let him sail tomorrow.

"What time is it?" he asked.

"Four in the afternoon."

He looked relieved. "That's not so bad. We were a day ahead of schedule, so even losing a day, we should still hit Key West by early Saturday morning as long as the weather cooperates."

"It's four in the afternoon on *Wednesday*," she said. "You've been asleep since yesterday morning."

"What!" He shoved the tray at her. "Here, take this."

She stood, picked up the tray.

"We'll have to sail through the night."

"You're not sailing anywhere tonight."

"Who's gonna stop me?"

"I am."

"And how do you plan on doing that?"

"By holding your clothes hostage."

"Then I'll just sail naked." Jeb swung his legs over the edge of the bed and, thankfully, kept the covers over his lap, but she couldn't avoid that bare chest.

Oh, gosh, if he stood up, she would see his full naked body again. Unprepared. She was woefully unprepared for this, for him. "You're too weak—"

He inhaled audibly, grabbed his head and muttered, "Whoa."

She settled the tray onto the desk and then turned to press him back against the pillow, making sure to keep the covers over him. "Lie down."

"I'm okay. Just sat up a bit too fast."

"You're getting better, but you're in no condition to sail and your body is trying to tell you that."

"Ever thought about becoming a drill sergeant? You'd be really good at it."

"I'm looking after your best interests."

"You know," he said, "if someone else uttered that line, I wouldn't believe them, but you…"

"But me what?"

"You really do put other people's interests ahead of your own. You really do care."

"You sound surprised."

"I'm surprised because there aren't many people like you in the world."

She rearranged his covers again. Her heart did a crazy dip-swirl thing. He seemed to know exactly what to say to flatter her. He truly had a gift for soft soap. *Lather me up.* "There are more than you think."

"You're too generous."

"And you," she said sternly, "need to learn to ride out the consequences of your choices."

"What does that mean?"

"You chose to spend the night in the rain and you got sick. You can't get well on demand."

"You're blaming me for getting sick?"

"No, I'm saying you have to accept the consequences of your actions."

"That's harsh."

"That's reality. You have a tendency toward magical thinking, Jeb."

He looked as if she'd just run him through with a skewer. "Wow."

"I'm not saying this to hurt your feelings."

"You didn't hurt my feelings. It's just that…" He trailed off.

"What?"

"You see right through me. Am I that transparent?"

"To anyone who's really looking at you."

"You see me as I am, huh?"

"I believe I do."

"And you still like me?"

"Who wouldn't like you?"

"My point exactly." He paused a long moment. "I've always believed I could do anything I set my mind to. You'd probably say it's because I grew up privileged, and maybe you'd be right, but I seemed to have the ability to get what I wanted with a smile."

The man did have a devastating smile.

"It never seems to work with you, though."

"I wouldn't say never."

He smiled then, big and playful.

And she fell for it. Smiled back. Hey, smiling wasn't going to hurt anything.

"You've got a point."

"You agree with me?"

"When I was six or seven, I got it into my head that I could live in the water like a dolphin. My dad had a waterfront home, Tampa Bay—this was between wife number two and wife number three—and I'd spend summers with him. My dad has this pedal boat for us kids to play on, and one day after I'd gotten in trouble for something, I decided I was going to go live with my real family, the dolphins. So I pedaled out into the bay."

"Alone?" Her insides tightened. She could just see him as a kid, totally heedless to the danger he was putting himself in. He must have driven his mother crazy with worry.

"Well, yeah. If I was going to go live with the dolphins, I didn't want to take any people along with me. That would defeat the point. I was just about to dive off the boat when I thought it might be a good idea to anchor the pedal boat, just in case I couldn't find the dolphins right off the bat."

"This story is making me nervous." She nibbled her bottom lip.

"Clearly," he said, "I survived, so settle down, worrywart. I pedaled back to the house, got a cinder block, tied a rope around it, stuck it on the pedal boat and went back out."

"And you were just six or seven?" She wrung her hands. "Where were your parents?"

He shrugged. "They were pretty lax."

She shook her head. No child of hers would ever be given such a free rein at such a young age.

"I dropped anchor. I was convinced that I was going to find a school of dolphins and swim away with them. I totally believed it deep down in my bones."

What an imaginative and adventuresome kid he'd been. Haley was hooked on the horns of his narrative. He had a way of spinning a story that reeled her in. He'd make a great salesman.

"I held my breath and dived in headfirst. Everything around me was dark and cold."

But of course. Jeb would never just dip his toe into something and ease into it.

"And I was really shocked when I couldn't stay under. I tried, but the water pushed against me and I just had to breathe. I tried to breathe underwater, but of course, I got a mouthful of ocean. Then it occurred to me that the reason I couldn't do it, couldn't breathe, couldn't find my dolphin family was because I'd anchored that pedal boat and if I hadn't had a fallback plan, then I would have been able to swim away underwater. I'd ruined my chances by casting a safety net, by not trusting in the magic."

"Did you try it without anchoring the boat?"

He shook his head. "My dad found me and I got a good bawling out. Not long after that, he sold the beach house, but honestly, I believed it was because my lack of belief had blown my chances forever."

"And yet you named your boat *Second Chance*."

A smile played at his lips. "I did, at that."

"You need to get some rest." She picked up the tray, moved to the door with it.

"You're not going to leave me here alone, are you?"

"That's the idea."

"I'm bored."

Honestly, so was she. She'd spent the past day reading ebooks on her cell phone in between checking in on him. She was more than ready for conversation.

"I've got some board games underneath the bench seating of the dining room table," he said. "Pick your favorite."

She was tempted. "If you promise to be good."

"Define *good*." He grinned impishly.

"Not getting up until I say you can."

"Not sure I can keep that promise." The sexy look on his face told her he was thinking of an alternate meaning for the word *up*.

Her cheeks burned. She sat down the tray, opened a drawer, pulled out underwear, cargo shorts and a T-shirt for him and tossed them at him. "Put these on and I'll think about playing a game with you."

"Don't think too hard, angel. That's your problem—you think too much."

"And your problem is that you don't think enough."

"Makes us a perfect match," he teased. "Two halves of a whole."

She picked up the tray again. "I wonder what your friend Jackie would have to say about that." Then she turned and walked out the door, blood pumping hot and fast through her veins.

JEB GOT DRESSED in the clothes that Haley had thrown at him and he waited for her return.

And waited.

And waited.

And waited.

An hour later, when he assumed she was just going to leave him hanging, a sharp knock sounded on the door, but she didn't wait for him to invite her in. Instead, she entered, carrying an armful of board games.

"I've never heard of any of these games before. Don't you have Monopoly or Scrabble or Parcheesi?"

"Nope."

She set the board games on the bed. "You pick one."

"Ah," he said, slipping the bottom game from the stack. "This one."

"'I've Never,'" she said, reading the name of the game, "'The Outrageous Game of Truth.' Hmm. Sounds interesting. I'm in."

"Actually, it's a drinking game. You need hooch."

"Well, I'm not going to let you drink. You're just recovering from a fever."

"Think of it as medicinal, Scotch and water, with lots of water so I don't dehydrate? Besides, I never lose at this game. You'll be the one doing all the drinking."

"Oh, ho, that sounds like a challenge to me. Consider the gauntlet thrown," she said. "I'm very competitive."

"So I've noticed. The liquor is underneath the bar."

She left and came back a few minutes later with a bottle of peach brandy and two tumblers. She poured an inch into each glass. "Sip when you lose."

"I'm not going to lose."

"We'll see," she said, giving him a knowing look that was so adorable he almost laughed. "How do you play this thing?"

"It's pretty simple. You roll the dice, move to that numbered square on the board and if the question written on the square is true, then you move forward a space. If it's not true, you have to take a drink, then roll the dice again for your next move."

"What's to keep someone from lying?"

"I don't lie. Do you?"

"No. This is a hypothetical question."

"If you're caught in a lie and you're called on it, you have to drink twice."

"Hmm, so this game turns you into a drunken liar."

"Only if you don't tell the truth."

"I'm ready to whip your butt," she said, rolling the dice between her palms as he opened the board up on the bed between them. She rolled a three, moved her game piece forward three spaces and leaned over to read what was written there.

"Hey," she said. "These questions are all of an adult nature."

"That's the game." He gave her a knowing wink. "Too much for you? We could always play Old Maid."

"Are you saying I'm a prude?"

"You *are* blushing."

"Fine." She ran a hand through her hair and pressed her lips into a prim line and then read the question on the game board. "'I've never been spanked in fore-play.'"

Jeb chuckled. He'd bet a thousand dollars that Haley had never done anything that outside-the-box. Not that a little spanking was very kinky. "True or false, angel? If it's true, you get to move forward one square. If it's false, you have to take a drink."

Hesitantly, she took a sip of brandy.

"Look at you," Jeb hooted. "Haley likes having her butt spanked. No wonder you wanted to whip mine."

"I didn't say I liked it." She tossed her head, but her cheeks reddened considerably. "Go on. It's your turn."

Jeb rolled. Landed on six. "'I've never had a three-some,'" he read.

"True or false?"

He moved ahead one square.

Haley snapped her fingers. "I challenge that. I say you're lying."

His eyes met hers. "I might have been something of a player before this past year, but I've never been to bed with more than one woman at a time." He purpose-fully held her gaze longer than he should have. Was it bad of him to tease her? "When I'm with a woman, she gets my full, undivided attention."

Haley gulped visibly, dropped his gaze as if it was plutonium.

"Take a drink," he said.

"Why?"

"If you challenge someone and they're not lying, then *you* have to take a drink."

"You didn't explain that in the beginning."

"I'm explaining it now."

She rolled the dice with a shaky hand. "'I've never been arrested.'" With a disgruntled look, she took another sip of brandy. "At this rate I'll be blitzed before we're halfway through the game."

Wow, he would never have expected this. "Quite the little jailbird, are we?"

She held back her shoulders in a cocky gesture. "What? It was a protest rally."

He read the square he'd landed on. "'I've never had sex on a water bed.' Nope, never done that, either."

"But you've had sex on a bed on the water," she pointed out.

"That's not what the question asked."

"I challenge that one, too."

"Haley, Haley, Haley. How old do you think I am? I wasn't born in the seventies at the height of the water bed craze."

"Well, neither was I, and I've slept on a water bed."

"But did you have sex on it?"

"No, but it's not my question."

"Touché. Take a drink."

"Why?"

"I wasn't lying and you challenged me."

She chuffed out a breath and took a sip so small she barely got her lips wet. "Fine. Happy now?"

He nodded. "Very."

"My turn." She tossed the dice again. Moved up two spaces. She was ahead of him on the board and on drinking. "'I've never drunk-texted an ex.' Ha! At last something I haven't done."

Jeb took his turn. "'I've never streaked.' Okay, I have done that." He took a swallow of brandy.

"You streaked?"

"Uh-huh."

"Where?"

"College graduation."

"Seriously?" She squealed.

"Not one of my finest moments, but yeah. It was a dare."

"And if the person had dared you to jump off a building, would you have done it?"

"Now you sound like my mother."

"I can't believe you streaked. How embarrassing."

"Hey, I didn't get caught. No arrests on my record, Miss Jailbird."

Haley read her next question. "'I've never slept with a married person.'"

A strange look came over her face and she peeked over at him.

It hit Jeb like a punch to the gut and he just knew she was going to lie.

"Nope, never did that." She moved her marker up one space.

He should let it go. No matter that his gut was telling him that she was lying, it was none of his business. It was a stupid game.

"Challenge," he said in a voice so steely it surprised him.

She startled. "Pardon?"

"I challenge. I think you *have* slept with a married man." Why did he care? Why was he suddenly so pissed off?

Her color instantly paled. "I don't want to play this game anymore." She hopped off the bed.

Jeb wasn't going to let her get away with that. He grabbed her by the elbow. "Haley?"

She yanked against his grip, but he didn't let go.

"Talk to me."

Tears brimmed in her eyes and it just about undid him. Immediately, he let go of her. What had happened?

She ducked her head, turned away and gave him her back.

"Never mind. I shouldn't have pressed. It's none of my business." He swept the game board and pieces back into the box. Why had he ruined a perfectly nice evening?

"I lied because I'm so ashamed of myself," she mumbled. "I didn't know he was married when we began the affair."

"Was it the rich guy? The one that prejudiced you against people with money?"

Mutely, she nodded.

Jeb had an impulse to hunt the guy down and punch his lights out for hurting Haley.

"That's why it gets all over me when you call me *baby*. He called me *baby*. Like I was a child, an infant. Of course, I really was as naive as a baby. I took people at face value. I thought if someone treated you nicely that it meant they were a nice person."

"Looks can be deceiving." Seriously, he was dishing up trite adages for her? Jeb clenched his teeth. He didn't know what else to say.

"It's the one thing in my life I regret most. I let myself down." She cried quietly, her shoulders trembling.

"Shh," he murmured and reached for her.

With her back still to him, she wilted onto the mattress. "Don't be so nice to me. I don't deserve it."

"You broke up with him when you found out he was married, right?"

She stiffened and a sick feeling settled in the pit of his stomach. She hadn't left the relationship when she'd learned he was married. Wow. So his idol had feet of clay after all. It was like finding out that the America's Cup trophy was made out of aluminum instead of sterling silver. How long had he had her up on a pedestal?

"I tried to break up with him," she whispered, "but that night…" She put a hand to her mouth, shook her head.

"Haley." He rubbed her back. "You don't have to tell me anything. You owe me no explanations."

She dropped her forehead to his shoulder and sobbed helplessly.

He wrapped his arm around her waist, drew her against him. Oh, damn…oh, hell. *Don't cry, angel, don't cry.* What had he started? "You loved him a lot, huh?"

She shook her head. "No, no, that's not it at all."

He hooked his thumb underneath her chin and gently guided it up until she was forced to meet his gaze. It killed him to see her looking so wrecked.

"It's okay. Whatever happened, it's okay now. You're here with me and you're safe." He pressed his lips against her forehead, but that only made her cry harder.

"He…" She swallowed. "He said we weren't done until *he* said we were done. That's when he…forced me into bed. I said no, but he was bigger and stronger, and in the end, I just stopped fighting. I wanted the whole thing over with."

"Are you saying he raped you?"

Silently, she nodded.

"You didn't report it to the police?"

"I did, but the D.A. said there wasn't evidence to bring the case to trial. Ultimately, it would have been my word against the word of a wealthy, prominent businessman, and I had been having an adulterous affair with him. I could tell the authorities didn't really believe my story." She buried her face in her hands.

Adrenaline shot through Jeb. His impulse to punch the guy turned dark and deadly. He wanted to strangle the son of a bitch with his bare hands. Flat-out kill him for hurting Haley. He had no idea he could feel so murderous. He was an easygoing guy. He didn't get enraged. But this…this was unforgivable behavior. Stringing the man up was too good for him.

Haley's tears dampened his shirt. He ran his hand through her hair, held her close, kissed her forehead again and again, softly and sweetly. Nothing sexual. Total comfort. The last thing she needed was some horny guy pawing at her. He reached for a tissue on the shelf above the headboard and handed it to her.

She dabbed her eyes. "I don't know why I'm crying about this. It was years ago. I was a freshman in college. Young and dumb, as they say."

"No, not dumb. Don't put this on yourself."

"Honestly, I sort of felt like I deserved the punishment. I should have suspected he was married."

"Haley!" How could she think that?

"I felt guilty and ashamed for having such poor judgment."

"You did *not* deserve that!"

"If I'd been smarter—"

"Shh, shh." He cradled her in his arms.

"I went to counseling," she said. "I thought I'd put it all behind me, but apparently there's still some lingering issues."

"Ah, damn, angel, I'm so sorry."

"It's not your fault. You didn't do anything, but in a way you remind me of him. In the beginning anyway, before I got to really know you."

Jeb gritted his teeth. "I hate that I remind you of him. No wonder you disliked me."

"It's not you." She shook her head. "It's me. I'm gun-shy—"

"Understandably."

"And I was terrified of getting involved with that kind of man again."

"I'm not like that. I would never, ever hurt you, Haley." He tipped her chin up, and she met his eyes.

"I know, I know, but there's Jackie. I know you're not married to her, but you want to be."

Yeah. Jackie. Jeb blew out his breath. He wasn't going to think about that for now. For now, he just wanted to comfort Haley. He rubbed a palm against her upper back. "If you want to keep talking, I'm all ears, but if you'd rather not say any more, I understand."

Haley let out a small sigh. "Honestly, I'm glad I told you. I feel better already. You're a great listener, Jeb."

"Anything else I can do?"

"Listening is enough. Thank you for that."

"I wish I could do more."

"The past is the past, and I've put it behind me," she said, sounding determined. "Let's focus on something else."

"What would you like to talk about?" he asked.

"Sailing," she replied staunchly. "The sailing bug has bitten me and I'm fascinated."

Now, that was a topic he could handle. "Anything specific you'd like to discuss?"

"Could you show me how to use navigation charts to plot a sea voyage?"

"Love to. We need to do a dead reckoning anyway."

"Dead reckoning? What's that?"

"It's how we figure out where we are and where we're going from here."

"Sounds very purposeful." She smiled. The dark emotions that had earlier clouded her eyes had vanished completely. "Let's do it."

That plucky, hopeful smile tugged his heartstrings. He admired her so much. Admired the way she was able to deal with such adversity and not let it cripple her. She was amazing.

*You're in trouble now, Whitcomb. She's gotcha wrapped around her sweet little finger like a telltale.*

# 10

**Dead reckoning**—*Plotting your course based on the distance from a previously known position*

On Thursday morning, they set sail at dawn. With Jeb's dead reckoning and the happy discovery that the wind was still at their backs, he predicted that if everything went smoothly, even with factoring in the delay, they could still make Key West by Saturday morning. It still gave them plenty of time to get through customs before Jackie's 4:00 p.m. wedding.

For her part, Haley tried not to think about how good it had felt to tell Jeb her secret. He'd been so kind, so understanding, so comforting, and he'd made her feel— Well, she wasn't going to analyze that.

The day had passed companionably. Jeb recovered so quickly it was almost as if he'd never been stricken with a fever, and Haley took him up on his offer to teach her more sailing tips, tricks and techniques. He guided her in taking the helm and she learned how to make the boat go faster through steering. Jeb's lesson there was "steer straight to steer fast." She learned about weather helm, which was a sailboat's tendency to turn toward the wind, and about all the forces pushing and pulling on it.

What surprised her most was that the boat pilot had to make small steering changes in order to keep a sailboat going straight. Whenever the wind changed in velocity or the boat shifted its angle of heel—she'd learned that *heel* was the term used for when a sailboat leaned or tipped to one side—the amount of weather helm changed, forcing the pilot to alter the rudder slightly to stay the course, but by the end of the day, she was already getting the feel of it.

They kept their conversations neutral, steering off hot-button topics like sex. Instead, they discussed books that they loved and they were delighted to discover they had the same taste in literature; both of them enjoyed hard-boiled detective stories, spine-tingling thrillers and biographies. They talked about St. Michael's and what they loved most about the island. They veered into other topics—childhood pets, vacations they'd taken, how to make perfect homemade ice cream.

The day passed pleasantly punctuated by salty sea air and a bracing wind that sent them soaring toward Florida. They stayed up late, lingering over the pasta dinner Jeb cooked and a nice bottle of Chianti, then they went to their separate sleeping quarters, neither one of them brave enough to act on the sexual feelings sparking between them.

By Friday morning, Haley found her entire perception of Jeb had shifted. Whereas before she'd really gotten to know him she'd thought he was frivolous and a bit full of himself, now she'd learned that he simply didn't like to dwell on the darker side of life and he had a talent for turning work into play. Who could fault him for that? It was a skill she sorely needed to learn.

He had a gifted way of making ordinary tasks enjoyable. No wonder everyone wanted to hang around him. And he made her feel entertained, dazzled and inspired. His unwavering self-confidence had a way of filling up the gaps inside her.

"I'm jealous of your self-discipline," he told her as they hoisted the sail at dawn.

"I'm envious of your ability to turn everything into a game." She pushed a strand of windblown hair back off her face. She hadn't once pulled her hair into a ponytail or bun since she'd come on board his boat. Having her hair down made her feel freer, easygoing. "And I thought you found me stick-in-the-muddish."

"I'm serious," he said. "You make me feel inadequate in that regard."

"Jeb, I don't mean to make you feel that way."

"You also make me feel like I have a higher calling and I don't want to let you down."

She thumped him lightly on the chest. "Just live up to your full potential."

"Is that all I have to do to win your respect?"

"You already have my respect."

His eyes twinkled with amusement. "When did I earn that?"

"It started the day you rescued the seagull, but it hit home when you told me how much you wanted to change in order to win Jackie back. I respect people who try to improve."

"You're a fair and honest woman, Haley French."

They stood looking at each other, the wind whipping around them. It was the most perfect moment, the two of them sharing a smile, a sail and their appreciation for each other.

"You know, I've had a really good time this week," she said. "In spite of the unconventional beginning."

"Me, too."

"I'm almost sorry it'll be over tomorrow."

"Almost?" he asked.

"Well, you know me. I can only live in a fantasy for so long. Sooner or later I have to roll up my sleeves and get back to work. Too much time in paradise makes me antsy."

He flashed her a row of his perfect teeth, gave that jaunty wink of his as the wind caught the mainsail and they were off. They'd been sailing for a little less than an hour when land came into view for the first time since they'd left St. Michael's.

"What's that?" Haley pointed.

"Pelican Island. It's a ghost island."

"What's a ghost island?"

"You know, like a ghost town. Once upon a time the island was inhabited, but a hurricane in the early 1900s wiped out everything but the lighthouse."

"I love lighthouses."

"I've always wanted to go ashore. The lighthouse is a popular rendezvous spot for people sailing from the Bahamas to Florida. Too bad we don't have time to stop and investigate."

"Too bad," Haley echoed.

"But we'll be sailing right by it. You'll get a close view of the lighthouse."

She left the sailing to Jeb and went to the bow of the boat as the *Second Chance* glided toward the island. The past few days had been an eye-opener. When she'd first found herself accidentally stowed away upon Jeb's boat, she had not expected to come out of this experience feeling…*cleansed.*

Her time at sea had been restorative, a mental vacation she hadn't even known she'd needed. Being out here on the open sea surrounded by nature reminded her of her own buried wildness. She loved the feel of sunshine on her face and the waves rocking beneath her feet. She was alert to life, fully awake to new experiences in a way she'd never quite been before, and it was all due to Jeb.

She darted a glance over her shoulder at him. He looked so commandingly masculine as his hands skillfully guided the boat. In the deepest, darkest, most intimate, most honest part of her, her muscles clenched in an ache so sweet and sharp, she had to close her eyes, moisten her lips.

He held the keys to a universe of sensations and delight. The man knew how to play. He was a sensualist. A gastronome. No doubt about it. Emotions flooded her. Feelings she'd kept carefully in check since she'd made a youthful mistake and fallen for the wrong man.

Was she doing it again?

Yes. Not because Jeb wasn't a good guy, but rather because his heart belonged to someone else. Haley could not, would not fall for him, but as strong-minded as she was, she could not seem to control her body's internal response. No amount of chiding could stop her smiling every time he looked deeply into her eyes.

Resolutely, she directed her attention back to the sea, and within an hour, they were upon Pelican Island. The lighthouse jutted on a rock pier. Images of a lonely lighthouse keeper swept into her mind. She could see him manning the light that kept boats from crashing into the island. Lighthouses were the stuff of romantic legends and lore—mermaids and sirens and hapless sailors dashed to death on rocky shoals.

The island was shaped like a crescent roll, a small inlet sheltering lighter blue water. She spied some kind of creature moving in the bay.

Was it a dolphin?

Haley squinted. No, the creature was too large for that and too slow, as well. It bobbled on the water, bigger than a cow, gray and lumpish. Elephant. It looked like an underwater elephant without the trunk.

A manatee!

It was one of Florida's famous manatees.

The thrill sent a shiver over her and she ran to Jeb.

"What's got you grinning?"

She put out her hand. "Binoculars."

"What is it?"

"I think there's a manatee over by the lighthouse."

"You sure it's not a ghost?" he teased, digging around in the box where he stowed his sailing gear and coming up with a pair of high-powered binoculars in a black waterproof case.

"There's no such thing as ghosts," she scoffed and hurriedly returned to the bow. She opened the case, took out the binoculars, brought them to her eyes and fine-tuned the focus. It took her a minute to find the creature.

Yes! It was a manatee, big and docile.

The manatee swam above water with lumbering movements, propelling itself forward a few feet and then disappearing from sight as it sank below the water. It came up for air a few seconds later in the exact spot that it had been before. It thrashed. Vanished again. The manatee surfaced once more, swam, submerged, repeating the process again and again.

Something was wrong.

She frowned. Tried to enhance the view by fiddling with the lenses, took another look. Was that a thin black wire wrapped around the manatee? Or was she seeing things?

"Jeb!" She waved him over.

He engaged the autohelm feature and came strolling toward her. Her pulse jumped and she swallowed past the lump filling her throat.

"What is it?"

"Look there and see if I'm imagining things." She passed him the binoculars. "I think the manatee has gotten something wrapped around him and he's trapped."

Jeb raised the binoculars to his eyes and studied the creature for a long moment. The wind whipped his cargo shorts around his tanned legs. He looked like summer. Clean and hot and lazy. Haley's mouth watered.

"I believe you might be right."

"What is it? Can you tell?"

"Not from this distance."

"What are we going to do?"

Jeb lowered the binoculars. "We're not going to do anything. Nothing we can do. Manatees are really big."

"But I heard they're very gentle."

"Haley, it's just not feasible. Logistically, it will be a nightmare trying to land the sailboat on those rocky shoals."

"Couldn't we anchor out here and swim to shore?"

"That sounds a lot easier than it is. The current is swift and unless you're a strong swimmer—"

"I am."

"We don't know that we can rescue him. We're not equipped for manatee rescue."

"We have to try. We just can't go off and leave him like this."

"I'll get on the radio and let the Coast Guard know. They'll send someone out."

"That could take hours. The poor thing could die by then. It's already exhausted itself."

"Haley," he said softly, "you can't save the entire world."

She snapped her mouth shut, crossed her arms and narrowed her eyes.

"You're giving me the stink eye?" he said.

"You deserve it."

"For what?"

"Oh, I get it."

He looked puzzled. "Get what?"

"You think it would take up too much time to help the manatee."

"Well, it would, with absolutely no guarantee of success. Plus, we'll be putting our own lives in danger. Much safer for both us and the manatee to let the Coast Guard handle it."

"You mean much easier for you. If we stopped it might keep you from preventing Jackie from getting married."

"Yes, there is that. It is the reason we're out here in the first place."

She couldn't believe he was being so rational. This

was the same impulsive guy who'd rescued the seagull with the plastic beer ring around its feet? "You're deluding yourself, you know," she muttered.

"In what way?"

"Jackie."

"Are you trying to pick a fight?"

Was she? "You think that just because you come sailing up, all Benjamin Braddock from *The Graduate,* begging her to run away from her wedding with you that she's going to do it."

The expression on his face told her she'd nailed it.

"News flash, if she wanted to marry you, she would never have broken up with you."

"She might not have wanted to marry the old me, but when she hears what I've done, she'll change her mind," he said stubbornly.

"That's magical thinking, Jeb. Can't you just accept the fact that she's in love with this other guy?"

His chin hardened and all the smile went out of his eyes. Haley had never seen him looking so bleak. "She just thinks she's in love with him."

Her stomach hurt. She put a palm over her belly. "How do you know that?"

"Because she's supposed to be with me."

"How do you know *that?*"

"Because she promised she'd give me a year and she didn't give me a full year. That's not like Jackie to go back on her word."

"My point exactly. Doesn't it strike you that this guy must be awfully special for her not to even tell you she's getting married, just sends you a text invitation, which, FYI, probably means she didn't really expect you to come?" Okay, so she felt as if she was ruining Christmas, but come on, it had to be said.

"Then why did she tell me at all? She could have just gotten married and let me find out about it after the fact. I think she was secretly wanting me to swoop in and sail her away."

"You've got some very romantic notions about women," Haley said. "Jackie probably told you about the wedding because you're a childhood friend that she cares about. She wants you there to celebrate her joy, not to break it up."

Anger flashed in his eyes. "You don't even know her."

Haley held up her palms. "You're right, but I also know that for all your devil-may-care attitude, you're not the kind of guy to leave a helpless animal behind when you could help it out. You did come to St. Michael's after all and almost single-handedly saved that island. Your motives might not have been the most altruistic, but what you did was admirable."

"Dammit." He snorted and stalked away.

"Where are you going?" she called after him.

"To drop anchor. Go put on that pink bikini, angel. We're going to save a manatee."

HALF AN HOUR LATER, with the *Second Chance* bobbing and anchored forty yards offshore, Jeb and Haley swam for the small bay where the manatee floundered. They'd swam rather than take the *Second Chance*'s inflatable dinghy because they were afraid the sharp rocks might puncture the raft, and since they were both strong swimmers, they figured it was faster and easier to just swim.

Up close it was easy to tell the panicked creature was in serious trouble. Carefully, they approached it.

The manatee's big sloe eyes were frantic. It floundered, splashed and made a high-pitched, weary squeaking noise like the sound of wiper blades rubbing against a dry windshield. The closer they got the more frantic the mammal's splashing became and the louder and longer its cries grew.

"Easy," Jeb cooed. "Nice and easy, big girl."

"How do you know it's a girl?" Haley asked.

"I don't."

"And here I thought you knew everything there was to know about the sea."

"The sea," he said sagely, "is unknowable."

They had to dog-paddle to reach the stranded mammal. She—Haley was just going to go with the manatee's femininity—stared at them. Her eyes seemed to beg, "Save me."

"We've gotta help her. We can't let this magnificent creature die here."

"Let me see if I can find out what's going on." Jeb dived out of sight and swam underneath the manatee.

"It's okay," Haley soothed. "He knows what he's doing." *I think.*

The manatee looked skeptical.

"I trust him with my life." It was true. She did trust Jeb. More than she'd ever trusted any man besides her father and brother.

Jeb came up, water rolling off his body. He scrubbed a palm down his face, spat out ocean. "Not good."

"What is it?"

"She's got what looks to be bailing wire wrapped all around her. And whenever she moves forward the wire constricts around her. When she relaxes, the wire loosens and she thinks she's free and she surges forward, pulling the wire tight again. No telling how long she's been here. She's pretty exhausted, aren't you, old girl?" A softness lit Jeb's eyes and he tenderly stroked the manatee's back.

Haley's chest tightened. She had given him a hard time, but Jeb had come through with flying colors. He was truly worried about the manatee. "If we could get her to stay relaxed, could we uncoil the wire from around her?"

"Maybe. It would be more efficient to get wire cutters and cut her out, but we need to keep her calm. She could injure herself so easily."

"Where are we going to get wire cutters?"

"I've got some on the yacht."

"I'll stay here with her, see if I can keep her soothed," Haley said. "You go get the wire cutters."

"Are you sure? While manatees are gentle creatures, they're still creatures. She's in pain and distress. No telling what she might do."

"I'll be fine. Go on."

He looked reluctant to leave her. "The water is over your head."

"I can handle myself, Jeb. I know how to float and dog-paddle."

"Okay, but you'll be out here all alone."

"Worry about yourself. You'll be swimming back and forth the entire time."

"Good thing I'm in excellent shape." He grinned, flexed.

"Good thing. Now go."

Chuckling, he swam toward the *Second Chance*. "I'll be back as soon as I can."

Haley's heart crawled into her throat. What a guy. Why had she ever thought him superficial? He was magnificent. Unexpected tears filled her eyes. What was *this?* She blinked, focused her attention on the manatee.

She treaded water beside the mammal and began humming softly. She patted the manatee's thick gray hide and she was surprised to discover she felt just like a wet elephant.

Haley's attention did seem to calm her. The manatee ceased thrashing so hard and just floated. Haley rolled onto her back, floated beside her.

"That's it, sweetie. Just take it easy and Jeb will have you fixed up in no time and you'll be hanging out with other manatees before you know it. That'll be nice, won't it? Just think about that."

Her nursing skills helped her soothe the creature. She thought of Jeb and the effort he was putting forth swimming to the boat and back. She was so proud of him. How she wished she'd gotten to know him better before now. He'd enriched her life in ways she couldn't have imagined. The strains of Phish's "Velvet Sea" pushed through her head and she started humming that song for the manatee, crooning, singing, petting and living in the moment.

She savored the time, pressed it to her chest like a favorite photograph. In the future, if anyone asked her about the defining moments of her life, she'd have to say this sailboat trip, culminating in a manatee rescue, was one of the most life-affirming things she'd ever experienced.

There weren't too many more things in life that could move someone—falling in love, marriage, having a baby. Most people got to do those things, but how many people got to save another living thing? She was so very lucky.

"'Velvet Sea,' huh?" Jeb asked.

Haley startled. She'd been so wrapped up in her thoughts and keeping the manatee quiet that she hadn't heard him swim up. "Phish," she said. "I thought it was appropriate."

"It's one of my favorite ocean songs," he said.

"Mine, too. Not that I have a compilation of seafaring songs or anything."

"I do." He grinned wide. The man was always smiling. "Maybe I'll let you hear my playlist sometime."

When would that be? After tomorrow, she'd never see him again. A sick feeling settled in the pit of her stomach.

"In the meantime," she said, "we have a manatee to save."

Jeb pulled wire cutters from the pocket of his swim trunks. "I'm on the job.

He was. And Haley's cheeks heated. She was terrified he could read the desire in her eyes, so she quickly glanced away.

"Keep up the singing. She's much more relaxed than when we got here. You have a nice singing voice."

Haley stroked the manatee's head, hummed Weezer's "Island in the Sun" while Jeb dived down. He clipped wires and then came back up for air. He would take deep gulps of air and submerge again to clip some more.

She worried about him. While he was in good

shape, that had been quite a swim and it seemed the frequent dipping and cutting was taking a toll. Each time he came up, his face was flushed and his lungs were heaving.

Finally, after a good fifteen minutes, Jeb had cut through enough wire so that the manatee could swing her fin like a paddle.

When he came up for air seconds later, blood was oozing from a cut on his forearm.

Haley gasped softly. "You hurt yourself!"

"Wire got me."

"I'll patch you up when we get back to the boat."

"You spent the whole trip playing nursemaid to me."

"Not the entire trip."

"Okay." He chuckled. "For part of it you played nursemaid to a manatee."

"Hey, what can I say? Birds gotta fly. Fish gotta swim—"

"Haley has to play nurse."

Jeb went below one last time, cut the final wire.

Giddy with freedom, the manatee lunged forward. Haley rocketed back, water filling her nose and her ears, burning her eyes. She came up sputtering, but feeling utterly reborn.

Jeb came along beside her. Together, they watched the manatee swim for open water.

"We did it," she said, pushing wet hair from her eyes. "We saved her."

Jeb touched her shoulder. "Feels good. I'm glad you guilted me into saving her."

"See why I like my job? I get to feel like that almost every day of the week."

"The feeling is hard-won." Wryly, he held up his bleeding arm.

"But worth all the battle scars."

"Yeah." His gazed zeroed in on hers. "It is. That's something I don't think I really realized until now."

"Seriously?"

"You've taught me the value of hard work and sacrifice, Haley."

She arched a skeptical eyebrow. "Are you making fun of me?"

"Not at all." His smile was sweet. "C'mon. Let's go ashore."

They floated toward the rocks, both too exhausted to swim. When the water grew shallow enough, they walked, slogging slowly to shore. Haley's knees were boiled noodles. Her head was stuffy and her skin felt too tight, while at the same time feeling too loose.

The afternoon sun beat down. She squinted her eyes at the *Second Chance,* anchored some distance away, wished for sunglasses and aspirin. She certainly didn't feel up to a twenty-minute swim right now.

Apparently, neither did Jeb. He collapsed, drooping onto his back on a big smooth rock. He lay there, an arm stretched across his flat, taut abs, the muscles in his legs shaking slightly. "That was a hellacious workout."

Haley dropped onto the rock beside him, brought her knees to her chest, rested her chin on her knees.

Jeb's eyes were closed.

She couldn't help staring at him. The man was amazing. Her imagination shifted into hyperdrive. What would it be like to have him inside of her? She yanked her gaze away, looked to where the manatee had disappeared. What was going on with her? Why couldn't she control her wild thoughts?

Nurse mode. Nurse mode always helped.

"Let me see that cut," she said.

He stuck out an arm.

It was a long, straight surface cut. No stitches needed, thankfully. She couldn't do anything for him here anyway. When they got back to the boat, she'd wash it out with antiseptic.

"Give it to me straight, Doc. How bad is it?"

"You'll live."

He opened his eyes, used the palm of his hand to shield his face from the sun. "You ready to swim back?"

"Even if I was, you're not. Your legs are still not steady enough."

"I can handle it." He bounced to his feet, but immediately wobbled. "Wow. Oops."

"You're probably dehydrated. Tell me that you drank some water while you were on board the boat."

He looked chagrined. "I didn't think about it. I was trying to get back here ASAP."

Haley sighed. "Between the sun and the exertion, your body is running on empty."

"I wasn't the only one out there."

A few feet away stood a cluster of palm trees loaded with ripe coconuts. "Coconut water would do the trick. How good are you at cracking open a coconut?" she asked.

"Pretty masterful."

"Coconut cracking in your bag of seduction tricks?"

"You never know when you'll be stranded on a desert island and need a piña colada."

Haley laughed. "I'll get the coconuts. You save your strength for the cracking."

She got up, dusted off her wet bottom and gingerly stepped over the rocks to the sand. At the base of the trees, she found two felled coconuts. She scooped them up and turned to find Jeb behind her.

"Since we're already here and we do need a good rest, why not check out the lighthouse?" She nodded in the direction of the old structure.

"I'm game if you are." He winked.

And damn if this wasn't turning out to be one of the nicest days she'd had in a very long time.

# 11

**Dew point**—*The temperature at which the air becomes saturated with water vapor*

AFTER JEB OPENED the coconuts with some expert smashing of hulls against the rocks, they drank the coconut water and ate the fruit. Once their energy returned, they decided to climb to the top of the lighthouse.

Haley's pert fanny swished up the circular stone steps ahead of him. Man alive, she had the finest backside this side of the gulf stream.

*Whitcomb, you've got to stop torturing yourself. This is the one that gets away so that the one you're after doesn't. You've spent your entire life flitting from woman to woman. It's time to take a stand and commit. Jackie is the one for you.*

So why was the sight of Haley in that pink bikini driving him insane?

She was sexy and he was human. It didn't mean he had to act on it. That was what he'd been telling himself this entire trip. At the top of the stairs lay a wooden landing, and beyond it, the arched opening where lanterns were once hung to warn sailors away from the shallows. History washed over him as he thought about the lives this lighthouse must have saved.

Haley moved to the arched opening, peered out at the landscape below. Jeb came up behind her, his pulse suddenly hammering hard when he caught a scent of her. Even amid the smell of salt and sea and coconut, he could smell her strawberry fragrance. Summer. She smelled like summer. He would never eat strawberries again without thinking about her.

His chest tightened strangely and he wondered what Jackie would have to say about that. Well, he and Jackie needed time to get reacquainted. Obviously, a year apart had changed things, but it wasn't anything that couldn't be put right again.

Yes, and speaking of Jackie, he might have blown everything by agreeing to save that manatee. It was already Friday afternoon and the *Second Chance* was still fifty miles off the coast of Key West. He had the Gulf Stream to navigate, so there was a good chance that he wouldn't make it in time to stop the wedding.

And if that happened? Then what?

*Don't panic. You'll make it. Just get the heck out of here now.*

He placed a hand on Haley's shoulder to tell her that they needed to go. She turned around, looked deeply into his eyes and smiled a smile so special he felt something in his chest unravel.

Jeb heard mermaids singing, ocean waves crashing, seabirds calling, every bit of it in his head and his heart. From the very moment he'd first laid eyes on Haley, he'd wanted her and fought it. Hard.

But here, now, looking at her, he lost his last shred of control. Jeb leaned in and claimed that pink strawberry mouth for his own.

She let out a soft moan, parted her lips and sank against his chest. Hell, there was only so much a man could take. He cupped her chin in his palm and held her face still while he fully explored that glorious mouth of hers.

She trembled against him. Aroused or scared or both?

He was turned on and scared, too.

They explored each other softly and slowly. When he reluctantly broke the kiss and pulled back, her blue-green eyes had gone murky and she gazed at him with an expression of such desire and confusion he could smell her indecision. Her body tensed in his arms. The blue vein at the hollow of her throat beat rapidly. She wanted to bolt.

And he couldn't blame her. He'd come on too strong. He should not have kissed her.

Even so, he could not resist kissing her again.

The sweet sound of pleasure ripped from her lips cut straight through him, and the next thing he knew she was pulling his head down in a kiss so blistering that if he were to walk buck naked in Antarctica he could not be cooled.

After a long, hard, soul-reaching kiss, she dragged herself away, her chest heaving, her eyes wide and her lips wet with his moisture.

They blinked at each other.

"Again!" she exclaimed.

Laughing, Jeb kissed her a third time. He gently bit her bottom lip and then rolled his tongue over her upper lip. He caressed the small of her back, pressing her tight against him. He kissed her chin, her throat, and he must have found an erogenous zone, since she gasped and clung to him.

"Haley, you taste like heaven."

She laughed nervously, shook her head. Her honey-blond hair tumbled provocatively about her shoulders. He ran two fingers over her cheeks, peered into her eyes, thought of a hundred things he wanted to say. *I want you. I need you. But I can't offer you forever.*

He heard the rumble of thunder, felt the wind blow cool air on their heated skin. He cast a troubled eye to the sky, saw gray clouds gather and bunch.

A storm was coming.

And whether they were ready or not, they were caught in it.

IT WAS FOUR-THIRTY by the time they got back to the boat and the wind was whipping at thirty knots in an easterly direction. Hoping to outrun the impending storm—or at the very least get as close to Key West as he could before the storm hit—Jeb decided to pull in sails and use the engine. He'd run as long as he could, even after dark until the rains came. After that, they'd drop anchor and wait it out. He prayed it would be a swift, quick storm.

Haley helped him secure everything. He was amazed at how much she'd picked up so quickly. He hadn't been exaggerating when he'd called her a natural sailor.

The clouds thickened at sunset, obscuring the sky,

and the air smelled heavily of rain. He kept his eyes on the sky and continued pushing the *Second Chance,* eager to get to Jackie before his feelings for Haley became too much for him to ignore. He was terrified he was falling back into old patterns, becoming easily distracted once he'd made a decision and chosen a course. This was Jeb's personal dead reckoning. His line in the sand. If he turned tail at this point, he feared it meant he would never be able to see anything through to completion.

"Our journey is almost over," Haley said.

"It's been a big adventure. Thank you for taking it with me."

"Jackie's a lucky woman."

He stood at the helm with Haley beside him, coiling up a rope, her eyes downcast. "Haley," he said, "I wish I'd met you at a different time in my life."

"I know."

"Jackie is…" He couldn't finish it. He could tell her how fabulous Jackie was, but she didn't want to hear that. Plus, Haley was just as fabulous in her own way.

This was the crux of his problem. Up until now, he'd been the kind of guy to love the one he was with. He'd fallen into old habits and he was looking at Haley as greener grass. It was his modus operandi, and the only way to break the cycle was not to give in to his desires, but he wanted her in the worst way. Wanted her so badly his bones ached. How was it fate had been so damned fickle as to land Haley here on his boat when he'd been trying to prove a point?

Maybe that was just it. Maybe fate had put her here to test his resolve.

Or maybe, just maybe, fate was trying to tell him that Haley was the one for him and not Jackie.

It was a traitorous thought. One he didn't want to look at too closely. *Everything will work out. Don't worry. Be happy.* Once he saw Jackie and she saw him, all would be resolved.

It sounded good. He'd been dishing up such garbage to himself since he was a kid. But would it really be all right? What if he hurt Haley in the process? It slayed him to think that he might do so.

"I'm going down into the galley," she said, "to make dinner before the storm hits. I'm thinking something simple. Grilled-cheese sandwiches and tomato soup?"

"Sounds good." Food was the last thing on his mind. He was thinking about storms and fate and choices made and desires that could lead you astray and lost loves and, and…

This wasn't like him. He didn't second-guess himself. He made choices, lived with them, moved on.

*So stop thinking.*

Determinedly, he turned his attention to the sky. The wind was whipping wildly now, the boat rising up on the swells, then roughly slamming back down. The clouds turned an ominous black. He hung with it until the first big splats of rain. Haley appeared at the top of the stairs, motioning him inside. "Come in!" she hollered at him.

She was right. This storm was more powerful than the last one. There would be no sleeping on the bridge for him tonight. Like it or not, he had to go belowdecks and ride out the storm, and he prayed he could weather it without falling into Haley's arms.

THIS WAS HER LAST CHANCE to have a night with Jeb.

He wanted it. She could see it in his eyes, but he was so terribly conflicted. But could she in good conscience seduce him? She wasn't the kind of person who stole another woman's man. Still, she couldn't help dreaming about making love to him.

*Stop it. Just stop it.*

They ate their meal and did the dishes together, feeling the heat of the storm grow stronger. The sailboat rocked and pitched. They had nothing to do to divert them.

No TV. No computer access. And she wasn't about to play board games with him again. The only thing to do was go to bed and sleep through it.

"You take your bed tonight," she said. "I've hogged it for too long."

"You're fine where you are."

"I'll sleep on the bench seating here."

"Can't. That's where I'll be sleeping."

"Jeb." She shook her head.

"Haley."

What she wanted to do was suggest they share a bed, but of course, she would not do that. "Do you want to shower first?" she asked, "or should I?"

They still hadn't washed the grime of the day off them after rescuing a manatee and climbing a lighthouse and eating coconuts and swimming to the island and back.

"I'll go first," he said. "That way I'll be out of your hair."

While he showered, Haley puttered around the galley kitchen, straightening things that didn't need to be straightened. Her heart felt heavy in her chest and her lungs didn't seem to want to fully inflate. She purposefully drew in several slow, deep, cleansing breaths, and by the time Jeb entered the galley toweling his hair dry and smelling of soap, she had herself under control. Somewhat.

Until he smiled at her.

"I left you plenty of hot water."

"That was nice of you."

He wore pajama bottoms and nothing else. It should be against the law for him to come strutting in here looking so damned available.

Haley pressed two fingers against her lips, remembering what his lips had felt like against hers.

She got up to slip past him, anxious to get to the bathroom for her turn at the shower, but as she went by, the boat lurched, tossing her against him just as the lights went out.

"You okay?" Jeb asked.

"Fine," Haley whispered. She should step away. She was going to step away, but the boat lurched.

The wind howled, picking up speed.

Haley shivered.

"Are you cold?"

No. She was anything but cold.

He stepped forward and rubbed his palms up and down her arms.

She gave in, just gave in and that was all there was to it. She sank against him, as pliable as candle wax.

He pressed his cheek against the top of her head. She could hear the loud, erratic thumping of his heart. Unnerved. He was as unnerved as she was.

Haley licked her lips.

His arms tightened around her.

The boat pitched, tossing them against the furnishings. "We need to sit," he said, "or lie down so that we don't get beat up."

"Yes," she croaked.

"C'mon, I'll guide you to the bedroom."

He took her hand and moved in the darkness. He whacked into something, mumbled a sharp curse. "Didn't need that shin anyway."

His fingers gripped hers gently. "Hold on. Let me take the brunt of the licking."

Licking. Hmm. She'd like to lick him from head to toe.

*Haley Jean French! Bite your tongue.*

Why did wanting him have to be so wrong? Why couldn't she have met him before he'd taken a vow of celibacy in his attempt to win Jackie? Why couldn't they have met before St. Michael's?

Because before then she would never have considered a torrid affair. She'd been trying to live down her past, trod the straight and narrow, avoid temptation at all costs. And here she'd ended up stuck at sea with the biggest temptation of all.

The rolling and thrusting of the ocean didn't help their progress to the bedroom. The *Second Chance* tossed and floundered one way, then the other. Haley had to admit it was pretty frightening, being out in the ocean with nothing between them and wreckage but a few pieces of wood, fiberglass and metal. She tightened her fingers around his. "Have you ever been in a storm this fierce while on the boat?"

"Yes," he said. "Don't be scared. It'll pass and the sun will come out and everything will be all right."

His optimistic, glass-half-full philosophy was comforting and she wanted to buy it. Oh, how she wanted to buy it. But even if the sun did come out tomorrow and they made it through the night safe and sound, there was always the knowledge that something special had passed her by.

"This way, angel," he crooned.

Angel.

He'd started calling her that the night she'd told him about Trey Goss. The night she'd completely broken down. She'd never told another soul on the face of the earth about what had happened that night, until Jeb. She still didn't know why she'd told him.

After a good five minutes of halting steps, they made it to the cabin. The boat was pitching like a gasoline-powered rocking chair jerking back and forth, back and forth. The rigging creaked and groaned under the onslaught. Lightning flashed. Thunder smashed. She cringed.

"Scared of storms?"

"Not normally, but being out here on the ocean in one makes me feel so vulnerable."

"But it's sort of exhilarating, right?"

In truth, it was.

"More fun than a roller coaster."

"And not nearly as safe," she said.

"Safety is overrated. It keeps you from seizing the day."

"Seize a live wire and you can end up electrocuted."

"Touché."

Wasn't that exactly what she'd done with Jeb? Seized a live wire?

A flash of lightning through the porthole lit up the cabin in a momentary flash of brilliant white light.

In a freeze-frame strobe, she saw Jeb's face and on it was an expression of total male desire combined with a sweet sense of awe and wonder as he looked at her.

"Here are your accommodations for the night, angel," he said, putting a hand around her waist and guiding her to the bed.

She stood beside him, her fingers laced through his. They were breathing in tandem. The storm shook, shouted.

The waves smacked against the boat with even more force than before. The *Second Chance* listed hard starboard, throwing Haley down onto the bed and Jeb on top of her.

His pelvis was pressed against her, his erection hard against her thigh.

"I'm sorry," he apologized.

"Hey," she whispered, "it happens."

"Not like this. Not like it does with you."

Her face flushed and she was grateful for the darkness.

He moved to get up, but the boat pitched again, throwing him right back down on top of her.

"Hang on," he said. "I'll make my getaway in the lull of the next wave."

It sounded good, but when he tried to get up again, the same thing happened.

"Looks like you're stuck here until the storm calms down."

"Just until the worst of it passes," he said.

"I'll just lie right here against the wall." She scooted over. "And you can stay right there on the outside."

"Good plan."

"Let's imagine an invisible line running right down the middle of the bed."

"Me on my side, you on yours."

"Exactly."

"No crossing."

"None."

"You don't touch me, I won't touch you."

"Deal."

"This won't be a problem. None at all."

"Nope. Easy peasy. We can share a bed without anything happening."

"We're adults."

"Fully in control of ourselves."

"Absolutely."

The silence lasted for almost a minute.

"Haley," he breathed in the darkness.

That was all it took. That husky whisper and she crossed that invisible line of restraint she'd had a tenuous hold on since the beginning of the trip. He was waiting for her, arms outstretched. His lips captured hers and he was kissing her with a hunger that stole all the air from her lungs.

The muscles deep in her feminine core clenched and released in a startlingly strong rhythm—aching, begging, craving. In a mad frenzy, they ripped off each other's clothing as the ship bucked and rolled. Thunder and lightning set the mood, rough and electric.

Jeb's mouth was hot against her breast, his wicked tongue challenging her nerve endings, a scrumptious threat. His body was stretched the length of hers, Haley's back pressed into the mattress. His erection a steel rod between them.

Her heart pounded so loudly in her ears she couldn't

hear anything else. She was lost at sea, storm-tossed and loving it.

Supporting his weight on his forearms, he hovered above her, his palms pressed on either side of her face. A flash of lightning illuminated his dear face. He stared into her eyes, his expression one of pure awe, pinning her to the spot.

A lump of emotion clogged her throat. She shouldn't be doing this. It couldn't lead anywhere, but maybe that was exactly why she should do it. Just throw out the rule book and let nature take its course. She was a nurse. She understood biological needs. It didn't have to mean anything more than that.

Sure. That was her plan. Just enjoy the physical and block out the mental and emotional. So what if her heart gave a wistful twist when the corner of his mouth lifted in a boyish quirk? A special smile meant just for her.

He moved his hands from her face; inquisitive fingers explored her body. At his touch, her breasts swelled and her nipples stood erect. His mouth played with her nipples, teased first one and then the other.

She moaned and threaded her fingers through his hair, encouraging him to keep doing the lovely things he was doing. Losing control, she tightened her grip on his hair.

A ragged chuckle rolled from his throat. "Let's see if we can make you do more of that," he murmured against her navel, the sound vibrating clear to her spine.

Yes.

Up they went on the ocean swells, the boat lurching, the waves pummeling an onslaught of sensation through their bodies.

He kissed her cheeks, her neck, and she came completely unraveled, her body clenching and releasing in widening waves. She drew in short, rapid breaths of air, savored the smell of this masculine man doing wondrous things to her.

As fun as it was to let him steer the course, Haley believed in an equal partnership. While his mouth and tongue did crazy things to her, she reached a hand down and stroked the velvet tip of his manhood poking against her thigh.

He let loose an appreciative groan and slid down the flat of her belly, his tongue licking and swirling, stoking her arousal. Finally, he raised his head, hair sticking every which way from where she'd mussed it, and he flashed her the most beguiling grin.

She smiled back at him, enchanted.

Gracefully, he leaned forward, his chest puffing up like a spinnaker filling with wind. "Hang on, angel, we're going body sailing."

"What?" she asked, a bit confused, but he answered her question with his body instead of words.

His fingers trailed from her waist, down the flat of her belly to the curve of her hip, and then traveled around her thigh until he found her most intimate spot. She exhaled on a sigh, every muscle in her body liquefied.

"I want to make love to you so badly I can taste it."

His declaration stirred her. She wanted him, too. She touched him again, letting him know it was full speed ahead, cupping the weight of his masculinity in her palm.

"You're so sexy," he crooned. "Haley, I can't believe you're even here with me."

She couldn't believe it, either.

He paused a moment, looked down into her face again. "Are you sure this is what you want?"

"Yes." She whimpered, unable to bear the thought of not having his body joined with hers. Only he could quench the fire burning inside her. Only he had the key to her lock. "More than anything!"

He reached for something in the overhead compartment and pulled out a condom. Ever ready for a sea adventure. Some nurse she was. So overcome by desire she'd forgotten about protection. Thankfully, Jeb was thinking. He tore open the packet with his teeth.

"Let me," she said, taking the condom from him and rolling it on the length of his throbbing, hot erection. When she finished, they were both breathing hard and desperate.

"Put your legs on my shoulders," he urged.

She obeyed. The position raised her hips up off the mattress. He was between her legs, the head of his shaft poised at her entrance. He was quivering, as excited as she.

Haley arched her back, tipped her butt down and stared up into his eyes. "I want you."

"I want you," he whispered.

Unable to resist another second, she brought his head down to hers for a long, heartfelt kiss.

He eased his body into hers—tender and loving. How good it felt. She closed her eyes, floating on the absolute bliss of the moment.

The timbers were shivering, along with everything

else on the boat. While the storm raged fiercely out-side, their passion raged even fiercer inside the cabin.

Jeb moved slowly, letting her get accustomed to him and she whispered her approval, used her legs to draw him more deeply inside of her.

"You are so tight," he murmured. "Beautiful."

She squeezed him with her internal muscles and he groaned. She slipped her hands around his forearms, holding on for the thrill ride of her life. How was it she'd lived so long without knowing sex could feel like this? Innocent. She felt like an innocent experiencing sex for the first time.

"I feel like a virgin," she whispered, "with you."

"Me, too," he said with such sincerity that she al-most believed him.

Over the course of the past few days, he'd taught her a lot about taking life as it came instead of always fighting against the current.

Certainly being with him was light, easy. All she had to do was relax into him. Have fun. He was so much fun to be with. He made everything a game. He opened her eyes to so many possibilities. In his presence, life was an exciting adventure waiting to be explored.

And right now, all kinds of heady feelings were flowing through her.

"Everything about you is intense, isn't it?" he crooned.

It was true. She came at life as if it was a battle to be won.

"Okay, that's the way we'll do this. Here we go, angel," he murmured, his voice raw and strained. "Overboard."

She thrust upward just as he thrust down, meeting him halfway, pushing and rubbing, caressing and stroking, until their bodies beaded with perspiration. Friction.

They were a craze of arms and legs, mouths and teeth and tongues. After a few desperate minutes, he changed the tempo, slowing down, dragging it out.

Haley whimpered with frustration.

"Let's make it last," he explained.

*Oh.*

He tightened his buttocks, eased out of her.

She whimpered louder.

He gave a self-satisfied laugh.

"Tease," she mumbled.

"A good tease never hurt anyone."

She rolled over onto her hands and knees, wriggled her fanny, and he let out a groan. "Ha, not so cocky now, huh?"

"I'm plenty cocky. We're just getting started."

"Promises, promises."

"Now who's being cocky?" He lightly swatted her fanny.

"Punishing me?"

"Never. This is all about your pleasure."

Her insides clenched hard and she was panting. "Do it again," she whispered.

"This?" His palm cupped her fanny again, gave her a short little smack.

Blood shot through her veins, rushing adrenaline to her heart.

"You like this?"

Mutely, she nodded. She wasn't sure how far she wanted it to go, but right now, her pulse sprinted like a racehorse and her entire body hammered with excitement.

Another quick swat.

They were all alone out here. Just her and Jeb and the ocean and the storm, but she trusted him completely. That surprised her most of all. She didn't trust easily, but somehow, she knew deep down inside that Jeb would never hurt her. Maybe that was why she felt so free to whisper her secret spanking fantasy into his ear. She wanted him more than she'd ever wanted anything in her life.

"Please," she whispered, without even knowing for sure what she was begging for. "Please."

He cupped her buttocks in his palms.

She buried her face into the pillow and he gently entered her again. Overjoyed, she wanted to sing.

"Haley," he called her name, and the sound of it pouring from his lips did strange and wondrous things to her.

Playful. Their coupling was playful and light-hearted, and in this sweet game, they found their release together, as their ecstatic cries were drowned out by the snarling storm.

# 12

**Ebb**—*A tidal current flowing out to sea*

"Now," Jeb said, "we're going to do it my way."

"Mmm," Haley murmured, reached up to trace an index finger over his bottom lip. "How is that?"

"Slow and sweet and I want you on your back so I can see your face."

"Why, Jeb Whitcomb, you're a traditionalist at heart. Who knew?"

Outside, the storm was ebbing, the lightning a weak flutter from distant clouds, thunder a muted grumble, but inside, Jeb was in tumult. He couldn't keep his hands off Haley. Couldn't think of anything but making love to her again, but in just a few hours, weather willing, they'd be hitting land in Florida.

And then what?

His chest tightened and his skin prickled.

Haley tangled her fingers in the hairs at his chest and her gentle tickling drove him wild. He closed his eyes, took in a deep breath, tried to grasp some small shred of control.

*Haley.*

She kissed from his chest to his belly, going to a place he longed for her to go, but didn't want to ask. A groan, half pleasure, half despair, slipped past his lips. There was no stopping now. He'd already sped past the point of no return. The woman had reduced him to rubble.

Her sweet lips touched the head of his shaft and it was all he could do not to lose it instantly. She took charge, closing her mouth around him.

Ah, hell, he'd wanted to make love to her face-to-face, look deeply into her eyes, but if she kept going the way she was going, he'd be spent before they got that far.

He tried to pull her back up, but she resisted, her tongue doing startling things to him. He grasped her hair in his fists, tugging gently. "Angel, I want to be inside you."

She give a wicked laugh and did a little maneuver that sent him over the edge. Without warning the orgasm overtook him.

*Haley.*

Clenching his jaw, he shuddered as he climaxed, shaking and chanting her name.

When it was over, she collapsed onto the bed beside him. "Turnabout is fair play." She laughed.

He could hear his own heart beat, taste the black, mysterious shadows of the darkened room. He inhaled it—the night—smelling thickly of their lovemaking and the ozone scent from discharged lightning.

*Haley.*

The sexy woman who challenged him to be a better man. The woman who'd captured his heart. He gathered her to him, hugged her close and kissed the top of her head.

They slumbered like that for a while, then he woke her sometime later with more kisses, got another condom from the cabinet and finally made love to her the way he'd ached to make love to her for months.

Face-to-face. Eye to eye. Just the two of them, in the quiet, reverent lull left by the vanishing storm.

WHAT HAD SHE DONE?

Haley lay in bed beside a sleeping Jeb, the sheet wrapped around her waist, staring up at the ceiling as tendrils of dawn blushed pink about the porthole. She looked over at him. The man was so handsome and for a second she forgot everything except how glorious it felt to be next to him.

*Wonder how many other women have been in this same spot.*

That made her stomach hurt.

She hitched in her breath, returned her gaze to the ceiling. See. That was what was wrong with this scenario, as nice—oh, who was she kidding, it had been incredible—as last night had been, he pined for this Jackie woman.

That was the thing. She would not romanticize what had happened between her and Jeb. The storm has tossed them into bed together and they simply hadn't been able to keep their hands off each other. Proximity and sexual chemistry equaled heady lust, *not* true love.

So why did it hurt so much?

She couldn't stop herself from peeping over at him again. His generous mouth was relaxed, welcoming. His square jaw was scruffy with a sandy-colored beard, and a lock of hair flopped boyishly over his forehead. Even when he was asleep, he was fun-loving. Really, it was better that they were going their separate ways. They didn't fit together. Honestly, what did they have in common?

Oreos. Double-stuffed. Kept in the refrigerator.

Cold Oreos were not enough to base a relationship on.

*As if he was even considering a relationship with you. Stop hoping. There's no hope. Snuff it out. You can't dare let him know that you're hoping for something he can't deliver. It will just make both of you feel bad.*

Besides, she'd violated her own code of ethics, making love to a man whose heart belonged to another woman. She deserved this. She'd known better and she'd allowed it to happen anyway.

Misery ate at her.

There was no other way to handle this than to pretend last night had meant absolutely nothing more than scratching an itch. He would be relieved that she had no expectations from him. When they made land in Florida, he'd go to Jackie, she'd return home to St. Michael's.

It was the only way to deal with the situation—deny her feelings. What were feelings anyway but fleeting emotions subject to change? It was the sensible solution and it would protect her from a mountain of hurt.

Her mind made up about the strategy to take, she turned over on her stomach and stuffed the corner of the pillow into her mouth so Jeb could not hear her sobs.

THE WIND WAS LIGHT and from the south, making crossing the Gulf Stream into Key West easier than usual.
With this early start and the calm after the storm,
they could just sail right in. He had an open channel
straight to Jackie.

Fate had spoken. Even with going through customs
and taking Haley to the airport to catch a charter plane
back to St. Michael's, he would have plenty of time to
stop Jackie's wedding.

Except, now he did not know if he wanted to do
that.

Jackie seemed so far away, part of another life.

What was real, what was genuine, was the woman
standing on the bridge beside him.

Haley.

He cut his eyes over at her.

She seemed so peaceful. A week ago if someone
had told him she'd be on his boat and that they would
make love and she'd seem so calm about it afterward,
he would have laughed. It was an image he couldn't
have dreamed of.

This morning, she'd gotten up and made breakfast and greeted him with a cheery smile when he'd
stumbled from the cabin, but when he'd tried to catch
her around the waist and give her a kiss, she'd slipped
away from him. Her shoulders stiffened and her smile
faltered.

Uh-oh. She was giving him the morning-after
brush-off. He knew because he'd used it on women,
and he knew with absolutely certainty that if they'd
been on dry land, she would have taken off in the
middle of the night.

The woman had turned the tables on him, giving him a dose of his own roguish behavior.

Except he'd been trying so hard to change. Wanted desperately to redeem himself.

Maybe Haley was the instrument of his final redemption. Even though he'd given in to last night's wild temptation, he was feeling firsthand what it was like to be used for sex.

The old Jeb would have lapped it up, but this new Jeb was ashamed to think he'd ever made others feel the way he was feeling now.

Taken advantage of.

"Last night—"

"Is over," Haley said brightly and shoved a cup of coffee into his hand. "I had fun, but there's no need to dissect it. Things got out of hand and we crossed a line, but there's no need to feel guilty or ashamed. I release you from any sense of obligation you might be feeling toward me."

"I...I..." He was speechless.

"We should get going," she said, "if you intend on breaking up a wedding."

She'd walked away, gone topside, leaving him with nothing to do but scoot after her.

Jeb didn't erect the sails, but instead powered up the engines for the ride into Key West.

Haley moved port side, sat down, looked out to sea, her honey-colored hair glistening in the dawn. She looked completely unaffected by what they'd shared last night and her cavalier attitude was a punch in the gut.

*She doesn't care. You should be happy about that. You have a goal, a plan, and Haley isn't part of it.*

Jackie. That was where his future lay.

Why, then, did his chest tighten and a sick feeling rise in his throat?

Why? He'd let Jackie down, he'd let Haley down, but most of all he'd let himself down.

That was the core of it. He'd wanted to prove to Haley that he was an honorable, ethical man. Her high standards had made him want to raise his expectations of himself, but he'd failed. Big-time.

He navigated the boat, but his mind wasn't on sailing; it was tangled up around Haley, as tight as fishing line. She must have sensed he was staring at her because she swiveled purposely and met his gaze, gave him a brief smile.

His heart capsized.

He had a hundred things he wanted to say to her, but didn't know how to start. *Thank you for the gift of last night. I'm sorry if I've caused you pain in any way. I'll miss you.*

She glanced away.

What was she thinking? He couldn't get a read on her. Which was odd. Normally, with Haley you knew exactly where you stood.

He opened his mouth; shut it. He donned his sunglasses.

She reached into the storage compartment where he kept supplies, took out a bottle of sunblock and squeezed some into her palm.

*Not gonna watch her. Not gonna do it.*

Jeb tilted his head, slid her a sideways glance.

Haley slathered the lotion over her tanned arms.

Moisture filled his mouth. He licked his lips. Swallowed hard.

Her long fingers massaged the lotion into her skin in slow, rhythmic circles.

He hardened instantly. This was bad.

Haley stretched out one long, shapely leg, rubbed it with a fresh squirt of lotion.

Sweat popped out on Jeb's brow. He blew out his breath and yanked his gaze away. *Drive the damn boat.* He clenched his jaw, did his best to think of Jackie and steered the *Second Chance* toward Key West.

HALEY SMILED AND SMILED and smiled, but it was all an act.

Inside, her heart was aching and nausea settled low in her stomach. Last night, she'd thrown caution to the wind and allowed her body to dictate her behavior. Mistake. Huge mistake. And why was she shocked?

She'd asked for this, but she hadn't expected just how much it would hurt to walk away.

The wind whipped her hair against her face and she kept her eyes glued toward the sea. She would be okay. She would survive this. She was tough.

A tear slid down her cheek. Quickly, she scrubbed it away. None of that nonsense. She'd cried all she was going to cry over him.

She drew her knees to her chest, smelled Jeb's scent on the T-shirt she wore thrown over the pink bikini. There was no escaping him. Not while she was on this boat.

Land lay ahead. Soon, her adventure would be over.

Jeb navigated the Gulf Stream like a hot knife slicing through cold butter. Haley couldn't help sneaking surreptitious glances at him. The wind blew his hair back off his handsome face, and his sturdy fingers gripped the wheel. Fingers that just a few short hours ago had been igniting her body in a hundred different ways.

He caught her eye and she quickly glanced away, feigned nonchalance, dipped her shoulder down and stroked the polished wood with her big toe. She missed the sails, how they would billow out wide in the breeze. Missed the sound of the rigging banging against the mast. Motoring into port instead of gracefully sailing in on the wind felt like defeat.

She was going to be okay. It was not the end of the world. Never mind that she was a wrung-out dishrag and her bones were made of rubber. She'd put one foot in front of the other, move through this, past this.

Key. Jeb had given her the key to a new way of being. She could relax and let go. She didn't always have to be in control, and that was a good thing. She was grateful for the gift he'd given her and she would treasure it forever, even if a hole gaped in the middle of her heart.

# 13

**Death roll**—*A capsize to windward; generally occurs while sailing downwind*

THREE HOURS LATER, they made it through customs in Key West. Jeb rented a white convertible and drove her to the airport, where he chartered a plane for her.

"Well," he said, as they stood in the reception area of Island Conch Charters, other passengers going to and fro, "I guess this is goodbye."

"It's been an experience I'll never forget."

Their gazes met. The tender look in his eyes held her and a bittersweet smile played at the corners of his mouth.

Outside the window, lightning flashed so close it sizzled brilliantly bright across the sky, immediately followed by a loud clash of thunder. Unnerved, Haley jumped. The ramp crew came running into the building, signaled to the receptionist, who got on the PA address system and announced that the ramp would be closed until the lightning passed.

"Looks like I've got a wait," she said, smoothing

wrinkles from the skirt of the little blue flowered dress she'd worn on board Jeb's ship six days ago. She'd changed so much in such a short amount of time.

Jeb guided her toward a leather couch in the lobby, sat down with her. She wished he'd just leave.

"I want to thank you, Haley," he murmured.

"For what?"

"Making my life richer."

If she'd made his life so rich, why was he running off after another woman? "You're the one who's enriched my life."

He reached out to take her hand.

She wanted to resist, pull back. She should have, but instead, she sank against him.

"I'm going to miss you."

"Ditto." She could barely push the word past her constricted throat.

"I want to write to you—"

She shook her head. "No."

"Just as friends."

"No." She stepped away from him.

He jammed his hands in his pockets, rounded his shoulders. "I know."

If only they could be friends! But he'd given his heart to another woman, and Haley was not going to come between them. She'd already crossed a line that she should not have crossed. She refused to compound an error in judgment by encouraging him.

"You should go," she said coolly.

"Haley—"

"I mean it. Just go." She jerked her head away, blinking rapidly to banish the tears collecting behind her eyelids.

"You're very special to me," he said. "I'd rather cut off my arm than hurt you. I never intended for any of this to happen. You've got to believe me."

Here was the issue. She *did* believe him, but it didn't change a darn thing.

He reached for her again.

This time, she was strong enough to ward him off. She held up her palm. Stop sign. "I know you didn't mean to hurt me."

"But I did," he whispered.

She wasn't about to give him that kind of power over her feelings. "I'm fine, Jeb. You didn't hurt me. Not in the least."

*He* looked hurt, then relieved and then suspicious. "You're just saying that to spare me."

"Honestly," she lied through her teeth, "I'm not shattered."

A sheepish expression crossed his face. "I like you, Haley. I like you a great deal."

"I like you, too, but that doesn't matter, does it?"

"What do you mean?"

"C'mon, even if you weren't on the way to stop your ex-girlfriend from marrying someone else, you and me..." She toggled a finger between them, shook her head. "We don't belong together, but you and Jackie Birchard? Now, that's a match made in high-society heaven. You're both rich, accustomed to fame and move in the same circles. You're both seafaring folks. You speak the same language. You and me? We're like hot dogs and caviar."

"Hey, you took to the sea like an otter."

Haley traced his face with her gaze. He was the epitome of a wealthy yachtsman and she carried bedpans for a living. No matter how she might try to convince herself otherwise, she would not fit into his world. "It was fun for a while, but you can't raise kids on the sea, and that's what I want one day—a husband, kids, an ordinary life. Let's face it. You're too extraordinary for me, Jeb Whitcomb."

"You're the extraordinary one, Haley French, and I'm the one who's not good enough for you."

"While we had a good time in bed, there's a big difference between heating up the sheets and being good together as a couple."

He sucked in his breath through clenched teeth and his color paled beneath his tan. "Yeah," he mumbled. "You're probably right."

"I *am* right."

"I wish—"

"No sense wishing things to be different. They are what they are." She forced a smile.

"Haley, I—"

Broken, she swallowed hard. "You better go or you'll be too late to stop the wedding."

"What if I were?" he said softly.

She pretended she hadn't heard him, stood up, turned away, because if she didn't, she was terrified that she would get down on her knees and plead with him to stay.

IT WAS 3:45 P.M.

With fifteen minutes to spare, Jeb drove into the Wharf 16 parking lot where Jackie's wedding was being held aboard the *Sea Anemone,* his mind glazed with sweet thoughts of Haley.

He sat in the rental car, picked up his cell to dial

her number. Put it down. Picked it up again and then realized he didn't even know her cell-phone number. How could he be crazy for a woman when he didn't even know her cell-phone number?

*Um, how can you be crazy for her when you're here to tell Jackie that you love her?*

That was just the thing, wasn't it?

He switched off the phone, watched the digital clock flip to 3:47. Wedding guests walked passed him on their way to the *Sea Anemone*. Wedding music swelled in the air—the Carpenters, of all things. That sounded too romantic and cheesy for Jackie.

Why wasn't he jumping out of the car, running up the gangplank, demanding that they stop the wedding? Protesting that he was speaking now instead of forever holding his peace?

He drummed his fingers on the steering wheel, felt his throat tighten. Haley had said that a seafaring lifestyle wasn't for her, but he'd seen the way she'd looked when she'd spied those dolphins—free, alive, *happy*. She said she wanted to get married and have kids some day, and for the first time in his life, Jeb realized he wanted that, too.

A car with a U-Haul trailer towed behind it pulled into the parking lot behind Jeb. A tall man in his early thirties wearing a leg brace got out of the passenger seat and hobbled toward the ship. Jeb recognized the man as Jackie's older half brother, Boone, but he didn't call out to the former Iraq war vet. Boone looked to be a man on a mission, his face set into a dark frown.

Jeb knew that he and Jackie had a lot in common— divorced parents, half siblings, money, their love of the sea. They would be perfect together.

Except whenever Jeb closed his eyes, Jackie was not the blonde he saw. Rather it was Haley's honey-colored hair that clouded his vision, Haley who made his blood pound.

Boone talked to an usher at the gangplank, went over to a building on the pier. It was now 3:50 and still, Jeb sat there.

Jackie and Boone came out of the building together. They were having a serious discussion. Jackie wore an elegant white dress and looked drop-dead gorgeous.

Jeb felt...well, hell, he felt nothing except happiness for her.

No desire. No sexual attraction. No burning need. No desperation.

Instead, he thought of Haley.

He could not say why he was so drawn to her. Sure, she was pretty, but he'd been with more beautiful women—Jackie was a case in point. Maybe it was because Haley had disliked him and he couldn't stand for people not to like him. In the beginning, he'd done everything he could to impress her, and the harder he'd tried, the less impressed she'd been. It had only been when he'd stopped trying so hard that he'd begun to win her over.

He thought of the fun they'd had—sailing, spotting dolphins, playing drinking games, saving a manatee, exploring a lighthouse.

Making love.

A rap sounded against the window and Jeb startled.

There was Jackie with the biggest grin on her face. She wrenched open the door. "Jeb!"

He got out and she folded him in an enthusiastic hug. "I'm so happy you made it. You're here and Boone showed up with his girl. My two favorite men in the whole world—besides Scotty, of course." Jackie blushed prettily.

Never, in all the years that he'd known her, had Jeb ever seen Jackie blush.

"We're holding up the wedding a few minutes so Boone and his girl can join us." Jackie held out her arms as if she wanted to embrace the whole world. "And now that you're here, too, my wedding day is complete."

"Jackie, I…" *This is it. The part where you tell her that you love her and that you don't want her to marry this Scott character.*

"Yes?" Her smile was as bright as the sun.

Jeb swallowed, a little stunned. "I'm happy for you."

It was true. He was happy for her.

Jackie linked her arm through his and tugged him toward the *Sea Anemone.* Dazed, he simply let her. He wasn't in love with Jackie. He never had been. Not in a romantic sense. He'd admired and respected her and they were friends, but he'd never felt for Jackie what he felt for Haley.

"What is it?" Jackie asked. "What's wrong?"

He told her everything.

"You came here to bust up my wedding?"

"Yes, but I no longer want to do that. I can tell from your face that you're madly in love with Scott."

"I am," she said with such conviction it bowled him over. "Now, tell me about Haley."

He smiled big. "She's the most amazing woman I've ever known."

"You're in love with her."

"Yeah," he admitted.

"So what's the problem?"

He shook his head. "She doesn't love me."

Jackie sighed and shook her head. "Men. You're impossible."

"In what way?"

"You told her you were coming here to stop my wedding, right?"

Mutely, he nodded.

"She thinks you're madly in love with me. She thinks you're making this grand romantic gesture."

"I was going to—"

"But somewhere along the way you fell in love with her."

"I did."

"But you were afraid that if you let yourself show how you felt about her that it would mean I was right about you when I accused you of being a fickle playboy who only wanted what he couldn't have."

"Yeah." He ducked his head, splayed his palm to the nape of his neck.

"Well, think about it from her point of view. If she's in love with you, she's certainly not going to admit it when she believes that you're either in love with another woman or a fickle playboy."

Jackie had a point.

"You think…" He paused, his heart pounding. Could it be true? Could Haley be in love with him? He was scared to hope.

"I think."

"What should I do?"

"Tell her how you feel."

Jeb clenched his jaw.

"Don't let fear hold you back. I know you've had commitment issues in the past—"

"It's not a commitment issue," he said. "I want Haley more than I've ever wanted anything in my life. I'm just trying to decide if I should drive to the airport before she takes off or if I should stay here for the wedding."

Jackie pointed to the car. "Go."

"And if she's already gone?"

"You catch the next plane and go after her."

He looked into his friend's eyes. Jackie was truly a good friend. "You don't mind?"

"I'll bean you over the head if you don't go. I had to learn the hard way, Jeb. When you find someone who loves you inside and out, for all your strengths and flaws, don't ever let them go."

# 14

**Fetch**—*The distance of open water that waves have to grow*

JEB RACED TO THE AIRFIELD in the rental car, pushing it past the limit and praying he didn't get pulled over for speeding. Could he convince Haley to forgive him? He'd been so dumb. So blind to what was right in front of him.

He'd dumped her off at the airport so he could go off to chase after another woman. Fool. He'd treated her cruelly. After the way he'd acted, he didn't deserve a second chance, didn't deserve to even beg for her forgiveness.

But he had to try. He could not let her slip through his fingers.

What if the plane had already left? It had probably already left, even with the weather delay.

Well, if the plane had already left, he'd get another plane and fly to St. Michael's after her, but he hoped it hadn't left. He couldn't wait to touch her again, even though it had only been a few hours. Kiss her again. Tell her that he loved her.

Because he loved her with a fierceness that took his breath away.

It would serve him right if she wouldn't forgive him. His stomach clenched and his hands froze on the steering wheel. No. He could not afford to think like that. She would forgive him. He *had* to convince her. Winning her love was the most important mission of his life.

The *only* mission of his life that really mattered, because without Haley, he was only half the man he could be.

Pulse racing, he darted into the airport parking lot. Jeb jumped from the car, rushed through the building of the fixed-based operator. "The charter flight to St. Michael's," he hollered at the receptionist. "Is it still here?"

"They're just about to take off."

He raced for the ramp door marked Employees Only.

"Sir! Sir!" The receptionist jumped to her feet. "You can't go out there. The plane is about to taxi out. Sir! If you go on the ramp, I'm calling security."

"STOP THE PLANE!"

Haley raised her head and glanced out the window of the small charter jet.

Jeb came running up, waving his arms at the pilot in the cockpit. "Stop the plane!"

"Who the hell is this joker?" the pilot asked the copilot through the open door of the cockpit as they completed their flight checks.

Heart in her throat, Haley sprang to her feet. "He's with me. Don't take off."

"Kill the engines," the pilot told the copilot.

Haley ran to the door, fumbled for the latch. "How do you open this thing?"

"Hang on." The copilot came to her rescue. "What's going on?"

"I don't know," Haley said, but she hoped, oh, how she hoped, that this was her second chance.

The door opened, and with it, automatic stairs came down.

Haley flew down the steps just as Jeb scaled up them. They met in the middle and their eyes hooked on each other.

Could it be...? She had no clue why he'd come to stop her from taking off, but she couldn't help hoping that he was here to grovel.

"What is it?" she asked. "Jackie turned you down so you came to claim second place with me?"

"No," he said. "I came to apologize for being the world's biggest idiot."

Her heart pumped blood through her ears so loudly she wasn't sure she heard him. Her chest squeezed and she felt faintly dizzy. "You can be pretty clueless," she conceded.

"Not anymore," he said.

"About Jackie?"

"About you."

"About me?" she whispered.

"You're the one that I want. The only one I need."

"You expect me to take that to the bank?"

"Haley." He looked miserable, threaded a hand through his hair. "It kills me to think I've hurt you."

"The only way you'll hurt me is if you don't truly mean the stuff you're saying."

Jeb sank to his knees on the step below her, clasped his hands together in a pleading gesture. "Haley French, I've never in my life professed my love to another woman."

Love! Her heart leaped. "Not even to your mother or your sisters?"

"You know what I mean. Pay attention."

"Not even to Jackie?"

"No."

"Not even when you got to the wedding?"

"No, because I realized that while I do love Jackie—"

Haley inhaled audibly, splayed a palm to her chest, felt her heart stumble.

"—I don't *love* her, love her. I love her as a friend and *nothing more*. That's where I kept getting tangled up. I had feelings for Jackie, but I didn't understand that those were feelings of friendship, not romantic love."

Haley folded her arms over her chest. "It sure took you a long time to figure that out."

"Not really," he said. "It just took me a long time to admit it. I've been falling for you since that sunset on Diver's Beach. I was just too scared to admit it, too afraid I was simply falling into an old, familiar pattern of hopping from one woman to the next as soon as things got serious."

"How do you know you're not doing that now?"

"Because I've never met anyone like you. Never felt like this."

"I'm not convinced," she said, ignoring her wildly fluttering heart. How she wanted to believe him!

"I named my boat the *Second Chance*."

"Because of another woman."

"Jackie might have set me on my journey," he said, "but the journey led me to you."

"Uh-huh." She was trying desperately to be cool when all she wanted to do was fling herself into his arms and kiss him until their lips were raw.

"Haley, I know I'm asking you to overlook a lot of things—"

"Like the fact that you're a womanizer."

"Was. That's firmly in the past."

"How do I know that you won't change your mind?"

"I've never told a woman that I loved her before. Not in a romantic way. For all my faults, I've never thrown that word around to get someone into bed. Love means something to me."

"Not even Jackie?"

"Not even Jackie. You're it, Haley. My one and only. I love you."

Haley moistened her lips. "Jeb."

Fear flared in his eyes as if an incomprehensible thought had just speared his brain. "Oh," he said, looking completely stricken, "you don't love *me*."

She couldn't keep torturing him this way. "Silly man, of course I love you."

"How's a guy supposed to know that? Especially when you went out of your way to tell me how wrong I was for you."

"I was trying to protect myself."

"But you love me." A grin kidnapped his entire face.

"I do."

He pulled her into his arms right there on the steps of the airplane and kissed her soundly. He took his time, his tongue leisurely coaxing and teasing.

"Okay," she said, breaking the kiss with a reluctant sigh, "we need to get something straight."

"I'm all ears."

She met sumptuous eyes the color of the sea. "I'm not the easiest person to get along with."

"Uh-huh." He leaned in to nibble her earlobe.

Haley's pulse skittered. "I have strong convictions."

"Don't worry, I know how to get you to relax."

He certainly did at that. He'd taught her that it was okay to enjoy herself once in awhile. That life didn't have to be a grim proposition filled with responsibilities and expectations.

"I have a tendency to judge first and give second chances grudgingly."

"I know." His fingers kneaded her shoulders.

"I'd had a bad experience with a wealthy man. I lumped you in the same category, but you fooled me."

"You're admitting you were wrong?"

"Don't get smug about it. You've got a few flaws yourself."

"Who, me?" He kissed the tip of her nose.

"You are given to grand gestures, like running up and trying to stop a plane."

"Guilty as charged."

"Not a smart thing to do."

"It worked, didn't it?" He tickled her lightly in the ribs and she chuckled. "But you were right about me. I was a cocky guy used to getting my way and being adored."

"I didn't think—"

"You did and you were right, but thanks to you—"

"And Jackie—she's the one who gave you the shove you needed to come to St. Michael's in the first place. I owe her a thank-you gift."

"I'm just grateful that I recognized how I felt about you. Honestly, I think it happened the day you got hit by the boom."

"And you kissed the breath back into me."

He peered into her eyes, held her tightly in his arms. "And I want to keep doing it for the rest of our lives."

What romantic words! They struck her heart like an arrow from a quiver. "For me," she said, "that night we played I've Never and I told you about my secret shame and you didn't judge or condemn me for it. In fact, you comforted me, held me in your arms. That was the night I knew it was more than sex or infatuation."

"But the sex is good, right?" He wriggled his eyebrows.

"Not even close."

"No?" He looked so crestfallen, she almost laughed out loud.

"It's the most amazing sex I've ever had."

"For me, too." He winked. "And that's saying something."

Playfully, she swatted his upper arm.

"What say we let these pilots have their plane back and head back to the *Second Chance?*"

"Under one condition," Haley said.

"What's that?"

"We change the name of that boat."

"Haven't you heard? It's bad luck to change the name of the boat."

"You changed it before and very good luck came your way. You're not superstitious, are you?"

"Not when I'm with you. What should we change the name to?"

"How about the *Happily Ever After?*"

"Exactly what I was thinking."

He took her into his arms once more, kissed her hard and long and sweet until Haley knew in her heart that from here on out, everything between them would be smooth sailing.

\* \* \* \* \*

**Twelve military heroes.**
**Twelve indomitable heroines.**
**One UNIFORMLY HOT! miniseries.**

Mills & Boon® Blaze®'s bestselling miniseries
continues with another year of irresistible soldiers
from all branches of the armed forces.

*Don't miss*

**THE RISK-TAKER**
by Kira Sinclair

**A SEAL'S SEDUCTION**
by Tawny Weber

**A SEAL'S SURRENDER**
by Tawny Weber

**THE RULE-BREAKER**
by Rhonda Nelson

**UNIFORMLY HOT!**

*The Few. The Proud. The Sexy as Hell.*

Dear Reader,

I had such a wonderful time writing *A SEAL's Surrender,* in part because I am the Queen of Goals, and the Soul of Stubborn. So I can relate to Cade Sullivan in a major way, because he is a man who believes in goals, too, and stubbornly refuses to give up on one—even after he's achieved it. But it was great, too, to explore Eden's challenges as someone who wants so much, and deserves so much—but isn't willing to actually ask for it. Oh, yeah, I can relate to that. Can you? I hope you'll drop me a note after you read the story and let me know.

And, as always, I love writing about the special fun that pets are. In this case, Jojo the goat, Mooch the mutt and Alfie the Yorkie—who is actually based on my mom's darling Yorkie. If you'd like to see Alfie, drop by my website at www.TawnyWeber.com and see his picture on *A SEAL's Surrender's* page. And while you're there, I'd love it if you'd peek around, check out the recipes and contests. Or drop by Facebook and visit me at www.facebook.com/ TawnyWeber.RomanceAuthor.

Enjoy!

*Tawny Weber*

# A SEAL'S SURRENDER

### BY
### TAWNY WEBER

First published in Great Britain 2013
by Mills & Boon, an imprint of Harlequin (UK) Limited,
Eton House, 18-24 Paradise Road, Richmond, Surrey TW9 1SR

© Tawny Weber 2013

ISBN: 978 0 263 90307 2
ebook ISBN: 978 1 408 99675 1

14-0513

Harlequin (UK) policy is to use papers that are natural, renewable and recyclable products and made from wood grown in sustainable forests. The logging and manufacturing processes conform to the legal environmental regulations of the country of origin.

Printed and bound in Spain
by Blackprint CPI, Barcelona

**Tawny Weber** has been writing sassy, sexy romances for Mills & Boon® Blaze® since her first book hit the shelves in 2008. A fan of Johnny Depp, cupcakes and color coordinating, Tawny spends a lot of her time shopping for cute shoes, scrapbooking and hanging out on Facebook. Come by and visit her on the web at www.tawnyweber.com.

With loving thanks to Anna Sugden,
simply for being awesome.

# 1

*I WISH FOR A GUY who worships my body, is great at sex and makes me feel like a goddess. Someone who loves me, for me. Inside and out. And is really, really good at it.*

And if he could be six foot two, with sandy blond hair and dreamy green eyes, a body that made nymphomaniacs weep and a smile that melted her panties, that'd be cool, too.

Eyes scrunched tight, Eden Gillespie let that visual play out for just a second. Then, with a deep breath, she opened her eyes wide and blew.

The flame went out. Thankfully. Because she'd blown so hard, the candle toppled from its perch on the chocolate cupcake. Good wishes did that, she told herself as she scooped up a fingerful of frosting and grinned at the woman sitting across from her.

"So? What'd you wish for?" Bev Lang leaned forward, her wild red curls bouncing like springs around her cheerful face.

"It's a secret. If I tell, it won't come true," Eden said primly before bursting into laughter. Yeah. Like she was gonna lose out on her body-worshipping lover because she put the word out that she was waiting? Still, she pulled her cupcake closer and, since it was filled with molten chocolate, used a fork to enjoy the next bite...and fill her mouth so she didn't blurt anything out.

Because you never knew with wishes.

"I can't believe you won't tell me. How long have we been friends?" Bev asked, putting on her best 'affronted' expression. It wasn't very effective since she still looked like she was waiting for a white apron and her boyfriend, Raggedy Andy.

"Eleven years?" Eden guessed, counting back to the first day of high school. That'd been the year her dad had died, leaving her mom too broke to keep paying the exorbitant tuition to the private school Eden had always attended. Secretly terrified, Eden had put on a brave face in hopes that the public school kids would accept her more than the private school snobs had. Bev had been the new girl in town, unaware that Eden wasn't acceptable because of her zip code. By the time she'd learned the ins and outs of Ocean Point social politics, she and Eden had been too good of friends for it to matter.

"Then as your best friend since ninth grade, I figure it's my job to help you with the wish," Bev decided, leaning back in Eden's faded and frayed Queen Anne dining chair and digging into her own cupcake. "I think this should be your year for sex."

"An entire year, dedicated to sex?" Eden asked with a laugh. She was sure there was nothing more than dust motes and the faint air of neglect floating through the formal dining room. But, still, it was all she could do not to look over her head to see if the wish was written there in the candle smoke.

"You should dedicate this year to the *pursuit* of sex." Bev scrunched up her nose. "I don't want to hurt your feelings or anything, but it might take a little effort on your part," she added.

When was the last time she'd had sex worth the effort? Definitely not with Kenny. Not with any guy, if she were being honest. Eden swirled her fork in the gooey rich chocolate, using it to make a design on the Meissen plate. After all, what better time for brutal self-truths than a girl's twenty-fifth birthday.

Kenny, the last guy she'd had sex with, had broken his foot trying to prove his manliness by doing it against a tree. Instead of accepting that he just wasn't he-man material, he'd blamed her.

No wonder her love life sucked. Look at what she had to work with.

"So I know why I should want good sex," Eden said, standing to clear their plates. "But why is my personal life on your radar?"

She didn't have to look to know Bev was following her to the kitchen. The rat-a-tat-tat of her high heels was a giveaway.

"Janie was in the shop yesterday," Bev said, sounding like her cupcake had been bitter lemon instead of rich chocolate. Bev owned Stylin', the best salon in town. And despite her penchant for wearing her own hair in rag doll fashion, she worked pure magic on everyone else. Enough magic to lure in the well-paying Oceanfront set.

"Ah." Eden didn't need to hear any more than that. She wasn't sure of the what, when and where, but she was sure she was the who the chatter had revolved around. That's how Janie and company worked. They wouldn't check in with Eden directly—they'd go to her best friend and mine for gossip.

"Don't let her get to you." Eden set the plates next to the sink.

"I'm just so tired of them talking about you," Bev grumbled, throwing the cupcake wrappers in the trash so hard that they bounced right back out. "They are all so snooty and rude, with their perfect lives bought and paid for by someone else."

"You think they have perfect sex, bought and paid for, too?" Eden asked, keeping her tone, and her expression, serious. She lost it, though, when Bev glared. Laughing, she asked, "What? You think I should get upset because they are talking about, let me guess… My love life, or lack thereof?"

"Well, it's not like they are saying nice things."

Eden shrugged, so used to pretending she didn't care that it pretty much came naturally to her now.

As if realizing she'd brought the bummer cloud to dim the party atmosphere, Bev clapped her hands together and exclaimed, "Presents! I'll be right back. I'm going to get your gift from the car."

Eden kept a cheery smile of anticipation on her face until the wooden screen door clapped shut behind her friend, then let it drop. She sighed, tossing the forks into the dishwasher and squirting liquid soap on a sponge.

Hot, happy sex.

Her chances of finding that were about as small and slender as the half-melted candle she'd just blown out.

What a waste of a wish.

She should have used it on her career.

Only out of veterinary school six months, she still had student loans and now a substantial mortgage on this house. It'd taken every bit of daughterly influence she had to convince her mother to let her buy it instead of putting it on the market. It'd also taken her entire savings account and the tiny trust fund left to her by her grandfather, but Eden loved her home and her heritage too much to see it sold to the highest bidder. And then there was the fact that there was enough property for her to set up her veterinary clinic.

With a shake of her head, she carefully dried the china and walked over to place it in the ornate cabinet with the reverence her great-great-great-gramma's plates deserved. Like most of the furnishings in her childhood home, the glass-fronted hutch was an antique. Rattling around here alone all the time, Eden sometimes felt like the house was just waiting for her to join the ranks of antiques so she'd better fit in.

It wasn't that she minded being alone, really. But like sex, sometimes a girl got tired of going it solo.

"The postman drove by when I was at my car," Bev said, returning to the room with a huge polka-dot box with a ribbon as curly as her hair. "I brought your mail in. Look, I think there are a couple of birthday cards here."

More because Bev was looking worried again than because of any curiosity to see who'd remembered her birthday, Eden took the stack of mail. Before she could get to the telltale bright envelopes, she noticed one from the bank. It was addressed to both her and her mother.

"What's up with this," she muttered, tossing the others on the counter and sliding her fingernail under the flap. She and her mother had no bank business together. And since Eleanor was tooling around the country, following the craft fairs in a new RV, Eden didn't hesitate to open the missive.

"What the…" She had to wait for the room to stop spinning and the buzzing to clear from her ears before she could read the letter again.

Nope. The words hadn't changed.

"I'm going to kill her," she muttered through gritted teeth.

"What? Who? Where's a shovel so I can help you bury the evidence."

"My mother took out a loan against the house." Fury pounded at her temples like a gorilla with a sledgehammer. Knowing the words wouldn't change, no matter how many times she glared at them, Eden crumpled the letter in her fist and threw it against the wall.

"I thought the house was yours," Bev said quietly. "I thought you bought it from her."

"My cousin Arnie is a lawyer. He wrote up a legal document that said the house was mine once I took over the mortgage, and then added my name to the title. But he'd advised against transferring it out of my mom's name at that point because I was still carrying student loans and needed the bank to approve another so I could start a new business."

But why hadn't he checked for loans against the property when he'd changed the title?

"She didn't warn you? Talk it over with you before taking out the loan? Give you a heads-up that you were about to get hit with a big ole bill? Nothing?"

"Warn me? She didn't even call to wish me a happy birthday," Eden said, her laugh only a little bitter, wishing she could be as shocked as Bev. "To her credit, she probably forgot."

"About the loan?" Bev scoffed, her freckled face furrowed in fury.

"About my birthday."

And how sad was it that the fact that her mother forgot her birthday hurt more than a bill for thirty grand. Eden reached for the phone, then curled her fingers into her palm. As much as she wanted an explanation, an assurance that the payment-in-full had been mailed to the bank, she knew better.

Eleanor Gillespie didn't worry about little things like money. She was too flaky to let the mundane rain on her creative lifestyle.

Glancing at the bank's letter, Eden cringed. Flake or not, her mother had made a mess of things. And, as usual, Eden was the one who had to figure out how to clean it up. Because if she didn't find some money quickly, she could lose the house. The property that'd been in her family for five generations. Her home, her place of business.

Her life.

As if reading her mind, Bev asked, "What are you going to do?"

Eden blinked fast to clear the dampness from her eyes. What she *wasn't* going to do was cry, dammit.

"I guess I'm going to find thirty thousand dollars." Where on earth was she going to find that on top of her other debts? And why hadn't her mother arranged for a repayment plan? Coming up with that kind of money in one fell swoop was close to impossible. Eden rubbed her fingers against the sudden pounding in her temple, then walked over to retrieve the letter. She'd have to study it, contact the bank, so she understood all the details.

"You're really going to take on your mother's loan?"

"It's against my property. I have to take it on. At least, until she turns up again and deals with it herself. But she's tooling across the country from craft fair to art show right now. I have no idea when I'll hear from her. Or when she'll come home and clean up her mess."

"How are you going to get the money?"

Hell if she knew.

Every penny she earned was earmarked. Despite her fancy address, she was living a ramen noodle lifestyle here.

There was nothing of value to sell. Oh, sure, she still had her great-grandma's china and there were a few antiques left floating around. But they were all she had left of her family. Well, those and her mother. And right now she was pretty sure the china was worth more.

Eden took a deep breath. There had to be a way through this. She just had to think. *Think, Eden.*

Her eyes fell on a square envelope embossed with ivy and roses. The monthly garden club meeting. She wrinkled her nose, wondering if they resented having to send her the invitation as much as she hated getting it.

Because she was the last person the socially upstanding ladies wanted invading their exclusive get-togethers. But the Gillespie name guaranteed her an invitation.

"The Oceanfront set," she exclaimed, snapping her fingers.

"What was the question again?" Bev asked with a confused look.

"I'll hit up the country club ladies."

"For loans?"

Eden cringed. Handouts? Oh hell, no. She was nobody's charity case.

"For clients. They are all big on their designer pets. I just have to get two, maybe three of them to start using my veterinary services, and more will follow."

"How much are you going to charge?" Bev asked, her eyes huge with a horrified sort of glee.

Eden laughed.

"Just enough that they consider the services exclusive. All it will take is a few of them using me as their vet, a little behind the scenes hype and pretty soon I'll have a well-heeled clientele. I might not be able to pay off the entire loan at once, but if I can get enough of a down payment and show the bank that I have the potential income, I'll bet I can swing a deal."

Maybe.

And maybe was all she needed.

Eden reached for the phone again, quickly dialing the head of the Garden Club.

Five minutes and three grimaces later, she hung up with a triumphant smile.

"Why'd you RSVP for two?" Bev asked, pulling her head out of the pantry to give Eden a suspicious look.

"Because you're going with me."

"Oh, no," Bev declared, emptying an armload of bins and jars onto the chipped tile counter. "I'm not a member. They won't let me in."

"You're my guest."

"They aren't going to want me there," Bev predicted.

"They don't want me there, either." Eden shrugged. "They'll just have to deal with us. Because I need you with me."

"For moral support?"

Eden wasn't sure how much good moral support would be when faced with forcing a tight-knit group of women to accept an outsider at one of their chichi meetings. But she did need someone to play off. Someone who could talk up her veterinary skills and give her the verbal setups she'd need to spike home her point if this plan was going to work.

"What are you doing?" Eden asked, eying the eggs and butter that had just joined the flour, brown sugar and peanut butter.

"This is clearly a cookie situation," Bev said, digging a bag of chocolate morsels out of the freezer.

Before Eden could decide if the two of them eating what, if the butter and eggs were anything to go by, would be a double batch of peanut butter chocolate chip cookies was a good idea, there was a rumbling outside.

Company? Or another birthday surprise? Maybe her mother had found a way to send the plague by UPS.

Or, Eden squinted, in a shiny new Jaguar.

"Hey, cool. It's like the birthday fairy heard your wish," Bev joked, joining Eden at the door to see who was pulling up the weather-pitted driveway.

Recognizing the car, Eden frowned.

Even though they were neighbors, Robert Sullivan never visited.

So the only way the birthday fairy was playing into this particular arrival was if his son, Cade, had hijacked the Jag and was driving up to make all of Eden's fantasies come true.

*Cade Sullivan.*

Tall, blond and gorgeous, with hypnotic green eyes and more charm than a proud momma's bracelet.

The sexiest guy to ever set foot in Ocean Point.

High school quarterback. Class president. Navy SEAL.

Her hero.

She knew most people in town who didn't have membership with the exclusive Ocean Point Country Club— and even a few who did—saw Robert Sullivan as a major asshole. But when she looked at him, all she saw was an older version of Cade. The guy who always rescued her from mishaps, who'd never made a tag-a-long girl five years his junior feel stupid.

The guy she'd had a crush on since she was seven. The one she'd spied on at the small, private lake that bordered their two properties. The man who'd formed her every basis for what spelled sexy in a guy.

Eden sighed.

Then Robert's car swerved.

Eden gasped.

The Jaguar made a beeline for the faded brick arch that welcomed people to the Gillespie house.

Eden hit the door running. Just as she made it to the

bottom of the steps, the car slid into the unyielding bricks with a sick crunch of crumpling metal.

"What's happened? Who is it?" Bev called as Eden sprinted across the lawn, skidding on the gravel driveway in her hurry to reach the car.

"Call an ambulance. Tell them to hurry." Eden stared at the older, colder version of her favorite fantasy, her breath tight in her chest. She checked the pulse at his throat to be sure, then gave a shaky sigh. "Robert's hurt. I think he might have had a heart attack."

IT WAS LIKE WATCHING a bunch of virgins tour a whorehouse. Lieutenant Commander Cade Sullivan shook his head at the current crew of Basic Underwater Demolition SEAL trainees slogging through the wet sand, each carrying a dripping log over his shoulder.

"Were we ever that green?" he wondered aloud.

"You weren't," Captain Seth Borden said with a laugh, clapping Cade on the back. "You were one of the most focused BUDS we've seen come through here. I've been a MTS a long time, but even I can't always tell which guys will make it through Hell Week. Sometimes none do. But when you came through, every instructor knew you'd graduate."

Borden was a Master Training Specialist. One of the top at Coronado's Naval Special Warfare Center, as a matter of fact. He was a machine. A guy who'd dedicated thirty years to the navy and scared the hell out of most people.

Cade considered him a crusty old bastard who drank like the sailor he was, cussed with flare and played a wicked hand of poker. And when they weren't in uniform or on base, he was Cade's favorite uncle.

"Why'd you haul me down here?" Cade asked, grimacing when one guy tripped over his own feet, taking three others down with him and sending his log flying ahead into the back of two more. "Wanted to make sure I appreciate how good my team is?"

He grinned when three wannabe SEALs sidestepped the downfall and just kept on going. Those guys, they had what it took.

"You need a reminder?"

"Nope." Cade's smile faded. He knew damned well that he served with some of the best SEALs in existence. Guys who gave their all, like his buddy Phil Hawkins, who'd given it right to the end. A familiar band of grief tightened in Cade's chest, as it did whenever he thought of the loss. The Three Amigos, Phil, Cade and Blake Landon had gone through BUDS together, had served in the same platoon, on countless missions together. They embraced everything that being a SEAL stood for. Brotherhood. Dedication. Excellence.

And now the Three Amigos were two.

"C'mon in. We'll have a cup of coffee."

Grateful for any distraction from the gnawing emptiness that had started to overshadow his SEAL career, Cade followed the captain to his office. He shook his head when Borden held up the coffeepot. While on tour, he might have to stick with field rations, but the rest of the time, he opted for quality. From the looks of that pot, the sludge in the carafe was barely digestible.

"So?" Cade prodded, knowing he didn't need to repeat the question.

"You're coming up on your PRD."

Cade wasn't surprised at the captain's statement. Borden figured he'd recruited Cade to the SEALs. Since being a SEAL had been Cade's goal from the time he was twelve, he didn't think recruiting was the right term, but he let the old man have his illusions.

"Not for six months," Cade said, referring to his Projected Rotation Date, the time when he'd be up for reassignment. He'd been based here in California for eight years. Chances of being sent to Virginia or Hawaii were slim, but possible. Maybe a transfer was a good thing, though. He could start fresh, get away from the constant reminders of his lost friend. "Why?"

"I want you to consider taking your MTS cert."

Cade laughed and shook his head. "Why the hell would I want to be certified as a trainer?"

"You're a freefall jumpmaster, took gold in the Excellence in Pistol Shot, and were awarded the Silver Star. You aced out of Sniper School. And then there's the advanced counterterrorism technology training. You're one of the elite. You got the goods, boy."

Cade rocked back on the heels of his jump boots and grinned. Yeah. That was a pretty sweet list of qualifications. He'd worked damned hard, and loved every second of getting all of them. But all he said was, "So?"

"So we could use you here. The certification, a year as a trainer—it'd bump your pay grade and move you a lot closer to those captain's bars."

Cade frowned. He didn't care about the pay or rank. But he did care about losing his edge, about this depthless funk he'd sunk into, dragging his team down, too. He glanced out the window at the grown men falling all over themselves in the surf, struggling like toddlers to reach their boats. Those guys wanted to excel. To be the best. And he could be damned good at helping them get there. But to do that, he'd have to quit being a SEAL. And he didn't quit. Not one damned thing.

So he shook his head. "Nah. I'm good."

"Don't you think it'd be mighty impressive?" the cap-

tain asked as he and his steaming cup of coffee settled
behind the desk.

"Borden, I'm already a SEAL. There's not a damned
thing more impressive than that."

"Sure, maybe to the ladies."

"Who else matters?" Cade laughed.

Hell, it was rare that he ever even had to pull out the
SEAL card to impress a woman. He looked good enough
that the women tended to fall all over him anyway. They
always had. And it wasn't ego talking. He credited genet-
ics for his sandy blond hair, sharp green eyes and chiseled
features and the navy for his ripped body.

He had nothing to prove to anyone else.

"You want to climb higher than Lieutenant Commander?"

Cade shrugged again. Rank and money didn't mean
anything to him. Neither one had the thrill, the excitement,
or the rock-solid satisfaction of being a part of Special Ops.
At least, up until last fall, when Hawkins had taken a piece
of shrapnel to the head while under Cade's command.

"I'll bet there are some people who'd like to see you
move up the ranks," Seth said, staring into his cup like it
held some fascinating secret. Or, more likely, because he
didn't want his expression to give away his trump card.

"I don't live my life for other people," Cade countered
with a grin, dropping to a chair and getting ready to play.
Mind games were almost as much fun to win as war games.

"What about Robert?"

Cade's smile fell away.

"I definitely don't live my life for my old man."

"Not saying you should. But I'll bet it'd go a long way
toward keeping him off your back for a while."

"You mean it'll keep him off your back?"

Robert Sullivan had married Seth's little sister Laura

thirty-five years ago and had probably muttered an average of a few dozen words a year to his brother-in-law since the reception. Less after they'd lost her to cancer five summers ago. But Robert somehow managed to find a few here and there to touch base with Seth for a little secondhand haranguing for his one and only child.

"Robert doesn't bother me," Cade's uncle said, dismissing him with a jerk of one shoulder. As if his ex-in-law was that easy to flick off.

Cade wished that were so. But he knew better. Robert Sullivan, of Sullivan Enterprises, specialized in tenacity, had the personality of a bulldog and the charm of a cactus. He'd been furious when Cade had joined the navy instead of taking his rightful place at the helm of the family's financial consulting firm.

"If he doesn't bother you, then why are you using him as bait?" Cade challenged.

"Because you're a damned good soldier. A fine SEAL and a strong leader. I don't want to see you derailed. You're on edge lately. That's the kind of thing that some people look for, try to take advantage of in order to make things go their way," he said, referring to Cade's father. "A break would let you figure it all out, before you're played."

His pleasant expression didn't change, nor did his body shift even an inch as a painful sort of tension spiked through Cade's system.

"No offense, Captain," Cade said with a grin as he got to his feet. "But I don't give a good damn what my father does. And nobody plays me. Not even the old man."

To Robert Sullivan, Cade was a pawn. A useful tool. He'd expected his only child to follow in his footsteps, to learn the ins and outs of finance and take over the vast Sullivan holdings if and when Robert deemed it time.

Cade had never been interested in any of that. Not even

as a kid. So he'd never let the old man in on his plans. He'd enlisted the day he'd turned eighteen, three months before he'd finished high school. Already knowing the value of good strategy, he'd waited to tell his father until the morning after graduation. And he'd left for basic training right after the ensuing big ugly fight.

It wasn't just that he didn't want to take some bullshit business major if his father covered tuition that made him decide not to go to college.

He simply hadn't wanted to wait to get started in the navy.

And then, like now, he hadn't given a damn about rank.

He just wanted to be a SEAL.

He was born for the military.

He just had to remember that and get through this damned... What did his squadmate and amigo, Blake's fiancée, Alexia, call it? Journey of grief. Stupid thing to call being pissed off over losing his buddy. And definitely not something he wanted to talk about. Not to Blake, not to Alexia. And definitely not to his uncle.

Before he could make excuses to leave, Cade's cellphone rang.

"Speak of the devil," he muttered, noting the number on the screen.

"The old man?"

"Close enough—it's my grandmother."

The only thing that kept Cade from turning his back on his family, and all the drama and crap that went along with it, was his grandmother. He would do anything, even play nice at holidays, to make Catherine Sullivan happy.

With that in mind, he gestured his apology to Borden and took the call. Five minutes later, he wished he hadn't.

"Robert had a heart attack," Cade murmured as he slid the phone into his pocket.

"Is he okay?" Seth asked, looking up from the paperwork he'd been pretending to do to give his nephew some semblance of privacy.

"He's in intensive care. They don't know if he's going to make it."

Seth frowned, coming around the desk. "Are *you* okay?"

Cade shrugged. He didn't know what he was. Numb. Despite a lousy, contentious relationship, shouldn't he care that his father might die? That he was hanging by a thread?

Cade's mind couldn't quite take it in.

He was a SEAL, specially trained in multiple ways to cause death. He'd served during wartime. He'd watched men die. He'd held one of his best friends as life drained away. It wasn't that he wasn't familiar with the concept.

But his father? He'd always figured the old man was too stubborn, too obnoxious, too uncompromising to allow it to happen on anything but his own approved timetable.

"You need anything?"

Cade gave Seth a blank look, then shook his head. "Gotta see my CO, get leave. Grandma wants me home."

Seth's wince pretty much summed up Cade's lifelong feelings about returning to the Sullivan Estate.

Cade grimaced in return. "Looks like I'm getting that break after all."

# 2

"DID YOU HEAR? Cade Sullivan is back."

Eden shook her head as twitters and giggles filled the room, women from the ages of eighteen to sixty-eight offering up a communal sigh. From what she'd seen, the members of the Garden Club rarely agreed on anything. Leave it to Cade Sullivan to bring women together.

But as hot and sexy as Cade was, he wasn't the kind of stud she wanted to talk about right now.

It wasn't like she wasn't a fan of Cade herself. She adored the guy. Heck, she'd love to *do* the guy. But she was here to talk up her business. To try and garner a few new clients. Instead, the entire conversation had been derailed by the homecoming of the town hero.

Cade was good at that kind of thing. Making women sigh, fantasize, and if rumors were true, have some mighty fine orgasms. At least, that's what the Cade-ettes, as those lucky few who were in the know liked to call themselves, claimed.

"I heard he's here for a month. He doesn't come back often, does he?" Bev mused, her eyes dreamy. No doubt visualizing Cade in some form of undress. "It's been, what? Ten years since he left?"

"Twelve," Eden corrected absently, leaning over to scoop up a bite of her friend's lemon chiffon cake. The fork halfway to her mouth, she noticed all the stares aimed her way and shrugged. "It's not like I'm marking off the years in my diary. He left for the navy the same week I broke my foot the first time. He's the one who carried me home from the lake."

"Did you know him well?" asked a pretty blonde whose name Eden didn't remember. The girl had married her way into the Ocean Point high society, so she didn't have firsthand knowledge of the almost mythical wonderfulness that was Cade Sullivan.

"Oh, please," Janie Truman scoffed, sliding into an empty seat at the table and taking a single grape from the bowl in the center. "You barely knew Cade Sullivan. Sure, he rescued you a few dozen times. But that's sort of what he does for a living, isn't it? You were like basic training."

Her laugh was too bubbly for Eden to take offense. At least, not unless she wanted to look like a bitch. That was the problem with Janie. She always came across as all smiles and charm, even while she slid her pretty jeweled knife between your ribs.

Eden sighed, wondering why belonging to this group was her holy grail. The ugly was always as subtle, but as real, as the expensive perfume. But only to outsiders, she figured. The only way to avoid being the butt of their jokes and pitying looks was to belong.

"I'd say growing up next door to the Sullivans means she probably knows Cade well enough," Bev defended, her irritation on Eden's behalf shining bright.

"Sort of," Eden demurred, not sure she wanted to share just how much about Cade she did know. Instead she settled on the simple facts. "Cade's five years older than I am, so we weren't in school together, didn't run in the same crowds. Cade was busy with football and the swim team and I was playing with animals and volunteering at the shelter."

How was that for an opening to talk about veterinary care, Eden thought, giving herself a mental back-pat.

"Captain of the football team. Class president, homecoming king," Janie rhapsodized, her sharp chin on her hand as she gave a dreamy sigh, ignoring any references that included Eden. "Oh, to be a Cade-ette…"

"Cade-ette?" Bev asked with a laugh. She gave Eden an *are you kidding* look.

Eden grinned. It was a little shameless, as far as titles went. Still, it carried as much cachet as an Oscar did for an actor. "It's silly. When Cade was in high school—"

"Junior high, even," Janie interrupted.

"Maybe," Eden acknowledged, wrinkling her nose. "That's awfully young, though. Not for Cade, of course, but for the girls? But nobody knows for sure, do they?"

"Knows what?" Bev prompted before Janie could launch into one of her typical attempts to prove that she did, indeed, know everything.

"Knows when it all started, what the rules are or even who's in the club," Eden said. "The story goes that Cade, while being quite the ladies' man even in his teens, knew he wanted out of Mendocino County and wasn't about to let anything—not even a girlfriend—keep him here. So while he played the field, he kept things simple, uncomplicated."

"In other words, he was really careful about sleeping around because he didn't want to be trapped. Not just because he's super cute, but because the Sullivans are filthy rich," Janie explained, eyeing the cake with an envious look before nibbling on another grape.

"But after a while, girls started bragging. I think the allure of having done Cade Sullivan was better than a pair of diamond studs, and they just couldn't keep from showing off." Eden remembered the almost mythical shot to fame the girls would get, being fawned over, buddied up to, romanced by other guys. "Pretty soon, the Cade-ettes had an even more exclusive membership than the country club."

"Exclusive, and elusive," Janie interrupted. "There weren't many who could make that claim to fame. Maybe a dozen at the most."

"How do you know they were telling the truth?" Bev wondered. "I mean, if he was determined not to get trapped, would he really sleep around, even with a dozen girls in four years?"

"Sixteen years," Janie corrected. "That dozen counts the girls he was with before—and after—he left for the navy."

"You mean the club still has openings?" Bev joked.

*I wish,* Eden almost said aloud. Horrified, she focused on shoveling cake into her mouth to keep it busy. She had a bad habit of looking before she leapt, and speaking before she thought. Usually, she didn't worry about the results. But this was Cade they were talking about. And she cared about everything that had to do with Cade Sullivan.

Which was why she'd never shared, not even with her best friend, how often she'd seen Cade at the lake behind their properties. Skinny dipping sometimes, practicing martial arts others. But usually with a girl. Eden had rarely seen the girl's face, but could see through the bushes clearly enough to know they both usually ended up naked.

He'd been gorgeous, even as a teen, with the body of one of the Greek Gods Eden had been fascinated with. Tan, sculpted and, well, huge, he'd been worth the many bouts of poison oak she'd gotten spying through the trees.

She dropped her fork onto the empty plate and reached for her iced tea, needing to cool off.

"So this rumor, you believe it?" Bev prompted.

"Sure." Eden shrugged. "I mean, the few who did try to claim they'd done Cade Sullivan were outed as liars pretty fast. Nobody but the Cade-ettes themselves know what the secret is that proves the truth. I guess they think it's a pretty good secret, too. Like I said, it's been twelve years since he left and they still aren't talking."

And while she'd only watched him a couple of times before embarrassment and a heart-crushing envy had made her avoid the lake altogether just in case he was there, she'd never seen any distinguishing marks or heard him use any special phrases that might stand out as tells.

"Everyone wanted to be a Cade-ette," Janie said with a sigh, either forgetting her constant diet as she scooped up a fingerful of chocolate from the cake in front of her, or envy making her so morose that she didn't care.

"Everyone?" Bev asked, her eyes questioning Eden.

Eden just shrugged again. She wasn't going to lie to her best friend, but neither did she see any point in admitting that she would have given anything to join the well-sexed crowd. But not for the title. Nope, she just wanted Cade.

"Ladies, time to get to work," Gloria Bell, the Garden Club president called, clapping her hands for attention. "The Spring Fling is just around the corner. Our biggest society ball needs the best flower arrangements, don't you think? Come on now, chop chop."

Most of the older women got up and gathered around the three head tables, discussing what kind of flowers screamed fancy party. That left Eden and a dozen women her own age seated next to the dessert buffet. A fact that seemed to pain half of them, since they studiously kept their gazes averted. Eden, who while carrying a plethora of issues and challenges, could happily eat anything and everything without gaining an ounce, just grinned.

This was the only way she stood out, a wren among

peacocks. They were grace, she was clumsy. They were as beautiful as money could buy, she was as average as broke could maintain.

"I can't believe nobody has shared the secret yet. Are you sure there is one?" Bev asked, wrinkling her nose. "I mean, it sounds like more of an urban legend than fact, you know?"

"Oh, it's real." Crystal Parker leaned forward, her eyes shifting to the matriarchs to see that her mother was occupied before she shared in a low tone, "My sister, Chloe, was almost one of the Cade-ettes."

"Almost?" gaped Bev. "How is one almost in the club?"

"She went on a few dates with Cade the winter before he graduated. The two of them were getting really friendly, if you know what I mean, during the high school Winter Bash and Chloe got a little loud. Then the principal, Mrs. Pince, walked in on them. Chloe said Cade charmed his way out of a lecture, but never did ask her out again."

She gave a good-humored roll of her eyes, as if her sister's getting busted making out still amused her.

"Of course, that couldn't have been as embarrassing as what happened to poor Eden here," Janie said with a giggle before patting Eden's hand. As if that friendly gesture made the joke any easier to take. "You never have told us the real story about what you and Kenny Phillips were really doing when he broke his foot and ended up covered in a nasty rash."

Eden pressed her lips together in a grimacey sort of smile, hoping someone, *anyone,* would change the subject. She didn't need anyone speculating about what particular sexual position Kenny had been in when he'd fallen.

Cade had rescued her then, too. Turning the tables nicely, he'd shown up at the lake to find her with his best buddy from high school. The poor guy had been rolling around naked in a patch of poison oak while clutching his broken ankle.

"Girls," Gloria called, gliding over like an elegant steamship. "Chitchat is over. Now it's time for work."

"I can help," Eden offered, gratefully getting to her feet. But in her desire to escape further sexual comparisons, her hip bumped the table, sending the unlit candles toppling, forks bouncing off plates and the grapes rolling over white damask to the floor.

"Oh, well…" Mrs. Bell grimaced, then shook her head. "Thank you, dear. But we need someone with a little better eye for color. Janie, why don't you and the girls come along now and see what you think of the plans."

En masse, all of the women except Bev and Eden migrated to the front of the room. To the popular section.

Eden sighed, pushing aside the last plate of dessert, this one a double-chocolate brownie.

"What's wrong? It's not like you to stop rubbing your super-fast metabolism in the princesses' faces before you've tried every dessert," Bev said quietly.

Although Eden noticed a few envious glances at three empty plates in front of her, all she could focus on was the giggling group of women all bundled together around the flower displays. All fitting in, all contributing meaningfully. All perfect, even if they couldn't eat more than two hundred calories at a time.

"Nothing. I'm just tired," she excused, not completely lying. She was tired.

Tired of being so easily dismissed.

Tired of feeling like a failure.

Tired of wallowing in mediocrity.

Just once, she wanted to be admired. To stand out—in a good way. To feel like someone special. To be part of the in-crowd.

And maybe she should wish for a time machine, too, and blast back to high school when she should have gotten over these silly issues.

"Oh, Eden," Lilly-Ann Winters, who sat at the next table, called, offering a charming smile. "I'm so glad you made it to the meeting this month. You so rarely do."

"I usually work Thursday afternoons," Eden said with a cautioning look toward Bev. Lilly-Ann had a trio of Parti Yorkies and a pedigree Persian at home.

"Oh, you still have that, um, job?" Lilly-Ann asked, a rapid flutter of her lashes probably supposed to be a distraction from her having no clue what Eden did.

"I opened my veterinary clinic six months ago, and yes, it's still in business," Eden said with a nod, amping up her smile and getting ready to pitch her real reason for subjugating herself to this torture. "You should bring Snowball in for a checkup. I have a wonderful new program for cats, an all-natural diet and supplements that are guaranteed to add luster to her coat."

"Oh, no. Snowball only sees Dr. Turner," Lilly-Ann said, her eyes wide with horror at the idea of taking her precious Persian anywhere but the most expensive vet in three counties.

"I understand," Eden said, pulling out the diplomacy she'd been practicing since she'd called in her RSVP. "Dr. Turner has a wonderful reputation. And he's so popular. Just last week someone was saying she had to wait a month to get her puppies in for a routine exam."

Lilly-Ann's smile tightened at the corners. Bingo. Eden knew the only thing the other woman hated more than designer knockoffs was having to wait for *anything*.

"Don't you worry about emergencies, though?" Eden continued, leaning forward and speaking in a hushed, let's-share-a-secret tone. "You can't take risks with a feline as delicate as Snowball. If you wanted to just bring her by for a checkup, I'd have her information on file in case, God forbid, there was ever a crisis."

For one brief, gratifying second, Lilly-Ann looked tempted. Then she gave Eden a once-over, as if to remind herself who she was dealing with, and shook her head. "No, no. Thanks, though. Dr. Turner has a pet ambulance. I'm sure we'll be fine."

With that and a giggling little finger wave, she got to her feet. Bev stood, too, an argument obviously on her lips.

Eden shook her head, gesturing to her friend to sit. What was the point? She needed clients desperately. She'd hoped a few of the women would, if only for faux-friendship's sake, give her a chance. But to them, and to most of Ocean Point, she'd always be the klutzy girl who'd broken Kenny's foot while having sex. A joke. An average, broke joke who was about to lose her home. Because she'd tried everything she could think of, even calling her mother—who hadn't answered—to find a way out of this financial mess. If she didn't come up with the money—or at least enough to negotiate a deal—within three weeks, her home, her heritage, would be gone.

"Brownie?" Bev offered again with a sympathetic frown.

Eden shook her head.

Some things, even chocolate couldn't help.

SHE WAS STILL ASKING herself what the point of it all was two hours later as she drove home.

"Well that was a total waste of a Saturday," Bev declared from the passenger seat, nibbling on the piece of cake she hadn't let herself eat in front of the other women. "I can't believe that in a roomful of thirty women, twenty-six of them have pets."

"And of that twenty-six, I couldn't get a single client," Eden mumbled, wishing she hadn't wasted Bev's time. "Still, it wasn't all bad."

She didn't have to take her eyes off the road to know Bev had shot her an incredulous look. Probably a sneer, too, if Eden knew her friend.

"Hey, I made contacts. That counts. They might not have signed on board today, but all it takes is one good word, one rich matron with a colicky dog, and I'm set." She slanted a sideways glance toward the passenger seat. "And, hey, at least dessert was good."

"Well, I'll give you the desserts point. But do you really think a matron or two using you as their vet is going to stop the bank from calling in the loan?" Bev didn't even bother with the skeptical look this time. Her tone, even wrapped around chocolate icing, spoke volumes.

"Until I come up with something better, this is the best shot I've got," Eden said morosely.

Damn her mother. Damn *herself* for not forcing Eleanor to sign herself off the property when Eden had bought her out. She should have known better. According to her personal bio, Eleanor Gillespie was a free spirit. A wild wind that couldn't be tamed. Eden sighed, her fingers clenching and unclenching on the steering wheel. A loving flake who specialized in making life difficult for her only child.

From preschool when she'd used all of Eden's classmates to test her politically incorrect, factually accurate and visually scarring nursery rhymes to high school when she'd volunteered as a parental chaperone at the senior all-nighter, then lectured everyone on birth control, sexual satisfaction and the benefits of a vegan lifestyle, she'd been a challenge. But she was also fun and bubbly, creative and clever, and loved Eden in her own self-absorbed, offbeat way.

Eden rounded the corner of narrow country road, tall trees looming on either side of the asphalt. But just as she passed the pretty stone gates that led to the Sullivan Estate, something white flashed. She lifted her foot off the gas, peering through the window. She saw it again.

White fur and gray spots.

She slammed on the breaks.

Bev's hand shot forward, bracing against the dash.

"What the hell…?"

Half on and half off the road, Eden killed the car engine and threw her door open.

"It's Paisley," she called as she hurried around the car toward the stately bank of large maple trees Laura Sullivan had planted when she was a young bride. "Mrs. Carmichael has been frantic since the cat ran away last week. We need to rescue her."

"That cat is evil," Bev muttered, following her. "Besides, do you really think *ran away* is the right term? That sounds so innocent. I heard it was more like a prison break, complete with injuries and property damage."

Eden waved that away. So Paisley was a little difficult. She was a rare snow Savannah. Being standoffish was a characteristic of the breed, as was the need for play and fun. Since Mrs. Carmichael wasn't much good at either, the poor cat had probably run off out of boredom.

Before she could explain the psychological makeup of Savannahs, there was a loud screech, then a crash boomed out from behind the women.

Except for a teeth-clenching wince, Eden froze.

Bev screamed.

Cringing, they both pivoted toward the car.

Eden had forgotten to set the parking brake.

She and Bev stared at the tree-hugging vehicle in silence.

Damn.

"This is a bad week for cars around you," Bev observed with a resigned sort of huff.

Eden groaned. It was like she was a walking, talking accident waiting to happen.

The car wasn't new, or even in very good condition, but it'd been big enough for her to transport anything smaller than a horse, was paid for and had looked decent enough not to irritate wealthy potential clients.

Now the passenger fender had formed an intimate relationship with a redwood.

After staring at the car for a solid minute, Eden sighed and deliberately turned her back on it to walk the rest of the way across the street.

"Aren't you going to do something? Where are you going?" Bev hurried after her. When Eden stopped under a tree and peered through the leaves, then reached up to test the strength of one branch, the cheery blonde gaped. "You can't be serious? You're still going to try to rescue the cat?"

"Why not? The car is already a mess—I might as well have something to show for it." A safe, secured pet was a reasonable price to exchange for a molested fender. And maybe, if she was lucky, this could be her chance to bond with Paisley and get in Mrs. Carmichael's good graces.

"Paisley," Eden called in a cajoling tone. The cat, perched high on a maple branch, stopped its upward bounce to toss Eden a disdainful look. "C'mere, pretty kitty."

"Why don't we just call Mrs. Carmichael and tell we saw her cat. She can come get it herself," Bev suggested when her stilettos slid on the dirt bank. "And give us a ride while she's at it."

"Sure, a sixty-year-old woman needs to be climbing a tree after her cat," Eden dismissed, her own stubby-heeled

Mary Janes not slipping at all—girls who tended to trip over their own feet wore stilettos at great risk—as she made her way around the base of the maple.

After a few more calls, a few snarky remarks from Bev and another dismissive look from the cat, Eden sighed. She looked up the road, then down, to make sure no cars were coming. She only climbed trees once in a blue moon, but somehow she always managed to get busted.

"You're lookout," she told Bev. She glanced down at her pretty blue cotton dress, then tugged the back of the pleated skirt forward between her thighs, tucking it into the wide black belt. "There, modesty intact."

"There, fashion destroyed," Bev said, shaking her head in dismay. "If anyone asks, I tried to talk you out of this. I pointed out the likelihood of you falling, of you breaking yet another bone or something horrible happening to your hair."

Eden's fingers combed through the thick swath of heavy brown hair at her shoulders and gave Bev a confused look. "My hair?"

"I think it's the only thing you haven't messed up so far. It's due."

Eden grimaced, then shrugged. Bev was probably right. Some people might lament their fate, others would spend hours in therapy. She figured that by simply accepting that she was a little accident prone, she was not only ahead of the game in terms of dealing with emergencies—because after all, she created at least one a month—but she was saving a fortune on psychiatric fees.

"Watch for cars," she warned again, reaching up to grab the closest branch.

"What do I do if I see one? Whistle? Throw myself across the driver's window to hide their view?"

There might be a few drawbacks to having a BFF with

a smart mouth, Eden decided as she levered her body onto the first branch.

"Just give me enough warning so I can hide," she said as she gained her balance and slowly stood upright to reach for another limb.

With Bev's voice droning in the background, covering everything from the fact that she'd never learned to climb a tree to the insanity of grown women acting like squirrels, Eden scurried higher.

A minute later, she was one branch away from Paisley.

"Hi, sweet kitty," she said in a soft singsong voice. "Are you up here playing Queen of the Jungle? You should be— you look like royalty."

She kept the soothing tone going, her outstretched fingers in constant motion to get the cat's attention.

It worked. After a few seconds and a cautious sniff, the exotic white cat was nudging her broad forehead against Eden's knuckles.

"Oh, aren't you sweet."

Unable to resist, Eden gave herself a moment to cuddle and pet the pretty cat before tucking her under one arm and slowly lowering herself until her butt met the branch. Like scooting down a rickety ladder, she went one branch at a time, with plenty of cuddling in between. Finally she was close enough to hand the cat to Bev.

"Why don't you put her in the car," Eden instructed, her belly flat against a wide limb that was about six feet from the ground. "Crack the windows, and there's a bottle of water and portable pet dish in the trunk. If you'll sit with her, she'll probably drink a little."

Despite her earlier opinion that the cat might be evil, Bev didn't hesitate to reach out and cuddle the gray-spotted feline. Paisley gave a meow of protest, and threw an injured look toward Eden, but didn't try to escape. Eden waited until her friend and the cat were safely inside the car, treats and water dispensed, before she lowered herself to the next branch.

There. She smiled her relief. Almost down.

It was the smile that did it, she figured.

Because she went from enjoying an easy descent to being suddenly trapped in the space of a heartbeat. Like an anchor, something held tight, so she couldn't move.

Breathless, Eden twisted to see what was wrong.

Then scowled when she saw that the strap of her shoe was caught on a branch. Eden tugged. The shoe stuck. She tried to slip it off, but the branch was too rough, scratching painfully against the soft flesh of her instep.

A minute later she added cursing to the mix.

"Haven't we been here before?" a husky voice asked.

Oh, hell. Eden froze. She hadn't even heard a car. Please, oh, please, let him be talking to someone else.

"That is Eden up there, right?" the voice asked.

Double hell.

She shook her head, hoping the move would shift the curtain of hair from blocking her view.

Her heart, already pounding like a freight train, sped up. What little was left of her breath escaped her lungs in a rush.

She twisted her torso, angling herself sideways to make sure the face matched the voice.

Gorgeous green eyes, a tanned complexion over sculpted cheekbones and a strong jawline. Wide, full lips stretched in a smile that bordered on laughter. And the sexiest man-dimple she'd ever seen.

Her eyes widened and she gave a long, lusty sigh.

Didn't it just figure? At least she'd tucked her skirt in so she wasn't flashing him. Sure, she might have a few dozen fantasies about sharing her undies with this particular man. But this position wasn't featured in a single one.

So she did what she always did when caught in an uncomfortable situation.

She smiled and made the best of it.

"Hi, Cade."

# 3

"Do you do these things just to keep me in practice?" Cade asked, grinning at his favorite perpetual-victim, her silky brown hair a dark curtain over a face he knew would be sliding into a sheepish smile.

Eden Gillespie always looked sheepish when she had to be rescued. Something, if he'd ever considered it, he'd have figured she'd have outgrown. He eyed her legs, smooth and bare all the way to the top of her hot-pink panties thanks to the way her dress was hanging. Her arms were wrapped around the tree limb and one foot dangled while the other was caught in a snarl of branches and leaves. Clearly he'd have figured wrong.

"Consider it my welcome-home present," she muttered, blowing a puff of air so her hair cleared enough that he could see the resigned amusement in her big brown eyes.

That was one of the things he'd always admired about Eden. She could laugh at herself. So many of the girls he'd grown up with, and the women he'd dated for that matter, took themselves and life way too seriously. They were so worried about controlling the impression they made, they didn't let themselves just live.

Without thinking, his eyes shifted back to Eden's legs.

Long and sleek, they wrapped around that big, hard branch. He frowned at the scrapes and faint reddening of her tender flesh, for the first time ever tempted to kiss away a boo-boo. All the way up to her panties. Practical cotton, he noted, his mouth going dry, but in a fun, sassy color. Since she was facedown on the branch, the curve of her butt was perfectly highlighted in that pink fabric. His fingers itched to touch, to see if her curves were as firm as they looked.

Whoa. Not cool, he lectured himself. Lusting after the sweet girl next door was walking an awfully close line to settling down. Nothing wrong with it in the big picture, but in his personal rulebook? Totally out of the question.

"Want some help?" he offered, wondering how many times now he'd had to hurry these rescues along because of a hit of inappropriate lust. After all, he was pretty sure he'd been hauling her out of scrapes since his pre-teen days. But it'd only been since *that* rescue, when he'd seen her naked, that the sight of her made him instantly horny. He sighed with relief. There, now he was only a standard guy, not a weird pervert with a superhero complex.

"I can do it," she muttered, tugging her foot to try and loosen it from the branch. Her shoe, a cute little black strappy thing, was good and stuck. She sighed and slanted him a rueful look. "But maybe you could just unhook my shoe for me?"

Cade didn't bother arguing. He reached up and pulled the twigs from her foot. Then he wrapped both hands around her surprisingly narrow waist, easily lifting her from the overhead branch. It was like doing a military press, he thought with a grin as he lowered her body toward the ground.

Except he hadn't counted on her shocked reaction. She gasped, struggling a little as if wanting him to let her go. Since he wasn't about to drop her three feet to the ground, he shifted. Her breasts skimmed his chin. He froze. Other than to gasp and grab on to his shoulders for support, so did she.

Cade had felt the same energy pounding through his body when he held a live grenade. Danger, excitement, all senses on full alert.

Wrong, his brain screamed. Eden was the sweet girl next door. The same girl he'd been rescuing for years. She wasn't supposed to inspire this degree of lust. The kind that made him want to take her, right there against the tree. He didn't care that they'd only said a dozen or so words to each other in years, or that her friend was over there, face pressed against the window of the wrecked car, watching.

It was neither of those things that had Cade ignoring the hot need in his belly, or his body's demand that he taste her, touch her.

It was the flutter of Eden's lashes. The way her pulse trembled in her throat. The tiny trembles of her fingers where they dug into his shoulders. He, and his wicked desires, were out of her league.

So, nope. Not giving in to the need.

But that didn't mean he couldn't enjoy himself up to that limit line.

Grinning, he slowly brought his arms down. He didn't let go of his hold on her waist, so her body had to slide, in one long glorious trip, down his.

His eyes never left hers. There was something heady, intense, in seeing the heat flare, then her gaze blur with passion.

As soon as her feet hit the ground, she pushed away like he was fire, too hot for her to touch.

"Thanks again," she said as she stepped backward. Her foot caught on a root and would have sent her sprawling if he hadn't grabbed her.

"Babe, I live for these moments," he told her in a husky tone, only half-teasing. Because he really did. Eden always made coming home fun.

"Me, too."

The look on her face, a mix of horror and chagrin, said loud and clear that she had, as usual, spoke without thinking.

He should let her off the hook.

It wasn't like he was going to give in to the heat between them. Ever since his first romp at the tender age of fourteen, he'd made it a point to stay relationship-free and keep his sexual encounters easygoing and simple. There was nothing simple or easygoing about Eden.

Except looking at her. That was as simple and easy as breathing. And talking to her. He'd never had any hesitation there. Listening to her laugh was pure pleasure.

Hell.

"C'mon, I'll give you a ride home," he said, his words a little gruffer than he'd intended.

"I can get home."

Cade didn't bother arguing. He just pointed to her fender, wrapped around that tree as intimately as he'd like to see Eden wrapped around his body.

"Oh. Yeah." She sighed, looking from the fender to her friend, then to Cade. Her gaze shifted again to the cat, then his car. Finally she shrugged. "Thanks. We appreciate the ride."

As soon as both women—and the feline—were settled in his borrowed BMW—the quiet redhead in the back and Eden and her rescue cat in the front—he started the car.

"So, you still seeing Kenny Phillips?" he asked, hoping like hell she'd say yes.

"Not anymore." She did that cute little nose-wrinkling

thing then shook her head. "He never quite forgave me for breaking his foot."

It'd been Kenny's screams that'd caught Cade's attention a couple years back, leading him to rescue a stunning, naked Eden. Cade was still baffled by that situation, since Kenny was nothing if not a missionary kind of guy. How the hell did a guy break his foot having standard, missionary sex? You'd think it'd take a swing, a tube of body lube and a few leather straps to reach that level of risk.

"I don't think you lost out on much. Dating is a full-contact sport," he told her with a laugh.

Unlike a lot of women, Eden didn't get that speculative, *how interested are you in playing the game with me* look in her eyes. Instead she just shrugged.

"I guess Kenny decided to sign up for a lower-risk league, then," she informed him as she rolled her ankle first one way, then the other. "And he took most of his teammates in town with him."

"Wimps," Cade muttered. What kind of jerks blamed the girl for their own incompetence? Sure, Eden was a little accident prone. But she was sweet and sexy in that girl-next-door way. She was fun and easy to talk to, and unlike so many others around town, she didn't play the user game. A guy would be lucky to date her. If he was interested in dating, that is.

"So you're saying you wouldn't be scared?" Eden challenged. Her chin was high and her tone light, but he could see the vulnerability in those gold-flecked brown eyes.

"Sweetie, unless a woman straps an explosive device around her waist and insists we go dancing, there's not much that will scare me." Cade laughed.

"So you'd date a girl who had a reputation for being a little clumsy?" she asked quietly.

Well, how the hell had he missed that trap? Cade

frowned, even as a gurgle of horrified laughter came from the backseat.

"I don't base my dating choices on things like that," he sidestepped. Then, to further cement the *keep out* message, he added, "Really, I don't see myself dating at all in the next little while. Between the old man in ICU and my grandmother needing me, I figure I'll be pretty tied up until I return to base. Gramma said something about some deals my father was trying to wind up when he had the heart attack, something with important timing. I'm probably going to have to take care of that, too."

Ah, silence.

He had no idea what'd caused it, but he'd take the stilted quiet over tap dancing around a verbal trap any day. Other than the uncomfortable shifting her friend did in the backseat, nobody made a sound. Even the cat quit purring.

Still, by the time they reached Eden's place, less than a mile up the road, tension tight enough to bounce coins off rippled across the back of Cade's neck. He drove down the long, circular driveway, his discomfort slowly fading as he noted how rundown the Gillespie place had become. The immediate yard around the huge house was still tidy, but beyond the fence, weeds were brushing the trees. Even the once vivid white paint on the shutters was graying, chipped and curling.

One of the outbuildings looked like the roof had collapsed and someone—probably Eden—had built a crude wire fence to pen up a goat and what looked like a horse-size dog.

"Thanks for the rescue. And the ride," Eden said when he stopped in front of wide bank of steps leading to her front door.

"Anytime," he told her. "Just try to keep your accidents

scheduled for my visits home. I hate to think of you hanging from a tree and only wimps here to save you."

She laughed, the pained discomfort chased away by amusement. "Would you believe that I usually manage to rescue myself when you're not around?"

Cade considered that for a second.

Then he shook his head. "Nope."

Her cheeks warm with a pretty pink wash, Eden gave him a sweet look from under her lashes. The kind of look that should make him feel protective. Or manly, like a superhero.

Not horny like a sailor on leave.

Time to go, he decided.

Leaning one elbow on the seat, he angled himself around.

"It was nice to meet you," he told the quiet redhead in the backseat. She gave him a wide-eyed, about-to-hyperventilate look.

Because he was a SEAL, trained in multiple ways to kill men and defend his country? Or because of his high school rep and near rock-star dating status?

Then the redhead blushed.

Yep. Rock star.

"Cade?"

He looked at Eden with a friendly smile, ready to politely brush off her thanks.

She was staring at the cat on her lap, as if one glance away would send it leaping out the window.

"Did you maybe want to get drinks with me? Sort of a welcome-home and thank-you combination?"

Drinks? Unless that meant standing in line together to each buy their own bottle of water at the corner market, drinks were a really bad idea. Drinks were code word for tiptoeing into dating territory. A precursor to, part of or windup from something more intimate.

A huge mistake.

It wasn't that Cade didn't date. And he was nowhere near being a monk. But here in his hometown, the rules were different. Here, the women tended to see him as Robert Sullivan's son. The guy who'd get the key to the Sullivan coffers. A great catch.

Not that women didn't have an agenda outside of Ocean Point, as well, but usually that had more to do with being able to say they'd been with a SEAL. Being a notch on a woman's lipstick case, he was okay with. Being the target of her engagement ring search, he wasn't.

Still, this was Eden. He'd need to let her down easy.

"Sure," he heard himself say instead. "A drink sounds good."

His momentary chagrin at giving in to the urge fled quickly at the look of surprise on Eden's face and the delighted shock on her friend's.

She'd expected him to say no. To be a wimp.

Her friend had figured the same, hopefully without the wimp part. He knew his rep, and the status-obsessed focus of a lot of the country club set that Eden ran with. The Sullivans were big shit around town. The Gillespies barely danced around the fringe. From the time he was fourteen, he'd heard hundreds of lectures on dating, all focused on the girl's last name, never her first. God, he hated that. That, and the way everyone always gossiped, judging each other's worth by who they dated or the limit on their credit card. Hell, before he hit the end of the driveway, he'd bet her friend would have texted twenty of her best friends to tell them the news.

Within ten minutes, forty more people would probably have texted her back with varying degrees of shock, denial and outright horror at the idea of a Sullivan lowering himself to date a woman like Eden. One who lived in a rundown house, whose sexual encounters resulted in broken bones and who wrecked cars to rescue cats.

Who didn't date for status.

Who liked him for him, not because of his last name.

Who made him feel like the hero she always teased him about being.

Any intention Cade had of retracting his agreement disappeared. He was going out for that drink, and he was going to make damned sure that Eden—and anyone else who might be curious—knew he was glad to spend time with her.

"Tomorrow night?" she asked, her casual tone at odds with the tension in her eyes.

"Six okay?"

She gave a tiny frown, her arched brows drawing together for a second before she nodded. Then she leaned down to grab her purse, gathered the cat closer and reached for the door handle.

"Let me," Cade offered. Giving in to rare mischief, he grinned, then leaned across Eden's body to open the passenger door from the inside. He let his forearm brush, ever-so-lightly, across her breasts. She gave a tiny gasp, her doe-eyes rounding with shock. Her scent wrapped around him, earthy and sweet at the same time, like honeysuckle at midnight.

He forgot about the woman in the backseat, ignored the purring mass of fur draped across Eden's lap. All he cared about was the woman staring up at him like he'd hung the moon, lit the stars and made the sun rise when he whistled.

Without thinking, he leaned down and brushed a whisper-soft kiss over her shocked mouth.

"Thanks for the welcome home," he murmured, immediately leaning back. He kept his expression light. Amused even. As if his own body hadn't just gone into overdrive at the taste of her lips under his.

"Anytime," she murmured, draping the huge cat over her shoulder and sliding from the car as if in a fog. He waited until her friend was out, too, then shifted the car into gear.

A quick glance in the rearview mirror confirmed that both women were still staring.

Cade grinned.

Maybe the next couple of weeks wouldn't be so bad after all.

THERE WAS NO WAY in hell he was sticking around another couple of weeks. Cade clenched his teeth to keep the fury inside, both because spewing it would upset his grandmother, and more to the point, because he refused to let his father know he was pushing buttons.

"You need to step it up, put in more effort," his father lectured from the crisp white sheets of his hospital bed. A chorus of beeps and buzzes accompanied his rant, medical equipment proving that a man could have a heart and still be a heartless bastard. "You've been doing the same thing for years now. When are you going to get a promotion? What's it take to get a raise in that military you serve? Don't my tax dollars pay enough for you to make a little more? Call up your ambition, boy. Push harder."

It didn't stop there. Cade made a show of inspecting his boots while Robert droned on.

And on and on.

And on.

It was like he was trying to spew out every demand, every put-down he could as fast as possible because he

knew the drugs and his body's need to heal would soon
take over and knock him back out.

Cade wished they'd hurry the hell up.

At first, he'd listened in sympathy to the slurred words
dragged down by drugs and age. He'd stared at the man
lying in the hospital bed, trying to reconcile the sagging
gray skin and fragile appearance with his no-bullshit father. Seeing him tapped every which way into wires and
machines, for the first time in his life, Cade had felt sympathy for his old man.

Once Robert had awakened, that sympathy had lasted
about five minutes.

Now, an hour later, Cade was once again asking himself if his mother, rest her soul, had bumped her head a
few times before agreeing to marry such a tyrant. He'd
served under some hard-asses in his years, had worked
with egomaniacs and assholes. But none held a candle to
his old man.

"You hear me, boy?"

"I'm not the one under medical observation," Cade said
laconically, rocking back on the heels of his boots and giving his father the easygoing smile he knew irritated him
the most. "My hearing is just fine."

The older man's eyes, just as green as Cade's though
blurred now, narrowed.

"I wasn't sure. You're always being shot at, or surrounded with bombs going off all around you. You might
have lost a few brain cells."

Cade's smile slipped a little. Nope. All he'd lost was
one of his best friends. But Robert Sullivan wouldn't give
a damn about that.

Hell, the loss of his wife had only slowed him down a
few weeks. If he missed her now, Sullivan-the-elder never
showed it. Cade wished, for the first time in his life, that

he had a little of that distance, that he could tap into that emotional void and just not care. Not feel the pain. Not carry the almost too heavy to bear weight of responsibility.

Gut clenched, he stared at the tubes pumping health into his father, focusing on the slender plastic until he could slam the lid shut on the gnawing pain.

"I've got to say, I find it difficult to believe you haven't made Commander yet. You clearly aren't applying yourself. You want me to die here, knowing my son quit for nothing? That he walked away from his familial obligations to play soldier and then didn't get anywhere?"

Cade's fists clenched and his blood boiled. He took a step forward, not caring that he was teetering on the edge of an explosion.

"Robert."

That's all it took. One word from Catherine to settle her son against his well-fluffed pillow. And, more likely her goal, to make her grandson stand down without challenging his father's obnoxious remarks.

Cade hated that the old man got to him. He didn't have a damned thing to prove to anyone. Still, he couldn't shake the tension knotting his shoulders or the fury coiling in the pit of his belly. Why had he come back? Why wouldn't his grandmother let him fly her to San Diego once in a while, or at least listen to his oft-repeated advice that she give up on that crazy illusion that they were a cozy family.

He needed to get out of here. And, if he was smart, he should go call Eden and cancel drinks. A night of thinking had provided plenty of reasons why it was a really bad idea. Mostly because all the images he'd had involved stripping those pink cotton panties off her.

"I'll be back to pick you up in a couple hours," he told his grandmother.

Catherine patted his hand with her own gnarled one,

her expression peaceful, even with the tiny line of worry creasing her brow when she gazed at her only child. It must be a mother thing, Cade thought, shaking his head. That ability to see something positive where nobody else could.

"I have a job you need to do," his father called out when Cade's hand closed on the doorknob. "I loaned one of the neighbors some money with their property as collateral. Turns out they took out a loan with the bank, too. If the bank decides to foreclose, I've got no leverage to get my money back. So I need you to collect before that happens."

Since there were only two tracts of land close enough to be considered neighbors, and one belonged to Cade's grandmother, that meant Robert was talking about the Gillespie property.

Cade was surprised his fist didn't crush the knob.

With the same caution, vigilance and care he'd take in facing an armed enemy, Cade slowly turned around.

"I'm not available for side jobs," he said, keeping his tone light, his expression neutral. Both because he didn't want to upset his grandmother, and yes, because he knew it'd piss his father off even more. Petty, he acknowledged, given that the guy was in a hospital bed. But he couldn't help himself.

"You need to do this one. If you don't the bank is going to take the property. I'll lose my money, and the Gillespie girl will lose her home."

"Eden borrowed money from you?"

"Eleanor did."

Robert didn't meet the shocked looks of his son or his mother. Looking frail again, he glared at the tubes in his hand for a second, then muttered, "She kept trying to sell me those ceramic things she makes. Erotic art, she calls it. I finally gave her the loan against the house just to get her to go away. Now she's off, who knows where, and not paying her debts. Figures."

Cade should be amused that someone could knock his father down a peg or two. But he was too busy worrying about the sweet girl next door.

"Eden has no idea?"

"As flaky as Eleanor is, I doubt it. I was on my way to tell Eden she was going to have to make good on her mother's debt when all of this…" he waved his tube-tapped hand toward the machines "…happened. I've been a little preoccupied since."

"You'd take the home out from under a girl you watched grow up. A neighbor? She made you cookies," Cade said, gesturing to the tray on the sideboard with a bright red bow and get-well card.

"The bank's the one that would be taking it out from under her. I just want to collect on what's due to me," Robert argued, shifting to his elbow to glare at his son. "Eleanor shouldn't have taken that loan if she couldn't pay it off. That's on her, not me."

"You're the one trying to kick Eden out of her home."

"The bank's going to kick her out. I'm the one stuck in this damned hospital bed peeing into a hose while I get screwed out of ten grand."

Maybe there was justice in the world.

It was something Cade had believed, once. Just like he'd believed he could make a difference. Now, he didn't have much faith in anything.

He couldn't stop his father from being a jerk, from hurting people. But he'd be damned if he'd help him.

But if he walked away, what happened to Eden? Cade remembered the state of the property. Run-down, rough looking. She didn't have the money for upkeep, which meant she probably didn't have enough to pay off his father. Or the bank.

He wanted to say screw it all. To get the hell out of here and go back to San Diego. For the first time since Phil had died, Cade wanted a mission. Something dangerous and intense. Something with a lot of guns, escalating violence and hopefully a shot at a little hand-to-hand combat.

"Cade," Catherine said, her quiet voice still loud enough to be heard over the sudden beeps and buzzing of the machines monitoring Robert. "That sweet girl is going to need help. Someone has to step in and keep the bank, and others, from taking her property. You'll take care of this for her until Eleanor gets back to pay her debts, won't you?"

Like a plug had been pulled on his fury, Cade sighed.

What was it about his grandmother? She never raised her voice, never said a harsh word. Yet nobody could say no to her. Including him.

"Sure, yeah, I'll take care of things," he promised quietly.

What else could he do? It was Eden. He couldn't, wouldn't, let her be tossed out of her house. It was the only home she'd ever known. Hell, until her mother had taken up mobile living, it was the only home the last four generations of her family had ever known.

He had to find a way to save it. To save her.

And, maybe, just maybe thinking of her as a mission, as a personal responsibility, would keep his hands off her sexy ass.

# 4

"IS THIS TOO MODEST?"

Eden turned one way, then the other, trying to see how she looked. Her bureau mirror only showed the top two-thirds of her body, though. So she couldn't tell if the borrowed skirt was sexy, slutty or simply stupid.

"Shouldn't you be asking if it's too revealing? Or," Bev leaned her head sideways and squinted, "if you should be wearing underwear?"

Eden clapped both hands on her butt cheeks, checking to make sure they weren't hanging out. The skirt wasn't that short, was it? After assuring herself it hit mid-thigh, she glared at her friend.

"Just because it doesn't leave panty lines doesn't mean a thong isn't underwear," she chided. And she wasn't about to ruin the look of her cute little black skirt with panty lines. Short, but not so much that she'd be in danger of flashing her goods, it fit like a glove, and showed off the benefits of being able to eat anything and everything and not gain an ounce. Her black blouse billowed, making her feel like a sexy poet with its wide ruffles and full sleeves.

Not a bad *just drinks, not really a date, but don't you wish it were* look, she decided. She leaned closer to the mirror to check her makeup. Smoky but subtle, like the magazines suggested. Glistening pink on her lips, just a hint of shimmer on her cheekbones and an extra coat of mascara.

She looked like herself, but not.

Exactly what she'd been hoping for.

This was it. Her chance to make one of her favorite fantasies come true. To make Cade Sullivan see her as more than a rescue operation, a charity case. A cute pet he needed to pull from the occasional tree.

"So?" she asked again, giving Bev an expectant look.

"You look great," the other woman said, sitting cross-legged on Eden's bed wearing blue jeans and a frown.

The bedroom, like the rest of the house, was a little worn. The last time the paint had been refreshed, Eden had been thirteen and going through her Grateful Dead phase. Thankfully, the years had faded the virulent purple to a smoky amethyst. Evening light, soft and gentle, wafted through the open windows, bringing with it the occasional bark from the barn. Eden had three dogs kenneled in what she affectionately called her veterinary hospital, but what most everyone else called a wreck. She'd spent the afternoon giving them, the horse and the goat extra play time and exercise to make up for the fact that she wouldn't be down to visit later. Because, please-oh-please fingers crossed tight, it'd be too late when she got home.

"This is the first time I've ever actually spent any time with Cade. He actually seems like a nice guy," Bev said, her tone implying he was pure poison. "Are you sure you want to go out with him?"

Trying to figure out what to do with her hair, because hanging flat was so boring, it took Eden a few seconds to take that in.

"What? You think I should only go out with guys who aren't nice?"

"No. But you have to admit, you don't have very good dating luck. Or should I say, the guys who date you don't have very good luck."

Which inevitably resulted in Eden not getting lucky. But that was beside the point. Or maybe it was the point, she frowned. Something to consider if tonight didn't work out. Maybe she should learn not to maim her dates or something.

"Cade's a navy SEAL. I'm sure he's been trained to handle dangerous situations," she said drily.

"Maybe," Bev allowed with a grimace. "Still, I don't think this is a good idea."

"Okay, what're you so worried about?" Eden asked with a sigh. When a friend brought over her entire collection of makeup, clothes and shoes for you to choose from, a girl was somewhat obligated to listen to her concerns.

"Nothing, just, well, you know how the women were talking yesterday. This guy's got such a reputation that they give out groupie insignia for being with him. Is that really the kind of guy you want to date?"

*Hell, yeah.*

Eden managed to keep the exclamation to herself, though. She didn't think it'd allay Bev's worries to hear her rhapsodize about how great it would be to finally be considered a part of the "in" crowd. To be worthy of an insignia, or even talked about in any way that didn't invoke pitying eye rolls. God, she hated the eye rolls.

"It's fine," she said instead. "Cade's just a friend and this is just a welcome-home, thanks-for-hauling-me-out-of-the-tree drink. Nothing more."

"He kissed you."

Eden's entire body went hot.

The memory of his lips, so soft yet firm, as they'd brushed hers had kept her awake half the night. His scent, rich and earthy, had wrapped around her. If she closed her eyes and imagined, she could smell him again. Still…

"That wasn't a kiss. That was just a peck, a friendly gesture. A real kiss requires tongue," Eden replied. Although she was pretty sure Cade could take her from tepid to boiling with just his lips.

Rumor supported her theory, as did the peeks she'd taken at his lakeside rendezvous. Cade Sullivan was the sexual bomb. She was sure of it. And she wanted, more than anything else, for him to make her explode.

"Look," she said, going for distraction before her blushes gave away how much she really wanted Cade, "I'm just having drinks with him. It's a good thing and it will help me out of the jam I'm in."

At Bev's quizzical look, Eden continued. "You know what the bank manager said. Because my mother took out that loan against the house while it was still in just her name, and because we just added my name to the title instead of transferring it when I took over the mortgage, I'm stuck. Cousin Arnie is sure Mom meant to pay that off. I'm sure she meant to pay it off. And as soon as I reach her, I'm sure she'll take care of it. But in the meantime, I need to make those payments."

"So?"

"So… People will see us, get to talking, and you know how the gossip chain is in this town. Everyone wants the inside scoop but doesn't want to look like a snoop. So they'll try to be casual, make appointments for me to see their pets. Or their mom's pet, or their neighbor's pet, whatever they can get." Eden wrinkled her nose, equally amused and irritated. "I'll get some new business, put the money toward a reasonable payment to the bank and buy some time until I can reach Mom."

Every word was true. Except that not one of them had anything to do with why she wanted to go out with Cade.

"You're using this guy to build your business?" Bev asked, her face all screwed up with distaste.

Eden paused in the act of twisting her hair this way, then that, to stare at Bev in the mirror. She made it sound so bad. Like Eden was one of those girls in the club, only after Cade's status. They didn't care if they dated him, or his father, as long as the last name was Sullivan. She wasn't like that.

She opened her mouth to explain that to Bev, then closed it right back up. Because explaining would require she give her real reason for wanting this date so badly.

She wanted to seduce Cade Sullivan.

She wanted to strip him naked, drive him crazy and make him wild for her. To become a memory that he could think about on those nights before a scary mission and smile. To stop being the cute, accident-prone girl next door in his mind and become the sexiest experience he'd ever had.

She wanted to experience wild, intensely fabulous sex. To find out if all those rumors about his prowess were real. She wanted to be a Cade-ette, even if nobody but she and Cade knew it.

She wasn't using Cade Sullivan for his name or connections or to better her social standing, dammit.

She was using him for his body.

But Bev wouldn't understand that. She was too much a romantic. And also just a little bit of a worrywart. The minute she knew what Eden was planning, she'd try to talk her out of it.

Eden pressed one hand to her stomach, trying to soothe

the dancing butterflies, and figured she wasn't in any position to defend her decision.

"It's just drinks," she finally said. "How much using can be done over a beer?"

"You don't drink beer."

"Cade does."

Eden huffed at Bev's narrow look. "So I know what he drinks. You drink rum and cola. Janie drinks cosmopolitans, Crystal likes lemonade spritzers and Mrs. Winters chugs Kahlúa. What's the big deal?"

"How do you know these things?" Bev asked, sounding amazed as she finally relaxed enough to come over and start helping Eden fix her hair.

"I usually end up on bartender duty at the Spring Fling," she said, shrugging as if not ever being asked out on a date since the broken foot fiasco didn't bother her.

"Oh." Bev didn't say another word. A deep frown etched on her face, she did some twisty fun thing with a few braids, a flip here and a tuck there and turned Eden's heavy blanket of usually blah hair into a kicky style.

"Wow." Eden twisted one way, then the other, her grin getting bigger with each turn. "This is so cool. It's casual, sexy but still me. How do you do that?"

"I keep telling you, I'm good." Bev stepped back and peered through slitted eyes at the style, then shrugged. "If you'd let me do more than give you a trim, you'd find out. You could totally rock a shorter style. Something sassy."

"I don't think I'm the sassy type," Eden admitted. Although she was doing a pretty good impression right now. Cute top, with just a hint of sheer to show her red bra. Sexy skirt, just tight enough to remind her to sit like a lady so as not to show off her thong. And killer shoes. She eyed the black pumps with their red soles and white polka dots and wondered how many steps she'd make in them before she twisted something.

"You know, there are other shoes that would go with the outfit. Flats would work."

Eden grinned at the worry in Bev's voice. Geez, a few minor twisted ankles, a broken bone here and there and a girl got such a rep.

"I'll be fine. Since you're giving me a ride into town, I don't have to drive in them. I'll only have to walk from the car to the club, and back again."

Eden would have rather driven herself, but with her car at the Larkin's Body Shop, her only transportation at the moment was a ten-speed bicycle.

"Why isn't Cade picking you up?"

"He called earlier to change the time and mentioned that he's at ICU visiting his dad. I figured it'd be easier to meet him in town instead of making him drive here, then back there."

"So it really isn't a date," Bev said with a relieved sigh.

"Nope. Just two friends getting together for a welcome-home drink."

And, if Eden had her way, it would mark the beginning of a very hot, very sexy, very intense, and more importantly, very short affair.

AN HOUR LATER, Eden walked into the Oceanside Bar like a pageant queen on a slick catwalk—with slow, careful steps and pure concentration. What had she been thinking, suggesting they meet for drinks here?

"Eden?"

Ignoring the shocked looks, she called her hellos, but didn't slow down. If she did, she'd have to get the walking momentum going again, and that might not happen.

She should have hit the liquor store and invited Cade

over to her place. It'd be less nerve-racking to try and seduce a guy in private, wouldn't it? Of course, then he could leave as soon as he'd accepted her welcome, thanks and cold brew.

Eden's foot slipped, her ankle taking a sharp left while her foot went to the right. Damn. She quickly regained balance, hoping nobody had noticed, then hurried her mincing steps to the bar's entrance and its lovely carpeted floors. Bev had been right. Flats would have been much smarter.

"Eden?" This greeting didn't carry that air of shocked amusement. Nope, Cade's voice was filled with pure, masculine appreciation.

And he looked just as good as he sounded. Dark jeans, a forest green button-up shirt and a charming smile made him the sexiest guy in the room. Of course, she was pretty sure he could have been wearing fatigues or grease-stained coveralls or nothing at all and still have taken the sexiest title.

Oh. Nothing at all. She gave herself one second to enjoy that image, then stepped forward to join him.

"Hi," she greeted with a smile, reaching out to give his forearm a quick rub.

"I'm sorry I'm late—there was a dog emergency. Not the medical kind, but the howling kind. I wasn't sure if your grandmother was staying at the Wayfarers Inn to be close to your dad, but just in case she'd gone home, I wanted to make sure it was quiet for her. So, you know, I had to settle them. The dogs," she finished painfully.

Staring into Cade's wide eyes, she watched him try to process her babbling. Well. There you go. She hadn't fallen on her butt, but had managed to make an ass of herself anyway.

She wanted to groan. She was supposed to be sexy. Seductive, even. She'd have turned on her exceptionally high heels and walked right back out of the room, except that, well, yeah, the heels were exceptionally high. And Cade did look really good…

Too good to walk away from after just one strike.

"Okay, then," he said with a laugh. "I've got us a table already. Let's have a seat and you can run that by me one more time."

She glanced toward the dimly lit, secluded tables at the back. But they were all taken. Eden did a quick survey of the ocean-facing deck, looking for an unclaimed spot there. Nothing.

"Right over here," Cade said, gesturing toward the first-date section. The not-sure-you-want-to-see-it-through seating area. Where there were plenty of people-watching opportunities to distract from boring conversations, no hint of romantic potential and easy access to all escape routes.

*Well.*

Her inner seductress wanted to huff herself into a pout, then crawl into a corner. But Eden was too practical for that. She'd invited Cade out for a "welcome home, thank you for rescuing me from the tree" drink. He didn't know he was about to be seduced.

Yet.

So she followed his gesture, swaying a little more than usual thanks to the high, high heels, and made her way through the questioning looks and outright shock to their very public table.

Maybe the skirt was a little shorter than she'd realized? When Cade held out her chair, she glanced over her shoulder to offer a smile of thanks as she gratefully—if not gracefully—slid into it. And saw the look in his eyes.

Smoldering hot.

Thigh-clenchingly intense.

The kind of look a guy offered just before he stripped a girl naked.

Her breath caught tight in her chest. Eden wasn't sure what to do, what to say. She wanted to turn the rest of the way around, wrap her hands around his shoulders and climb up his long, hard body. She wanted to shift upward just a little, and try out that kiss from yesterday again. But this time with tongue.

She wanted to make him wish he'd gotten one of those dark, secluded booths, dammit.

Before she could give in to any of that temptation, he straightened. She had to force herself not to whimper when he moved away to round the table.

Then he sat down.

The look in his eyes was gone, as if it'd never existed. Instead, his gaze straddled the line between neutral and friendly. Like, now that he'd thought about seeing her naked, it just wasn't that interesting.

"Hey, Eden, I didn't know you were the buddy Cade was meeting," the waitress said, stepping over with a friendly smile for both of them. "What can I get you?"

*Buddy?* Eden, her teeth hurting from being clenched so tight, debated. She could be obvious and order a Screaming Orgasm or a Suck, Bang, Blow. Or try for sophisticated and order a glass of Chablis from the Naked Winery.

After a second, though, she sighed and went for the old standby. "A pomegranate margarita, blended. Thanks."

"Another beer," Cade added, lifting his bottle. As soon as the waitress left, he gave Eden one of those friendly, distant sort of smiles that she was sadly used to here at the Wayfarers. But never from him.

Despite the heat she'd have publically sworn was flaming between them the day before, he was suddenly acting like he barely knew her. What happened to treating her like she was a cute kid? Or his personal rescue victim. Neither role was one Eden particularly cared for—especially since neither one would get her into his pants any time soon. But they were better than being treated like a vague acquaintance from back in the day.

Determined, calling up the same stubborn focus she'd used to put herself through veterinary school, to build a business from the ground up in her hometown, in order to save the family property instead of moving anywhere easier, and to face down countless jokes at her expense, Eden squared her chin. She wanted Cade Sullivan, and by damn, she was going to have him.

"So what've you been up to lately?" he asked, leaning back in his chair. "Graduated high school, college. What else?"

"What else have I done since I graduated high school seven years ago?" she asked, snark overriding her seduction plans for a brief second. Thankfully her margarita arrived before she could say anymore. That gave Eden a second to mentally regroup. By the time Cade had said thanks for his beer, she'd decided on a plan.

It was one she figured Cade would approve of. Ready. Aim. Fire.

*Ready.*

She took a deep breath, the kind that added a little interest to the filmy fabric of her blouse, donned her sexiest, most seductive pout and leaned forward.

*Aim.*

"Do you know what I haven't done in, oh, I can't even remember how long?" she asked in a husky tone. The kind she'd use to share pillow talk, sex secrets and her favorite fantasy. The one that involved a naked Cade, the lake at midnight and a little light bondage.

Cade blinked. The neutral, aren't-you-a-cute-stranger

smile faded. He leaned back a little, like he wasn't sure what she might do next.

*Fire.*

"I haven't gone to the cliffs at night to watch the ocean," she told him. Unlike the lake, which had always been Cade's private love nest on his own property, the cliffs were just a mile away and open to the public. They were also a notorious makeout spot. She gave it a second for the words to sink in, for the visible tension to leave his shoulders, before reaching across the small table and running her fingernails gently over the back of his hand. "I love the power of the water at night, don't you? The crashing intensity. The uncontrolled, wild excitement. When was the last time you were on the cliffs, Cade? When was the last time you felt that kind of…excitement?"

Eden leaned back in her chair, lifting the margarita and sliding the bright pink straw between her teeth. Her eyes locked on his, she gently pursed her lips around the plastic and sucked.

"Mmm," she murmured before giving him a slow, inviting smile.

She put everything into that curve of her lips.

The heat of every fantasy.

The strength of every drop of sexual knowledge she had.

The hopes of every birthday wish she'd had since she was sixteen and first saw Cade Sullivan naked.

CADE WASN'T SURE what'd just happened.

One second, he was rolling nicely along, Eden playing her assigned part as the cute girl next door. The next, with just the flutter of those long eyelashes, she'd sent his body into overdrive.

This wasn't SOP.

And he was a guy who, once he'd decided on a course of action, followed standard operating procedures. His standards. His plan.

Neither of which included sporting a hard-on in the Wayfarers bar for a girl he'd already deemed off-limits. A girl who, whether she knew it or not, needed his help to keep from losing her home.

"Nope." He had to clear the desire from his throat before he continued. "No cliffside visits for me."

"That's too bad." Eden tilted her head to one side, a long silky strand of hair sliding over her cheek and down her throat like a caress before she tucked it away behind her ear. Her eyes, rich and dark, didn't leave his as she took another sip of her margarita.

Damn, she was good at that.

He licked his lips. Were hers as tasty as they looked?

Then something touched his leg. The slightest bump, then a slower, firmer press of her foot against his calf.

Cade damn near jumped out of his chair.

When had he lost control?

When had Eden become the kind of woman to take control?

And when had the entire idea become such a turn-on?

"So how's business?" he asked, shifting his legs a safe distance from hers. "You're working with animals, right? At the vet's or something?"

"I am the vet," she told him, slipping out of the seduction role for a second to give him a resigned look. "Maybe you missed it yesterday when you dropped me off? It's on my business card, too. The one I gave you with my phone number. You used it to call me to change times for this evening."

Cade winced. He wasn't sure which was better. To admit that he hadn't noticed anything except her the previous day. Or that he hadn't bothered to look at the card because he'd had her phone number committed to memory for years.

"So, really? You're a vet?" That was a safe topic. And a pertinent one, if he was going to figure out a way to help her pay off his father. "That's hard to believe."

"Why is it so hard to believe? Don't you think I'm smart enough? Good enough? Capable of keeping anything more troublesome than a dandelion alive?" She rolled her eyes before offering a disappointed shake of her head. "I didn't think you were the kind to buy into rumors. Just because I'm a little clumsy—and honestly, how it is that the few accidents I do have these days only happen when you're around is beyond me—does not mean I'm not great at my job."

*Ouch.*

Sore subject?

He might not live here anymore, but Cade knew the Ocean Point social games well enough to recognize a victim of them when he was lusting after her.

"That's not what I meant," he corrected with a frown. It was probably better that she thought he saw her like everyone else. But he didn't like being lumped in with the crowd, nor did he want her believing anything but the truth. Even if the truth meant he'd have to work a little harder to control his urge to grab her and kiss her like crazy. "I just meant you're really young."

"I graduated veterinary school a year ago, then interned in Sacramento for six months before opening my own clinic," she said, her chin lifting a fraction as she gave him a disappointed look.

"So you don't have to do four years of residency at a local veterinary hospital in order to practice?" he teased.

"Maybe if I'd gone into veterinary surgery," she said,

relaxing enough to smile at him again. "My focus is on companion animals." At his questioning look, she added, "Pets."

"Cats and dogs."

"Mostly, yes. I've worked with small farm animals, too. Not that there's much call for that around here," she said with a shrug.

"Didn't I see a goat at your place yesterday?" he remembered.

"That's Jojo," Eden told him. Then, after a hesitant look, she pulled her cell phone from her purse. A couple of taps and she held it up to show off a picture of the goat and an elderly man. "She belonged to a guy named Lloyd Flanders. He passed on a few months back and nobody knew what to do with her, so she came to live with me."

"Was he a friend?"

"He was a curmudgeonly old grump who lived in a senior center and kept a goat for a pet," Eden said, laughing and suddenly looking even sexier than she had sucking on that straw. "I volunteer at the Gentle Hands society. It's a non-profit group that brings together pets and the elderly. Or, in this case, finds homes for pets when their elderly companions pass on. Pets are a wonderful way of keeping people involved in life. They bring a lot of joy and love and even a number of health benefits. But they grieve like people do when they lose someone."

He didn't know why, but hearing that was like a punch to the gut. Cade stared at his beer for a second, trying to reel in the images flashing through his mind. He knew what that was like. The pain of losing someone you cared about, the intense emptiness that ate away at you, leaving a hollow shell that felt like it could never be filled.

Suddenly, he was feeling mighty empathetic toward that goat.

"I'm sorry," Eden said suddenly, reaching across the table to brush a gentle caress over the back of his hand. "I didn't mean to bore you. I know not everyone is an animal fan."

"You didn't bore me," he denied. But she had given him an idea. If he could get his grandmother to adopt a pet, and to use Eden as her vet, he'd bet Catherine would persuade a few of her friends to do the same. It wasn't brilliant as far as finance schemes went, but given that Cade had spent most of his life trying to avoid educating himself in anything having to do with his father's profession, it wasn't a bad start.

First, though, he had to tell her about the loan.

Cade grimaced. He'd faced guerrilla insurgents with more enthusiasm than he could muster up right that second.

"So how's your mother doing these days?" he asked, figuring that was as good a segue as any. Right up until a rarely seen fury flashed in Eden's eyes. She looked like she might chew the flame off the tabletop candle.

Whoa. He quickly changed the subject back to animals, asking about the cat she'd found the previous day.

Ten minutes later, he'd have been hard-pressed to offer up proof of her claim that not everyone was an animal fan. While it'd all clearly been a guise to gather dirt for gossip, four people had stopped at their table under the guise of asking Eden various vet-related questions, from what her hours were to did she treat pigeons. A couple of groups had made their way over to welcome Cade home and used the *how is business, are you setting him up with a pet* gambit to try and see why the two of them were together.

When a large party, mostly made up of people he'd gone to high school with, came through the door, Cade gave up. There was no way he could talk to her about the loan here.

"Would you like to go?" he asked. "Maybe somewhere quieter where we can talk."

Eden sucked in her bottom lip for a second, then released it so the soft pillow of flesh glistened temptingly. Her lashes fluttered and soft color washed her cheeks before she nodded.

There she was. That sweet girl next door. Some of the tension that'd gripped Cade, mostly in the southern regions, eased.

Then she lifted her drink and wrapped those lips around the straw again, giving a long, gentle suck. Cade was pretty sure the instant rush of blood to his dick might be a health threat.

"I'd love to go somewhere else," she said agreeably, setting her empty glass on the table and giving him that look again. The one that said she was pretty sure she knew what he looked like nude, and was just as sure that once she got him that way, she intended to bring him to his knees.

Cade was so freaking tempted to let her. Except for two things.

One, she was Eden. And he had a strict policy against getting naked with good girls like her. The kind that came with strings and ties and expectations.

And two, she was *Eden.* Which meant he was probably imagining all the sexual innuendo. This heat, flaming toward an inferno, was probably all in his imagination. And his pants.

"I haven't been to the cliffs lately," she told him as she rose, the soft fabric of her blouse settling around her slender curves in a most intriguing way. "Why don't we head that way and see how they look tonight."

Cade blinked.

*Uh-oh.*

# 5

EDEN WANTED TO DO a giddy happy dance, but she was horribly afraid that, even sitting in the passenger seat of his car, she'd somehow fall right off these shoes and break her neck. So she settled on giving Cade a wide smile as he parked at the gates leading to the cliffs. When he shut off the car, she waited for him to do the gentlemanly thing, coming around to the passenger's side.

This was it. Her chance. She called on every seductive wile she had in her body, every naughty idea she'd garnered from years of reading sexy romance novels.

When he opened the door, she looked up to give him her most seductive look, then made sure her body brushed against his taller, harder one as she straightened. The contrast of feeling him against her softer curves was like an erotic charge shooting through her body with the intensity of an electrical current.

Her head spun just a little and heat pooled, damp and sticky, between her thighs. She'd never felt anything like this. The want. The need. Like the very air around them was fueling her passion.

"It's gorgeous tonight, isn't it," she said a little breathlessly, leaning against the car for a second to get her balance. And, if she were honest with herself, to clear her head. He was so intense, so gorgeous, and so mouth-wateringly sexy. But she could handle this. She might be a little—okay, a lot—out of her league, but she was a quick study.

"Gorgeous."

But he wasn't looking at the stars, or toward the cliffs, Eden noticed. He was staring at her.

Hoo-boy, she breathed. Maybe she couldn't handle this.

It wouldn't be the first time she'd overestimated her abilities.

But she'd never let overestimating, or worrying, slow her down. So she ignored the nerves and offered him a bright smile before taking her first step toward the cliffs.

Too bad she tripped.

"Careful," he said with a laugh, reaching out to take her hand and lead her oh-so-carefully toward the ocean's view.

Again with total gentlemanly concern.

She wondered if that translated to his sexual technique. Was he a gentleman there, too? Always letting the lady come first. What did it take to push him over the edge? To make him so crazy that he lost all control.

Could she find out? Did she have it in her?

For another brief second, she worried that she was in over her head. A cautious little voice in her mind warned that she could ruin things between them. That she'd forever lose her hero, the guy who always rode to her rescue. And there was the very real possibility that she'd end up disappointing at least one of them, if not both.

Of course, with her breaking some bones was always a possibility. Or, given her track record, she might send them both tumbling over the cliff into the ocean.

Then again, who better to take that dive with than a navy SEAL, she laughed to herself.

Lust and amusement shushed the little voice, shooing it back to the quiet corner where it belonged. She wanted Cade and this was her shot. She wasn't going to be scared away from it by silly little fears.

"Not too many people come this way anymore," she told him as they stepped carefully, the moonlight their only guide along the overgrown path. Her words weren't quiet, but they were still almost drowned out by the pounding crash of the ocean beyond. "The view is better up the coast, the hike a little easier. But I like it here."

"Me too," he said, giving her a cautious smile. Not like he was afraid of her, or worried, really. But like he knew she was up to something and just wasn't sure what trap she was about to spring. Eden didn't mind. His knowing that she was playing the game made it that much more interesting.

"So why do you like it here better?" he asked. "The lack of tourists? Because it's closer to home? Or does the less manicured, more wild nature appeal to you?"

"Sure. But really I like it here because it's makeout point," she told him with a wicked laugh, her fingers curling into his as he helped her over the log separating the parking area and the tall grasses leading west.

His fingers tensed around hers for a second, as if he was going to yank her against him. Then he released her hand and, with a charmingly distant smile, gestured that she take the lead.

Well, well. Wasn't he Mr. Military Control?

No problem. She had more weapons in her arsenal. She'd just have to play through them until she found the one that worked. That pushed him over the edge and broke that control.

As if testing her resolve, or her balance, Eden's shoe twisted on the dirt path, her ankle going in the opposite direction. She grimaced. Falling at his feet wasn't quite what she'd had in mind.

"Maybe we should head back," he suggested. "Come back in the daylight, to check out the cliffs. Maybe in tennis shoes."

"I'm good," Eden told him with a stubborn shake of her head. No way. It wasn't that she thought tonight was her only chance with Cade. But she wasn't positive how long she could make that worrisome, cautioning voice stay quiet. She'd learned a long time ago that if she wanted to have any fun, to do anything exciting, she had to stay one step ahead of that voice.

So she took the next curve more carefully, determined not to ruin her chance to be seen as something other than one of Cade's rescue projects.

Then her toes caught an exposed root. Her breath wooshed and her stomach spun as she stumbled. Cade's arm shot out, catching her before she lost her balance.

"Oops." She laughed, righting herself. "Maybe I should just try this barefoot."

"Here," he said with a rueful shake of his head. He reached out to pull her against him, his arm steadying her wobbling gait. "Hang on to me."

Her stomach was doing the tripping now, falling all over itself as her body shifted closer to his. She caught her breath, the salty brine air mixed with the scent of Cade's cologne. Ocean meets forest, all wrapped up in the heady possibilities of nighttime.

She leaned closer, shivering a little as her body aligned with his. Mmm, mmm, Eden hummed. Chalk one up for klutziness.

His legs were so long, reaching almost to her waist, even in her heels. The muscled strength of his arm was comforting, but steady around her shoulders. Her mind flooded with visions of his body, just as strong and steady, guiding her into all sorts of tricky sexual positions. Wasn't that going to be handy?

For a second, that little voice peeked out of the corner to warn Eden that she was crazy, and quite possibly morally questionable to be chasing after a guy simply for sex.

It wasn't just sex, she argued with herself. It was her only chance to live out the fantasy. To have this one last shot at Cade before she likely had to move and say goodbye for good.

The voice, probably stocking up its energy for *I told you so's,* scooted back into the quiet corner.

Leaving Eden to figure out how to go about her poorly planned seduction.

"Do you spend a lot of time at the ocean?" she asked, wondering what he did when he was living his real life. Besides all the hero stuff, of course. "I mean, navy, ocean. I know you probably see your fair share of water."

Cade's shrug was a lesson in delight, since it meant his chest did a subtle shift against the side of her breast. Eden's nipples perked up while desire stretched, like a waking cat, in her belly.

"Not so much anymore," he said. "I used to. A couple buddies and I spent a lot of time at the beach. Phil was from the Midwest, so being by the water was his idea of hanging out at a candy shop."

There was something in his words she'd never heard before. A heaviness. Her heart ached, though she didn't know why.

"Did he get tired of candy?" she teased as they reached the cliffs. The ocean, pounding power in the night, was a study of black noise. "Or did you just get tired of all the bikini-wearing babes throwing themselves at you?"

She felt his silent laugh against her shoulder.

"Does that ever get old?" he asked, sounding amused. But that…something. Pain? She wasn't sure what it was in his tone. But she wanted to fix it. To make it—and him—feel better.

Since he hadn't actually answered either of her questions, Eden waited. Even though they were still now, she didn't step out of his arms.

"Other than work, I don't go to the beach much these days," he finally admitted, his words so low they were almost carried away by the ocean breeze. Tension radiated from him, tight and edgy. Like he wanted to explode, but knew the damage would be catastrophic. Eden wondered what it was like, having that kind of control.

She didn't say anything. She just waited. But she did tighten her arm around his waist. It wasn't like she thought he *needed* her support. But she didn't mind offering it, just in case.

"We lost Phil last year," Cade finally said, his gaze locked on the churning waves. "I guess you'd call it a routine mission, although they never really are. He was taken out by shrapnel to the head. Never felt a thing."

*No!* Horrified, Eden's fingers tightened on his waist. She knew Phil was one of his best friends. Phil, a guy named Blake and Cade were in so many of the pictures Catherine loved to share. Once, about five years back, Cade had brought the two men home with him for the holidays. Eden hadn't met them, but had heard they were great guys. And in the few, rare times Cade ever spoke of his SEAL work, he always mentioned Blake and Phil.

To lose one of his best friends? He must be devastated.

"I'm so sorry," she whispered.

Beyond hurting for his loss, wondering how he was dealing with it, a fear she'd never felt took hold in Eden's gut. Cade was a hero. A SEAL. He went out and did the impossible, like Superman. To her, he'd always been invincible.

The sudden realization that he wasn't was terrifying.

"Hey, it's a risk of the job. We all face it," he said, shrugging and giving her that charming smile he'd perfected. A smile that pushed people away, she realized, her eyes widening in the dark. That smile put up a wall so solid, most people wouldn't even realize it was there.

He acted like it was no big deal. But she knew better. She couldn't imagine losing a best friend. A comrade in arms. One of Catherine's favorite photos was of a young Cade just out of boot camp. Eden was pretty sure one of the guys in that sterling framed picture was Phil. To lose that?

She took a deep breath. And here she'd been worrying about getting a little fantasy nookie before her life fell apart. What did that say about her?

"You're not gonna get all girly on me, are you?" he asked, looking down and giving her a laughing sort of shoulder nudge. Then he frowned and shifted, so he was standing in front of her instead of at her side.

She didn't realize she was crying until he reached out, sliding his index finger over her cheek to wipe away a tear.

"You're sweet," he said, his smile shifting. It was still charming. After all, was that gorgeous face capable of anything less? But there was a warmth there Eden hadn't seen before. Something beyond charm, that touched her heart. That scared the hell out of her.

"And you're a hero," she told him, trying for a teasing smile. It was a little shaky at the corners, but it was the best she could do.

"You ever think about setting aside those rose colored glasses?" he asked, a hint of cynicism shining through for a second before he pulled the charm back around him like a cozy blanket. "You're gonna get taken advantage of if you aren't careful."

She'd rather just be taken.

But for the first time since she'd hurled herself into this crazy plan to seduce Cade, she wondered if she really knew him.

Realizing she was on the verge of talking herself out of making a move, she figured it was now or never.

She wet her lips, then, before good sense could warn her to stop, she stood on tiptoe, her fingers pressed to his chest for balance, and brushed her lips over his.

Much like his goodbye peck the day before, it wasn't threatening. Instead it was soft. Gentle. Almost sweet, except for the needy aching heat it inspired low in her belly. For just a second, his lips moved against hers, welcoming. Warming.

She'd never wanted anything, *anyone,* like she did Cade Sullivan. Never needed anything more than for him to want her, too.

Eden slowly pulled back, her eyes searching his.

"Is that a belated thank-you for getting you out of the tree? Or a payment in advance for helping you walk back to the car without breaking a leg?" he teased, his expression more avuncular than hot and bothered.

She dropped back to her heels, working hard to keep from letting the pout take hold. That's it? She worked up all her nerve, finally made her first move and he brushed her off? Eden glared past Cade's shoulder, staring at the water while she tried to gather a little composure.

Give it up, she decided, wanting to cry again but for a very different reason this time. She forced herself to plaster a little fake cheer on her face and tried to smile as she looked up at him.

And saw something.

Maybe?

She peered closer.

He had that same chilly, distant smile going on. His expression was as neutral as Switzerland. But his eyes had a glow. Maybe it was the moonlight reflecting off the water, but she'd swear she saw heat there. Passion. Desire.

Her stomach tightened. Her breath caught and excitement swirled through her entire body.

He wanted her.

Oh, he clearly didn't want to want her.

But he did.

She should focus on the message in his smile, the coolness in his tone.

But it was so much more fun to see what she could do to encourage the passion in his gaze.

"Last week was my birthday," she said impulsively.

"Yeah?" Looking delighted at the safe subject, he gave her a playful shoulder pat. The kind you'd offer a puppy who'd finally mastered a clever trick. "Happy belated birthday, then. I hope you have a great year."

Eden knew he wanted her to stick with her friendly girl-next-door role. It was safer—he didn't have to worry about complicating things with sex. Or brushing her off, she reminded herself, trying to swallow past the imagined nasty taste rejection would leave. That was probably complicated, too. And not nearly as fun. She tilted her head to the side, grateful for the salty ocean breeze cooling her warm cheeks.

Safe route?

Or dive in with both feet.

"I think I will. You see, I made a birthday wish. It's the same wish I've made for the last handful of years."

"What's your wish?" he asked in a slow, cautious tone. Well, he wasn't a well-trained special ops guy for nothing.

"To have sex with you."

CADE WAS PRETTY SURE Eden could have kicked him in the balls at that moment and he wouldn't have felt a damned thing. Nope, his brain was frozen in shock, while his body was inflamed with need.

He gave a quick, contemplative glance at the cliffs. How far was the jump? He'd gone deeper—he'd probably survive. And it'd be less risky than what he faced at this moment.

Because right now, the threat wasn't the cute little brunette standing in front of him. Nope, it was his own desires. Desires he shouldn't feel, knew better than to entertain and usually pretended didn't exist.

Cade had rules. Strict ones that he lived his relationships by. The first being that there were no strings involved. Past, present or future. And with Eden, Cade had lifelong relationship ties that went all the way back to hauling her off her trike when she'd run it into the bushes at the base of his driveway.

They had a history.

They had a friendship. The closest he'd ever had with a woman.

What they shouldn't have was heat. Passion. Sexual needs that arced between them like a live electric current, threatening to burn down anything it touched.

"Look…"

*What?*

How did he explain his rules? Ask her to promise not to get ugly when he walked away? To accept that once he walked, they wouldn't be playing again the next time he was home? To other women, it was easy. But to Eden? He'd sound like a prick. And while he might laugh off her always calling him her hero, he wasn't excited about the idea of destroying that myth *and* hurting her feelings all at the same time.

"Poor Cade," she laughed, like she thought it was funny that she'd tied him in knots then forced him to choose between his morals and his body's pounding needs. "It's hard, isn't it?"

Oh, baby, she had no idea.

Then her gaze changed. Went from amused to smoldering. She leaned back a little and made a show of giving him a long look. Down. Then up. Then back down again.

His dick throbbed. Her actions were probably some kind of sexual Morse Code for *do me and do me now*.

"Hmm," she murmured, those luscious full lips smiling now. Not the friendly smile he was used to, either. This one was pure sexual challenge. It was like she could read his mind. Which only added to the needy ache pressing against his zipper.

"All you have to do is tell me you don't want me," she said, giving him a look of sweet challenge through her lashes. As if testing his resolve, and daring him to lie straight to her face, she stepped closer.

Close enough that the tips of her breasts brushed his chest. That her breath was warm on his face. That he could see the sparkling humor in her dark eyes.

That was the thing that slayed him about Eden. No matter what was going on, what current disaster she'd dropped herself into, she always found a way to laugh. To enjoy herself.

Why the hell was that so sexy?

Why was she so damned irresistible?

"Look," he tried again. What had she said he could do to make her back off? He couldn't remember.

"Haven't you ever been a birthday wish before?" she asked when he couldn't find any words—or thoughts—to stop her. "Something you really, really wanted and knew you couldn't get yourself. Something that was going to take a little bit of magic."

"There's no such thing as magic," he managed to grind out as he tried to keep from moving too much. Every breath was a lesson in torture, pressing his chest closer against those soft, gloriously full breasts. He wanted to touch them. To feel them. To weigh them in his palms while running his thumbs over her nipples.

Oh, God. Her nipples. Nothing turned Cade on more than a set of gorgeous breasts.

"You don't believe in magic?" Upping the torture, she traced the fingertips of one hand up his arm, a whisper-soft journey toward his shoulder. Then she changed the angle, so her nails scraped ever-so-gently down his chest. "I think it's very real. Some might call it luck. That special something that brings everything and everyone into the right place at the right time so something special can happen."

"We make things happen," he said, barely aware of his words since the few drops of blood that weren't pounding their way south were totally focused on her fingers, now winding a path of torture around his hardening nipple.

"Of course we do," she agreed, her eyes molten now. So hot, so filled with passion and power that he was surprised they weren't shooting flames. Talk about magic. All she had to do was give him that look and he was done. All of the rules, all good sense, gone.

"But since I did build up a lot of years of birthday candle wishes, don't you think it's about time we made some *very* good…"

Pressing closer, close enough that he could feel her nipples through her bra, she stood on tiptoe.

"Things."

She scattered whisper-soft kisses along his jaw, her warm breath a vivid contrast to the cool ocean breeze.

"Happen."

Her teeth scraped along his throat. Cade growled. Sweet he could resist. But this sexy side of naughty?

He had no more willpower.

It was like she'd found the key to the part of him he kept locked tight. The part he mostly denied. The part that wanted her, wanted a future, believed he could actually have a relationship. The part that pretended the statistics regarding military relationships didn't apply to him. That he could beat the odds. That he wanted to try.

Or, more likely, she'd hit his horny button and he was about to explode.

Either way, there was no holding back any longer.

# 6

GRABBING EDEN BY THE WAIST, Cade pulled her tight against his hips, grinding his hard, throbbing dick against her soft warmth. He took her mouth. His lips slanted, finding the right angle, pressing and sliding against hers. Why did she fit so perfectly? Her mouth opened to his, inviting him in with a soft moan.

His tongue swept in, testing.

Tasting.

She was delicious.

His hands rushed over her body with desperate haste. She, on the other hand, was taking the slow, leisurely route, her palms smoothing his biceps before her nails scraped the muscle gently. He shivered. Freaking shivered. He'd been with plenty of women. A lot who saw his body as a damned fine example of masculine perfection.

But he'd never felt worshipped before.

Never felt that this—the sex—was as much about him as it was the end result. Doing it with a SEAL. Doing it with a Sullivan. Getting to the orgasm.

But Eden was all about him.

The real him.

Cade wasn't sure what swelled more at that thought. His ego or his dick.

Said dick did a little throbbing dance in his pants, as if to yell, *Yo, dude. This is my time. Egos check it at the zipper.*

Taking his cue from below, Cade focused.

*On Eden.*

She was perfect. Her mouth fit his like they'd been made for each other, her lips gliding over his mouth in a whisper-soft caress that seduced all the more because of its sweetness.

*On her body.*

It was delicious. Soft, curvaceous and welcoming as she snuggled up against him.

*On how she made him feel.*

Like the hero she joked he was. Like he could do anything, be anything, because she believed in him. Like making her feel as incredible as he did. Like giving her the kind of sensual delights that would blow her mind, make her scream with pleasure, send her body melting into orgasmic overload.

Yeah. He could do all that.

He took the kiss deeper.

Slower.

Their tongues danced, sliding hot and slick against each other. In and out, twirling and licking. The dance was slow. Sensually sweet. Cade felt like he was spinning in a gentle eddy, floating softly around the edges of passion as it pulled them in tighter, closer to the center.

He relaxed as the cool ocean breeze skimmed his bare arms, wondering when he'd ever felt this mellow during a kiss. Usually it was all hard, driving force, with passion pounding, demanding, taking control.

This was nice.

Sweet.

Easy.

Then Eden shifted, her fingers digging into his shoulders and her breasts pressing, hard, against his chest. Cade's body reacted like she'd just poked at his passion meter with a cattle prod. She sucked his tongue deep inside her mouth. He growled, every single muscle in his body going rock hard. It was like an inward orgasm. Sensation exploded inside Cade, making him quake with desire. His fingers shook as his hands raced down her back, cupping her ass and pulling her tight against his throbbing erection. Her moan reverberated against his tongue, adding a whole new dimension of pleasure to the delights she was offering.

She wrapped one leg around his thigh, so her hot core was pressed against him. He was breathing like a freight train now, desperate, needy, craving her like a drug he couldn't live without.

Holy hell. He'd thought she was nice and sweet?

Clearly, Eden knew a thing or two about torture.

On the edge of losing all semblance of control—and with it the image he always carefully maintained in Ocean Point that he was a gentleman—Cade pulled back. Just a little. Enough to see the passion fogging her dark eyes, to delight in the sexual need clear on her face.

Her need for him.

A need he was suddenly desperate to satisfy.

"You know what I like?" she asked quietly, her head falling backward, leaving the long line of her throat bare in the moonlight. "I like having my nipples tweaked. I want to feel what it's like to have you suck them into your mouth. To swirl your tongue around and nibble on them."

Cade was pretty sure his brain exploded right then and there. His knees almost gave out. His dick pounded against his zipper, determined to get out and play.

All this time, he'd figured her for a sweet, shy girl next door. Instead she was a sexual siren, a seductress with amazing sensual powers. It was like she'd delved into his deepest sexual fantasies and decided to bring them to life.

"I'll bet you taste delicious," he muttered, stepping back so he could clearly see her body, hidden in moonlight and fabric. He couldn't do much about the lack of lighting, but he could damned sure get rid of the material.

His fingers made frantic work of the buttons of her blouse, spreading the filmy fabric wide. Her skin glowed like white silk in the moonlight, a vivid contrast against her red bra. Cade traced the curve, just there, where the satin was edged in black ribbon. His mouth watered. He wanted to taste her. All of her.

But he knew his limits.

Her breath was coming faster now, those satin covered breasts quivering with every inhalation. Cade wanted to rip the red bra away. To touch, to taste. But he couldn't. The minute the bra came off, he'd lose every last bit of control.

So he feasted on her breasts with his eyes, but kept his mouth away. And his hands occupied.

Otherwise he'd take her with hard, fast desperation.

For no other woman would he ignore most of his rules of engagement so he could feast on her sexiness. But this was Eden. His sweet girl next door. The one who'd haunted his dreams for years. He had to taste her. Just a little taste. He had to hear her come, just once. But that was it. Just once, just a taste. He couldn't have more—wouldn't allow himself satisfaction—until he'd talked to her about expectations, made sure she knew the rules.

And there was no way in hell he was having that talk right now, with her body so hot and ready for him.

Unable to resist any longer, he cast a quick, desperate look around. There, ten feet to the north, was a crop of rocks. Picnickers used them, he remembered. They'd be good enough, except he had a different treat in mind.

"Over here."

He didn't wait for her to follow.

He simply swept her into his arms and carried her across the rocky ground.

"Afraid I'll fall at your feet?" she teased, her hands sweeping around the back of his neck, fingers tickling the hair at his nape.

Cade grinned down at her, suddenly feeling more like the romantic hero she saw him as than the horny guy in a hurry he knew he was.

"More afraid I'll fall at yours," he admitted, sinking his face into the silky strands of her hair and breathing deep before setting her gently on the broad stone surface. "You're a handful."

"Surely I'm not too much for you?" she asked, her tone not teasing anymore. Cade had to wonder what kind of guys she'd been hanging out with to ask such a crazy question.

Instead of answering, or releasing her, he held her gaze with his, refusing to let her look away. He leaned in slowly, taking her mouth with his. Softly at first. Just a glide of lips over lips.

She sighed.

He slipped his tongue along the edge of her teeth, sucking gently on the full pillow of her lower lip.

She whimpered.

He plunged his tongue deep, in and out, intense and fast.

Her nails bit into the back of his neck as she hung on, groaning in delight.

Cade shifted, angling his body to bump his hips against her knees. As if she'd been reading his mind forever, she shifted, clamping one thigh on either side of his and pulling him closer.

He'd found heaven, right here between her legs.

Suddenly desperate to explore more, Cade let go of Eden's waist, his hands rushing over her hips and down the fabric of her skirt to find the soft flesh of her thighs.

"Your hands are so warm," she breathed against his mouth. "So strong."

"Shh," he told her, releasing her mouth to trail tiny kisses down her throat. His hand skimmed up her thigh, under that tight little skirt. "You talk, you forfeit the fun."

"You mean you're calling all the shots?" she clarified, the last word coming out a squeak when his finger found the edge of her panties.

"I plunder, you surrender," he confirmed with a grin. She caught on fast.

"I never surrender," she breathed as his fingers curled under the elastic, sweeping inward, combing through her damp curls.

"Sure you will," he vowed.

He was going to make sure of it.

EDEN HAD SPENT a lot of time over the years imagining her and Cade together. She'd written stories in her mind, created visual odes to sexual pleasure starring the two of them.

She'd had no clue.

Not a freaking single one.

He was amazing. Incredible. He was going to ruin her for every other man for the rest of her life. And she didn't care. After all, just the fantasy of him had ruined her for all men up until this point. Why ruin a perfect track record?

His hands were so hot, his fingers sure as they skimmed

her thigh, teasing their way under the edge of her panties. Her body throbbed, wet, needy.

She wiggled a little, trying to entice his fingers. Hoping he'd touch her. Needing him to relieve the pressure that was building, tight as a spring, low in her belly.

He angled himself between her thighs, lifting her with both hands and scooting her further up the rock. The contrast of his warm body, hard muscles and unforgiving stone added an extra erotic edge to the passion coursing through her. His hand swept down her legs to her ankles, making her shiver as he gripped her feet just above the little leather straps of her shoes. Still gripping her ankles, he lifted her feet so they rested flat on the rock with her knees aimed at the sky.

"I feel like a sacrifice to the sea gods," Eden laughed breathlessly, propping herself up on her elbows to watch him through passion-hazed eyes. He looked so hot, so sexy. And so much better pleasuring her up close than he'd ever looked with someone else far away.

"They'd have parted the water for you," he told her before pressing an open mouth kiss against her knee, just inside where it curved. She shivered, delight skimming up her thigh like hot water over a hot skillet. With his eyes locked on hers, he kept the kisses climbing. She held her breath, her body getting tenser the higher he climbed. By the time he reached the tautly stretched fabric of her skirt, she was ready to pass out from lack of oxygen.

As he continued pressing kisses up her thigh, he slid the material higher with his palms, skimming their hard warmth along the outside of her legs as he went. He felt so good, those fingers so powerful and strong against her soft flesh.

"You're gorgeous," he said, his words husky and low, hanging on the night air.

"You're looking at me in the dark," she teased.

"I've got excellent night vision. And even better night skills." He pushed her skirt up to her waist, so her cherry-red thong was on full view. Even with the moon behind him, she could still see the glint of passion in his gorgeous eyes.

"Night skills?" she asked, her words hitching higher when her now-bare butt settled back down on the cold stone. "Is that a military thing?"

"Why don't we find out," he told her, lifting her legs and draping both knees over his shoulders. "You ready to surrender?"

Surrender? Eden wasn't sure she could even think.

Had she ever been in such an erotic position? Had a man ever looked at her like he was going to eat her alive, and make sure she loved every second of it?

She'd haul out the white flag and wave it like crazy.

Except then the game would be over.

"Oh, no," she breathed instead. She gave him her best *go ahead, I dare you* look. "You haven't won yet."

"Maybe not. But you're about to," he promised.

Then he got down to the feast.

His hands cupped the firm flesh of her butt, lifting her to the perfect angle for his mouth.

Keeping it slow, reining in the desperation, he used his tongue. Licked a wet path from the inside of her knee, all the way to her now sopping wet curls. Breathing in, as if he were addicted to her musky scent, he blew a puff of air against the quivering flesh between her thighs.

Eden gasped. Her fingers curled, then uncurled, like she was trying to grab the rock.

He slid his tongue along her clitoris.

Eden moaned.

He slipped one finger, then two, into her hot, aching depths. Swirling, pressing, then sliding back out.

Oh, baby.

He was incredible.

She wanted him like crazy. More, she wanted him to want her. To ache for her. To be more desperate for her than he'd ever been for anyone else in his life. Eden wanted to be special.

That need, that hope, overcame all of her inhibitions.

Remembering the intensity in his eyes when he'd looked at her breasts, the way he'd reached for them then stopped himself, she reached behind her back and unhooked her bra.

Quick, with a grace she rarely showed in anything else, she slipped out of her blouse and bra, then lay back on the stone again so her body was bared to the night sky, the ocean air, and Cade's hot eyes.

"Holy hell," he breathed against her thigh. She wasn't sure if the new wetness there was her own dripping juices, or if he was drooling.

Oh, please, her fragile ego begged. Let him drool over her.

With that in mind, she cupped her own breasts, using every move she wanted him to do on herself. She squeezed. She ran the tip of her fingers around her sensitive areola. She scraped her nail across the pebbled nipple, making herself gasp.

She could feel his eyes on her breasts. They were hot, intense as he watched from below. Even more turned on by his stare than she was with her own ministrations, she worked herself harder, her fingers swirling, plucking, teasing. His tongue swirled, plunged, sipped in time with her movements. She set the pace. She held all the control. She'd never had this much power, this much pleasure.

Then she cupped both breasts in her palms, the nipples jutting between her knuckles as she squeezed. Her hands worked the soft mounds, heating her own flesh as the cool ocean breeze nipped at the beaded tips in an erotic contrast. Her moans rose, her butt along with them as she pressed closer to his mouth, entreating him to take her higher.

His tongue stabbed, in and out. His thumb worked her throbbing clitoris, pressing, then skimming the swollen surface.

Her breath came in pants now. Her body rose higher. Her mind shut down. All she could do was feel.

His teeth nipped.

She exploded.

A fireworks of stars bombarded her closed lids, her head full back against the hard rock as she dug her heels into Cade's shoulders to press herself higher. To wring every drop of ecstasy out of the orgasm.

She just kept coming and coming.

Wave after wave of sensations poured through her body.

In time with the crashing ocean below, the power of her climax was overwhelming. It was like being swept away on a sea of passion, helpless against the intensity.

Slowly, so so slowly, she floated back into her body. Awareness seeped in as she felt Cade's body, still between her thighs. His hands slowly caressed her thighs, her butt. Like he was gently guiding her back.

Her own fingers soothed now, petting her exhausted flesh, warming her nipples as the passion eased, as her body settled.

"Wow," she finally breathed. "As in, oh, my God. Wow."

Cade's laugh sounded pained. Like he was hurting.

Poor baby.

Eden forced her eyes open, using every bit of strength she had to tilt her head upright. Her lashes fluttered, eyelids so heavy as she forced them open to stare at her sexy hero.

The skin was taut across his face, as if he was facing high levels of pain. If his body was anywhere near as turned on as hers had been, he probably was.

And she was just the girl to take care of that for him.

Excitement giving her new levels of energy, Eden's mind raced with all the things she wanted to do to him. On that body. Oh, baby.

She sat up, shoving her bra and blouse aside. She didn't care that her skirt was bunched up around her waist and her panties probably feeding the sharks in the ocean below.

"Yum," she said with a soft laugh. "I have to admit, I think you got my surrender there. But now it's your turn."

CADE'S ERECTION PRESSED against the stone's surface, throbbing so hard he was surprised it didn't jackhammer the surface to dust.

Before it took over, snapping his tenuous hold on control, he pushed away from the rock and put some much needed distance between him and Eden.

"What…?" Her shock was clear as the words rang out in question.

He was in trouble.

He'd gone over the side of an aircraft carrier once. He'd had total faith in himself, his training and his calculations. Still, there had been one brief second when he'd jumped that he'd questioned his own sanity. The dive had taken forever, and had been over in an instant.

That's how he felt now.

Like he was in over his head, and no matter how much he thought he was controlling the situation, there was every chance that it could all go to hell as soon as he landed.

She was five feet away, and yet, it was like she was still wrapped around him.

He could taste her, rich and heady, on his tongue.

He could feel her, soft and welcoming, against his body.

Her cries of delight, low and husky, would echo through his dreams tonight.

She was…

Wow.

And she was sliding off the rock and coming his way.

Oh, God.

Her skin glowed white in the moonlight, a vivid contrast against the black skirt she'd thankfully tugged into place. Her berry-red nipples were still swollen, well-worked by her skilled fingers.

Cade tried to shove his hands in the front pockets of his slacks, but the fabric was pulled so taut, they wouldn't fit. So he settled on crossing his arms over his chest and glaring at the ocean.

"Is that how it's supposed to end?" Eden asked, her tone a combination of amusement and sexy contentment as she came closer. She didn't touch him, thankfully. He wasn't sure his slacks could handle it. But she stopped close enough that her scent, honeysuckles again, invaded his senses. Close enough that he could feel the warmth radiating off her slender body.

End? It shouldn't have started. God, what was he thinking? He was supposed to be telling her about the loan his father was calling in. He should be helping her fix the mess her mother had left, one she didn't even know was about to crash down on her.

Instead, he'd gone down on her in a public park.

Wasn't he a prince.

"That's how it should end," he said. Then he realized how callous that sounded and almost groaned aloud. This was why he never did good girls—especially not here, in his hometown. He always stuck with ones who knew the game plan well before the panties were torn off.

But it was too late. Eden's panties were who knew where, and she was looking at him like she wasn't sure if he was the greatest thing since milk chocolate or a big mean ogre who was about to ruin her dreams.

He knew he should take the ogre route. He should be a hard-ass, tell her the way things were, and apologize for not filling her in before he'd stuck his tongue inside her body.

He should let his mistake be the perfect excuse to end things quickly and cleanly, before they got complicated. Or ugly.

Except this was Eden.

So things were already complicated. And he never, ever wanted to make her life ugly.

So instead of explaining, even nicely, why this had been a mistake, he did the most stupid thing ever.

He pulled her into his arms. Still staring at the ocean beyond, he sighed.

"I've got to get back to the hospital," he lied. "So I guess only one of us gets to win tonight."

Unable to resist, he brushed a kiss over her soft hair and added, "Sorry, babe. It was incredible."

# 7

THE NEXT DAY Eden sat at her desk, staring out at the green fields beyond the barn that served as her veterinary clinic and swore she could still feel tiny little aftershock orgasms. And she had to assume, given that it'd essentially been a solo party, that on the sexual Richter scale that'd been an average quake. She couldn't wait to find out what a full-blown, totally naked, penetration-rocks explosion was going to feel like.

"The question is," she murmured to the dog weaving between her feet and the chair legs, "will I get to find out? Cade wasn't exactly beating the drum for a do-over last night."

It was more like he was doing his damnedest to hurry her along before she got ideas. Either sticky ones that would require him to make excuses, or dramatic girly ones that would inspire him to run like hell.

But she hadn't done either. After he'd practically carried her back to the car, since she was even less sturdy on her high heels after he'd rocked her world, they'd kept up small talk. Friendly, meaningless social chitchat, as they'd both been raised to excel in. Then he'd walked her to the door, brushed a kiss over her lips and hurried off to see his father in ICU.

She'd wanted to ask if that was just an excuse, since everyone knew Cade wasn't a big fan of his father. And she wasn't sure if ICU was open at ten at night. But for a Sullivan, usual rules never applied. The insecure part of her, the one she tried to pretend didn't exist, had immediately wondered if Cade regretted their little love-fest.

The rest of her, the part that liked to dive headfirst into life and deal with the fallout later, shrugged off the worry. What good would it do to obsess? If he'd hated it, she'd deal with that when she saw him.

Or she'd sit here and freak out.

Sighing, Eden chewed on her thumbnail, wishing the knotted nerves in her stomach would unravel enough so she could eat something more nutritious for lunch.

A late lunch at that, since her clinic had had people in and out all day. Other than the three scheduled appointments, she'd had seven visitors, all casually moseying through to see how her day was coming along.

The first three had amused her. They'd all been schoolmates from town who'd wanted to congratulate her on trading up. Trading from what, she wasn't sure. The next two visitors were harmless irritations, both social-climbing hangers-on who were clearly looking for something juicy to make them popular with the Oceanfront ladies. But the last two, who Eden actually didn't know, had apparently learned their interviewing skills from the paparazzi. Or the inquisition.

Since none of them had pets, or the brains to pretend they might be checking into her services as well as her personal life, she didn't feel bad about sending them away without a speck of fuel for their gossip.

Now she was hiding with the stack of files sent to her

by local animal shelters and groups. The Shady Acres Retirement Home had five new residents this month and Eden wanted to visit in the morning with a list of possible pets for them to adopt.

"Eden…?"

Trying not to growl, Eden laid down her pen and eyed the dog.

"Think we can pretend we're not here?" she asked the small gray mutt. "Because you know, they're only after gossip."

"Eden?" the voice called, louder and more insistent.

"Back here," she admitted, rising resignedly to meet the eighth interruption of the morning. "In the office."

Some—mostly the Oceanfront set—would say that calling a small room in a barn an office was a little on the ambitious side. But, hey, it had a desk, a phone and internet access. A few framed certificates, her veterinary license and a huge orange filing cabinet completed the office requirement checklist.

"Oh, there you are, dear," the older woman said breathlessly, reaching the doorway before Eden had even crossed the small room. Eden eyed the stubby legs beneath that vivid floral dress. Had she run?

"Hi, Mrs. Carmichael," she greeted cautiously.

"I brought Paisley in," the heavyset woman said, stating the obvious since the cat was draped over her shoulders. She, not the cat, glowered at Mooch, who was cowering behind Eden's feet. "I don't want her scared, though."

"She got to know Mooch the other day when she was here visiting," Eden said cheerfully, holding out her fingers for the cat to sniff. With a jaw-snapping yawn, the feline arched her back, then stood on her owner's shoulder to leap into Eden's arms.

"Whoa, well, hello," Eden said with a laugh, falling

back a step under the sudden weight of the cat. "Aren't you the sweetheart? And a take-charge sweetheart, at that."

Impressed that the older woman could cart the twenty-pound feline around like she did, Eden decided comfort was more important than trying to prove she was as strong as a sixty-year-old. Hooking her foot around the wheel of her chair, she pulled it over next to the visitors' chair. Just in case Mrs. Carmichael was the stay-close-to-her-pet type.

As soon as they settled—Eden with the cat in her lap—Mooch came over and stood, front paws on Eden's legs, to say hi.

"Watch that," Mrs. Carmichael cautioned, half rising as if to throw herself between the dog and cat.

Eden's heart, always a sucker for anyone who loved animals, went soft.

"She'll be okay," she promised. But she put a cautioning hand on the dog's collar, just in case.

It only took two sniffs before the cat was purring and rubbing her white-spotted face against the dog's ear.

"Well, will you look at that?" Mrs. Carmichael gave the pair a baffled glance before turning, wide-eyed to Eden. "She never gets along with other animals. Or people, for that matter."

"Savannahs are known for being cautious," Eden agreed, rubbing her knuckle under the feline's chin. The cat was not only purring like a motorboat now, but doing the comfy circle dance in Eden's lap. "But once they make a bond, it's a pretty tight one."

"Hmm."

"What's wrong?" Eden asked, smiling at the grumpy-faced older woman.

"I didn't realize you were quite so well-read on rare cats. Or that you had such a way with animals."

"It is my job," Eden added, figuring it was easier to

smile than to grind her teeth. Even though that would have felt a hell of a lot better. What was up with people? They thought they had her so easily pegged? *Nice-enough misfit, a little klutzy, always good for a laugh.*

"Well, yes, but I suppose I thought you mostly tended animals like this one." The older woman gestured to Mooch, who was sniffing around her shoes like they were made of bacon.

"I try not to discriminate," Eden said gently, offering the raggedy looking mutt an indulgent look, even as she continued to rub her fingers under the chin of a cat that cost more than her car. "Mooch was abandoned when his owner died. He'd been with her for twelve years, and in the end, he was her only companion. Her only company. When she had a stroke, he shredded a window screen to escape, ran back and forth in front of the house, barking until he got someone's attention."

Mrs. Carmichael's polished lips rounded as she looked—actually *looked*—at the dog.

"All the owner's family wanted when she was gone was her money, anything they could sell for profit. They were going to have the dog put down."

"No!"

As if Eden had just taken a gun and aimed it at the canine, the older woman snatched him up and cuddled his wriggling body close in her arms.

"It happens a lot," Eden said sadly. She hated that. Hated that she couldn't do more to stop it. Her estimation of the other woman had sure taken a high leap, though. "The shelters, rescue groups and other vets know I take in special cases and try to find them homes. One of them called me about Mooch and I convinced the new owners to let me keep him."

"Does he have a home, then?"

Hmm. Quickly shielding her considering look, Eden shook her head slowly, letting her chin droop just a little. "He doesn't. I'm trying to find him one, though. I can't keep too many dogs here myself—it's just not fair to them."

Mooch, the consummate player, chose that moment to lick the older woman's chin and give a friendly yip. Mrs. Carmichael laughed, hugging him close.

"Well, that's a shame. I can't bring a dog home myself because Mr. Carmichael is allergic. But I have friends…"

Eden grinned.

Mooch was as good as placed. Mrs. Carmichael had a reputation for never saying anything she didn't mean—and quite a bit she did but should keep to herself. And given the tax bracket of her friends, Eden figured Mooch stood a really good chance of finishing out his golden years in prime style.

Five minutes later, Mooch on her lap, Mrs. Carmichael finally wound her way around to the real purpose of her visit.

"I heard that sweet boy, Cade Sullivan, helped you rescue my Paisley."

*Sweet boy?* Eden's lips twitched.

"Actually I'd already rescued Paisley. Bev was in the car giving her water when Cade showed up," she corrected meticulously. Then she laughed and leaned forward to admit, "It was me Cade was rescuing."

Mrs. Carmichael's eyes rounded, right along with her mouth.

"I figure you're here to get the really good inside dirt, right? And only Bev, Cade and I know that part. So there you go, I've just provided you with lunch fodder for an entire week." Too amused to be offended, Eden grinned.

The older woman tried for a look of righteous indignation, but couldn't hold it for more than a few seconds. Smiling back, she reached over to pat Eden's hand. "Sweetie, you're the best gossip this year. You didn't think I was going to waste my advantage, did you? Especially not when I've got the inside track."

"Is Paisley your inside track, then? I should charge you for an office visit for this," Eden teased, her fingers combing through the cat's soft fur. The Savannah purred her approval. Surprisingly, so did Mrs. Carmichael in the form of a harrumphing hum.

"Good point." The older woman looked around the office, noting the various animal photos, inspecting the certificates and then giving Eden a considering look. "Why don't you go ahead and give my baby a checkup. Make sure she's faring well after her little adventure. We'll see how that goes."

For a solid heartbeat, Eden just stared. What? A real appointment? From one of the Oceanfront matrons? Warning herself not to get too excited, Eden scooped the cat up into her arms and tilted her head to one side to ask, "Adding legitimacy to your pending story?"

The older woman laughed, rising too and waiting for Eden to lead the way to an exam room. "I'm meeting the Spring Fling planning committee in the morning. And you have to admit, your rescue and subsequent examination of my baby gives me an exciting co-star status in gossip central's latest favorite topic."

"Well…" Eden set the still purring cat on a stainless table and, one hand still rubbing her ears, reached for the stethoscope, "I think Paisley's the actual co-star."

"I'm her agent," Mrs. Carmichael deadpanned.

"She's a lucky cat," Eden decided ten minutes later after giving the cat a thorough and surprisingly easy exam. Savannahs weren't known for being agreeable, but the feline, who weighed more than Mooch, had purred through the entire checkup. "And in excellent health. You might want to supplement her with some fish oil. Omega-3s are good for the immune system and will make her coat even shinier. From the scent of her fur, you're taking her to the salon Dr. Turner recommends. They're lovely and do a fabulous job of pampering the pets. But after a month on the fish oil, you won't need those conditioning baths. Also, Savannahs often have a taurine deficiency, so if you aren't already, you might want to begin supplementing."

"I suppose you sell this taurine?"

Eden looked up from her inspection of the feline's nails to shake her head. "No, but I can recommend a few brands, though."

Mrs. Carmichael gave another humming humph, then nodded.

"You're very good at that," she decided with a considering look. "Paisley doesn't take to most people, let alone veterinarians. She hates the techs at Dr. Turner's. They've started asking me to sedate her before visits."

"Oh, that's a shame," Eden said, giving the huge cat a sympathetic hug. "I know Savannahs can be considered persnickety, but you'd think a veterinary clinic would understand that about the breed."

"You'd think," the other woman murmured before asking about the charges.

Eden gave the cat one last scratch, then leaving her with her owner, stepped over to the computer to print out a bill.

"So, where did you and the sweet Sullivan boy go after drinks last night?" Mrs. Carmichael asked, making a show of pulling her checkbook out of her Hermès bag. "A walk on the cliffs, perhaps?"

"Oh, my God," Eden breathed, the bill hanging limp in her fingers. Horrified images of YouTube videos, Instagrams and mocking humiliation for not moaning correctly during an orgasm all filled her head. "Did someone follow us?"

The older woman laughed so hard she snorted. Then, after wiping a tear from one eye, she took the paper and patted Eden's hand.

"Sweetie, you are such a rookie at this."

Eyes huge, Eden shook her head in denial. "That was a setup? But how'd you guess?"

"Process of elimination. Cade's BMW headed west when he left the Wayfarers. That meant you either went to the cliffs or up the coast. Since word is that his car was in his driveway two hours later, the cliffs were the best bet."

"We could have circled around, made a turn somewhere."

"Cade's too practical for that, sweetie. Please, if you don't know him better than that, how are you going to keep people guessing about what happened?"

Before Eden could process that, or even wonder if she'd totally underestimated the depth and reach of the Ocean Point gossip chain, the other woman handed her a check.

Eden glanced at the amount, then forcibly yanked her jaw off the floor.

"Um, I think this is a mistake." She tried to hand the slip of paper, with its overabundance of zeros, back.

"That's for the rescue, and the reward I'd have had to offer. For today's visit, which I'm assuming since it's a Sunday and your posted hours don't include weekends, means this is considered emergency time, and a retainer for monthly checkups for the next three months. At that point, we'll reevaluate."

With a grunt, she lifted the twenty pound feline, draped her over her shoulder like a purring stole, and gave Eden a nod.

"I'll be in touch during regular business hours to set up

Paisley's schedule. I'll expect you to have those supplements you recommended for me then, too. And don't forget to have Mooch ready for visitors. I'll send a few people out to meet him."

Between the buzzing in her ears and the feeling of standing on a very unstable cloud, Eden was sure she said something. Hopefully it included the words "thank you" and maybe "goodbye." But she couldn't be sure.

Still standing there in shock, Eden stared after the departing floral steamship.

Then she looked at the check again.

She'd done it.

Oh, she hadn't saved her home yet. But she'd gotten a new client. One who was married to the bank owner's brother, and had just handed her enough to pay off one-thirtieth of the loan.

Hips swinging, Eden happy-danced her way back to her office.

She'd told Bev that dating Cade should bring in some gossip gawkers who'd use their pets as an excuse to troll for dirt. But she'd just said that to throw Bev off Eden's true dating intentions. She hadn't really believed it.

But now?

"Mooch, we just might make this work after all," she said, tossing the dog a treat. Then, figuring if anything deserved celebrating, this did, she dug into her emergency chocolate stash and had one herself.

A screaming orgasm, a possible home for Mooch and a wealthy new client. This weekend was working out pretty darned good.

# 8

CADE WASN'T SURE what it'd take to make the weekend much worse. A plague, maybe. A natural disaster or two.

Or another visit to the hospital.

"Your father is out of ICU now. He's all settled in a private room and getting a little testy with the doctors' order that he not have a computer or work-related paperwork. After this morning's incident, they even restricted his access to the newspaper," Catherine said with a worried frown. Moving with the ease of someone much younger than her eighty years, she bustled around the brightly lit kitchen. Pouring coffee into a large custom mug with a picture of a fluffy baby harp seal and the caption *My Grandson*, she handed it, and a plate of cookies, to Cade. Then she gestured that he take them to the sitting room.

"I'm sure he's fine," Cade said absently, waiting until she took her cup of tea—in fine china with no seal—and was settled into her favorite chair before taking his own seat. "The doctors know what they're doing. If he listens I'm sure he'll be home with a private nurse by the end of the week."

Which meant Robert would be in the hospital for at

least two weeks, and probably cause at least three nurses to take mental health leave. Cade didn't care.

Now that he knew the old man would live, he'd done his duty by coming home. Now to get the hell out of here.

"He's going to be horribly bored," Catherine mused, as if terrorizing nurses and browbeating doctors wasn't entertainment enough for her son. "Maybe you could go by and visit this afternoon?"

"I don't think my visits are that good for his health," Cade said, offering a teasing smile to balance the bitterness in his words. As much as he loved his grandmother, he didn't see any point in perpetuating her naive hope that someday, somehow, her son and grandson would bond.

"It's good for both of you to spend time together," Catherine insisted, taking a dainty bite of her cookie before dipping the shortbread in her tea. "And it's a relief for him to know you're handling those little business issues."

"One issue, which is his trying to evict a neighbor you used to have over for teddy-bear tea parties," Cade pointed out. "And I haven't done anything to handle it so far."

"But you will, won't you?" Catherine leaned forward, her eyes intent as she gave her grandson the harshest look in her arsenal. The one that shot guilt like a laser. "Whatever your feelings about your father's business practices, Eden needs your help. You're going to help her figure out a way out of this, aren't you? Take care of her, please."

He'd taken damned good care of her last night.

But that was definitely not the kind of care his grandmother was talking about. Nor was it the kind he should even be thinking about, let alone wanting to repeat a few dozen times. He needed to forget about it. Pretend it had never happened.

Before he did something stupid.

"Mrs. Sullivan," Dora called from the door. "There's a phone call."

The live-in housekeeper offered Cade a friendly smile, but didn't give any other indication that she spoke to him on a monthly basis with updates on Catherine's well-being. If grandmother knew he was checking up on her, she'd pitch a fit. She'd probably follow it up with a hug and a plate of cookies, but Cade figured it was better to keep her fits to a minimum.

"Probably another person wanting to know all about your tête-à-tête with Eden last night. For someone who hasn't handled things, you've sure started a lot of chitchat around town," Catherine said, rising with an ease that belied her years. Her green eyes, so like Cade's own, twinkled behind round spectacles. "When I come back you can give me the details so I know what to tell people. And then you can fill me in on what really happened."

Holy hell.

And he was worried about doing something stupid?

He'd pretty much already covered that.

Cade managed to wait until his grandmother was out of the room before he buried his face in his hands and groaned.

God, what had he been thinking, going down on Eden like that?

Yes, she was fun and sexy and cute.

She was also a tie to the hometown he couldn't walk away from as long as his grandmother was alive. A tie that came with expectations. Responsibilities. Serious repercussions.

None of which Cade was willing to take on.

But, oh, God, she was delicious.

His mouth watering at the memory, Cade jumped to his feet.

Crazy. This was why ignoring his own rules was emotional suicide. Why getting involved with a friend was insane.

Unable to stay still, he paced the room. He scooped up a handful of cookies off the gilt-edged plate, tossing them, one at a time, in his mouth. Like always, he felt as if he was tiptoeing through a child's dollhouse here. Dainty furniture, gilt and crystal decorations. The surfaces were scattered with fresh flowers in everything from Baccarat to a mason jar, the bright scent of spring filling the air.

He wanted to leave. To get back to…what?

The base in Coronado?

What did it say about him that he had no interest in returning to the one place he really considered home?

Tension did a little tap dance along the back of his neck as Cade wondered what had happened.

He'd always been itching for another mission, amped up to dive into action.

Now?

Now he had nothing.

No enthusiasm.

No energy.

No interest.

Not in his career.

Definitely not in being back in his hometown.

The only thing that'd sparked any excitement was Eden, and she was off-limits. He'd stepped over the line, lost his head the night before. He was smart enough, savvy enough, to make sure it didn't happen again.

No matter how much he wanted it to.

One thing he could thank his father for, the old man had taught him young that you didn't always get what you wanted.

Tossing another cookie in his mouth, Cade stopped at

the grand piano. He hated that thing. It'd taken him a year to get out of the mandatory lessons his mother had insisted on. And at the tender age of six, the instrument had prompted his father to call him a quitter for the first time.

Good times.

His gaze skimmed the photos. Eighty years, plus, of framed memories scattered, dust-free, over the glossy black surface. His father's baby pictures, a variety of weddings, his own life in photos.

His eyes landed on an ebony frame. It was like a punch to the gut. Grinding his teeth, it took all his effort not to grab the photo and toss it out the window.

It was a photo of Cade, Blake Landon and Phil Hawkins on the day they'd graduated basic training. He used to laugh when he saw it. They were the epitome of the Three Amigos—Blake's uniform was perfectly pressed and his expression indulgent, Cade wore his dark shades looking like he was posing for a military ad, and Phil was cutting up by doing his Popeye impression. *Boy Scout, Slick* and *The Joker.*

They'd each earned—and lived up to—their nicknames.

Right up until one of them had died.

Cade's guts knotted, emotions wrapping around and getting them in a stranglehold.

It wasn't like he thought they were invincible. He'd always known the risks, reveled in them actually. They all had. And it wasn't like his belief in what they fought for, in their mission, had slipped any. He was still one-hundred percent on board.

But he was tired, dammit.

It felt like he'd been fighting, full-tilt, since he was a kid. First to get into the navy, then into the SEALs. Then, well, his job was to fight. Because he was damned good at it, he got to do it a lot.

Now?

Now he wondered how much fight he had left in him.

How long he could keep pushing before he hit the wall, burned out. Made a fatal mistake.

Cade hated that thought. Hated himself for entertaining it. He was grateful beyond words that his grandmother chose that moment to return. He almost grabbed her for a tight hug, so happy for the distraction from his miserable thoughts.

"That was Reba Carmichael. We're having lunch tomorrow to chat." Cade waited for his grandmother to take her seat before dropping into his own. "She said she has news, plus she wants me to see how much her cat has grown. I understand you met her yesterday?"

It took Cade a few seconds to shift his thoughts. Then another few to shove the lingering misery aside. He'd given up on eradicating it.

"Mrs. Carmichael?" he finally said. "I think I met her when I was in first grade."

"The cat, dear."

Oh. Cade replayed his grandmother's words.

"The cat Eden rescued?" At Catherine's nod, Cade shrugged. "Yeah, I guess so."

"That dear Eden. Reba said the sweet girl charmed her cat, who isn't easy to impress, truth be told. And incidentally why don't you tell me what you were doing with that sweet Gillespie girl last night if you weren't discussing your father's loan?" Catherine asked, watching him over the rim as she sipped her tea. There was a calculating look in those eyes, rarely seen, that clued Cade in to where his father had got some of his shrewd sense.

"You know, you're pretty lethal." Cade laughed drily. At his grandmother's chiding look, he gave a jerk of his shoulder. "It was just drinks. We never actually got around to talking about anything substantial because the town gossips kept stopping by and interrupting. I finally gave up and took her home."

With one short, incredibly delicious break between the bar and her house.

*Not thinking about it in front of your grandmother,* he scolded his body.

"But you'll help Eden before you leave, won't you? Make sure all this silly loan business is taken care of so she doesn't have to worry about her home?" Catherine prodded like a white-haired, velvet-covered steamroller. "She can't be made to pay for her mother's carelessness. That just wouldn't be fair, dear."

Why didn't she just tell her son to get off Eden's back? She had as much, no more, influence in this situation as Cade had. If it had been anyone else, he would have snapped. But this was his grandmother. For whatever reason, she never directly forced her son's hand. But she clearly wanted—with good reason—the threat to Eden's well-being dealt with.

How could he deny her that? Cade took a deep breath, leaned forward to pick up the cookie plate and offered it, and his most amiable smile.

"For you, Grandmother, anything," he promised.

His reward was a tittering laugh, a flutter of the lashes and his grandmother waving the last cookie toward him.

Yep, he thought as he bit into the buttery treat, charm always won out in the end.

"Now tell me, when are you going back to San Diego?" Catherine asked, those shrewd eyes still locked on him. "You've some decisions to make once you get there, don't you?"

Cade had to swallow the cookie crumbs that had just turned to dust in his throat before he could answer. What the hell? Did he have a sign over his head, proclaiming that his life was going down the toilet?

"Not as many as you'd think," he sidestepped. "I follow orders. That tends to take a lot of the decision making off my shoulders."

"But some things aren't ordered from higher up, are they?"

Like what to do with his career?

Or how to overcome the gut-wrenching feeling that he was betraying his own self by wanting a break from playing hero?

Then, a thought occurring to him, Cade narrowed his eyes and leaned forward to prop both elbows on his knees. He gave his grandmother a chiding look.

"You've been gossiping with Uncle Seth again, haven't you?"

"Don't be silly." As if her cheeks hadn't just turned bright pink, she tut-tutted before hiding behind her teacup again.

"So you're saying that Uncle Seth didn't call and talk to you about some possible changes in my MOS?"

"MOS, dear?"

Cade's smile widened. Oh, she was so good. He knew perfectly well that she knew more about military designations and terminology than most. But he knew the game, and how much she liked playing it.

"Military Occupational Specialty," he supplied, crossing one leg over the other and settling into the chair. "You know, job title."

"Oh, that MOS. I actually hadn't talked to Seth since the end of January. He calls every other month or so to keep me up to date on things." She gave a regretful look at her empty teacup, then set it down with a delicate snap before arching one elegant brow. "So, what would your uncle have told me about you changing jobs if he'd broken tradition and called early?"

Cade shook his head. Nope, not going there. The last thing he needed was more people weighing in on his career and trying to tell him what they thought he should do.

"If you weren't asking about my assignment, what were you referring to?"

"I had a lovely note from your friend, Blake."

What the hell? Blake was ratting him out now? Other than curling his hands into fists, Cade didn't show any reaction. But the minute he got a hold of his best friend…? His fingers throbbed.

"So…Blake wanted to inform you of, what? My current job performance evaluation? Isn't that a little above his pay grade?"

Not that it mattered that Blake was a Lieutenant and he was a Lieutenant Commander. Cade had never saw the rank difference as more than a couple of training choices, since Blake had spent two years focused on linguistics while Cade played with guns.

But still, where did the guy get off talking shit to Cade's grandmother? Wasn't he supposed to be a friend? What happened to covering each other's asses?

Catherine gave him a long, considering look before getting to her feet, crossing over to where he sat and grabbing the cookie out of his hand.

"Bratty mouths don't deserve sweets," she said primly. With enough force to turn the treat to crumbs, she smacked the cookie on the plate, then sat back down like nothing had happened.

Cade stared at his grandmother, then at the plate.

Damn. Regretting more than the loss of his snack, he sighed.

"I'm sorry," Cade said honestly. "Why don't you tell me what Blake was contacting you about."

Because it hadn't been about Cade, his job or anything personal. Blake didn't do that. The guy took his commitments—and friendship was a major one—as seriously as his missions.

"His lovely fiancée sent an engagement announcement, and I replied. We know her family, after all. She mentioned that Blake would be having you stand as his best man. So I, of course, contacted him directly to offer my congratulations."

"Oh."

*Best man.* Cade shifted, trying to adjust the fit of his shirt as it suddenly seemed to be squeezing his shoulders. Why was Blake even thinking about getting married? The guy was crazy.

"Oh, indeed. Now you can go brew me more tea while you consider why you are so surly."

*Surly?*

Cade bit back the response, offering a genial smile and nod instead and taking the teacup and empty-except-for-his-confiscated-crumbs cookie plate with him to the kitchen.

He didn't need the five minutes it took to boil water and pour it over a pile of dried flowers to know what had him on edge.

Everything was wrong. His edgy, exciting life—the one he'd dreamed of and planned for and, dammit, loved—just wasn't anymore.

Wasn't exciting.

Wasn't what he'd dreamed.

Wasn't what he loved.

Everything had changed.

Now Blake was changing, too. Getting married, for

God's sake. Why? Sure, Alexia was hot. Funny and smart and perfect for the Boy Scout. But it wasn't like she was holding out for a ring. Maybe it was because her father was an admiral, and could make Blake's life hell.

That had to be it. Why else would a guy, a SEAL, put himself or anyone else through the insanity that went hand in hand with being married to special ops?

There. That's why he was surly.

Because his life was off track, out of whack and his best friend was making a huge mistake.

Nothing a little time wouldn't fix.

Then he glanced out his grandmother's kitchen window.

Eden.

This wasn't surly he was fighting.

It was horny.

Even from this distance, the sight of her lithe body sent a wakeup call to his libido.

He warned his body to stand down. Talk about marriage material. Eden practically had "I Do" stamped over her head. Not because she seemed like she was interested in the wedding ordeal. But because the town would expect it. His grandmother, if she thought there was something between him and Eden, would totter right out to her greenhouse and start gathering lilies for the ceremony.

He winced when the goat butted Eden, using enough force to send her sideways. Surprisingly, for a girl prone to accidents, she didn't lose her footing. Instead, she turned and threw her arms around the goat's neck for a hug. She was too far away to hear but Cade could imagine her gurgling laughter as she played with the animals.

Damn, she was something.

He sighed.

If he left before the loan was settled for his father, Robert would start foreclosure action faster than the bank.

Eden would lose everything. And Catherine would smack him upside the head.

If he stuck around, he didn't think he could resist Eden. Not for long. Not after tasting her. Feeling her. Hearing the noises she made when she came, saw how she responded to sex. How would she look when he got her completely naked? Would she be as demanding and assertive when she touched him as she had been with herself?

What did her nipples taste like? How did it feel to slide inside her body? Did she like it on top? On bottom?

She bent over to scoop up the dogs' ball.

He groaned.

Did she like it from behind?

Realizing he was hard and horny in his grandmother's kitchen, Cade groaned and forced himself to turn away from the window.

Tea. Cookies. Torture.

He had to get the hell out of here.

Unable to resist, he looked at Eden again. The dogs romped while she watched, one arm draped affectionately over the goat.

And maybe he'd just figured out how to escape.

Knowing better than to get cocky, because plans had a way of being shot to hell, Cade still felt pretty confident when he strode into the sitting room.

"Grandmother," he asked, offering her tea and a fresh plate of shortbread. "Have you ever considered getting a pet?"

# 9

My, how things could change in just a few days. Pretending she wasn't a little shell-shocked—and pessimistically positive it wouldn't last—Eden circulated between clients in the clinic lobby, taking a payment from one and offering another's puppy a treat while telling the third she'd be right with him.

Five days ago, right after her night with Cade, dozens of people had come in to get the inside dirt on their date. When they'd realized she wasn't giving anything away free, the smart ones had made appointments for their pets. For the price of a checkup here, an inoculation there and the occasional heartworm test, they'd gotten damned good veterinary service to go with the coy responses Eden had liberally dished around.

She'd been delighted when she'd tallied her receipts from all those nosy new clients. Given that the bank manager was an old family friend, and the fact that Eden hadn't known anything about the loan, he'd agreed to accept a one-time payment against the interest, and extend the loan another thirty days. So she had a month to get her mother home to deal with it—or to find thirty grand to pay it off herself.

"Eden, I want to make an appointment for next week. You'll be around, won't you? Not jetting off somewhere with Cade?"

Eden's smile was a little shaky around the edges as she assured the woman she was taking appointments all month. Hurt tangled with disappointment, but she wasn't about to confess that she hadn't seen or heard from her hot, sexy date since Cade had dropped her at her front door.

"Thanks so much for bringing the kitten in for a visit," she said to the next client as she handed her the invoice. "If you decide to go ahead and get her vaccinated, let me know."

Eden had to resist the urge to shake her head. The woman had obviously already had her cat to a different vet, gotten a thorough checkup and all the accompanying care. But, hey, everyone knew by now that Eden wasn't offering info for free.

"Mrs. Went, would you like to bring your goldfish back now? We'll see if we can figure out why she's swimming slower than normal," she offered, keeping her smile in place. If they wanted to pay for her to meet their pets, that was on them. And maybe one or two would be impressed enough to make the next visit real.

Eden figured she'd be ready for her Pollyanna tattoo before the weekend.

Two hours later, her feet were hurting, her smile wilting and her mood edgy. She watched the last customer leave for the day, then hauled out the mop and cleanser. Maybe she should offer housebreaking classes. At least then her new clients would go away with something other than frustration.

She wondered what it said about her that she was so happy to share that particular feeling, even if she wasn't sharing any gossipy news.

Because *she* was frustrated. And angry. And feeling like a damned fool.

What had she been thinking, trying to seduce Cade Sullivan?

Now, instead of a buddy, the sexy guy who fueled her fantasies and hauled her out of trees, he was *that guy*.

The one she'd gone too far with. Not physically. That particular experience hadn't gone nearly far enough. But she'd gone too far counting on him. Actually thinking he'd finish the bone-melting job he'd started. That he'd be interested enough after a taste to come back for the whole banquet.

Instead, he'd pulled a dine and dash.

According to his grandmother, if the ever-so-reliable gossip that'd kept her doors open the last few days was to be trusted, Cade was only gone for a few days.

According to the miserable knot that was now living in Eden's stomach, everything was ruined.

Her easy, comfortable relationship with Cade.

The pride she took in just being herself, and pretending that she didn't care if people accepted that or not.

And her secretly cherished fantasy that after one kiss, he would be so crazy for her that he wouldn't be able to resist showing her every sort of delight she'd heard he had to offer.

She slammed the mop into the sink and smacked the knob to send water spraying everywhere.

She blamed Cade, she decided as she quickly adjusted the flow. She really did.

If only because he made her think she could have everything she'd dreamed of.

Before she could slide into the pout that had become her almost-constant companion over the last day or so, the phone rang. Turning off the water, she hurried across the room.

"Gillespie," she answered.

"Eden, how's business?"

Bev's good cheer floated across the line like music, upbeat and chipper.

And totally irritating.

"Booming, thanks to the gossip ghouls," Eden snapped. Then, like a geyser, all her frustration came spouting to the surface, casting a verbal splatter all over the place. "What is with these people? It's bad enough that they think they can bullshit their way into getting me to unwittingly spill information. It's another to be so blatant about it that it becomes an insult to both me and to themselves. You'd think they'd care enough to at least try to be clever with their snooping."

Bev's laugh rang over the telephone line, doing more to ease Eden's frustration than any coddling commiseration could have.

"Well, as lousy as they are, I've given three perms, touched up two color jobs that are so fresh I can still smell the toner and given six kids their first haircut."

"Pumping you for information, too?" Eden leaned against the counter and shook her head before giving in to the laughter. "That's just sad."

"At least we're making money out of it."

"I wonder if we can drag this out for another two months," Eden muttered, figuring it'd take that long at her current rate of would-be clients to pay off the bank loan. Especially if the bank manager charged her the seventeen-percent he'd mumbled about when they'd made their appointment.

Before Bev could offer encouragement, or some wild

new idea to capitalize on this newfound popularity, the front door opened.

*Damn.*

"I've got to go," Eden murmured, not waiting for her friend to disconnect. As she always did when faced with the Oceanfront girls, Eden wished for a mirror. Silly wish, since there wasn't much she could do to fancy up a ponytail, jeans and purple T-shirt.

"Hey there," she greeted Janie and Crystal as they stepped into the converted barn as gingerly as if the linoleum floor were covered with horse droppings. "I'm sorry, but I closed about a half hour ago. Unless you were here to make an appointment?"

Since neither woman had a pet, she didn't figure that was the case.

"Oh, no. We just stopped by to visit," Janie said, sniffing surreptitiously before letting the door close behind her and coming into the center of the lobby to look around in fascinated curiosity.

Poor thing, she obviously didn't get to go slumming very often.

Eden had to give them credit, though. Unlike the townspeople, and a few of the other Oceanfront set, at least they didn't bother with subterfuge.

"Visit?" she prompted, since they'd never, in all their years of growing up together, sought her out before. "Really?"

"We're here about the Spring Fling," Crystal said, walking over to the cat cage where three kittens were snoozing after a busy day of chasing visiting pets. "It's going to be so fun. And the dresses this year are to die for. You're going, aren't you?"

The cats woke, one of them pouncing on Crystal's finger like it was a toy mouse. Eden waited for the woman to complain, but instead she giggled and reached between the cage bars to rub the furry ears.

"I haven't missed a year yet." Wondering if she'd mis-judged Crystal, Eden walked over to unlatch the cage. The cats scrambled out to climb all over the pretty blonde, who laughed with delight. "Why would this one be any different?"

"Well, you haven't brought a date in a lot of years, either," Janie said, her smile brightly cheerful. "So we wanted to offer to help you this year."

"To help me...? What? Get a date?"

Both women giggled like she'd just recited a naughty limerick.

*There once was a girl on a rock*
*Who developed an intense craving for Cade's—*

"Of course not," Janie said with a wave of her Kate Spade purse. "I'm sure you've got that covered. I mean, I know it's been a few years since you broke Kenny's foot the weekend before the dance, but it's not like anyone's keeping track to see who you bring."

"Or who brings me?"

They wanted to know if she was going to the big coun-try club party with Cade. The knot in Eden's stomach tightened, making her a little ill.

"So why were you here again? Just to do a party head-count?"

"Oh, no, we're not on the RSVP committee," Crystal said, holding two cats now, her face buried in their fur. "We're on the decorating committee."

"We're driving down to San Francisco tomorrow," Janie explained, her tone upbeat and suspiciously friendly. "You know, shopping, lunch, fun stuff like that. We thought you might like to go."

Once upon a time...heck, was it only a month ago, she'd

have done anything for that kind of invitation. To be asked to join their exclusive little world. To be accepted, even on the fringes.

Now it held about as much appeal as being shaved bald and forced at gunpoint to sing "Achy Breaky Heart" while break dancing.

Because even if they did accept her, the minute they realized Cade was out of the picture and Eden wasn't great gossip fodder any longer, they'd push her right back out.

Smiling, so she wouldn't give in to the stupid tears burning her eyes, she crossed both arms over her chest and arched one brow. "Because, what? You think I need to be decorated?"

"Of course not. You have wonderful taste in clothes," Janie said in a humor-the-deluded tone. "We just thought it'd be fun for you. You know, maybe even throw in a makeover, and if you wanted, some lingerie shopping."

Oh, nicely done. Eden barely kept her sarcastic applause to herself.

The backhanded-insult attempt to garner information. She wished she could tell them that she didn't need lingerie, because Cade liked her better naked. That'd wipe the smirks off their faces so fast, they wouldn't be able to smile for a week.

"Ladies."

Eden jumped, her heart pounding at the sudden pivot from anger to surprise. She hadn't heard anyone come in. From Janie and Crystal's expressions, they hadn't, either.

While the other women made a show of girly excitement, complete with hands waving in front of their faces and one grabbing the counter as if to keep from falling, Eden eyed Cade, then the door. He must have caught the bell before it could chime. Extensive special-ops training for sneaking up on gossiping women, no doubt.

All three of them moved toward the center of the lobby to meet Cade, but unlike the other two, Eden didn't giggle, twitter or preen. Nor did she greet him with a smile.

Why would she? He'd brought her to a screaming orgasm, patted her on the head and disappeared.

Like he'd heard she'd been in a sexual drought and figured that was the next area of her life he'd sweep in and save.

And now that she was under mean-girl siege, he just happened to show up? Did he have an Eden's-up-the-creek beeper or something?

"Playing hero again?" she murmured with a scowl.

Neither Janie nor Crystal gave any sign of having heard her. Cade did, though. He arched a brown and shot her a wicked, *what else were you expecting* sort of look.

Eden didn't know what she had been expecting.

She just knew that she'd given up on expecting *him*.

CADE HATED BULLIES.

Even when those bullies were women. More so, he realized, since the female persuasion seemed to take an extra catty delight in knowing exactly where to stick the knife.

He didn't know what they'd been giving Eden crap about—he was just glad he would step in and stop it. He hadn't expected it to be quite this easy, though. Instead of doubling down on their bullying, they'd both plastered on friendly, there's-nothing-to-see-here innocent expressions before offering bubbling, friendly greetings.

Eden didn't look quite so thrilled.

As a matter of fact, he'd never seen her look quite as unthrilled to see him. Instead of the usual mischievously welcoming smile he was used to being greeted with, she just stared.

Cade twitched his shoulders, trying to throw off the feeling of guilt that was trying to settle there.

What? He hadn't made any promises. Oral sex on a rock under the moonlight wasn't a binding commitment, dammit. And he'd had to get away. The drive down the coast to San Francisco, a couple of days with Blake and Alexia—he'd needed that to clear his head after...

After losing it to the taste of Eden. After getting so tied up in worrying about her expectations that he'd essentially done the one thing he hated, the one his father always liked to toss out. He'd run away.

Still, he'd come back.

And if the crap she was taking was any indication, he'd arrived just in time.

"Cade," the tall woman said, tottering over with less grace than Eden had shown at the cliffs wearing crazy heels. Batting her lashes like they'd help her balance, she squeezed his arm and pressed her boobs against his shoulder in greeting. "Welcome home. I haven't seen you yet to tell you how sorry we were to hear about your father."

We? Was she wearing a crown?

"He's not dead," Cade said, shrugging off her comment and her hold on him.

"But he had a horrible heart attack. Triple bypass—that had to be scary."

"You're talking to a guy who faces down automatic weapons, live grenades and sings cadence with a bunch of guys," Eden said dryly. "I think he sees scary in a slightly different way than you do."

"Oh, Eden," the taller woman said, shaking her head and looking to Cade as if for sympathy. Why, he had no idea. "I'm sure he's been frantic with worry, which is just like fear, isn't it? Your poor father. The Garden Club ladies were at the hospital just this morning to check on him. You must be so glad he'll be home tomorrow."

Since his gramma would smack him for saying otherwise, Cade kept his response behind closed lips.

He looked back at Eden, wondering how she managed to look so much better, fresher, sexier than the two dolled-up tarts standing next to her.

He'd missed her.

He shouldn't have.

He never missed people. Not from his hometown, none of his friends, not even his family. Hell, he didn't even miss Phil, but that was probably because he refused to let himself think about his old buddy.

But he'd missed Eden.

Missed her smile, her laughter, and the sweet sexy scent of honeysuckle that seemed to float around her like a soft cloud.

He'd missed the taste of her.

How could a guy become addicted after just one small taste? And once hooked, how did he get over her without tearing up both of their lives?

"Hey, Eden," he greeted, his tone low, and probably a little friendlier than she wanted, given the audience.

"Cade."

Hmm, maybe that missing had been one-sided?

"Sorry I was gone so long."

He'd had to remove himself from temptation, sure if he'd stuck around, he'd have done something crazy. Like beg Eden to sleep with him.

But the minute he'd gotten back into town, he hadn't been able to resist coming to see her. And so far, so good. No begging yet.

"We were just talking about the Spring Fling," the tall woman interrupted. What the hell was her name? He tried to remember it as she did that lash-fluttering thing again. She must be hell on wheels during allergy season. "All the girls are wondering if this is the year you'll finally bring a date. A real one, not just your grandmother."

Subtle. Cade looked at Eden, whose eyes were dancing with delight. At his expense, no less.

"I'm not really into the country club events," Cade side-stepped.

Not far enough, though.

"Oh, this isn't just any event. You probably know your grandmother is hosting this year, and dedicating the auction funds to her veterans' program. She must be thrilled you're home, since your presence alone will guarantee people bid even more."

Well. Guilt, served up with a side of eyelash fluttering. He wasn't buying it, though. Still, afraid she'd grab his arm again, Cade shifted away, heading toward Eden. Not safety, he wasn't stupid. He knew damned well she was the most dangerous person in this building. But her kind of danger, he wouldn't mind sampling a few more times.

"You're going, aren't you?" the blonde prodded.

Cade debated. He didn't want to go, but he knew the power of a good show. If he put one on, he might have a better chance of manipulating his father into cutting a deal over the loan. And if the rumors he'd been hearing since getting back that morning were anything to go by, his going would likely toss a whole lot more business Eden's way. A win-win.

"Yeah, I'm going," he said. Then, tired of their snotty-ass attitudes toward Eden, he fully committed to the danger zone and stepped over, wrapping his arm around Eden's shoulders. He had to hold on extra tight when she almost jumped across the room.

Amping up his smile to keep the two barracudas' attention on himself, he added, "With Eden."

IT WAS LIKE BEING WRAPPED in a warm blanket of sexually charged delight and facing a barrage of poison arrows at the same time.

Eden didn't know whether to sigh in pleasure, or duck and run. Given the fury in Janie's pretty blue eyes, running wouldn't matter. The other woman was going to catch up sooner or later.

So, what was a girl to do?

Figuring spite over his disappearance wasn't worth keeping herself from enjoying whatever game he was playing, Eden leaned into his body, absorbing the warm, solid comfort he offered. She wasn't sure where the comfort came from. Maybe her usual, sexually overloaded reaction was inhibited by the women glaring at them. Hard to be horny when the voyeurs wanted to scratch your face off.

"You're taking Eden to the Spring Fling?" Janie asked in the same tone one would use to humor a two-year-old who'd just claimed they were going to fly to the moon on their teddy bear.

"And me, with nothing special to wear," Eden deadpanned, thrilled to throw Janie's words back at her.

Cade leaned closer, his breath tickling her ear as he whispered, "Something that goes with that red bra would be nice."

Despite her irritation over his disappearance, Eden gurgled with laughter and slanted him a naughty look.

"How interesting," Janie snapped, tucking her purse under her arm and grabbing Crystal with her other hand. "I guess we'll just have to do that shopping trip without you, Eden. See you at the ball."

With that, a chilly look and a tug on her stunned friend's arm, Janie glided out like she was floating on ice.

"Aww, I think you upset them," Eden said, still laughing as the front door slammed shut. "It's going to be painful, given that they came in for gossip and you sent them off with the best of the season. But Janie's going to have to choose between spreading the word or being pissed that you're claiming to take me to the social event of the season."

"Claim? I don't lie." At her doubtful look, Cade frowned. "Why wouldn't I take you?"

Easing out from under his arm so as to reboot the circuit to her brain, Eden rolled her eyes.

"Why wouldn't you take me, in their opinion? Or in reality?"

She blinked a couple times at the flash of fury in his eyes, but before she could do more than bite her lip, it was gone.

"Let's get their opinion out of the way, since it seems to matter to you."

"Oh, no," she exclaimed wide-eyed, giving a dismissive wave of her hand as if she could as easily shoo away the truth. "I don't care what they think. Although this will put an interesting spin on the *Who's Cade With Now* chitchat."

She could imagine the shock, dismay and questions. Drinks at the Wayfarers were one thing. Bringing the equivalent of a poor relation to the biggest social event of the year? That was like stepping up to pitch in the gossip major leagues.

"You have a problem with your name being linked to mine?"

Eden's lips twitched, wondering if he knew he sounded like a pouty ten-year-old.

"It sounds like you're the one worried about gossip,"

she said, gathering up the kittens and putting them back in their cage. Then she went to the supply closet to finish up her closing cleaning routine. "And their reasons are three-fold. I'm not wealthy. I might break something of yours they're going to want to use if you date them. And taking me means you're not taking one of them."

There. Three simple reasons, presented in her best non-whiny fashion.

"And what about you?"

"Me?" she asked, glancing up from her task of cleaning one of the cat boxes. "I'm closer to poor than non-wealthy. I never try to break things—it just happens. And I'm sure the perception that you already have a date will keep them from dogging you in hopes of getting asked out."

When he didn't respond, she finished the last cat box, then made her way through the lobby, reception area and exam room to empty trash bins. She returned two minutes later to find him still standing in the center of the room, arms crossed over his chest and a grumpy frown on his face.

"Do you have an excuse lined up?" she asked, hoping they were good ones. She'd realized that being blown off after starring in the *How'd She Get Him To Do That* gossip was going to be quite a slap. "Will you say you were called back to duty? An overseas emergency?"

"What are you talking about?"

Leaving the garbage bag by the door, she pushed a stray hair behind her ear and gave him a chiding look. "Well you're not really going to the Spring Fling with me, and I can't not go because I promised your grandmother I'd help out. So what excuse are you going to give?"

"I'm going with you," he insisted.

"Oh, please, you are not. You just said that because Janie was being a brat. That was a typical Cade Sullivan rescue."

His frown turned deadly.

Eden tried to swallow, but the look in his eyes dried up her throat.

Wow.

She'd always thought of Cade as a charmer, an easygoing guy who looked sexy as hell in a navy uniform. But she rarely thought of him as military. Until the other night when he'd mentioned losing his friend, she'd never thought of him as a fighter.

But that look, the one right there on his face?

That twisted her perception all around.

And made her shiver with apprehension. He wasn't just the boy next door. There were depths there, things he'd done, things he could do, that were beyond her ability to relate to. He wasn't just the guy she'd always crushed on now.

Now, he was a dangerous man who was suddenly way more than she could safely handle.

"A typical rescue?" he repeated, his words low, with a cold edge. Like he was seeing her in a whole different light, too.

Eden didn't care. She couldn't, wouldn't, pretend to be something she wasn't. Which included being meek and sweet just to get her forever crush to like her. Dammit, she wasn't in eighth grade and this wasn't child's play. Even if it did include an end-of-season dance.

"Of course this is another Cade Sullivan rescue. You've never attended the Spring Fling with a date, and nothing you say will convince me that you wanted to this year. The only reason you said you were taking me was to get Janie and Crystal to back off," she dismissed, irritated that her words came out shaky and hoping he'd take that as nerves instead of hurt.

"That wasn't bullshit," he denied. "I want to take you to the party."

Her heart leaped, excited and hopeful. She stomped it down quickly, since the defensive tone and quick flash of regret on his face didn't scream *happy date* to her.

"Why?" she asked, suddenly tired of being his pet project. Someone only worthy of his attention if she needed rescuing. Well, dammit, she was tired of having him see her as a mission. If he couldn't want her as a woman—a desirable, strong, worthy-of-him woman—she wished he'd just leave.

Again.

"Why?" he repeated, frustration and anger clear on his face.

"Yes," she challenged, lifting her palms to the air. "Why."

Cade's jaw worked, emotions chasing too fast through his eyes for her to keep up. Then, clearly reaching a conclusion—one that looked like it was going to scare the hell out of her, if that dark look was any indication—he stomped over.

"What—"

Before she could finish asking what he was doing, he grabbed both her arms and lifted her off her feet. Pulling her body tight against his, he bent low.

"This is why," he told her just before he took her mouth.

Eden melted, sinking into the kiss with a low moan.

He was so yummy.

And he wanted her.

That cautious—and totally inconvenient—little voice screamed out a warning. He was out of her league. So far out that she didn't have the first comprehension of what his real life was like. Four days ago, he'd been her hero. The boy next door who always pulled her out of the tree. But he was bigger and sexier and scarier and more intense now.

Slowly, reluctantly, she forced herself to pull away from

the most delicious kiss of her life. She barely held back a
protesting whimper.

Her lashes fluttered as she made herself meet his gaze.
His green eyes were like lasers, looking past her soul and
into that corner where her fears hid. He saw everything,
could do anything.

She slid out of his arms before she could curl up closer
and beg for another taste.

She wanted him.

And she was desperately afraid she was falling in love
with him.

# 10

"WELL," EDEN SAID, breathless as she pressed her fingers to her lips, looking like he'd just shocked her all to hell and back. "That's a good reason for a lot of things. But are you sure you want to do them in public? Because there's nothing more public than this event."

Hands fisted in his pockets so he wouldn't grab her again, Cade paced to the window to glare at the overgrown paddock.

What the hell was he doing? He'd wanted to see her, yes. But his reasons for coming here were much more practical. He needed to fill her in on the loan his father was trying to collect from her mother. And he wanted to arrange for her to get a pet for his grandmother. Next thing he knew, he was throwing out public declarations and playing grab-ass like a desperate sailor on his first leave.

He'd lived within specific protocols long enough to know he was stepping way over the line. There were times you took one for the squad, you risked it all for the mission. And then there was going so far off the deep end that you were practically AWOL. Doing this? Going after Eden? That was the equivalent of going rogue.

He knew what he was supposed to do.

He'd spent four days solidifying his mission plan and choices, outlining the known factors, considering the options and detailing his escape routes.

The mission was to get out of Ocean Point with everything the same as when he'd arrived. Which meant no crazy commitments, no broken hearts, no emotional drama.

The choices had been simple. Give in to his desire for Eden. Or do some damage control, convincing her that nothing had changed between them.

Known factors?

Eden was the girl he rescued, and even though she didn't know it, she currently needed his help.

She was tied to Ocean Point, and would have to face the gossips and innuendos long after he left.

She was deliciously sweet, in more ways than one.

She was fun and cute and made him feel like he could leap, fly and save the world.

If it wasn't for his dedication to the military, to his career as a SEAL, she was the kind of girl he'd want to settle down with. Which made her about as dangerous as a mountain of explosives in a lightning storm.

So her pushing him away?

It was the best thing she could have done for both of their sakes.

"Are you saying you don't want to go to the party with me?" he asked, totally aware as the words left his lips that he'd crossed the line.

"I'm just saying that I don't think it's a really good idea," she told him, her words slow and careful, as if she were measuring each one before she let it cross her tongue. "It's not like it's two buddies going out for a drink, you know? If we went to this event—because the dance isn't just another country club party—we'd be making a statement."

"You mean the gossips will go crazy talking about us, making up all kinds of stuff and trying to outdo each other with their brilliantly manufactured insider information?"

Eden's lips twitched and she rolled her eyes as if to say he was being ridiculous. Good. He was glad she could see how stupid it was to let other people factor into whether or not they went together.

"Exactly."

"Exactly, what?" Cade frowned. Was she agreeing with his gossip assessment? Or had she tapped into his thoughts and was reassuring him that she'd be totally on board with having a no-strings relationship with him in front of the entire town?

"The gossips would go crazy over the news that you were dating me. They already are, actually. It won't matter that it's a pity date thrown out in another of your routine rescues."

Cade wasn't sure which phrase sent his pissed meter through the roof. Pity date, or routine rescue. Both were pretty damned insulting.

"You think that's all there is between us? Pity rescues?"

She winced, then lifted her palms and gave him a sad look. "What else is there?"

He'd had it. He was so tired of denying his wants, turning away from his needs. He was sick of being the nice guy, dammit.

"What else is there? Do you need a reminder," he asked, giving in to the need to pull her close again. He took her lips before she could voice the protest he saw in her dark eyes. It only took a few seconds before passion blurred her gaze and she kissed him back.

He couldn't get enough of her.

His lips shifted, his mouth angling to take hers deeper. Why was this a bad idea again?

His need for her overruled everything.

Even his ability to think.

"Stop," she whispered, her mouth still moving against his.

"No."

His hands skimmed her hips, up her waist and cupped her breasts. He groaned, reveling in the wonder of her softness. Her fullness. He squeezed, loving how she filled his palms, making his body ache for more.

He angled his body closer, so his hardening length pressed tight against her hip. She moaned, soft and low, making his fingers tighten before he slipped one hand over the curve of her waist to tug the soft fabric of her T-shirt away from her jeans.

Before he could find flesh, though, her hand shot up and grabbed his wrist. Eden pulled her mouth away from his. Her eyes fluttered open and she stared for a second before giving a regretful moan. She brushed her lips against his, super-fast, then ripped herself from his arms to scurry a few feet away.

"I can't… Here… Um…" She shoved both hands through her hair, loosened now that he'd tossed her ponytail holder somewhere on the floor. "I work here."

"So? We can do other things here, too," he reasoned, reaching for her again. His fingers barely skimmed her waist before she skipped away.

"Nope. Not here," she said shaking her head. She didn't look like she wanted to stop, though. Her eyes were eating him up like candy, the heat in them enough to melt his shorts.

"Why not?" he finally demanded, wanting to hear her tell him to his face that she wasn't interested. Because her nipples were still saying the opposite as they pressed, hard and pebbled, against her T-shirt.

Before she could say anything, the front door opened. In came a handful of women, a gaggle of kids and, weirdly, the goat.

They all stopped, looks of shock and speculation chasing over their faces.

"Hey, Eden," one of the women greeted. A chorus of hellos followed. "We're here for the 4H meeting. Thanks again for letting us use the back room."

"Sure." Eden look flustered for a minute, then shook her head like she was tossing off a fog and gestured to a wide set of doors. "It's all set for your meeting. Just lock up when you leave."

The women slanted curious looks their way but didn't ask questions as they herded the kids toward the room. He did see one give another a hip bump and a giggle before glancing back and blushing.

Looked like another segment of Ocean Point had something to talk about now.

"When is this over?" Cade asked, wondering which would come first, talking himself out of sex with Eden, or exploding from pent-up frustration. If her meeting ran more than fifteen minutes, either one was distinctly possible.

"The 4H meeting?" Eden glanced back as one attendee led the goat into the room before looking at the clock. "They should wind up around four-thirty."

"They?"

"I'm not in the 4H," she said, her shrug a little wistful. Cade wondered why she wasn't, since she was totally into animals. Was it anything like why she wasn't a part of the Oceanfront snob patrol, even though she had the family pedigree to qualify?

"So you don't have to stay?"

"I usually don't."

The girl with the goat and the one with the wicked hip bump both stood in the doorway, pretending to inspect the dog food display. Cade was pretty sure they were tilting sideways, considering how close they were leaning to try and eavesdrop.

"Let's go," he suggested, wondering if it sounded like begging to everyone else in the room or if that was just in his head.

"Go?"

"Yeah," he said, grabbing her hand and pulling her toward the door. *"Go."*

"WHERE ARE WE GOING?" Eden's nerves were jumping all over the place as excitement, fear and anticipation wound through her system. She wanted to show a little pride and pull away, proving she wasn't a pushover. That she wasn't going to let him give her another wildly intense, mind-blowing orgasm and then just waltz away without a word.

"Let's go somewhere private. Your place is close," he suggested with a wicked smile, his fingers twining through hers.

Eden glanced toward the house for a considering second before sliding her eyes to the cars parked in front of the barn-slash-veterinary-clinic-slash-4H-classroom.

The house was close. A little too close to the barn-slash-vet-clinic filled with kids and curious adults. Many of whom she was sure had their noses pressed against the window at that exact moment.

She couldn't deny that she'd enjoyed reaping the benefits of the gossips this week. Cade was better than an ad, a coupon and a social-media blitz all rolled into one. But maybe it was time for a little caution. Because it wasn't just her reputation on the line here.

She was horribly afraid it might be her heart, too.

"How about we walk?" she countered, unable to deny herself more time with him despite the risk. She gestured to the path that traversed between both their properties. "We can take the lakeside trail. It's always so pretty along there."

"You want to go to the lake?" he asked, his voice dropping. It wasn't until she saw the flash of heat in his green eyes that she remembered. If he hadn't been holding her hand, she'd have used it to smack herself in the forehead. The lake was his spot. Initiations, sexual escapades, good times. She knew that. She'd fantasized about it so many times that the suggestion must have popped out of her subconscious.

Eden clenched her teeth in case some of the butterflies in her stomach escaped. Here it was, her only birthday wish of the last handful of years, ready to come true. All she had to do was let it.

"You sure you want to revisit the lake?" he asked, his words teasing and low. So low that he had to lean closer, so his warm breath washed over her, to deliver them.

Had he seen her all those times? Did he know she used to watch him there? Nerves flickering, Eden licked her lips. She gave him a wide-eyed look, then glanced toward the woods before asking, "What's wrong with the lake?"

"You don't have very good luck there, do you?"

"I beg your pardon?" What? Was he the only one who got to get lucky at the lake?

"Two years ago, I had to rescue you there, remember? Kenny Phillips was rolling naked in a batch of poison oak, trying to scare you away from sex."

Well, there it was. Now Eden knew she *could* cringe and laugh at the same time.

"How do you know I didn't scare him away from sex?" she asked, saying aloud what was usually whispered behind her back. "Word is he's never been the same, performance-wise."

Cade shrugged, his hand tightening as he helped her climb over a large fallen log in the path. "I don't know what you saw in the guy, but from what I recall, Kenny never was what I'd call a go-getter. He was second string, junior varsity, class presidential runner-up. You know, the kind of guy who never could go all the way."

Eden pressed her lips together to keep from admitting that those comments could easily be applied to Kenny's lovemaking skills, as well. After all, she'd broken the guy's foot. It'd just be rude to add insult to injury, even two years after the fact.

"I can't believe you showed up when you did two years ago," she said instead, still wondering how that'd happened. She hadn't even known he was coming home, so it wasn't like she'd had her rendezvous there in a subconscious attempt to send him some sexually charged message. "What are the odds?"

"I'd say the odds were pretty good since you're my, what'd you call it? Routine rescue?"

Eden grimaced. She should have known he'd throw that back at her. But she couldn't deny it. And, if she was honest, she didn't really want to. It was kinda nice, having her own personal hero.

"I didn't mean for that to sound so dismissive," she said quietly, following the pressure of his hand as he pulled her off the path, through the overgrown—but poison oak free—grasses toward the remote lake. "I really do appre-

ciate you being there to haul me out of trouble. Or to step
in when it seems like someone's picking on me."

"You're talking about the Spring Fling?"

"It was a sweet gesture," she said earnestly. It really
was. Even if it made her feel like crawling under a rock.
Eden sighed. She just wished, just one damned time in her
life, that someone could want her for her. Not for what they
could get or out of obligation. "But it's only going to put
you in an uncomfortable position. That's a lousy thank-
you for all the help you've given me."

He grimaced. He looked like he was going to say something—agree or protest, she wasn't sure. But before he
could, they stepped through the tight ring of trees to the
clearing surrounding the lake.

Eden hummed in appreciation, a combination of sensual energy and relaxation wrapping around her like a
sexually charged, but cozy, blanket. The setting was gorgeous. A serene blend of earth tones gave a gentle background to the mossy green water. Rocks as tall as her
hip, rounded by years of weather, stood sentinel. Sunlight
glinted through the overhead leaves, warming the cool
glade with a soft glow.

"You're the one who was looking uncomfortable. The
gossips are a pain but you don't have to let them bother
you. Why do you deal with snobby chicks like that Janie?"

Because she kept hoping for acceptance. Belonging.
History.

Since the first two sounded pathetic, she went with the
third.

"My family helped found Ocean Point. On both my
mom and my dad's side, they were integral to everything,
from founding the library to creating laws. My great-
grandfather actually donated the land the country club is
built on. That all makes me a part of the Oceanfront set,"

she said. No need to add that because her family was broke, her father gone and her mother dancing on the crazy side of irresponsible, some of the set would happily ignore that history and let her fade into a footnote in the town ledger. Cade already knew all that.

"Why not just move away?"

*Huh?* Eden blinked a couple of times, trying to process the idea. "I can't leave Ocean Point."

"Why not?"

"Because this is my home."

He just arched one brow. Panic grappled and clawed its way through Eden's stomach. Her life might not be everything she wanted, but she'd always lived it here. She might not fit perfectly, but at least her rut was dug in and familiar.

"Every place has its games and rules and drawbacks," she said with a shrug. "But here, I know the players, I can work the rules and sidestep the drawbacks. But more importantly, there are things here worth doing all that for."

"Like?"

She narrowed her eyes, realizing he wasn't just being argumentative. He really didn't see the benefits of his home town.

"Like knowing everyone, having those ties that go back. Not just to kindergarten or T-ball. But all the way back, generations. Like the familiarity of the places. Knowing where to get steak on Saturday or jam in the summer. Knowing who tells the best jokes and where to go for a good drink." She gestured to the lake. "Knowing the best makeout places, and learning from years of experience so you don't damage yourself while having a good time."

As she'd hoped, that made him laugh. Cade's entire face lit up, the remnants of anger behind his eyes fading as he looked around the lake with an affectionate smile.

"Best makeout places, huh?"

"Word is, this is yours," she said, not only ready to change the subject, but desperate to see what kind of magic happened when the lovemaking was done right.

"You don't say?" he asked, shifting around to face her, his hands cupping her hips and his gaze intent on her mouth. "You know better than anyone that gossip isn't always reliable."

"Word is," she repeated in a whisper. Eyelids heavy, she stared at his mouth, reveling in the soft fullness of his lips and hint of stubble that kept his face just this side of pretty.

His fingers were gentle as he reached up to glide over her cheek, tucking her hair behind one ear, then leaning down to brush his lips over her jaw.

"Word isn't everything," he said quietly. "Gossip always skims the surface, but never touches the truth."

"Are you trying to say the gossip isn't true? That this wasn't your special place?" she asked, already knowing the answer but wanting to hear it from him. Wanting him to say something, anything, that'd make her feel like she was different than the other girls he'd brought here.

That she was more.

That she was special.

But he didn't say a word.

He just looked at her.

The expression in his eyes was intense. Like he was searching her soul. Weighing, waiting. She didn't know what he found, or what he'd do with the discovery. Was she worthy of him, of his special place?

Nerves added a painful edge to the desire coursing through Eden. Before she could figure out what to do, find anything to say to break the tension, Cade skimmed both hands into the thick strands of her hair, cupping his fingers behind her head and angling her mouth to his.

His lips flowed, like a whisper, over hers. She barely

had time for a taste before he moved on, brushing kisses over her cheek, along her jaw and down her throat.

Her system spun into overdrive, passion smothering the nerves as she melted under his touch. Her fingers tingled as they skimmed over the hard muscles of his shoulders, down his back and cupped his tight butt. His body was a work of art. One she wanted to fully appreciate this time. To study, to explore, to enjoy.

Cade's kisses trailed along the rounded collar of her T-shirt, soft and sweet, as his fingers danced down her side, down to where the hem met her jeans. His hands, hot and powerful, slid under the fabric. She sucked in her breath, flattening her belly as his fingers pressed higher. They trailed the wide band of her bra, scraping the length of her torso with his fingernails. She shivered, her breath catching on a low moan.

Desire flamed.

Need pounded.

She grabbed the back of his shirt, tugging hard to pull the material from the waistband of his jeans. As soon as the shirt cleared, her fingers were scrambling for skin, smoothing over the hard, hot flesh of his back before skimming around to tangle in the delicious sprinkling of hair climbing from his flat belly up to a vee between his pecs.

His body was freaking awesome.

And his hands.

She moaned when he cupped his entire palm over her now bare breast. When had he unhooked her bra? He rubbed in circles, warming, caressing, tormenting her nipple into a hard pebble.

She knew it wasn't a race, but she still hurried to keep up, angling so she could scrape gentle nails over his nipples. He growled.

Before she could take another breath, he'd stripped

her shirt and bra off, tossing them somewhere toward the bushes and grabbing her by the waist to lift her high.

For a second, he just stared. His eyes were slits, passion flaming like a conflagration in the green depths as he took in the sight of her. Eden, needing more, desperate to push him over the edge, unbuttoned her jeans and gave a gentle push so they slid off her hips. They caught on her shoes, leaving her naked from the knees up except for a tiny pair of purple lace panties.

His groan was lost as his mouth latched onto her breast, his lips skating over the soft flesh to the aching tip. He sucked, hard. Her body convulsed, her core as hot and wet as he was making her nipple. There was something amazingly erotic about being so much at his mercy that she was practically floating on air.

He nipped, his teeth scraping her flesh, his mouth still sucking hard. Eden's fingers dug into his shoulders and she gave a whimpering cry of encouragement.

"More," she insisted. "Make me come."

"I'm gonna make you come more than once," he said, pulling back to stare into her eyes. The intensity of his look echoed the promise in his words.

"Big talk," she teased.

He laughed, then set her on the ground, but his hands didn't leave her waist. A thrill of delight shivered through her at the idea that he didn't want to let her go, even for a second.

"Off," he demanded, his words low.

"You first," she shot back.

He frowned, then, his fingers tightened for a second before he released her. His clothes were tossed aside so fast, Eden wasn't sure he had any buttons left, even on his jeans. She kicked off her shoes, toed off her socks and in the second it took her to step out of her jeans, he was naked.

She almost tripped over her pile of clothes at the sight.

"Oh, my," she breathed. Eyes huge, she tried to take him in. He was gorgeous.

Golden skin stretched over a body that would make a goddess weep. Sculpted muscles flowed in swimmer form, wide shoulders tapering down to a narrow waist and thighs...

Her mouth actually watered.

Oh, his thighs. Long, lean and roped with tight muscles, they were the perfect frame for the jutting length of manhood waving hello between them.

Eden's own knees got a little weak at that point.

"I guess you've got what it takes to live up to that *more than once* promise," she observed, her tone almost reverent. Unable to resist, she reached out to run her fingers along the hard, long length of him. He hissed. She angled a wicked grin his way, then did it again.

Before he could grab her and take control, she dropped to her knees. Palms flat, she ran her hands up the back of his legs from his calves to his upper thighs, then grabbed his butt for a little squeeze. At the same time, she leaned close and blew a puff of air on the rounded tip of his erection.

He growled.

She swirled her tongue around the head, lapping at the velvety knob before sucking, just that tip, into her mouth.

His fingers tunneled into her hair, the tips digging into her scalp as if he was afraid she'd pull away.

As if. She'd just been served up a huge portion of the tastiest treat she'd ever seen. She might never be done. She didn't think she could ever get enough of him.

Her lips tight against his flesh, she slid her mouth as far down as she could, then pulled back to just the tip, sucked, and did it again. And again. And again.

Cade could only take so much. Flesh quivering, he shifted, stepping backward. From her position on her knees, Eden slanted him a pouty look. And why not? He'd just taken away her treat.

He bent, grabbing his jeans and digging out his wallet before tossing them aside.

"While you're down there," he suggested, handing her a condom.

"My pleasure," Eden murmured with a wicked smile, sure it was going to be just that. Her eyes locked on his, she tore open the foil wrapper. Before she slid the latex over his burgeoning length, though, she leaned in for another kiss.

"You're wicked," he claimed, somewhere between a laugh and a moan. His fingers slid into her hair, a combination of a plea and a caress. Eden didn't know when she'd ever felt this wonderful, this powerful.

She had her hottest fantasy, panting over her.

It was amazing.

Ready to see just how much more amazing it could get, she slid the condom over his erection. Before she could move, he lifted her off her knees and in a single fluid motion laid himself back on the grass and positioned her above him.

"You're gorgeous," he told her. His eyes feasted on her body as she settled her knees on either side of his hips, his hands going to her breasts like they were magnetically drawn. His fingers tweaked the tips even as his palms held the weight, cupping and squeezing gently.

Eden's body heated, wet and needy as if every shift of his hands pushed her higher, hotter. Her hands braced on his chest for balance, she leaned over to kiss him at the same time she slowly, oh, baby, so incredibly slowly, lowered herself on the hard length of him.

He filled her.

Completed her.

Like they were custom fit, her body took him all, shivering and pulsing around him. For a second, Eden couldn't move. She could only feel. Sensation after sensation rippled from her core to her nipples and back again.

Cade groaned.

Swallowing hard, she lifted her hips. Then slowly, twisting a little, brought them back down so her core was pressed tight against the thatch of curls at his groin.

Cade growled.

Eden did it again. She moved faster. Up and down. Sliding, undulating. Her body grasping at his in desperate need. He moaned his approval, letting her set the pace.

Her eyes still on his, she watched his face tighten, his eyes hooded as they languidly moved from hers, then down to her breasts where his fingers were working pure magic, then back again. It was like he was fascinated with her body. Obsessed even.

The very idea made her come a little.

More excited than she'd ever been, Eden moved faster. The power built, tighter, needier.

Her head fell back, her body on fire as she rode the waves of sensations crashing around her. Her pounding heart echoed the power of her orgasms, beating like a conga drum.

Hands trembling, she gripped Cade's shoulders.

His fingers tightened, holding her breasts high as he angled his body upward to lick one, then the other nipple. Back and forth his mouth went, making her crazy as the climax coiled, tight as a spring, in her belly.

Then he nipped, his teeth tugging one nipple into his mouth to be sucked, laved, teased. His fingers twisted the other, then he tugged.

Eden exploded. Her moans were whimpers now as she

rode the waves, ebbing and flowing with pleasure. He followed her with a guttural growl of delight, his body pulsing inside hers.

It was like floating on a cloud of passion. Spikes of pleasure shot like lightening through her, but didn't change the foggy haze of delight that she was riding.

"More," she whispered, leaning down to press a soft kiss against his chin, then scattering more along his jaw and cheeks. "You're yummy, and I'm hungry."

"Feast, baby," he encouraged, his tone just as satisfied as the look on his gorgeous face.

# *11*

EDEN GRADUALLY DRIFTED AWAKE on the bank of the lake. Was this what an out-of-body experience felt like? Gloriously delicious, as if everything had a surreal tint to it. From her body, which ached in the most deliciously satisfied way, to her senses. She slowly lifted her eyelids to peer into the evening light. The sun was setting, the lake bathed in a rainbow of pinks, oranges and purples to reflect the evening sky. Cade's body was wrapped around hers, protective and warm.

She blinked a couple of times, not sure what'd woken her. She was limp with sexual satisfaction. So why the sudden tension? Like she should be worried, or even scared.

Then he muttered in his sleep, his hands gripping her waist as if he'd just been shoved off a cliff and she was his only hope of not plummeting to the ground.

Eden came fully awake, but was still standing on the edge of a terrifying nightmare. She couldn't see it, but she knew it was there. And it was attacking Cade. She could feel the waves of misery pouring off him.

"No!" His denial was guttural, desperate, even though it was only a whisper.

Frowning, she tried to shift. But his fingers dug in

tighter. She tilted her head back, peering up at him. Fear melted into sympathy. Her heart ached at the desolation on his face, at the pain in his voice.

"Cade," she whispered. She reached up to his shoulder, giving him a gentle shake. "Wake up."

"No. Return fire. Stop. No!" He didn't yell. He barely muttered the words. But the intensity, the horror in them ripped at Eden's gut, terrifying her.

"Cade. Wake up," she demanded, shaking harder now. "What?"

For one second, she could see it all in his eyes. The miserable pain, the devastation. The soul-wrenching loss.

Then he blinked. All it took was a second for him to tuck it all away. Charm and a rueful sort of self-derision replaced the raw emotion on his face.

"I think we wore each other out," he said, his smile a shadow of its usual wattage, his laugh a little rough around the edges. "I can't believe we fell asleep."

"You were dreaming," she said, ignoring the hint to let it go. "Are you okay?"

His jaw clenched, then he shifted, so he could skim his bottom hand down to cup her bare butt and his upper hand toward her breast.

Before he could cup her already aching flesh, she grabbed his wrist.

"You were dreaming," she said again. At least, if being under emotional attack in one's sleep counted as dreaming. Eden's eyes flew over his face, trying to see if he was okay. Stress etched lines in the corners of his eyes, bracketed his mouth. But his lips were curved in his usual, charming smile and his beautiful green gaze was determined. To fight the demons? Or to push her away?

"That's what people do when they are asleep." Whether because he saw how determined she was, or out of pique that she wasn't ready to roll around on the bank again, Cade shifted. He pulled his arms away and sat upright. "It's going to get cold, though. We should head back."

Eden gave him a long, considering look.

Here she was at the lake, that magical place of sexual-fantasies-come-true. With the sexiest man in the world. One who'd just rocked her every idea of what pleasure was supposed to feel like. If she ever wanted to feel that rocking pleasure again, she was pretty sure she should let it go. Just let the subject change, gather up her underwear and drag him back to her bed for another round.

But she couldn't.

This was Cade.

Her hero.

The guy who was always there for her. To save her from falling out of trees. To shoo away the mean girls. To show her that her fantasies had nothing on reality.

Didn't she owe it to him to be there for him, too?

Even if it ruined her shot at another mind-blowing orgasm?

Feeling very self-sacrificing, and just a little worried, she ignored the tense ball of stress in her stomach and rubbed her hand over his bare shoulder.

"Cade," she prompted softly, her tone as sweet as it was stubborn. "What's wrong? Were you dreaming about your friend? The one you lost last year?"

Maybe she should have got up and kneed him in the balls. He'd probably have looked less betrayed.

"Gossip again?" he asked in a tone as chilly as one of his father's worst put-downs. "I thought you knew better than to believe the whispers on the street."

"You told me yourself that you lost your friend, Phil," Eden countered, irritated at being lumped into the same category as the gossips, but deciding to letting it go. If she was hurting, she'd lash out, too. "I know how close you were because your grandmother speaks of him often. Last year she showed me a huge stack of pictures of the two of you and your other friend. Blake, right? She's referred to you three as *those sweet boys* ever since you brought them home for Christmas a few years ago."

For just a second, he closed his eyes as if the memory was too painful to see. Then he looked at her, his eyes as cold as she'd ever seen.

Eden swallowed hard, suddenly very aware that she was naked.

"Grandmother shouldn't be talking about my friends. Or about me. I didn't realize she was as much of a gossip as the rest of the town," he groused, shoving his hand through his hair and glaring across the water.

"She needed help putting photos into the family album," Eden said, irritation banishing her self-consciousness. How dare he so easily assume they were gossiping. "Your father has no interest, you weren't home and she doesn't like to let just anyone poke through her pictures. I'd stopped by to bring her a pie and offered to do it for her. She didn't gossip. She simply told me the names to write next to each entry."

"Oh."

He sounded like he'd rather have had that kick to the balls.

As he should.

"Yes, oh," Eden snapped back, sitting up and grabbing his shirt to wrap around her, definitely uncomfortable with her nudity now. His was fine, though. Even irritated, she could appreciate perfection when it sat naked in front of her. "Maybe instead of jumping to rude conclusions, you should consider how much Catherine worries about you. How much she loves you."

His shrug was a guilty jerk of one shoulder.

Eden pulled her knees up to her chest and took a deep breath. She felt like crying. Both for Cade's misery, and at the realization that she'd been so, so shallow.

All she'd ever seen was the gorgeous guy next door. The hottie who pulled her out of scrapes, who kept her supplied in fantasy material. That he was a navy SEAL only added to his sexy persona.

Sure, a few days ago on the cliffs, she'd clued in that his job had risks. That there was more to being a hero than just riding in with a charming smile and great timing. But she'd sort of let that fade into the back of her head. Not because it didn't matter, she realized, wrapping her arms tighter around her knees. But because it was scary to think of what he must face on a regular basis. To admit, even just to herself, to the possibility of something happening to him.

"I'm sorry you had a—" What? Bad dream sounded so childish. Nightmare was too B movie-esque. "Troubled sleep. I wish the sex had been a little wilder. Maybe then you'd have been too exhausted to dream."

She offered a tremulous smile, giving him her best *aren't I cute* look.

For a second, he just looked stunned. Then he burst into laughter.

"Oh, I don't know. I thought it was pretty wild," he said, reaching back to give her a quick, one-armed hug. He didn't keep up contact, though. Just as soon as his arm fell away, so did his smile.

Eden's heart ached.

As always, unable to sit quietly in the face of suffering, she rubbed a comforting hand on his shoulder again.

"I'm so sorry," she murmured. "And not sorry, in a hey, open a wound and share it with me kind of way. I just hate to see you hurting like this. And hiding from the hurt."

She wanted to tell him that it didn't do any good to hide like that. That he should get it out, whatever it was. Air the pain so it could start healing.

But she couldn't. She knew whatever she was imagining, whatever she'd lived through, couldn't compare to his pain. Who was she to tell someone how to grieve?

All she could do was be there for him, ache for him.

After a handful of miserably long minutes, Cade shrugged again.

"It was my mission," he finally said, his focus so strong on the water, it was like he was confessing a sin to the lake gods. "I planned it, I led it."

"Was it your first?"

"Nah." He shook his head. "I've led dozens. Not just like this, no two are exactly the same. But similar. Same region, same objective."

"Something went wrong?" she asked quietly.

"Phil was hit. Shrapnel to the head. One minute he was cracking jokes, the next he was gone. He still had a smile on his face when he hit the ground."

Tears trickled off Eden's chin, horror filling her heart as she imagined how he must have felt to have that happen right before his eyes.

"It wasn't your fault," she protested, shifting across the grass until she sat next to him. She shoved aside the sudden cascading barrage of terror that'd come along with recognizing the reality of his job and tried to focus on helping Cade. He still didn't look her way. Just continued to stare at the water, his face as hard as marble.

"The mission was my responsibility."

Eden didn't know what to say to that. She understood responsibility. Knew the heavy weight of it and how tempting it was to shoulder it alone. But she also recognized guilt. Why did the two always seem to go hand in hand?

She should let it go. She should make a joke, change the subject, slide down his body and offer a blowjob as a distraction.

Anything to keep him from thinking about his friend.

But she couldn't. Not when he was so clearly hurting.

"Could you have stopped it from happening?" she asked quietly. "Could you have done anything to change it?"

He still didn't look at her. Just stared at the water. His lips were white in the moonlight, his shoulders rigid. Finally, after long, miserably drawn-out seconds, he shrugged. "The powers that be don't think so."

"Do you?" She bit her lip, knowing she'd be better off backing away. But she'd never been able to take the safe route. "Does your friend Blake?"

That got his attention.

Cade's gaze shot to hers like a sniper's bullet. Iced fury flamed in those green depths, made all the scarier because the rest of his features were now shrouded in the dark.

The charming facade that most people took as the regular Cade Sullivan cracked, showing the real man beneath the usual charismatic amiability. Eden almost took a step back.

"I'm just saying…" She almost stuttered, then took a deep breath and continued, "Maybe you shouldn't be blaming yourself. I've seen all those pictures of you and Phil and Blake. You look like really good friends. Would Phil blame you? Would he want you carrying this?"

"Phil isn't here anymore," Cade snapped. "So what he would or wouldn't have wanted is immaterial."

Eden's heart broke for him. The pain, the loss, the misery. Without that protective facade of charm he usually held between himself and everyone else, she could see them all so clearly on his face.

She'd only been interested in the fantasy. In hot, wild

sex and a chance to live out all those things she'd dreamed of for so many years with a man she had always hero worshipped. Now he was more than a hero. Cade was a man, all man.

A man that she was terrified to realize she could easily fall in love with.

CADE WANTED TO TELL HER this was hardly the love talk he usually enjoyed after incredible sex. He liked the manly feel of cuddling in the afterglow. He preferred a slow buildup to round two, maybe a little kissing and sucking.

A woman poking at his most vulnerable parts, and not the one between his legs, wasn't the makings of a turn-on.

"You're a hero, Cade. Not because of your job, or because you've earned a chestful of medals. But because of who you are inside. Because you care, deeply, about people and about doing what's right." Eden bit her lip, then sighed and gestured to the patch of grass across the lake. "You take responsibility for everyone. For everything. Even when it's not yours to take."

Cade sighed. She wasn't going to give it up, was she.

"I was in charge," he said, appreciating her attempts to make him feel better but not willing to sidestep reality. "That means the responsibility was all mine."

Eden nodded.

Then, as if she'd heard his mental instructions, she shifted closer to his body, smoothed the palm of her hand up, then down his chest. The vulnerable part he wanted her interested in stirred to life as she pressed a soft kiss to a scar zigzagging down his shoulder.

"That must be rough. Taking all those untrained, unskilled, and what? Unwilling guys into a battle."

Shocked fury shut down his libido in a flash.

"What?" He ripped his gaze from the safe view of the

trees to glare at her. "That's bullshit. My team is the best. They are SEALs, dammit. We never ran a mission unless they were totally on board, were totally ready to kick ass. There's nobody unwilling to serve in my squad."

Eden didn't say a word. She waited a beat, then arched one brow.

Cade's frown turned ferocious.

"I'm not saying Phil didn't know what he was doing, or that he wasn't damned good," he snapped, getting the message loud and clear. "But—"

"Either your guys are damned good, highly trained and totally prepared, and the loss of one of them was a horrible result of going into battle," she interrupted. "Or you were responsible for every single thing, from the weather to the enemy to the state of mind of every man under your command."

Unable to find a valid argument that'd shoot her down, Cade finally settled on a glare.

She gave him a sympathetic smile, cupping his cheek in her palm and pressing a kiss against his lips.

Then she shifted, rolling quickly so her body angled over his. Straddling him, her thighs gripped his hips and her glorious breasts pressed against his chest.

"What are you doing?" he gasped as his body sprang to full alert.

"Exhausting you," she said with a watery laugh. Thankfully, her face was dry now, clear of those tears that ripped at his gut. "I don't know of any other way to distract you from making yourself miserable."

Cade wanted to protest. To claim that he wasn't miserable. But she wasn't leaving him any room to argue.

Or much space for self-pity.

Because it was impossible to feel bad when her body was making his feel so good.

Damn, Cade groaned as she snagged another of the condoms and rolled it over his throbbing length. Then she slid back up, her thighs gripping his sides as she slowly— so, so slowly—impaled herself on his rock-hard erection.

She was delicious.

Glorious. Like a triumphant Valkyrie warrior, fighting his demons for him, then sweeping him away to the heavens.

He was usually the one who rode to the rescue. Who dove in and saved the day.

Just before he took her mouth again, he had to wonder...

Who was going to rescue him?

CADE CROSSED HIS HANDS behind his head and propped one bare foot on the other, waiting for Eden to join him in bed.

This was pretty damned awesome. He'd never done this domestic thing with a woman before. A night here or there, a few days at a plush resort once in a while, sure. But all week long, everything from meals to sleep to showers? This was a whole new world. One he'd have sworn he'd hate. Instead, he was loving it.

He suddenly understood what Blake was talking about. That feeling of completion. Of happiness. It was freaky. Hell, another few days and he'd be writing bad poetry and crying over afternoon specials. A week and he'd be thinking about baby names and retirement property.

Cade grimaced, feeling like a girl all of a sudden.

Maybe he should drop to the floor and do a hundred pushups. Go flex something in the mirror.

His cell phone buzzed. Grateful for the distraction, he reached over to check the incoming text.

*Did you get my money?*

Or maybe he'd go beat the hell out of something to relieve frustration, he added to the previous litany.

Damn, his father was a pain.

Cade's fingers hovered over the text keyboard. He wanted to write back that the loan wasn't Eden's to pay. That Robert was an idiot for lending Eleanor money so it was his problem to collect. That Cade wasn't his damned errand boy.

But he didn't type any of that.

Because none of it would make a damned bit of difference. The minute he tossed this back in Robert's face, the old man would come after Eden directly.

She was doing great. Getting her business going, paying off the bank loan her mother had dumped on her. She didn't need this, too. It was Eleanor's responsibility, just like the bank loan. Cade wasn't going to let Eden get railroaded into paying Robert. After trying for a week and a half to reach the elder Gillespie, he'd finally had to accept that it wasn't going to happen before he went back to Coronado.

So…on to Plan B.

Cade glanced at the bathroom door. He couldn't hear the shower anymore. She'd be out any second now. So he took a deep breath, made one of those split-second decisions that made him an effective SEAL and texted back:

*You'll have a check tomorrow.*

Cade tossed the phone on the nightstand.

So the check would have his name on the signatory line, not Eden or Eleanor's. Robert could just deal with it. Then, when Cade finally heard from Eleanor, he'd make arrangements for her to pay him instead.

There, he gave a mental clap of his hands. All taken care of.

Except maybe he should tell Eden about it.

But what good would that do? It'd just stress her out, add to her worries and mess up his last days with her.

He closed his eyes, taking a deep breath and shoring up his determination.

He'd tell her later. After sex.

And after he told her he was heading back to San Diego in four days.

Never, since the day he left for boot camp, had Cade wanted less to return to duty. And not just because of the gorgeous woman joining him in bed.

Although she was a big part of the reason.

But so were the nightmares. The intense, gut-wrenching pain of missing Phil. The doubts about his leadership, the second-guessing of his decisions. Cade wasn't sure he had what it took to do a good job anymore. He wasn't sure he could be a SEAL.

For a man whose confidence had always topped out at supreme, this wasn't just humiliating, it was confusing as hell. He didn't know what to do.

So he wasn't going to do anything. For now, his entire focus was Eden. On fixing her issues, making her life easier. His, he'd deal with later.

"WELL?" FEELING FRESH and sexy after her shower, Eden sat cross-legged on her bed and leaned over to peer into Cade's face. "Aren't you going to say anything?"

He peeled one eye open and gave her a languid look. It took all her control not to giggle, but she managed to keep her expression impatiently expectant.

"I could say I'm looking forward to some good lovin'. Or I could say good-night, since it's almost midnight and you had me up early this morning to take care of a goat." He sounded a lot happier about the former than the latter.

Probably because Jojo hadn't taken too kindly to a man in her pen and had tried to headbutt him right back out.

"It won't be good lovin'. It will be great," Eden corrected primly. Then she arched one brow. "And you had a nap while I saw clients this afternoon, so I'd think you caught up on sleep just fine."

Eden wasn't quite sure what to make of her new life. She just knew it was wonderful. Somehow, in the week since the lakeside lovemaking, Cade had sort of moved in with her. Sort of, because neither of them had actually said a word about it. But his clothes were in a drawer she'd cleared. His toiletries sat next to hers in the bathroom. And the last three nights, she'd come in from a packed day at the clinic to find dinner waiting on the table, Cade in his stocking feet reading the paper and looking about as content as she'd ever seen him.

Business was booming, her love life was rocking and her social life… Holy cow, her social life. Suddenly she was the most popular girl in town. She'd been invited to join committees, to luncheons and just yesterday, Crystal had called to chat and ask about adopting the kittens.

It was like she suddenly belonged.

All thanks to Cade.

"Okay," her naked hero said, opening both eyes now and giving her a questioning look. Beneath the query and sexual heat, though, she could see something else. A pain that wrenched at her heart. A pain she didn't know how to fix. How to heal. All she could do was the same thing she'd done all week. Distract him with sex. But as deliciously wonderful as the results of that were, she knew that sooner or later, he had to face the pain. She just didn't know how to help him.

"What were you asking about?" At her blank look, he

arched a brow and added, "You asked if I had anything to say, remember?"

"Remember? Oh, yeah," she said with a strained laugh. "You visited with your grandmother today, right? How is she doing with Alfie?"

The look on Cade's face was pure doubt. "Are you sure that's a dog? It sounds more like one of the squeaky toys you find at the pet store. It's about the same size, too."

"Alfie's an AKC-registered Yorkshire Terrier," Eden said with an offended sniff. Then she grinned. "Isn't he adorable? As soon as you told me that your grandmother wanted a companion dog, I knew he'd be perfect. The lady who'd been taking care of him almost refused to give him up, but she already has ten dogs of her own."

Cade's jaw dropped. "Ten? Granted, they're so small, it would take about ten of them to equal the size of a real dog. But…ten?"

"She's a breeder who takes in fosters from time to time," Eden chided gently. "We're lucky she had the perfect pet so quickly. Sometimes it can take months. But I think it was love at first sight for both Alfie and Catherine."

"Yeah, she's totally into the dog," he admitted. "She was personally making it oatmeal and steamed carrots when I stopped by this afternoon."

"That's great. Alfie's fourteen and used to a whole-food diet." Eden gave him a narrow-eyed look. "What's the matter? Are you jealous of your grandmother's new pet?"

"She has a cook, but she insists on doing it herself. I don't think she's made me lunch since I was two," he muttered, making Eden grin.

"You are jealous," she said with a laugh.

"Only of the time you spend away from me," he admitted, his hand skimming up her thigh and underneath her nightgown.

Eden's breath caught. Desire shimmered, low in her belly.

"I'm with you now," she said.

"So you are." In a swift move, he rolled over, taking her with him. Laughing, Eden cuddled into the pillow and looked up at his sexy face.

"Let's go away this weekend," he suggested, burying his face in her throat for a nuzzle. "Just us. We'll go anywhere you want. Dancing all night in the city. A romantic balloon ride in wine country. You name it."

"I can't. We can't," she corrected. "This weekend is the Spring Fling, remember?"

"We'll skip it."

"Your grandmother would kill us both."

Cade's groan reverberated against her throat, but he didn't argue further. If anything, he got serious about turning the heat up on his kisses.

Eden shivered in delight, her hands cruising over the hard breadth of his shoulders.

As much as she wanted that feeling of being a couple, taking a trip together, she wanted the memory of walking into the most prestigious event of the year on the arm of Cade Sullivan. The most popular guy in Ocean Point.

That memory would be the cherry on top of a deliciously sexy, mind-bogglingly amazing fantasy come true. Walking in with Cade would cement her place in society.

The joy faded a little, happiness taking on a dim edge. Her heart drooped like a flower in desperate need of water as she forced herself to finish that thought.

She'd have wonderful memories. She'd be a part of the clique that she'd been born into, but only skirted around the edges of for most of her life. She'd have enough clients to pay off her mother's loan, a solid business and a strong foundation to build her future on.

The only thing she wouldn't have was Cade.

# 12

THE SPRING FLING. Ocean Point's most prestigious social event of the year, and here she was. Not helping the bartender, or sitting at the hostess table by the entrance, checking off RSVPs.

Nope. Eden was dressed in her fanciest gown, wearing her sassiest shoes, dancing in the arms of the sexiest man in town.

She gave a little shiver of delight. Wow, so many wonderful things were happening in her life, it was as if the dreams-come-true fairy had dumped a whole bagful of wishes on her life.

It felt magnificent.

Almost as magnificent as dancing in Cade's arms. Except instead of looking like he was having the time of his life, Cade was tenser than she'd ever seen him. Oh, the usual charm was right there, front and center. And he was just as gorgeous today as he'd been two weeks ago, or even a year ago. That hadn't changed. But Eden was pretty sure this was the first time she'd ever seen him so ill-at-ease. She rubbed a soothing hand over his back, grateful to feel some of the tension drain as he gave her a little smile.

Torn between the delight of the moment and needing

to make Cade feel better, Eden hesitated for just a second. Then, unable to do otherwise, she leaned in to brush a kiss on his cheek.

"Catherine and the Spring Fling committee did a wonderful job with everything. But maybe we could cut out early. Go home, get naked, heat up some cherry-flavored body oil," she added with a teasing wink.

She'd learned to read him pretty well over the last week or so. To look beyond his eyes, which hid everything behind a layer of charm, and instead notice the tiny wrinkles that pinched the corners of his eyes when he was stressed.

And despite her offer of warm body oil and a quick escape, the wrinkles were still there.

But all Cade said was, "Now that's an idea. But I promised my grandmother I'd introduce the Veteran's Auction."

"Then we'll leave as soon as it's over?"

"The very second."

Figuring she'd better enjoy the few dances she'd get, Eden cuddled closer into his arms with a sigh and glanced around. It was a magical scene. The chandeliers and candles all glinted warmly. The scent of lilies filled the air, melding with subtle perfumes and rich cologne. Like Cinderella at the ball, Eden reveled in the sight of everyone dressed so beautifully, looking so fancy.

Well, hell. A lot of those beautifully dressed people weren't just looking fancy. They were staring. Hard.

"So this is what it's like to be royalty," she murmured, giving Cade a flutter of her lashes as she burrowed a little deeper into his arms as the string quartet's rendition of The Doors's "Light My Fire" played. "I feel like I should be doing the princess wave."

From a few of the looks shooting her way, the wave would be returned with a single-finger salute. Of course, those were all single women who had crushes on Cade, so she shouldn't be surprised.

"I'd rather you kept your hands on me instead of waving to the gawkers," he said, taking his attention away from her face for just a second to cast a derisive look to the staring crowd. Not that they were the only ones on the dance floor. But they were the only ones cell phone cameras were being aimed at. "Just ignore them. We're here to dance, to help my grandmother raise a bundle of money, then to get the hell out and have fun."

With a tiny shiver in honor of the last round of fun they'd had, Eden smiled her agreement. Dance, help, money, run. She was good with all of that. And maybe if she focused on those steps, she could ignore the stares. Was this what he had to deal with all the time? The paparazzi-like frenzy from his friends and hometown acquaintances? She hadn't realized how bad it was for him, always being the center of attention.

A flash of color caught her eye, the vividness of Janie's dress commanding Eden's, and quite a few other people's, attention. The green tulle was just a few shades brighter than the jealous heat in her eyes as she glared.

Eden shifted, missing a step and almost stomping on Cade's foot. Before she could even wince, he easily incorporated her stumble into their dance steps.

"What's wrong?" he asked.

"Just feeling a little self-conscious," she answered, pulling her gaze away from the crowd. For a second she stared at his shoulder, before lifting her eyes to meet his. "I think I'd be more comfortable dancing without the audience."

"Could we be naked?"

She blinked, then burst into laughter. Her fingers curled tighter around the back of his neck and she gave him a flirtatious look.

"We could. Or better yet, we could take a radio down to the lake and dance there. Naked *and* under the moonlight."

They grinned at each other for a second. Then, remembering how many times they'd made love by the lake, and in her bedroom, her kitchen, her office, her bathroom, heck, everywhere but her car because it was still in the body shop, they stopped.

"Why don't we go outside and practice?" he whispered huskily, his breath warming her ear before he brushed a soft kiss against her cheek.

"A walk outside would be nice," she finally agreed, giving him a shadow of a smile. It would give her a few seconds to regroup, maybe a kiss or two to remind herself of why being with Cade was a wonderful temporary fantasy that she should enjoy every second of, and then, she'd be just fine.

Warm and comforting, his hand curled around hers as he led her off the dance floor. They'd made it about halfway to the wide expanse of French doors when Cade's steps slowed. She looked up at him.

His smile had dimmed and tension deepened the wrinkles in the sides of his eyes, stiffened his shoulders. Eden followed his gaze, grimacing when she saw his father settled into the corner with his glass of scotch, unlit cigar and group of toadies.

"I guess I should pay my respects," Cade said in the same tone she figured he'd use to accept an order to throw himself on a live grenade.

Eden's smile didn't waver, but she did take a deep, fortifying breath before entwining her fingers tighter with his and nodding. "Sure, let's say hello."

"You're going with me?"

"You sound so shocked."

"I am. Why would you want to talk to him? I sure

wouldn't if I had a choice." He slanted her an odd look, like he was about to change his mind about greeting his father.

"Moral support," she said, nudging him with her shoulder and pulling him another step forward. "C'mon. Let's get it over with so we can make out in the garden."

That got both a smile, and more importantly, his feet moving. They didn't make it two yards before their path was intersected by another man dressed in navy whites.

"Uncle Seth," Cade said in shock. "What are you doing here?"

"Can't a guy drop in to visit his favorite nephew?"

"I'm your only nephew."

"Then let's call it a friendly visit," the older man said before giving Cade an arch look and nodding to Eden.

Cade shook his head, as if clearing a ringing from his ears, then lifted Eden's hand in his. "Uncle Seth, this is Eden Gillespie. Eden, my uncle, Captain Seth Borden."

"Captain?" Eden offered a smile and a warm handshake. "Do you serve with Cade?"

"We're on the same base. But I'm in training. Something Cade here will be great at. I'm hoping he'll take me up on the offer to come work with the BUDS."

"You moonlighting as a recruiter now?" Cade asked. His smile was friendly, but his tone had a sharp edge to it.

Tension spiked, sharp and dangerous. Unlike the two men, Eden was unused to battles, so she felt like it was going to smother her. She shifted from one foot to the other, trying to find something to say to defuse the situation.

What had the other man said? Why was his offer— whatever it was—such an issue?

"Nah, just a guy with an intense interest in your future." Seth's smile shifted, worry lighting his eyes as he gave his nephew a long look. "A guy's got to know when he's approaching burnout. When it's time to take a break and look at some options."

What was he talking about?

Cade was approaching burnout? She gave a tiny grimace, noting that he looked more like he was battling fury rather than exhaustion.

"Eden, will you excuse us?" Cade asked, not taking his eyes off his uncle.

"Sure," she said, her own gaze huge as it sprang from one man's tense face to the other. "I'll mingle. It was a pleasure to meet you."

Other than Seth's absent nod, neither of them acknowledged her. Instead, after Cade gestured toward the open patio doors, they both strode out like they were going to strip down and beat the crap out of each other.

Eden's heart raced, nerves jangling.

Cade was a big boy.

He'd cut his teeth on society events, and this one was sponsored by his grandmother. He wouldn't do anything to cause a scene.

And he definitely wouldn't appreciate any interference on Eden's part.

Now that she had all of those reasonable, well-thought-out details solid in her mind, Eden gave a satisfied sigh.

Then looked around for Cade's grandmother.

She was going to need some backup when she went out to interrupt that little talk.

*There.*

She saw Catherine across the room, holding court in a Valentino gown and a diamond necklace and holding a tiny dog in her arm.

Aww, Alfie was here? Even if she didn't want, desperately, to congratulate the elderly woman on breaking rules with such panache, Eden would have rushed over just to see the dog.

She was almost there when someone called her name. Frowning, she glanced over to see Robert, his usual glower in place, beckoning.

"You bellowed?" she asked with a friendly smile as she approached his table. He sat in the corner, away from the dance floor, where it was quieter. With just the flick of his fingers, he sent his buddies away and gestured to the now vacated seat for Eden to join him.

"I can bellow if I want. I just had surgery," he said, chewing his unlit cigar.

Eden slid into the seat opposite him and gave his hand a sympathetic pat. "You've always bellowed, though. But you did, indeed, just have surgery. So why aren't you in bed resting?"

She couldn't help it. She knew Robert was a curmudgeonly old grump, a vicious businessman and a complete social snob. But she sort of liked him. Probably because his eyes were that same piercing green as Cade's.

"I've got business to take care of," Robert said, giving her a gruff look under his brows. As if she'd done something wrong. Eden frowned, wondering what it might be, other than having a brick wall inconveniently placed in the path of his car.

"Business? At the biggest social event of the season?" Eden noted his glass was empty and gestured to one of the waiters, then gave a tiny shake of her head when he headed for the bar. *Water,* she mouthed.

"More business is done at social events than in an office," he said, leaning forward and folding both hands together, as if preparing to prove his point.

Clueless about what kind of business he could want to talk to her about, Eden lifted her brow.

"So what's Seth doing here? Is he going to help the boy out? Did he give any indication about what he wanted to talk to Cade about?"

Was this fatherly concern? Worry over his son's recent loss? Nerves did a little dance up her spine. She wanted to help Cade, but Eden didn't think talking to his father about personal issues—any issues, actually—was a good idea.

"I'm not sure why Cade's uncle is here, or what they are discussing," she finally said.

"And you wouldn't tell me if you knew."

Eden's lips twitched but she didn't say anything. Just gave a slow shake of her head.

"You and my son, you're a thing now, right?"

Nerves were chased away by joy. She and Cade were a thing. The town thought so. The mean girls thought so, if Janie's glare on the dance floor was anything to go by. Now, even Cade's father thought so.

That meant something, right? Even though Cade was probably leaving in the next couple of weeks, this meant there might be some kind of future for them. Maybe?

The nerves were back, this time beating around inside her belly like giant bats. She'd only counted on the fantasy. The intense excitement. She hadn't let herself think about—hope for—anything after Cade left.

"It's bad enough he ran off to play hero all these years, but now he's going to give it up? For what? To be a glorified teacher?" Robert glared at the garden. Then he shifted his steely gaze back to Eden. "If he's going to drop out of the SEALs, he might as well come home and take his place at Sullivan Enterprises. You talk to him. Convince him to come back."

Drop out of being a SEAL? Shock ricocheted through Eden. Cade was leaving the SEALs? But, that's what he was. Who he was. How could he leave? Was that what his uncle was talking about? A million questions flew around her head, all of them moving too fast for her to focus on.

"Cade isn't going to change his career for me," was all she finally came up with.

"The boy just wrote a check for ten grand for you, girlie. He'll listen. But you'd better talk to him quick. He's heading back to San Diego in a couple of days. If you let him get back to that base, all bets are off."

Changing jobs?

Heading back?

Cade was leaving?

Eden's head buzzed, tears filling her eyes.

Why hadn't he told her?

She opened her mouth to ask when Cade was going. The closed it again.

What the hell did Robert mean by ten grand?

"I don't understand." Baffled, Eden shook her head again. But before she could ask what he meant, the waiter exchanged Robert's empty glass with a full one.

Without looking at it, the older man tossed back his drink. All of a sudden, his face turned red, his eyes bulged and he started coughing like crazy. He glared at the glass, then at the waiter. The man, looking terrified, pointed at Eden.

"Are you okay?" she asked, hurrying around the table. Before she got halfway, Robert's personal physician cut her off.

"It was just water," she protested, horrified that she might have sent Cade's father into a relapse.

Dr. Shaw shook his head and gave her a reassuring look.

"He should have been drinking water all along. It was just the shock of putting something healthy in his system. Don't worry, he'll be fine," he said. "He just needs to rest for a bit. C'mon, Sullivan. Let's visit the clubroom. You need some downtime."

Eden watched them totter away, her head spinning as a feeling of loss and pain wrapped around her like a tight shroud. The glow of her magical evening gone, she wanted to leave. To go home and cuddle with her animals until she came to grips with the pain that Cade was leaving.

Pressing one hand against the nausea churning in her belly, Eden tried to process the fact that the impression everyone had of the two of them being something special was a total lie. Clearly, Cade didn't think what they had was important. If he did, he'd have told her that goodbye was looming.

Not sure if she should go find Cade, or dive face-first into the chocolate fountain, Eden slowly made her way toward the garden.

She didn't make it halfway across the room before she was surrounded by a giggling gaggle of women. Even though she wanted nothing more than to talk to Cade, she knew that wasn't how the game was played here at the country club. So she forced herself to smile at the five faces circling her and greeted each by name.

"What happened to your date?" Janie asked, her tone mirroring the green of her eye-watering dress. "Cade got bored already?"

"Don't be silly. There was nothing boring about that dance. Whew, girl, you and Cade were heating up the dance floor," Crystal said, her tone teasing. Eden had to smile. Ever since the blonde had adopted those kittens, she'd been super friendly.

"Right. Not boring at all," Janie repeated with a subtle eye roll for the other women. When only one of them giggled, she quickly added, "So where is your hot date?"

"Cade's visiting with his uncle." Eden cast a quick

glance at the patio, but couldn't see anything. Were they talking about the job? Was he really thinking about leaving the SEALs? Eden had a million questions. Which made standing here all the more frustrating.

"So the rumors are true?" Janie asked, crossing her arms over her chest and giving Eden a narrow look.

What rumors? Who had time for rumors and gossip and games at a time like this? Eden was about to brush Janie off, to push through the crowd so she could continue her search for Cade. Then one of the women shouldered in front of Janie and held out her hand.

"Hi, I'm Mia. I don't think we've met. Crystal and I are cousins."

"Um, hi." Eden gave her a quick smile, but before she could offer her excuses, the woman continued.

"I know this is a lousy place to talk business, but I was hoping you had a second?"

"I hear more business is done at these social events than in an office," Eden murmured, forcing her feet to stay still. But she didn't care about the business of rumors, or the latest gossip about her and Cade. She cared about reality. And finding out just exactly what that reality would be.

"Oh, I won't go into a big spiel," Mia said with a laugh, tucking a long strand of jet black hair behind her ear. "I just wanted to make an appointment to come into your clinic."

Eden's feet stopped twitching. "The clinic? Sure, did you want to bring in your pet? I don't have my book with me but you could call tomorrow morning and I'll let you know what openings I have for Monday."

"You take calls on Sunday?" Mia exchanged a look with Crystal, who shot back a triumphant look. "Actually, I have a proposition for you. I'm a veterinarian, too. I operate a mobile unit out of Fort Bragg and would love to expand my territory. I wanted to discuss the possibility of us working together."

Wow, Robert really knew what he was talking about. Eden blinked a couple of times, trying to process the proposal. A partner? A mobile clinic? Thoughts chased ideas in an excited circle through her brain. She was going to need a little time and space to sort through them all. Ready to offer a gracious social sidestep, she gave Mia a warm smile.

"Why?" She winced. Apparently her mouth hadn't got with the program yet. Clearly, there was a reason she didn't do these social things very often. "What I mean is, I have a lot of questions. Why don't we meet tomorrow morning? My clinic, around eight?"

Mia's eyes danced as she nodded. "That's perfect. And you can thank Crystal for the why. She's been raving about her kittens for a week now. I've heard good things about your work before, of course, but there's nothing like a personal recommendation."

"A personal recommendation?" Eden gave Crystal a grateful smile. "Thank you."

Before Crystal could respond, Janie rolled her eyes and elbowed her way in front of Mia.

"Fine, fine. Pets will get care and all that great stuff." She gave both women her patented fake smile, then arched a look at Eden. "What's really important now, though, are the rumors about you and Cade Sullivan. Everyone's talking about how the two of you are a thing. But I figure that's probably as likely as The Rolling Stones showing up here to play tonight."

Eden had known she'd face curiosity.

She'd known there would be questions. Innuendo. Speculation, gossip, prying.

What she hadn't expected was hatred.

But that's what was gleaming from the pretty brunette's eyes.

"Rumors about Cade and me, hmm?" Eden said slowly, casting a quick glance around the group. Crystal looked uncomfortable, like she'd be happy to follow a topic change and Mia walked away with a show of checking her cellphone. The other surrounding women, however, looked like bulldogs. But Eden wasn't about to throw them a bone.

"Well, there are the rumors about us running off to Tahiti together to live in a grass hut and drink umbrella drinks from coconuts. Mrs. Carmichael told me that one. Then there's the one about Cade using my veterinary clinic as a base for a secret SEAL operation. Did you hear about that? I wonder if he's going to let Jojo the goat help out?"

A few lips twitched. But Janie just glared.

Eden's stomach clenched.

Nerves danced, making her ears buzz a little with stage fright.

This was it. Her chance to cement her spot in the popular hall of fame. To claim Cade-ette status and revel in adulation for the rest of her single days. This would wipe out talk of Kenny's broken foot and at least three other clumsy debacles people brought up when they talked about her.

She opened her mouth to stake her claim, but no words came out.

"Oh, please," Janie dismissed, dropping the society facade altogether in her irritation. "I knew there wasn't any truth to the rumors. This whole dating thing is just another one of Cade Sullivan's rescue missions. If you had anything real going on, you'd have applied to join the Cade-ettes."

"Is that like applying for a job? Is there an interview? Do you think they need my social security number?" Eden asked, suddenly pissed.

And not, as she should rightfully be, at Janie. But at herself. What the hell had she been thinking? She suddenly felt like a total idiot. First, for letting herself fall so hard for Cade. Second, for caring so much what these women thought that she'd let herself get into this situation, with her heart at risk.

She couldn't do it.

The words, ones she'd been wanting to say for years, stuck in her throat. She bit her lip, trying not to cry. Not because she couldn't seem to admit having achieved her dream goal.

But because of why she couldn't admit it.

What she had with Cade was special. It wasn't a goal or a rescue or a game. It was magic. And even if it was only magic on one side and friendship on the other, or if it lasted a couple of weeks before fading into a glowing memory, it was still hers. It was still special.

She pressed a shaky palm against her churning stomach and tried to take a deep breath through the lump in her throat.

Well, this was a sucky time to realize she was in love with him.

# 13

"You're quiet." Cade's words were mellow over the gentle hum of the car engine. She could feel his gaze on her but wasn't ready to face her Spring Fling epiphany. "Did I miss something while I was talking to my uncle outside?"

Other than her realizing she was madly in love with him?

"Not much," Eden murmured, finally pulling her gaze from the passing road to look his way. Even in profile, with those gorgeous eyes fixed on the night-blackened road, he was the sexiest man alive.

"You seem a little upset."

Sexiest, and most perceptive.

"I'm just…" Confused, terrified, worried, freaked out. "Overwhelmed."

"By the party? Were the gossips and gawkers a pain?"

For the first time that Eden could remember, the gossips and mean girls had been the least of her woes. Heck, after that scene with Robert, they'd practically been anticlimactic.

Oh, hell. Cade's father.

"Um, something did happen with your father." Eden

winced. "He sort of had an incident while we were talking."

"What kind of an incident?" He shot her a quick look. "Why would you talk to my father? What did he say?"

His father was fresh out of the hospital. So why did he sound more angry than worried? Eden frowned, twisting a little to get a better look at Cade. Wait a second. What was it Robert had said? Between trying to con her into manipulating Cade's career decisions and choking on water?

Something about a check?

"Your father's okay," she assured him, despite the lack of concern. "But there was a little incident. Doctor Shaw was right there and took him off to rest."

Brow furrowed, Cade slowed the car to pull into Eden's driveway. He parked in front of the house, but didn't get out. "So that's all? He had an incident? Nothing else?"

"Yep. That's all."

She waited until the tension poured out of him, his fist unclenching from the steering wheel, then added, "Oh, and he mentioned something about you writing a check for me. Something about ten grand?"

Cade cussed under his breath.

"I told him it was taken care of," he muttered. "What the hell, he thinks a country club dance is the place to bring up your mother's debt to him? The man is unreal."

It was like someone sucked all the air out of the car. Eden's chest throbbed and she couldn't catch her breath.

"Seriously?" she asked, her voice a faint whisper. Her mom had taken out *another* loan? How many more were there?

Fury and hurt tangled, making her head throb from the pressure of not screaming.

"Does nobody tell me anything?" she wondered aloud. "Is there some sign over the top of my head claiming I'm incapable of handling the truth? Some notice that was sent around suggesting I be treated like an idiot?"

"You know how Eleanor is," Cade excused, his words rushed, like he was trying to convince her that everything was going to be okay. "She's a little undependable, but I'm sure she intended to take care of everything. Nobody thinks you're an idiot."

"No? Then why didn't you tell me about this added debt?"

Eden didn't wait for Cade's excuse. She was suddenly so mad, she threw open the door and jumped out of the car. Pacing in front of the little porch didn't shake off her fury, so she headed for the wide side yard where she could stomp around freely.

"Wait a second," Cade said as he caught up to her. That he had to shorten his step to keep pace with hers only irritated her more. Eden wanted him panting, struggling to chase her down. Instead it was darned near a leisurely stroll for him. Which pretty much typified everything about their relationship, she realized.

"You aren't blaming me for this?"

"Blaming you for having vital information about my financial situation, and not telling me? Blaming you for knowing that my mother made yet another horrible judgment call that could affect my business and home, but not give me a heads up so I could make sure it's the last one she does? Blaming you for writing a ten-thousand-dollar check…" She was so mad now, she couldn't even walk. Eden stopped and poked her finger at Cade like she was drilling the words home. "To bail me out instead of trusting me to handle the situation myself?"

"Look, you had enough going on, trying to pay off your mom's first loan, keeping up with all the new business. Nosy busybodies. Stuff like that." For just a second, he looked defensive. Like an argument was right there on the tip of his tongue. But then he lifted both palms as if to say he gave up. "I was just trying to help."

Eden's heart, still reeling from the shock of facing her love for him, wept a little.

He was so sweet. So special.

Unable to stop herself, she reached up with both hands and cupped his cheeks, then stood on her tiptoes to brush a kiss over his lips.

"You're just about the sweetest guy in the world," she declared, loving him even more. "But you always do this, Cade. You treat me like I can't take care of myself. I'm not a rescue mission. I'm not the perpetual victim, just here to help you earn your hero badge."

"I'm not using you to get a hero badge," he muttered. "And you're not a victim."

"Oh, let's see. There were three tree rescues, a flat tire, an invitation to the Spring Fling, the two times you got me out of lousy dates and then there is the infamous naked Kenny rescue," Eden said, ticking the items off. "Shall I keep going?"

Cade stood there, moonlight glinting off his navy whites, looking like she'd just bitched him out for rescuing her kittens from a burning building.

"I think you're overreacting just a little bit here. I've never seen you as a victim."

What had he seen her as, then? The girl next door, always there waiting whenever he came home? Did he see her as a temporary fling, the same as she'd tried to convince herself she saw him? Of course, she'd thought that temporary was at least a month. Not two weeks.

"You didn't even tell me you were leaving," she blurted out. Then, slapping both hands over her mouth, Eden groaned, turned on her heel and spun away. Oh, hell. Why had she said that? She had a good reason to be mad. Why was she throwing sad in there, too?

"How'd you find out?"

The anger and defensiveness were gone from Cade's tone now. Instead, he sounded sorry. Tired, even.

"Does it matter?" she asked, turning back to face him. Outing his father for the second time wasn't going to do anybody any good. "Why couldn't you tell me yourself?"

He shrugged, grimacing. "I didn't want to upset you."

"Another rescue?" she whispered, wanting to cry. Again, he was trying to save her. Even from herself. Did he see her as that needy? That pathetic? How could she think they had a chance of being more than just a fantasy if he didn't see her as an equal?

Maybe that was the real fantasy, Eden realized, trying not to cry. Believing that she and Cade actually had a chance.

"Come to San Diego," he said all of a sudden.

Still wallowing in the heartache, Eden frowned, then shook her head. "What? To visit? Shouldn't you wait until you're back, see where you're assigned?"

In the time they'd been together, he'd never talked about his missions, hadn't mentioned any locales or places he'd been. Other than describing the physical training he did on a regular basis, he hadn't referenced his job at all. But she knew from his grandmother that Cade was often outside of the U.S. for months at a time.

"Sure. I'm thinking about a transfer. Out of SEALs, into the training program. I'd be one of those hard-ass drill sergeant types, molding the next wave of SEALs. It'd mean no more travel." He hesitated, his face a study of doubt. Then he gave a shrug. "Maybe I could get an apartment instead of living on base. You could come, stay with me."

Joy and shock tangled with a dozen other emotions, all rushing through Eden like a hurricane.

"Why would you do that? Why would you leave the SEALs?"

"I'm not happy," he said simply. "Something's missing. Something vital."

"But to leave the SEALs? Are you sure you want to take that big of a step? Maybe you're just suffering from burnout. We all hit it once in a while. I'll bet you just need a little more time off," she suggested. *Maybe a month or so, right here in Ocean Point.*

"Lives depend on me, Eden. On me being one-hundred percent. If I can't give that, I shouldn't be leading. Shouldn't be on the team." He walked over to the paddock, staring across the land toward his father's house. "I figure I'll give training a try, see how that goes. See if I still have a career with the navy."

He sounded so sad.

But when he turned to face her, he wore his usual charming smile. "And, hey, now we have a chance. The odds of things working out if I'm a SEAL are slim to none. But this way, we can see where things go. You can visit me in San Diego. I can come up here. What do you think?"

What did she think?

Eden pressed her hand against her churning stomach.

She thought it was an incredible idea.

To see if this heat between them could last, could grow. She thought it'd be so much easier knowing that Cade was safe.

This was so much bigger than her birthday wish fantasy. So much more than she'd ever let herself hope she'd have with Cade.

He valued her enough to base the biggest decision of his life on her opinion. All it would take was one word

·from her and he'd take a safer job. One that'd keep him in one place for long periods of time. One that would give them a chance.

Eden had spent so much of her life wanting to be special to someone. Special enough that she'd matter so much that her opinion, her feelings mattered.

It felt as if she was teetering on the edge of that now. This thing, the heat and laughter and comfortable joy between her and Cade, it was special. It could be more. It could be everything she'd ever dreamed of.

All she had to do was tell him to leave the SEALs. But he was using her, using this career choice, as a way to hide. To avoid dealing with the pain of losing his friend. Eden knew Cade well enough to read between the lines. In his mind, the only way they could stay together was if he left the SEALs.

But if he left, he'd never heal.

All her life, she'd wanted to be special. To be wanted, just for her. To belong.

Now, when she'd finally found the one person who made her feel that way, she was thinking about sending him away.

"You need to ask yourself what it is you really want," she said quietly. "Don't think about your father. Don't think about Phil. Don't even think about me. Just focus on you."

Cade shook his head, as if that was an impossible request. Eden took a deep breath, blinking fast to clear the hot tears from her eyes.

She turned away, staring at the small barn that housed her clinic. Her dream.

Years of watching Cade, of being rescued by him, of obsessing and fantasizing about him gave her a strong insight. She knew this man inside out. She knew what made him smile, and now she knew what made him groan with

pleasure. She knew his likes and dislikes, his fetishes and,
her heart sighed, she knew his fears.

She knew exactly why he was talking about giving up
his career. And it had nothing to do with her.

And everything to do with him.

So, for the first time in their lives, she was going to
turn the table.

This time, she was going to rescue Cade.

And then she was going to crawl into bed and cry for
a month.

"LOOK, YOU'D REALLY LIKE San Diego," Cade said, talking to Eden's back. His words were edgy, a little desperate, but dammit, she wasn't reacting the way he'd hoped.
Hell, he'd just tossed relationship promises out there and
she hadn't jumped in to grab a single one of them. "I'll
introduce you to Alexia, Blake's fiancée. You'll like her.
She's an animal kind of gal."

Actually he couldn't remember if Alexia liked animals
or not. He could barely remember his name after that chat
with Seth. His uncle was worried. Afraid Cade was pushing himself too hard. He'd been the one to put the idea in
Cade's head that Eden come to San Diego. But as soon as
the thought was there, Cade couldn't get it out. He wanted
it, wanted her.

And she was acting like she wasn't even interested.

Damn, tonight sucked.

Finally Eden turned around. Her face was set, chin
high and shoulders pulled back. What the hell? He'd seen
enough people prepare for battle to recognize that look.

"You are so wonderful." Her eyes were clear as she
stared up at him, but Cade had the feeling there were tears
behind them somewhere. Why, though? This was good,

right? They were talking about their future, making big plans. Didn't women love that kind of thing?

"So why don't you sound like you want to be into wonderful?" he asked. His tone was teasing, but he didn't stop searching her face for clues.

"This thing—" she gestured with her fingers between them "—between us… Cade, it was just for fun. You know, a good time."

"Yeah, we did have a good time. But we had more than that, too." Poor thing, she was so used to dating idiots like that Kenny that she probably didn't realize she was making her declaration sound like a prelude to dumping him.

"No." Eden shook her head, her eyes sad now. Shuttered. Like she was pushing him away. "That's all we had. Fun. A fantasy. A birthday wish, remember?"

"What's between us is bigger than just a fantasy," he protested.

They had laughter. They had passion and joy and a connection that went deep. They understood each other. And dammit, they comforted each other. He found peace when he was with Eden. The nightmares didn't ache when he woke to find her face on the pillow next to him. He could shove aside the memories just by focusing on her, on how she made him feel.

Cade stared down at Eden's closed expression. Her lush lashes cast a shadow on pale cheeks, silky hair fell in soft curls around a face he knew as well as his own.

He didn't know when it had happened. Maybe this week. Maybe years ago. But he loved her.

Simply loved her.

*That* was what they had between them.

"Look…" Suddenly nervous, he tried to gather the words. He'd never told a woman he loved her before, so they weren't coming easily.

As if she knew he was about to make a major declaration, she backed away shaking her head. Cade grabbed her hands to pull her back.

"No," she said again. She gave him a look that made him feel like he'd crushed her heart. "No, Cade. We were really good together. But that's not enough to make it long term. It's not something you leave your job for. You don't quit a career you love for a good time."

Spine stiff against the accusation that he was quitting, Cade ground his teeth together to keep from arguing. After all, maybe, for her a good time was all they were?

"Is it my job? The risks?" He saw something flash in her eyes, enough that he figured he'd nailed the issue. Taking a deep breath, a part of him feeling like the quitter his father always declared he was while the rest was thrilled not to have to think about it anymore, Cade declared, "Don't let that be a problem, okay? Like I said, I'll be changing positions. There's not much danger in yelling at recruits."

"You won't be happy walking away from the SEALs, Cade," she told him, her words certain.

Since a part of him was currently doing backflips over the idea, Cade had no problem disagreeing. "I think I know what I want, Eden."

"And I know what will make you happy. I know you inside out, Cade. You, the man."

Cade didn't know why he suddenly wanted to leave. To be done with this conversation. But the idea of getting the hell out of there before she revealed any of the truths in her eyes was so freaking tempting.

"Look, I've got a pretty solid handle on my happiness," he lied. "Nobody knows me better than I know myself."

"The man loves his grandmother," she said, lifting one finger.

Before Cade could point out that description could be

applied to most non-psychopaths, she took a step closer
and continued.

"Despite being brought up to be a Class-A snob, the
man prefers beer in a bottle and burgers in wrappers to
wine and filet mignon." Two fingers and another step
closer. Cade was too proud to back up.

"The man is the kind of friend who goes to the edge for
people he cares about. One who cares so much, he holds
their loss in his heart in order to honor them." Three fingers jabbed the air this time, but Cade could barely see
them through his blurred gaze.

His jaw clenched against the barrage of feeling her
words brought on. As if she'd opened that memorial he'd
created in his heart for Phil and forced him to truly see it.

He was so engrossed in those feelings, he barely noticed that Eden was standing, high-heel-to-boot in front
of him now.

"The man is so heartbroken, he's willing to hide from
the pain he feels instead of honoring where it came from.
To take on a relationship he doesn't want so he can ignore
the one he's lost."

It was like getting sucker punched in the gut.

Who the hell was she to rip open the safeguards he'd
built around his heart and force him to see what was inside?

"You're a wonderful man, Cade. But you're trying to
use what you *think* we have to hide from what's missing in
your life. You're trying to turn our little fantasy into something more. To convince yourself it'll be enough to fill the
huge, gaping hole that'd be left if you leave the SEALs."

What a bunch of crap. But he was too used to standing up for Eden, to hurrying to her rescue, to say that to
her face. But just because he didn't tell her that she was

so far off base she was writing fiction, didn't mean he wasn't thinking it.

Even as a part of him wondered if maybe she wasn't just a tiny, little bit right.

"What we have is special," he claimed, focusing on the only part of her argument he was willing to discuss. This was stupid. He wasn't letting her cold feet, or whatever she was dealing with, ruin things between them.

"No," she said, her words so quiet they almost flew away on the gentle evening breeze. "Like I said, we were just a fantasy. A wish."

He could hear her swallow, like the words were a painful lump in her throat, before she continued.

"You came to my rescue, as always. But this time you didn't even realize it. Our relationship got me more attention than anything I could have done on my own. The gossips, the busybodies were so excited about us, they made my business a success. And you, us, this affair—" Her voice broke. Then she lifted her chin and gave him a chilly smile. "This affair guaranteed my social standing in town. So, again, thanks for the rescue."

"What?" No. He couldn't have heard her right. Cade shook his head to try and throw off the buzzing in his ears. She was bullshitting him. There was no way Eden would use him like that.

"I'm a Cade-ette now. I've finally got a secure spot in Ocean Point's social register. I won't have to ever worry again about getting invited to all the right parties. You not only gave me a couple of weeks of incredible sex, Cade. You guaranteed my business would be a success."

All he could do was stand there in the moonlight and stare at her. If she'd pulled a machine gun out from under her dress and opened fire, he couldn't have been more shocked.

But she didn't pull anything out. She just gave him a long, sad look, then turned on her fancy high heels and walked toward her house.

Cade just stood there, watching.

She never looked back.

He wanted to yell.

To punch something. To attack. To fight.

Cade wasn't sure he'd ever felt as betrayed as he did in that second. He knew he'd never been as hurt.

Fists clenched at his side, he wanted to grab onto the fury, to revel in the anger. But the pain was so much stronger. He couldn't use anger to hide from it, because Eden had never promised him any more than sex. She'd never indicated that she was fishing for a ring.

Nope, right from the get go, that night on the cliffs, she'd said she wanted the fantasy.

Could he blame her that she was willing to let the fantasy do double duty? To give her both pleasure, and a little security?

Still, not even losing Phil had made him feel this miserable.

He'd listened to Seth tonight as his uncle outlined all of the reasons why Cade should give the SEALs a break. The only point his uncle hadn't made was that Cade had lost his edge when Phil had died in combat.

Because that was the only point that really mattered.

The one Eden had beat him in the gut with.

He wanted to go after her. To tell her she was right. That he needed to heal, but didn't know how.

Except Eden didn't care about that.

She'd gotten what she wanted.

She'd gotten her fantasy wish. A whole lot of good sex, and a Cade-ette T-shirt.

Instead of following her, though, he slowly made his way to his car.

As he started the ignition, he congratulated himself.

He should be happy. He'd escaped a potential nightmare. Changing his career, just for Eden? To give them a chance at a future?

What a mistake that would have been, given that there wasn't any.

At last, not to Eden.

## 14

SHE SHOULD BE DOING BACKFLIPS.

Yesterday, she'd met with Mia Warren about trying out a partnership. Mia had an extensive client list, but no physical clinic to operate out of since the old vet she'd worked with had retired last year. Eden would get access to those clients, in exchange for Mia using the clinic one day a week. There were still a lot of details to discuss, but, so far, it was sounding like a dream come true.

She'd fielded four phone calls, happily turning down two requests that she serve on committees, had blown off Kenny Phillips's offer of drinks and dinner sometime, and had accepted Crystal's invitation to go shopping, on the condition that Bev join them.

And she'd only thought of Cade, oh, a million miserable times.

Not bad for a day spent wishing she was curled up in her bed, the covers drawn comfortably over her head. That, or cozied up in McCall's Bakery stuffing herself with chocolate fudge muffins, apple fritters and cheesecake brownies.

This pain would go away. The heartbreak, the misery, they'd fade. Eden figured if she kept promising herself that, sooner or later she'd buy into the hype and start believing it.

In the meantime, she'd just keep on moving forward. Enjoy the blessings that were rolling into her life. All she'd had to do to bring in all of those blessings was get that first wish out of the way, and then it'd snowballed. It had broken her heart, too, of course. She really shouldn't forget that part of the equation.

But she was determined not to let it turn her into a whiny baby who hid her chocolate-smeared face under her pillow.

Her determination to keep that from happening was the reason she was here at the Oceanfront Country Club. She trudged across the parquet floor on her favorite pair of perky and cheerful ballet flats, wondering why Catherine had called this morning, insisting she come to breakfast.

"Eden, darling."

Reluctantly pulled out of her reverie, Eden looked around. A genuine smile curved her mouth when she saw Mrs. Carmichael floating toward her in a brilliant blue caftan and earrings the size of gold dinner plates.

"Good morning." Eden's greeting ended in a surprised squeak when the older woman engulfed her in a hug.

"You are a miracle worker, my dear. My Paisley has never looked better. Those supplements and the diet changes you recommended are wonderful."

"I'm so glad. You'll have to bring her in to see Mooch again. I've never seen him take to a cat the way he did Paisley."

"That's exactly what I wanted to talk to you about. Adopting Mooch."

"But I thought Mr. Carmichael is allergic to dogs." Trying not to get too excited, Eden shook her head. "I want

Mooch to have a loving home, but not at the expense of your husband's comfort."

"Pshaw, I think he's more allergic to walking a dog than anything else. But, it won't be my house Mooch will live in. My niece, Kelly, moved back to town. She wants a pet and he'd be perfect." Mrs. Carmichael gave Eden a narrow look, then added, "Kelly's about your age, dear. You come to lunch next week, and the two of you can get to know each other. You'll be good for her. You can introduce her around, help her settle in."

"Me?" Shocked, Eden shook her head again. "Don't you want someone more, you know, in with the right crowd?"

"What? One of those society leeches like Janie Truman? That girl and the ones in her circle, they are all takers. You're a sweet girl. You help, contribute, make a difference." With that and a pat of her chubby hand on Eden's shoulder, Mrs. Carmichael turned to leave. "We'll have lunch on Wednesday at my house. Bring Mooch, please."

Eden could only blink a few times and try to process that while watching the other woman float away. Well, look at that. More good news.

She wished she could be excited.

Sighing, she approached the hostess station.

"I'm meeting Mrs. Sullivan," Eden told the woman.

The pretty redhead leaned forward to give Eden a big smile. "I'm so glad to see you. I was going to call this afternoon when I get off shift."

"I beg your pardon?"

"My cat had kittens. Under the front porch, no less. One of them is tiny. I'm kind of worried and was hoping I could make an appointment to bring them all in to see you. I know it's short notice, but maybe today or tomorrow?"

Eden blinked a couple of times, wondering if she'd heard right. "You want to bring your cats in to see me?"

"Is that okay?"

She should be excited. Business was great, everything was working out. Instead, she wanted to cry.

Keeping her chin stiff, she said, "Of course. Why don't you bring them by anytime tomorrow?"

"Awesome," the hostess said with a grateful smile as she came around the podium and gestured toward the dining room.

Eden followed her through the crowded tables, smiling at a few faces here and there. It was like walking through a sea of whispers. She heard her name, and Cade's, at least a dozen times. The gossip never ended. That would follow her, an ever-present reminder of the cost of having her wish. A part of her wanted it to go away. But that'd mean giving up her time with Cade. And even though it had ended, even though her heart felt like it had shattered in two, she couldn't wish that time away.

Blinking away tears, she was so focused on not breaking down, she didn't see the other two people sitting with Catherine Sullivan until she reached the table.

Shock rocked her back so far, she was glad she was wearing flats instead of heels. Otherwise she'd have landed on her butt.

"Mr. Sullivan," she greeted quietly, wincing at the slight gray cast to his skin. Obviously he still hadn't quite recovered from his encounter with the glass of water the other night. And if his steely stare was any indication, he hadn't forgiven her for it, either.

No matter. It was obviously going to be a non-forgiving kind of get-together, she decided as she shifted her gaze to the third person at the table.

Fury, frustration and a surge of love all twined together as Eden lifted her chin and in her chilliest tone greeted, "Hello, Mother."

As far as parents went, Eleanor was a stunner. Traveling across the country had clearly agreed with the woman, who glowed like she'd just had a luxury spa treatment.

"Darling, it's so good to see you." Eleanor made as if to get up and offer her only child a hug, but Eden wasn't having any of that. She quickly slid into the chair next to Catherine instead, so her mother had to settle for patting her hand.

"You must be surprised," Catherine said in a gentle tone. She gave Eden a sympathetic look from those eyes so like Cade's and smiled. "I was afraid if I told you who would be joining us, you might find an excuse to refuse breakfast."

"I never refuse breakfast," she said with the closest thing to a smile she could muster. "Actually, breakfast is my favorite meal. I'm especially fond of the stuffed French toast they make here. That, and the breakfast biscuits. They're as flaky as they are light."

"Eden—"

Eden's jaw clenched. Before she could snap, Catherine sent Eleanor a chiding look, then gestured for Eden to continue.

"Speaking of breakfast," Eden added, after taking a deep breath. "The special-blend kibble you ordered for Alfie arrived yesterday. I have it in my car to give to you before we leave."

"Alfie will love that, dear." Catherine took a sip of her tea, then launched a soliloquy on the wonderfulness that was her new pet.

In the next five minutes, Eden discovered three things. Robert Sullivan hated being ignored. He looked like he was about to burst, his face was so red and tight. And she wasn't sure how much longer her mother could go without saying a word, but she was impressed that Eleanor's upbringing was so solidly ingrained that she managed to keep her friendly smile in place, even while she wore her fingernails down tapping them on the table.

But best of all, she realized that Catherine was a total imp. The society matron knew perfectly well that she was torturing her son and driving her guest crazy, but from the way her eyes were dancing, she didn't care. All she seemed focused on was talking about her sweet little Yorkie.

And, Eden realized, putting her at her ease.

Almost moved to grateful tears, Eden decided she'd taken advantage of the older woman's machinations long enough. She took a deep breath, then offered a hesitant smile.

"Mrs. Sullivan, I have to apologize for leaving the Spring Fling early. I wasn't feeling my best. But that's no excuse for my rudeness in not staying to help out."

As if she'd been waiting for Eden to get to that point, Catherine nodded, then gestured to the other two people scowling at the table.

"You shouldn't feel bad for needing to leave, dear," she chided. "From what I understand, my son was horribly un-couth, tactlessly discussing matters that had no business being mentioned at a social event."

Eden's lips twitched when Robert actually hung his head at that, still frowning despite his abashed look.

Since there was nothing she could say to top that chas-tisement, she turned her attention to her mother instead.

"I've been trying to reach you for two weeks. What made you finally decide to come home?" she asked, try-ing to keep her tone neutral but afraid it still had a strong layer of bitterness on top.

"Cade reached me in Connecticut yesterday. He insisted I return." Eleanor leaned forward and, ignoring Eden's glare, took both of her daughter's hands. "Oh, darling, I'm

sorry. I didn't mean to be so out of touch. I'd met a wonderful couple at my first craft fair who suggested I try the
eastern circuit instead of the southern route. Oh, sweetie,
it was wonderful. My erotic pottery was a huge hit. Then
I got so distracted with the shows, the new people, that I
totally forgot about checking in with you."

No surprise there. Eden's anger, fueled by the hurt of
always being forgotten by her own mother, faded a little.
It was hard to hold a grudge against Eleanor for simply
being her usual self-absorbed self. Still, she'd gone behind Eden's back, borrowed against the house, then ran
out on her debts.

"I tried calling you, Mother. I left a dozen or more mes-
sages. You never returned any of them."

"I forgot to charge that silly phone."

"Then how did Cade—" Eden paused to swallow the
lump in her throat. It even hurt to say his name. "How did
he reach you?"

"He had me arrested."

Robert's snort drowned out the sound of Eden's gasp.

"Arrested?"

"Well, I guess that's what you'd call it." Sunlight glistened off the dozen rings on Eleanor's fingers as she waved
her hand. "I was picked up by the military police in Gro-
ton."

Eden narrowed her eyes, then shook her head. "You
don't seem very upset for someone who was detained,
Mother."

"Well, the boy who stopped me *was* very cute. And so
polite. What a lovely credit to the navy he was. Much like
Cade, of course," Eleanor said, giving both Catherine and
Robert a bright smile. "What a sweet man he's grown to
be. As angry as he had to be, he sent his uncle to meet me

at the airport and bring me here in time to meet with the three of you."

Cade had arranged this. He'd tracked down her flake of a mother, called in military favors and made all these arrangements. He really was her hero.

"I didn't mean to get you into this mess, Sweetie. I simply lost track of time and forgot the payments were due."

"Speaking of payments, I have a proposition for you and your mother," Robert interrupted, pulling her attention back to the less friendly faces at her own table.

"What's that?" Eden asked, not caring since she knew anything he proposed wasn't going to be in her favor. Still, she couldn't be rude with Catherine sitting right there.

"You use your influence on my son. Convince him not to take this new assignment." Robert reached into the pocket of his suit jacket and pulled out a check. The one Cade had written for ten thousand dollars, Eden realized. "You do that, and I'll forgive your mother's loan. You want to help your mom, don't you?"

Eden's mouth dropped. She didn't know what was worse. That he would try to bribe her to con his own son, or that he thought she would consider it.

Before she could say anything, or even try to talk over the strident scolding Catherine was serving up, her mother interrupted.

"Oh, now that's just silly. Eden isn't responsible for my debts. Robert, I told you that I'd pay you. Time just got away from me."

"The loan was due last month, and you missed that deadline. Now we're discussing new terms."

"Robert," Catherine whispered, her face a study of anger.

"Don't be silly. The terms we agreed on are just fine," Eleanor said with a flutter of her lashes. "Even though you didn't cash that check from Cade yet, taking it was implicit acceptance of payment, after all. I'd planned to give the cash directly to him, but this is easier."

Eleanor leaned over to lift a suede bag from her feet, setting it on the table with a dull thud. She tugged open the drawstrings, and the fabric fell away, revealing a foot-tall pottery sculpture with a pile of neatly bundled bills at its feet.

Eden knew she should be gaping at all of those dollars. Ten thousand of them at least, she figured. But it was hard to tear her eyes off the vivid pink color and distinctive shape.

"What the..."

"That's a little bonus. A sort of thank you for being so patient," Eleanor told him, giving the large ceramic vulva one last proud pat. "It's part of my Evolving Woman series. I have other pieces if you'd like a different color."

"You've got to be kidding," Robert protested. "What are you doing, making that, that...?"

"This is art. I used to call it a craft. And then I did this little trip and learned the difference. I, my dears, create art," Eleanor declared. "Art that earns me a tidy bundle. Enough to pay you back, pay off the bank and repay my sweet Eden. You should learn to expand your horizons a little, Robert."

"Expand my...?"

Eden's lips twitched. The man was actually speechless.

"We should always be true to ourselves, after all. Look at my Eden, here. She's worked hard to follow her dreams. Going to school all those years, getting her degree and coming back to open her veterinary clinic here." Eleanor's smile beamed across the table, warming her daughter. "And your Cade. You must be so proud of him, of all he's done. Not because he's a SEAL, but because he's followed his dream. Because he's been true to himself. That's all we want as parents, isn't it?"

Eden was so busy doing an emotional tailspin, she missed the rest of her mother's lecture on parenting from the heart.

She *had* followed her dreams. She was seeing her wishes come true and even more dreams manifest. She didn't know if it was because she'd been so excited, so confident and empowered after she got her wish for fantasy sex with Cade. Whatever it was, she'd been making her own decisions all along. She'd chosen to have sex with Cade. She'd been the one to maneuver all the gossips into bringing in their pets if they wanted to be nosy. Right up until the Spring Fling, when she'd elected to walk away from Janie's taunts instead of using her relationship to gain a coveted spot as a Cade-ette.

Suddenly feeling a little ill, Eden gulped iced lemon water and tried to pretend her mother wasn't petting ceramic girly bits.

She'd made all those choices.

But she hadn't let Cade make his own decision.

She'd tried to rescue him.

Instead of letting him rescue himself.

Exactly what she'd accused him of doing.

Eden's heart sank.

Even if she'd ruined things between her and Cade, she had to fix her mistake.

Eden got to her feet so fast, the ceramic vulva teetered. Eleanor gasped and grabbed the statue. Robert growled. Catherine gave a serene smile.

"Mr. Sullivan, please take my mother's payment and consider this matter closed." Eden interrupted his stutters and leaned across the table, giving him a stern look. "And consider this. You are lucky to have a son as wonderful as yours. If you want a little advice, you might start appreciating what you have. If you want something from Cade, talk to him. Be truthful. These silly games are beneath you."

Advice she'd do well to listen to herself.

With that, and a quick kiss for both Catherine and her grinning mother, Eden turned on the heel of her very practical shoes and glided from the room.

It was, if she did say so herself, the most graceful exit of her life.

CADE STUMBLED DOWN the stairs, wincing as the bright sunlight pierced his sleep-deprived eyes, and felt his way into the kitchen. Who the hell was making all this noise?

His grandmother's rules drilled into his head, he automatically pasted on a smile filled with as much charm as he could muster with a hangover and yanked open the door.

As soon as he saw who was on the other side, his smile dropped, along with his mood—which hadn't been too perky to begin with.

"What? You need an affidavit signed stating you qualify for the Cade-ettes?" he asked, leaning his bare shoulder against the doorframe and giving Eden a distant look.

"Clever." Eden gave him a shaky smile that fell away quickly when he didn't smile back.

She looked so damned good. Her hair was slicked back in a tidy braid, her face glowing in the morning light. There wasn't a hint of misery or even a smidge of a hangover in her big brown eyes.

*Damn her.*

"Can I come in?"

"Why? Catherine isn't here."

There. He wanted her to leave, that should do it. Cade steeled himself against the hurt he expected to see on her face. But Eden lifted her chin and gave him a look that said she was more determined than dissuaded. *What the hell?*

"I need to talk to you." She bit her lip, then offered a big, bright smile. "I need your help."

Cade's jaw dropped.

"You're kidding, right?"

She was kidding, right?

Instead of assuring him that this was a joke, Eden brushed past, gave his arm a quick pat, then hurried into the sitting room.

Cade wanted to believe it was shocked curiosity that had him following and not the fact that, even now, he couldn't refuse her a single thing.

"You need my help?" he repeated, trying to smother his automatic call to action. "With what?"

Seating herself on his grandmother's antique settee, Eden opened her mouth to respond, then her eyes went wide and hot. Cade glanced down and grimaced, realizing he'd stormed down the stairs in just a pair of jeans. He should excuse himself and put a shirt on at least.

But he liked that look on her face. He watched her eyes heat as they trailed over his body like a hot caress. He liked the way she wet her bottom lip and took a deep breath, as if the sight of him was a total turn-on.

It didn't matter that they were through, or that she'd used him. He couldn't stop his body's reaction.

"What do you need help with?" he asked again, wanting her eyes back on his face before his body's reaction became any more apparent.

"What?" She blinked a couple of times, then puffed out a breath. "Oh. Right. Um, first, before we get into that, I wanted to say thank you."

"For what?"

For getting her into an exclusive club?

For giving her two weeks of mind-blowing sex?

For falling crazy in love with her?

"For hauling my mother home. Making her face her responsibilities and take care of the mess she'd left." Eden looked down at her knees for a second, as if smothering a smile. "She paid your father this morning, and is meeting with the bank manager this afternoon. So thank you, yet again, for rescuing me."

Cade frowned. He hadn't pickled his brain so much that he'd forgotten her accusations just two days ago. That he saw her as a perpetual victim, that he didn't believe she could take care of herself. She'd yelled at him for rescuing her all the time. And now she was thanking him for it?

He rubbed at the throbbing pain in his temple. What was she trying to do?

"I don't get it," he confessed. "Now you're glad I rescued you?"

"Yes." She said the word so fast it was practically a rush of air. Then she bit her lip again and gave him one of those sweet, big-eyed stares.

"Why?"

"Because I realized that it's not a judgment or sign that you don't respect me. It's proof that you care. A way of trying to help. Of stepping in to keep me from getting hurt."

*Right.*

His frown deepened. He narrowed his gaze.

"What are you up to?"

Eden jumped up from the couch and started pacing. Fireplace to window, chair to piano. After two rounds, she took a deep breath and met his gaze.

"I sort of have something to confess."

Did she want to confess that she really cared about him? Admit that she was miserable without him?

Beg him to strip her naked and do wild and naughty things to her body?

From the scared look on her face, Cade figured it was probably none of the above.

"I sort of didn't tell you the truth the other night," she said, her words murmured to her toes instead of his face.

"I beg your pardon?"

Even after she'd told him she'd used him to get into that stupid club, Cade didn't think Eden had it in her to actually lie.

"I didn't really try to get into the Cade-ettes. I refused to tell Janie what we had between us."

"Then why'd you say you did?"

"I was afraid you were going to throw your career away. That you'd make this huge decision and regret it later. I figured if you didn't have me as an excuse, you'd stick with the SEALs until you really knew if you wanted to leave or not."

Cade's mind reeled. But one clear fact stood out in the spinning confusion.

"You were trying to rescue me?"

Her smile was half-grimace, half-wince.

"I was afraid you'd give up something you loved for the wrong reason."

"You think leaving the SEALs for you is the wrong reason?"

"I think leaving the SEALs because you can't get over the loss of your friend is the wrong reason," she said gently, lifting his grandmother's framed photo of him, Blake and Phil graduating bootcamp.

Cade stared at the picture.

It was like he was at war with himself.

A part of him was tired. Just so damned tired. A year would give him time to decide if he wanted to stick with the SEALs or shift focus. It would give him time to get past the loss of Phil, to process his feelings about command. To heal.

Damned if he'd even known he was wounded until Eden made him face the truth. Just like he wouldn't have realized he was in love with her until she'd walked out on him.

The real question wasn't what he was going to do about his job. The question on the table right now was what was he going to do about his life.

"You were right," he finally said.

"I was...?"

"Right," he repeated. Cade shoved both hands through his hair, then shrugged. "I wanted to use you to avoid making a choice. To avoid admitting that I might want to do something other than be a SEAL."

"And now?" Her words were whisper soft, but so loaded with understanding that Cade felt as if she'd come over and wrapped him in a big hug.

"And now I know what I'm going to do. Just like I know I need to quit hiding and face the loss of my buddy." It hurt to say the words. To admit that he was ready to take that first step toward healing. It'd be like saying goodbye to Phil all over again. But he couldn't have a future if he was stuck in the past.

He looked at Eden, and knew.

He wanted to make her his future.

EDEN WAS SO GLAD she hadn't stayed at the country club long enough to actually eat anything, because her stomach was doing all sorts of crazy backflips.

All her life, she'd wished for more. She'd blown out candles and watched for falling stars. She'd dreamed of what it'd be like to have her perfect life.

But today, she'd finally realized that all the wishing

in the world didn't matter. It was the doing that made the difference.

And she really, really loved doing Cade.

She took a deep breath, knowing she needed to confess everything before she lost her nerve. Or jumped his body. Her eyes ran over the sleek silken glow of his muscles again and her mouth started to water. The odds of both things happening were running pretty even at that moment.

"What you said the other night made me realize that I've spent years sitting idly by, waiting. Hoping that if I was good enough, nice enough, that everyone, someone, *anyone* would see that I was worthy."

He looked like he wanted to argue as if the idea of her thinking that she was less than perfect simply pissed him off. Eden loved that about him. Loved how strongly he wanted to defend her.

"But you always saw me as worthy. Even when you hauled me out of trees or kept me from falling on my face, you made me feel like I was special. Even when all there was between us was a mutual street sign and a lot of rescues, you accepted me. So, now I'm through waiting," she said, her heart pounding so loud she wouldn't have been surprised if he could hear it. But it was beating with excitement, rather than fear. Because even if he turned her down, she'd have tried. She'd have given them her best shot.

"What're you through waiting for?" he asked slowly. Clearly his training had clued him in that he might be in danger.

"I'm through waiting for all of my wishes to come true." Eden took a deep breath, then walked over until she stood in front of him. Her fingers ached to touch, but she kept them at her sides.

"I realized today that I do make things happen. I made the right choices that led to opportunities, or the lack thereof. I might need to be rescued once in a while because I'm chasing the dream. But that's okay, because I'm the one choosing to run after it," she whispered.

His eyes gleamed, the smile starting to play at the corners of his mouth giving her a little encouragement.

"So what're you planning to make happen next?"

"This," she told him, launching herself into his waiting arms. Both hands cupping his cheeks, she ravaged his mouth. Cade, gentleman that he was, ravaged her right back.

"I love you," she breathed against his mouth. For a split second, she wanted to grab the words back. To wait and see if he said them first. Then she lifted her chin and met his eyes. Nope. No waiting. Not any longer.

"I love you," she repeated, her words strong and sure this time. "I want to give us a chance. I'll spend time in San Diego, whether it's once a year when you're on leave or a few times a month if you're doing training. Whatever you decide, for whatever reasons you see fit, I want to be there for you."

For just a second, he looked shocked. Then a smile like she'd never seen—one filled with little-boy joy, delight and hope—split his face.

"I'd say we have one hell of a chance," he decided, sweeping her into his arms and carrying her to the couch where he settled with her tight in his arms. "Because I love you, too."

Eden was pretty sure her heart stopped.

She stared, wide-eyed, for two breaths until it started again. Elation surged as she met his lips, their kiss as raw and honest as their declarations of love.

"Looks like my birthday wish came true," she said when they came up for air.

"Yeah? The one about us having a lot of sex?" He pulled

her more firmly onto his lap, the hard length of his erection pressing against her thigh, letting her know he couldn't wait to start.

"I do like that part," she agreed with a laugh, wriggling just a little to tease him. "But the part I've always wished for, even before sex with you, was to have my very own hero."

Cade's smile softened, his eyes warming hers as he pressed a kiss of promise against her lips.

"I'll always be your hero."

# *Epilogue*

CADE LAY ON THE BED, his hands crossed behind his head while he contemplated just how damned great his life was. It had been nine months since the infamous Spring Fling and he and Eden were as strong as ever together.

So strong, he actually believed in taking chances now instead of following the tried and true. In his jacket pocket was his mother's engagement ring. His father had suggested he use it when he'd told Robert and Catherine that he was asking Eden to marry him.

Nerves danced for a second while he tried to decide how to ask. She'd say yes, wouldn't she? Thanks to her partnership with Mia, she'd changed her veterinary schedule to spend a week or two each month with him in San Diego. He spent all of his breaks between training sessions here in Ocean Point with her. She'd even started working with pet-placement groups in Southern California. Those were good signs, right?

The nerves in his belly got a little more active.

"Blake and Alexia should be back from their honeymoon next week," he said, grateful for the distraction when Eden stepped out of the bathroom, steam from her shower billowing around her. "You up for a week or two in San Diego? We'll take them out to celebrate married life."

"Maybe."

He frowned in surprise at her response. Eden and Alexia had become pretty good friends. In fact, within a week of meeting her, Alexia had adjusted her wedding plans to include Eden as a bridesmaid.

So what was up?

Eden stopped at the foot of the bed, her worried frown driving everything from his mind.

"What's wrong?" he asked, jackknifing into a sitting position. He knew her face, her every expression. She was scared. Anxious and happy all at the same time.

*What the hell?*

"Um, well, I think I— We broke something."

Cade looked around. No damage.

He shifted to take in her body, from the top of her silky brown hair, over the tiny red nightie and down to the tips of her pale pink toes.

"What?"

Eden bit her lip, then, with the soft flesh still tight between her teeth, she held out a stick.

Cade looked at it, frowned and gave a shrug.

"What's that?"

"It's, um, a pregnancy test."

*What?* Cade's gaze flew from the stick to her face and back again. Then it landed on her stomach, flat as ever under her silky nightgown.

"A condom broke?" he confirmed in an awed tone.

Wincing, she gave a little shrug, then nodded.

He threw back his head and laughed.

God, could life get any better?

Loving it, loving her, he leaped from the bed and swept Eden into his arms to spin her in a wide circle. On his second time around, he grabbed his jacket in one hand then dropped to the bed with Eden in his lap.

"Talk about accident prone," she muttered.

"Babe, this isn't an accident. This is a blessing, pure and simple."

To prove it to her, he scooped the little velvet box out of the pocket, letting the jacket fall to the floor as he flipped the lid and held out the diamond.

Eden's eyes widened, then went soft with so much love that Cade had to blink.

"Will you marry me?"

"Did you already know I was pregnant?" she asked in shock, reaching out to touch the ring with one unsteady finger before pulling her hand back.

"Nope. I knew I loved you. I knew I wanted to spend the rest of my life with you." Cade caught her hand in his, brought it to his lips and brushed a kiss over her knuckles before twining his fingers with hers. "You being pregnant only adds to the perfection we've got together. It's like a sign that I'm making all the right choices, that I'm living my life for my own dreams instead of trying to prove something to my father. Something to myself."

Eden's smile was a little shaky at the corners.

"I don't expect you to give up being a SEAL. I know the BUDs training was just a temporary thing. I don't want you to think you have to give up going back into Special Ops."

Cade had to close his eyes for a second, he was so overcome by emotions. She was incredible.

"Babe, I love training. It's like I was made for it. I love being stationary, able to come home to you every night. I love the idea of building a life together, of bringing a new life into the world with you." He watched the worry fade from her dark gaze, then slid the ring on her finger before kissing her with all the love and passion he had in his heart.

When she was breathless and limp, he pulled back to give her his most charming smile. "Bottom line, I love you."

Eden's laugh was so soft, it was more a puff of breath over his face than a sound. She cupped his face in both hands and kissed him again.

"My hero."

\* \* \* \* \*

# The World of Mills & Boon®

There's a Mills & Boon® series that's perfect for you. We publish ten series and, with new titles every month, you never have to wait long for your favourite to come along.

---

## Blaze®
*Scorching hot, sexy reads*
4 new stories every month

## By Request
*Relive the romance with the best of the best*
9 new stories every month

## Cherish™
*Romance to melt the heart every time*
12 new stories every month

## Desire™
*Passionate and dramatic love stories*
8 new stories every month